By Thomas H. Raddall

Novels

HIS MAJESTY'S YANKEES
ROGER SUDDEN
PRIDE'S FANCY
THE NYMPH AND THE LAMP
TIDEFALL

Short Stories

THE PIED PIPER OF DIPPER CREEK
TAMBOUR
THE WEDDING GIFT

Nonfiction

WEST NOVAS
HALIFAX: WARDEN OF THE NORTH

Tidefall

A NOVEL BY Thomas H. Raddall

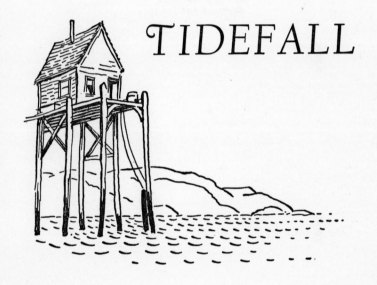

TIDEFALL

McClelland and Stewart, Limited · Toronto

Thou art a man remarked to taste a mischief,
Look for't; though it come late it will come sure.

Tidefall

PORT Barron was a nick in the shore of a lonely cape
that lay on the coastal chart like a thumb, with a tip
called Gannet Head. Once it had been covered with
a windy forest of spruce and fir, but long ago a bush fire
had scalped it and left a black desert in which after many
years a moorland growth of sheep laurel, bayberry and
other tough shrubs had crept abroad. In a few swampy hol-
lows, where the ancient fire had not penetrated, there were
clumps of sickly hackmatack trees, and on the Head itself a small wood of cat spruce had survived the flames by
a shift of wind. This tuft of cat spruce was gnarled and
pressed into dense thickets on the seaward face by the
force of the Atlantic gales, so that seamen coming along
the coast saw the cape as a badly worn toothbrush lying on
the sea.

South and east and west of the cape spread the gray
wet mass of the North Atlantic, but the view to the northwest was dotted with small islands, a scattered archipel-
ago straggling on for fifty miles, some covered with dark
spruce woods, some with bushes and grass, and some
mere heaps of rock. Through them passed the strong scour
of the Fundy tide. The nearest railway point was Eglinton,
where the line cut across the base of the cape on its way
along the coast, and from it once a day the mail went out

to Port Barron in an old fish-reeking motorboat. In this craft on a cold March day in 1931 there traveled two passengers, both of whom had got off the westbound train at Eglinton. One was a salesman probing every lonely hole in the coast in search of business. The other was a dark stocky man of thirty-five named R. Saxby Nolan, whose errand was of another kind.

At Port Barron they put up at the only hotel, a small white-shingled building facing across the main street towards the harbor, in reality nothing but a boardinghouse inhabited by several retired couples of simple means and by occasional transients like the salesman and Sax Nolan. The town was like a hundred others of its kind in the more remote parts of the Canadian east coast: a single street winding about the harbor shore with a few rocky lanes running up the slope; a straggle of small wooden houses, some painted but most of them bare and weathered to the tint of a winter sea; short rock-and-timber jetties for the fishing boats and a long pile wharf, somewhat decrepit, at which a fair-sized ship could dock. About the head of the long wharf lay the town's center — a church, a school, an Odd Fellows' Hall, the hotel, a few warehouses and a branch office of the Royal Bank of Canada. A large store occupied the street face of one of the warehouses, with the name *J. C. Caraday & Son* in crumbling gilt letters across the plate-glass windows, and this name appeared again on the side of the warehouse and over a gateway leading to the wharf.

The town had a fringe of pastures, narrow and stony and enclosed by low walls of rock wrenched from the thin soil, and behind these ran the dun barrens of the cape, a wilderness of bushes, winter-bare, in which great boulders rose like islands in a sea. The only trees in Port Barron were a few salt-bitten apples and poplars in the back

4

yards of the houses. Most of the winter's snow had gone but the shrunken remains of big drifts survived in the lee of the pasture walls and between the warehouses, where even in summer no sunshine ever fell. The street was a porridge of mud and slush, the aftermath of an unusually early thaw. A reek of fish and decayed lobster shells hung about the waterfront and crept about the houses on the cold breeze from the sea. The whole history of Port Barron was one of exposure and hard living and it was written on its face.

Three times a week a movie show flickered in the ramshackle Odd Fellows' Hall, running old films, mostly westerns of the silent sort. The audience was composed of fishermen in thick frieze-cloth trousers, Mackinaw shirts, long rubber boots with the tops folded below the knees and spangled with fish scales, and long-peaked caps which they kept on their heads throughout the performance; and women and girls in shabby coats, with handkerchiefs bound over their hair, all chattering away in direct competition with the bored girl hammering a piano under the screen. To this din was added a continual thump and rumble and the clatter of wooden pins from the bowling alley overhead.

After the show Port Barron died. Not a house showed a light except the hotel, where a nightly poker game that had been going on for thirty years occupied a group of cronies until midnight. These meager diversions and the stormy March weather, the rains and snows, the icicles dangling like witch locks from eaves and ledges on the south side of the street, the nightly frosts putting a crust on the puddles, the reek of fish and gurry from the slips, the silence and darkness of the street at night, the cold chuckle of tidewater about the jetties, the whole brooding aura of the place that whispered of eternal struggle

5

with a harsh sea and a stony soil, all made Port Barron a place of horror to traveling salesmen at this season of the year. Indeed few came at any season, and none stayed any longer than he could help.

But to Sax all this was familiar and he did not mind. He had hated the place as a boy and left it with glee, but over the space of seventeen years and twenty-five degrees of latitude he had thought upon Port Barron with a growing nostalgia, looking forward to this time. He had no intention of staying, of course. There were other places in Nova Scotia where life was comfortable and a man with money could settle down and enjoy it. But first he had promised himself a sight of this dull little backwater, and he had the secret hankering of any self-made man to show himself in the role of local-boy-made-good.

For two days he indulged these old desires, but in the chief one he was disappointed. Nobody remembered him. His first casual inquiries revealed that his parents had drifted off long ago to some other poverty-stricken corner of the coast, no one knew where, as they had drifted to the cape in the first place. Even the familiar shack far out of town at Herring Point was a ruin. No loss, the people said. A shiftless man and a sour silent woman, they remembered that. Inwardly Sax was relieved. No call for his charity there. He had never loved them, indeed he had despised them, for he had known even then that the world was divided into two kinds of people, the smart ones and the fools.

He paused outside the school and called up a vision of himself trudging up the steps in old rubber boots clotted with the mud of the path from Herring Point. He had been a sallow youngster then, with a round face and a mop of black hair, very strong in a quick stocky way and with an air of sly self-confidence. He had been clever at

6

his books. The kids at school had called him Monkey Eyes — not to his face, because he was very ready with fists and boots in moments of resentment, but he had come to know the name. Long afterward in a tropical port he had seen a monkey on a chain, and it had startled him to see in the little beast's eyes the wary, calculating and somewhat cynical look that greeted him in the mirror whenever he shaved.

And now Monkey Eyes was forgotten in Port Barron. It was natural after all. He was only one of the eternal procession of restless youngsters who went away and never came back, or at best returned for a day or a week and then shook its mud off their shoes forever. The people he passed in the street regarded him with the casual curiosity given to any stranger, seeing a swarthy man of thirty-five with small dark eyes that were never still, with an odd little smile that came and went like April sunshine, and dressed in a kind of clothes that came obviously from the States. The hotel proprietor reported that the stranger called himself Captain Nolan and that, oddly for a seafaring man, he did not smoke or drink. Moreover, he had refused an invitation to join the nightly card party in the parlor, saying that he never gambled except on a sure thing. A witty fellow, it seemed.

∿ ∿ Chapter 2

B Y the morning of the third day Sax had seen enough of Port Barron. He decided to leave on the morrow; and since he had an empty afternoon to fill, and because the shabby sign of J. C. Caraday & Son intrigued him, he followed his curiosity across the street. There was an advantage in being forgotten. After the first day or two you could walk about unnoticed, like the chap with the invisible cloak in the old tale. There was not much to see. The Caraday warehouse was empty except for some hogsheads that rang hollow at the touch of his boot, and some odds and ends of sailing-ship gear, like rope and blocks, a ship's boat, dry-rotten and gaping at the seams, a binnacle, a heap of rat-gnawed canvas.

The planking of the wharf was worn and rotten and so were many of the spiles. The adjoining shipyard had the same air of disuse; the two slips were decayed except where they dipped into the tide; the forge, the shipwrights' shed, the sail loft and mold loft were deserted and dusty. An old tern schooner, obviously beached to prevent her sinking, lay on the foreshore, stripped of sails and deck gear. The name *Pamela Caraday* appeared on her stern in flaked gilt paint.

The store facing the street seemed to be the only active part of the business, a big old-fashioned shop cluttered with goods of every kind, from codline to women's shoes. Much of the stock had been long on the shelves. Sax noted on a high shelf some dusty shoe boxes bearing the trade-mark of a Halifax firm defunct for years. Not a customer was in sight. Two women clerks of a spinsterish cast stood warming their behinds at a pear-shaped iron stove. When he inquired for the boss they passed him on to an office at the back of the warehouse, a roomy chamber whose windows faced on the wharf. Four high bookkeepers' desks and chairs made a wooden island in midfloor about another pear-shaped stove, and there were two flat desks under the windows.

At one of these sat a fleshy old man slowly turning the leaves of a ledger and peering at them through steel-

8

rimmed spectacles. He got up and blinked as the stranger came into the room.

"My name's Nolan — Captain Nolan, to give you a handle," Sax said carelessly. "Been walking around your place. Hope you don't mind."

"You come in reply to the ad?" the old man said.

"I don't know what you mean."

"Been puttin' an ad in the Hal'fax papers the past two years, off and on, offerin' the business for sale."

"I didn't see it. Just walked in out of curiosity. You the owner?"

A solemn smile. "Name's Bostwick. I'm just the man-ager — the bookkeeper really." And a little pompously, "Seen the time when I had four clerks under me here in this room, and a girl typewriter besides. The owner's Mrs. Caraday. Lives out the shore road a piece."

"What's she like?"

"Mrs. Caraday? Oh, she's a woman gettin' on a bit, fiftyish. She don't know much about the business, tell you the truth. Nor'd her husband for that matter. Dead now. Roger, that was. J.C.'s son. Things weren't like this in J.C.'s day, I tell you. Hustler, he was. 'Course times have changed. Pretty hard right now. You weren't thinkin' of buyin' the business by any chance? Store's the main thing now. Biggest in Port Barron. Full stock. See for yourself."

"I've seen," Sax said bluntly. "The warehouse and wharf seem to be falling apart. So does the shipyard, and that old hooker lying on the beach. The whole show looks as dead as old what's-his-name."

Bostwick sucked his false teeth with the hissing sound of one in pain. He flashed an indignant look through the spectacles. But his voice was mild.

"Things are bound to go down a bit in hard times, sir.

Hard times here ever since the war." And with some spirit, "Not but what a bit of capital wouldn't put the whole thing back on its feet again. Good old firm, sir. Highly respected still about the coast — clear up to Hal'fax."

"Why?"

"People remember. All the things we did. Used to have a fleet of schooners in the cod fishery. Sent one or two up north sealin' every spring. Rendered the seal oil in a boiler plant behind the shipyard — torn down now. Wintertime the vessels'd take our dried fish to the south'ard. Timber, too, from the sawmills up to Eglinton. Cuba, Jamaiky, Porta Reek, Demerary, sometimes down to the River Plate. 'Cross to Portugal and Spain sometimes — people ate a lot of our salt fish over there, time past. The West Indy ships'd bring back sugar, molasses, rum, that kind o'thing. The Spain and Portugal ships'd bring loads of Iviza salt for the fishery, sometimes a cargo of wines for the liquor merchants up to Hal'fax. And we built all our own ships, mind. Right in that yard out there. Built ships for other people too, o' course. Matter o' fact we la'nched our last job, schooner for Newfoundland parties, only three or four years ago. Ah yes, things used to hum around here."

"Um." The faint smile played about Sax's lips. He knew it all, and he was tempted to observe that everything around here now had finished humming — like the flies in the spider webs that adorned the high corners of the office.

"You mean to say the Caradays hope to sell all this" — he swept a hand that took in the wharf, the shipyard, the warehouse, the shop, even Bostwick himself — "as a going concern?"

"Yes."

10

Sax raised his black brows. He surveyed the old man with an amused contempt.

"For how much? If that's a fair question."

"You'll have to see Mrs. Caraday about that, sir, if you're interested. But I guess you'd better see the bank manager first."

"Why?"

The bookkeeper put on a cautious air. "That's not for me to say."

Sax made a mouth and shrugged, nodded and went out. He felt around him still that quaint illusion of a magic cloak that enabled him to move about prying into secrets, and himself invisible. A bit of a shock though to see what seventeen years had done to J. C. Caraday & Son. In his youth the firm had been the strong beating heart of Port Barron, the life of the place. He was curious to know how it had come down to this. He walked up the street and into the bank.

The bank manager was a slender man with a thin in- tellectual face and silver hair brushed up from the tem- ples in the sweeping curves of a ship's bow wave. He was about forty-five, but the hair, the gaunt lines of his face, the starched gates-ajar collar and carefully knotted cravat all gave him a much older look. His eyes had the pink in- flamed lids of a man whose sight has been strained by years of studying columns of figures but who from some queer little vanity refuses to wear glasses. He glanced at Captain Nolan's card and invited him to sit in the small inner office, where large framed photographs of King George, Queen Mary, the current president and two past presidents of the Royal Bank of Canada all looked down from their separate places on the walls with a rather for- bidding air.

"I don't know what Bostwick was making a mystery

11

about," he said briskly when Sax asked his question. "Naturally the Caraday firm has always done its business with us and in recent years we've had to carry them to some extent."

"To what extent?"

"At the present time they owe us twenty thousand dollars and accrued interest."

Sax arched his brows. "The whole outfit's not worth that. Not today."

"Including the residence — Caraday House?"

"I don't know anything about that. I mean the warehouse, the wharf and shipyard and all that. Except for the store the whole thing's falling down."

"Of course," the manager said carefully, "the name and good will of J. C. Caraday & Son are worth a lot. No doubt Bostwick's mentioned that, he's very proud of the old firm."

Sax twisted his lips. Name and good will. All these hard-up shipping firms trumped up name and good will when they couldn't think of anything else. In his journey along the coast from Halifax, getting off the train at small ports here and there for a day's inquiry, he had met the phrase at every turn.

"Well," he said, "I won't deny I'm sort of interested in shipping firms that aren't too big and have a decent reputation. I'm told the Caradays used to be the great firm of this place. What's their story?"

"It's rather a long one."

"Can't you reef it a bit?"

The banker sat back in his chair and placed the tips of his lean fingers together in the conventional gesture of bankers everywhere. "It's quite a common story in a way. I daresay you could find a firm with a history like the Caradays' in various places between here and Newfoundland. The founder was John C. A young sailor wrecked here on the cape in the 1870's. Married a local girl and settled down. Built a small house on the tip of the cape at Gannet Head and went into the fishery. A lonely spot but a good one for the lobster fishing especially. Caraday had lots of brains, energy, character — an admirable man — and before long he was making a bit of money. Other fishermen joined him, built small shacks and cottages about Caraday's Cove — it's still called that, you can see it on the charts — and in fact created a small village there. Caraday let 'em have sites for their cottages on lease — wouldn't sell a foot. Gave him the whip hand. Nothing mean about him, understand. Man of old-fashioned principles, death on drinking and all that. Ordered the people to put up a church, provided the timber himself, and held service every Sunday morning, reading the Scriptures himself and giving the sermon in a voice like thunder. When some sin had been committed at the Head they claim you could hear him clear up to Port Barron. Big man with a red beard. They used to call him King Caraday."

"He sounds pretty poisonous to me," Sax said. He had heard it all before and long ago. What he wanted was the firm's more recent history, the tale of their decline and fall, but it amused him to let the banker ramble on.

"Ah, he was, to people he didn't like. But everybody respected Caraday, even the ones he kicked off the Head for breaking his rules. He knew the sea and how to make money out of it and he was willing to let the others cash in with him. After a time he moved into Port Barron and built a lobster cannery. Then the shipyard. Shipbuilding took him into the West Indies trade with salt fish and lumber and all that, and he went on from there, all sorts of things, including the big shop across the street. When he died in 1910 he owned half a dozen schooners in the Bank fishery, a couple of big square-riggers in the Caribbean trade, and he owned all of Gannet Head and half Port Barron. He must have been worth at a guess well over a hundred thousand dollars — a big fortune for these parts. A dollar was worth a dollar then."

"I see. What happened when he died?"

"His son Roger inherited the lot. Roger's mother had died when he was young and he was sickly himself, born you might say with a medicine spoon in his mouth. He'd grown up tall like the old man but thin and stooped and wrapped up in books, you know the type. Caraday sent him to college at Halifax. Several times his health broke down and the old man used to ship him off in one of the Caraday barkentines to spend the winter in Jamaica. Eventually he got his degree. Came home full of education but with no more business sense than a child. You can guess the rest."

"Shirt sleeves to shirt sleeves?"

"Something like that. Not all Roger's fault, of course. Times were changing when the old man died. Steam coming into everything — tramps on even the petty West Indian routes, trawlers in the fishery, steamers out of Newfoundland taking over the sealing — everywhere you looked. And then in '14 the Germans started the big war and that changed everything in the world. Queen Victoria had been dead for years but it was Kaiser Bill who really buried her and all she stood for."

"This Roger Caraday," Sax said with some impatience.

"Ah! Married a girl he'd met at college at Halifax, daughter of an English officer in the garrison. A lady, you understand. She didn't like it here but she put up with Port Barron in the summers and of course they spent every winter in the West Indies for his health. Left the business in Bostwick's charge. You've seen Bostwick. Honest old fellow, very precise with his figures, still calls his office the 'counting room' sometimes, like a character out of Thackeray. What the firm needed — still needs — is a character out of the present day, a modern type of old John C., some smart energetic chap who knows ships and fish and how to adapt an old business to new times."

At this point the banker gave Sax a careful stare. There was a little silence. His voice went on, "Poor old Bostwick did his best but he couldn't see any farther than the end of a ledger column. No judge of men. Things bungled right and left. You'd think any firm with a few ships, even windjammers, could have made a profit out of the war. A good many did. But Bostwick lost thousands, trying to run things in the old-fashioned way. After the war the firm began to borrow from my bank. On my advice they sold their ships — all but the *Pamela* — for what they could get. A wooden ship was a liability after '21. When they sold a ship they'd pay off a bit of the loan. Then they'd borrow more. Finally I had to say No. That was in '27, when Roger died — four years ago. After the slump of '29 I told Mrs. Caraday and Bostwick there was only one thing to do — advertise the business for sale."

"Any offers?" Sax said.

"You know what things have been like since '29. Loose capital's as rare as the passenger pigeon. I'm telling you all this frankly because you've seen the firm's properties for yourself, and I take it you're a seafaring man and you know what's what."

"And," added Sax with a monkey-imp gleam, "you think I might be the character you mentioned a moment ago — the modern bloke who can put the whole thing back on its feet. Well, it's flattering, I'll say that. It might even be true. But you're not giving me that kind of talk because you like the cut of my jib. You see a chance to collect that twenty thousand dollars plus interest if you can sell me the mortgage your bank's holding on the properties. Isn't that it?"

An expression of distaste flitted over the banker's face. He turned a small glass paperweight in his fingers and examined it carefully before replying.

"Captain Nolan, I've been here a good many years. I've known the Caradays all that time. In a place like Port Barron there isn't much social life of a congenial kind and my wife and I and the doctor have always enjoyed the friendship of the Caraday family. There's such a thing as loyalty to one's friends."

Sax uttered a snort. And with another monkey gleam, "Is that why you let the Caradays have all that money when you knew the firm was leaking at the seams?"

"I lent the money to a business I considered fundamentally sound," returned the banker coldly. "The hard times in the '20's, especially the big crash of '29, upset my calculations as they did everybody's. For the past two years my district head office has been pressing me to liquidate the Caraday loan. Their last letter was — um — peremptory. On the face of it that means foreclosure and selling the properties for anything they'll fetch. But you realize what else it means? Of course you do. It means putting Mrs. Caraday and her daughter into the road without a cent, without a home, without relatives, without even friends except the doctor and myself — and do you think for one minute they'd accept charity from us?"

Sax itched to laugh in the banker's face. His words had a familiar sound, an echo from those old tearful plays that wandering road shows used to put on, for one night only, in the Eglinton theater years ago. There ought to be a violin somewhere scraping "Hearts and Flowers," and a

16

paper snowstorm coming down. The banker paused as if for an answer to his cue, gazing at the faintly smiling mask across the desk. At last he went on, turning his face towards the window, "No doubt you think I'm an odd sort of banker. We aren't supposed to mix sentiment with business. But let me impress upon you this, Captain Nolan. It's my business sense, quite apart from sentiment, that objects to selling out the Caradays just for the bank's twenty thousand. The firm's assets, its name and good will with the rest, are worth at least twice that, even in these times. And think of its opportunities!"

"What opportunities?" Sax said cynically.

"You know, I think. As many fish in the sea as ever; as many hard-working fellows hereabouts who know how to catch and cure 'em, and how to sail the stuff to market. Down in the West Indies and South America there must be as many people ready to eat salt codfish on saints' days and Fridays as ever there were. Whole populations. The Nova Scotia fishery was built on that long ago, and it's still a good foundation." At this point the banker cast aside his air of chill reserve and leaned forward with an eager face. "Look here, you seem to me a man of energy and experience and I take it you've got some capital to invest or you wouldn't be here at this cold time of year asking questions about J. C. Caraday & Son. I put it to you that here's an opportunity to invest your money and yourself, bring a fine old firm back to life on a modern basis and reap the reward. The man who founded it made a fortune out of it. So can you."

The little smile played about Captain Nolan's lips. "Mr. — MacIlraith, is that right? — Mr. MacIlraith, I hope this bank pays you a nice fat salary. Because they're getting quite a spellbinder for their money. You make this Caraday thing sound like a trunkful of government bonds with

17

a sentimental novel in the lid. Trouble is, I'm not a sentimental man, myself. I don't mix business with anything. I got my money the hard way and that's the way I part with it. If you want the truth I'm not a damned bit interested in the Caradays, the firm, the name and good will or anything else about 'em, including the town they're in. I don't mind telling you I'd like to buy a good little shipping business somewhere on this coast if I can get it cheap enough. I've looked in every port from here to Halifax and I've seen one or two that might be okay. The fact is, I'm looking for more than just a business. I've put in a lot of tough years abroad and now I want to settle down in some place where I can be a bit of a swell and enjoy some swell society — not what you're doing, chumming up with some old girl that's living on memories and the small change from the village store — but some real Class. I don't see anything like that here."

Mr. MacIlraith looked surprised. He also looked thoughtful. He played with the paperweight again. "I'm afraid you're seeing Port Barron at its worst right now, Captain. In summer it's a very pleasant place indeed. And from a business standpoint it's one of the handiest places on the whole coast for the fishery, stuck out in the sea like this."

"Fish! You keep talking fish," Sax snapped. "Fishing's not what I've got in mind. What's on my mind is some sort of coastal shipping business. Two or three smart auxiliary schooners, say. Buy a small steamer somewhere, lots of tramps laid up now. Run the whole thing from an outport, where I don't have much taxes to pay; place where I can refit my vessels at my own wharf, on my own slips; place where I can operate in peace without some nosy government official or seamen's union breathing down my neck all the time. All that. See?"

"Yes, Captain. Yes, of course. And I still say Port Barron's the place you're looking for. Look here, we're talking in confidence; may I ask how much you might invest altogether — just a rough figure — in the business you have in mind? Including the purchase of new schooners and the steamer and so forth?"

Sax allowed himself a glow of self-satisfaction. But he made his voice casual.

"Oh, I'd say something like eighty thousand dollars. A bit more, maybe."

The banker's eyes widened. He passed up a slim hand and brushed one of those silver waves with a nervous gesture. "Let me make a proposition. It's quite a simple one. Why not take over the Caraday firm just as it stands, leaving Mrs. Caraday the house and a certain share of the business? In that way the purchase won't cost you, in actual cash I mean, any more than the bank's mortgage on the properties. You can use the rest of your capital for development. You'll control the firm entirely — by virtue of your major interest — and Mrs. Caraday will take the chance she's always had to take, that the firm makes enough profit to give her a living."

Sax felt hilarious now. He wondered if this quill driver really thought he'd fall for that heap of junk across the street, and with Caraday's widow for a partner. What a lark!

"And what would you call 'a certain share'?" he asked smoothly.

"I'd say, to be quite fair, Captain, to be absolutely just in the matter, she ought to retain a quarter of the business. That's to say a twenty-thousand-dollar share, reckoning your total investment at eighty thousand. Any further money you chose to invest naturally would increase your share and decrease hers. Easily work that out when the time comes. Matter of book work. And the agreement should include a clause by which you buy out her interest for cash any time she chooses to sell."

"Ah! Very anxious to protect the lady, aren't you?"

"After all I've a double responsibility — to my bank and to my client."

"And what about me?"

Mr. MacIlraith opened his hands with their long pale fingers and polished nails. Sax imagined them picking up and putting down cards politely and precisely in some semiweekly bridge rite at Caraday House, along with his wife and the doctor and the widow of Roger Caraday, all in the pink shade of lamps and with a faint rattle of teacups in the offing.

"My dear Captain," said the banker with this open gesture, "you surely realize that your success in putting the Caraday firm on its feet is a matter vital to the whole town of Port Barron and therefore to my bank. I've every reason to consider your interests. We're the only bank here and I assume you'd do your business with us as the Caradays have in the past. I'm not asking you to buy a pig in a poke — not at all. Indeed I'm urging you not to make a snap decision one way or the other without looking into the thing. Why not go with me to see Mrs. Caraday and talk the matter over — tomorrow afternoon, say? I'll send her a note if you like."

MacIlraith leaned forward over those appealing hands. His air of frosty dignity was quite gone. Sax regarded him with the eyes of a mischievous ape.

"Okay, why not? I warn you I'm cold on the deal."

"But you'll come?"

"Sure."

~ ~ *Chapter 3*

IN the hotel that evening, sitting in his room in the growing dark and staring out upon the silent street, Sax thought of the morrow and called up a vision of things past. There was a good deal to think about, and now in the dusk it was easy to see himself once more as a boy tramping in from Herring Point to school, or dragging a small handcart with fresh lobsters or the first run of mackerel to sell at the kitchen doors of merchants and other white-handed folk who touched fish only with knife and fork. Often he had dragged the cart all the way out to Caraday House, and he could see himself there too, chaffering with the cook about the price.

In such ways he had earned and saved enough dollars to buy his first suit of store clothes. And then the bicycle, the wonderful bicycle that enabled him to get to town in ten minutes instead of trudging half an hour — his first glimpse of the power of money. He was seventeen then, with sudden interest in girls. On a memorable summer Sunday he had ridden sedately up and down the street when the girls came home from church, his black mop slicked down against the skull with pomatum, his first long trousers neatly clipped about his ankles, his mail-order necktie flying in the breeze. He had felt magnificent, but he found that the girls laughed behind their hands and said "Monkey Eyes" to each other in voices that carried cruelly on the wind.

He had returned to the shack at Herring Point, sitting in one of his moody fits beside the shore and promising himself that someday, somehow, he would master one of those tittering creatures and satisfy the hatred and the longing that he had for them. It was the first of his ambitions and it had blended later into that dream of going away and getting rich and coming back to show them all what Monkey Eyes had done.

At eighteen he had left for Eglinton, armed with a letter from the schoolmaster saying that R. Saxby Nolan had passed out of the school with top marks in arithmetic and trigonometry. With this he had got a job as junior clerk in an Eglinton bank, and a year or two later, with the 1914 war in progress and young men going off to join the army, he had been promoted to fill the vacancy in the teller's cage. The pay was only fifty dollars a month, but the feel of all this other money was marvelous; and the gilt-barred window of the cage gave him a discerning view of the people who made money, and often how they made it and what they did with it.

As the war rolled on conscription came, and with it the crisis that had changed his life. It was 1917. He had no personal fear of battle. He had always loved to fight at school because he was smart as well as strong and it gave him a fierce pleasure to hear the other fellow howl. Of course war was a different thing but even so he had been tempted to enlist, especially when he saw how the girls regarded anyone in khaki. What killed the notion was the army pay. Only a fool would chuck up his job and risk his neck for a dollar ten per day.

Now they were saying that healthy young men had to go, and already parties of army police were riding the trains and checking exemption papers in the country towns. On the day Sax got his army call-up notice he rode his bicycle down to the Eglinton docks and found a tramp schooner loading pine boards for Jamaica. She was an old three-masted thing called *Albertine* and she had been rotting in a disused dock for years when the war made shipping scarce. Her present skipper had bought her for a few hundred dollars, recaulked the hull in a local shipyard and fitted her with new rigging and sails.

His name was Halkett, a lean, blue-jawed, drawling man with hard slate eyes. Captain Halkett had a taste for rum and with one or two drams under his belt he would spin long yarns about his bygone ships and voyages. He would say with one of his sudden wide smiles, "Oh I've had my ups and downs, I tell you," and he would tell you, and then he would glance about the cabin of *Albertine* with a cold gray satisfaction that left you no doubt that this was one of the ups. When Sax discovered that Captain Halkett lacked a few men, he did not hesitate. At first the skipper was astonished. "You?" he exclaimed, looking Saxby up and down and taking in the sallow face, the thick white hands, the neat serge suit and the bicycle clips on the trouser cuffs.

"Why not?" replied Sax with another of his monkey looks, the who-are-you-damn-you stare of the ape who has found a way to slip the chain. It was Halkett who looked away first.

"You're no seaman," he said.

"Were you, when you first went to sea?"

"Ah."

"I'm strong, brought up in a fishing town. And I'm smart."

"I don't doubt that," Halkett murmured, amused.

And so it was arranged. On the day before sailing Sax signed the ship's articles as an ordinary seaman at fifty dollars per month, and within twenty minutes he had stowed his suitcase in the dim ratty forecastle, changed into dungarees, and was busy with mop and bucket on the afterdeck. He was just twenty-one.

23

It would be hard to say which learned most on the voyage to Jamaica, the green hand or the captain. Sax learned about ships and the sea, especially about *Albertine*. She sailed on a fair wind but against the tide, which raised a nasty chop in the mouth of Fundy. Sax discovered at once that he had a natural pair of sea legs. He ate his meals with appetite, even gusto. And he was as smart as his word. It did not take him more than two days to learn the principal ropes and their uses and to do a fair trick at the wheel. He was surprised, even a little contemptuous, to find that handling a tern schooner on the broad sea was a simple matter after all. He revised this premature opinion later when they ran into storms, especially one off Bermuda that nearly sank the ship, but it was all part of an education and he took it in that spirit. He enjoyed the riding motion, the steep heel of the deck, the big sails leaning against the sky, the enormous privacy of the sea, which the old schooner seemed to tread alone.

The crew consisted of Halkett, his mate, a boatswain, a cook, two able seamen and Nolan. The mate and bosun were quiet middle-aged Bluenoses. The cook, a gaunt profane creature with a consumptive cough, had been lured from the stove in a lumber camp by the prospect of West Indian sunshine. Norris, the better of the able seamen, was a Grand Bank fisherman shipping south for a change. Brownrigg, the other, was a hulking ill-tempered man whose only testimonial seemed to be the tattooing on his arms and chest. He had been "in steam" he said, but it was clear that he knew a good deal about sail, and it was whispered by the cook that he had lately spent a long stretch in Dorchester penitentiary.

Brownrigg and Sax disliked each other at first glance. Just before sailing there was an argument over bunks. The affair progressed during the first meal, also in the forecastle, where Brownrigg uttered a loud and obscene opinion of soft-handed young punks who didn't know a jib from a jetty and sat down at table with a seaman like himself. Nothing happened, however, and as these matters took place out of Halkett's knowledge the captain was not prepared for what followed. The Fundy tide had now reached the full, and with slack water the lumpy sea kicked up by the opposing wind became a steady southeasterly swell. Halkett was below. The mate took the wheel and ordered the topsails set, and the cook was called out of his galley to give the others a hand. The cook knew no more than Saxby about setting a topsail but he joined the cool man Norris, who put a rope in his hands and told him to pull. This left Sax no choice but to help Brownrigg, who was throwing a halyard off a cleat at the mizzenmast, while the bosun was busy forward.

Like the cook, Sax was willing but uncertain in his movements, but Brownrigg was not disposed to suffer this awkward kind of help as patiently as Norris. Halkett, stepping out of the companionway, heard an oath and a blow, and there was the green hand, Nolan, sitting absurdly on the deck. Brownrigg hoisted the topsail alone. While he was doing this Captain Halkett watched the movements of the green hand with much interest. Sax came to his feet and quietly took off his shirt, baring a thick trunk and a pair of arms too long and large for proportion with the rest of him. A thicket of black hair extended over his chest and stomach and disappeared under his trouser band. Another lay like a fur cape across his shoulders and down his back. But it was not mere hairiness that caught the skipper's eye. What made him suck at his teeth was the sight of the bunched muscles and taut sinews of those long furry arms.

As Brownrigg turned from the cleat he found this apparition facing him with fists uplifted for battle. Brownrigg was not afraid. He was a notable brawler by his own account and he gave a shout that might have been contempt or even joy. The bosun had come to the foremast and stood now with Norris and the cook, gazing with relish on the prospect of a fight. Halkett stood by the mate at the wheel, casting a glance aloft at the newly set topsails from time to time but anxious not to miss any part of this affair. His notion of discipline was an easy one — it had to be with the kind of wages he paid — and it seemed to him that a good beating given each other by the surly a.b. and this cocky young lubber might save him trouble later on.

All were disappointed — all but Sax. The affair was one-sided and short. Sax drove one of his thick white fists into the other's belly to bring the tall man's jaw down, and his other fist smote that jaw with a thud that sounded the length of the ship. Brownrigg's figure sagged, and as it sagged those busy fists smote his eyes, his nose, his gaping mouth. He fell into the scuppers and in a moment the green hand was upon him, grasping his throat and beating his skull against the hard plank of the waterways.

Halkett ran to them, crying startled oaths. He found the bosun beside him and it took their combined strength to drag Nolan off the senseless object of his wrath. The skipper cried angrily, "Cut it out, you fool, d'you want to kill the man?"

"Yes," Sax said. But now the fighting bull-ape glare faded from his eyes and the glint of monkey mischief took its place. "I'm a peaceful bloke, Captain," he murmured, with his strange little smile. "But I don't like to be monkeyed with." Captain Halkett choked, as if the stub of

cigar between his teeth had suddenly filled his lungs with
hot smoke.

"By anybody," Sax added, looking the skipper full in the
face.

"I'll have no more of this kind o' thing," Halkett said
uncertainly. And in a stronger tone, "You put your shirt
on, and after this keep your hands to yourself. I'll tell
Brownrigg the same when he comes to — if he ever does.
We've got a dam' long way to go, young feller, and it
won't all be plain sailin' like this here. Norris, you and the
cook take Brownrigg to his bunk."

"I'll give 'em a hand," offered Sax promptly. But the
captain shook his head. He took the cigar from his
mouth and tossed it over the side. "I don't trust you,
Nolan. You lay aft and take another lesson at the wheel.
You've still got a lot to learn about this ship, and it might
as well come from me."

The incident was closed. When Brownrigg revived he
was a grotesque object. Each eye was reduced to a slit in a
blue-black plum that filled the whole socket, the nose
was crushed and shapeless, the lips puffed and split,
and queer green-tinged bruises were spreading over both
cheekbones. When the crew reminded each other that all
this had happened in a space of two minutes they stared
at Sax with a new respect and some uneasiness, as if they
were in the presence of something not quite human. For
his part Brownrigg ignored the presence of Nolan as if it
were not there. From the time of the fight until *Albertine*
reached Jamaica, through storm, through calm, through
every sort of petty duty about the deck and every con-
tact in the forecastle, not a word passed between them.
In Kingston, Brownrigg demanded to be paid off, and he
left the ship with the glazed look of a sleepwalker.

A little later, when Sax knocked on the jamb of the open door, the captain was sitting in his cabin aft with the ink of Brownrigg's shaky signature still wet on the article sheet before him.

"I'd like to pay off here too," Sax announced, adding "sir" as an afterthought. Halkett gave him the gaze of one calculating slate eye and shut the other. "You signed for the round voyage, Nolan."

"I know. But I want to quit here. You've let Brownrigg go."

"I let him go because he was no dam' good when you got through with him. That skull of his'll never be the same. Besides, what d'you want to do down here?"

"Private business — sir."

Halkett caught a flicker of the imp in Nolan's eyes. He grunted. It was hot in the cabin despite the open ports and the canvas wind scoop rigged through the skylight to catch the Caribbean breeze. From above came the cheerful yammer of black stevedores and the slither and drop of planks.

"Sit down," Halkett said. He pushed a rum bottle across the table. "There's a pitcher of iced lime juice at your elbow. Mix yourself a stingaree."

"No, thanks," murmured Sax. But he sat.

"T-T?"

"Yes."

"I've noticed you don't smoke either."

"I don't do anything that costs money and isn't some use to me."

"Well said." The captain took a sip at his own drink and put it down. His fingers tapped the glass. "Y'know, you're a clever young feller, Nolan. I never see a green hand catch on the way you did, comin' south. A seaman born, if you only knew it. And look at the way you fixed up the winch when it broke down, and the job you did on the pumps after she started her seams in that hard blow off Bermuda. As good as a machinist. Where'd you learn?"

"In a machine shop."

"Thought you came from a fishing town."

"I used to hang about a machine shop in Eglinton in my spare time. I like to know what makes things tick."

Captain Halkett ran a careful eye down the article sheet. "You write a pretty good hand too — for a fisherman." He looked up and met a malevolent stare. "Don't get me wrong," he said. "I ain't shovin' my oar in your affairs. I just wondered if there wasn't anything you couldn't do, or wouldn't do, say, for a bit of extra money. Point is, I can use a feller like you. Fact is, I ain't takin' this old hooker north again, the shape she's in. You saw what happened off Bermuda — and that was on'y a nice warm blow. Can you see her in home latitudes, thrashin' into the northerlies, and winter comin' on? Why, even water's heavier up there, it hits a ship harder and there's more of it — the width of the whole dam' North Atlantic on your beam."

"You get some big winds down here too," Sax suggested, remembering his school geography. "Hurricanes, eh?"

"Ah sure." The skipper waved a hand. "But that's just in the summer months, and here amongst all these islands you've always got a bit o' warnin' and a chance to find a lee. Tell you what's on my mind. I'm thinkin' o' goin' into the island trade, with a run across to New Orleans or Galveston now and then, or up to Key West maybe; or maybe a cruise along the Venezuela coast and the banana belt — there's a wide choice any way you look at it. Pickin' up freights wherever I can. All nice easy sailin', warm weather, the kind o' thing rich blokes pay good money for. Why, this is a windjammer's paradise, Nolan. This is where all the old Nova Scotia hookers are sold when they're no good for anything else. A hooker that wouldn't last another season on the Banks'll hang on here till kingdom come, provided she's coppered ag'in the worms and kept well south o' Hatteras.

"I know what I'm talkin' about, Nolan. I been in the Caribbee trade afore, when it wasn't nigh such good pickin's as now. Right now the war's pullin' all the steamers off to the North Atlantic, and there's sugar and rum and what not piled up on every wharf in the islands, and every merchant from Cuba to Trinidad hollerin' for trade goods from the States. That's where we come in — me and *Albertine* — and you if you've got half the sense I give you credit for. Look, Nolan, the mate and bosun's agreed to stay down here with me six months. The cook and Norris won't need much persuadin' either. Tell you what I'll do. I'll shove your wages up to seventy-five dollars a month. At the end o' six months' sailin' amongst the islands you'll know as much as the mate, and I'll give you his berth when he goes home. That means a hundred bucks a month, Canadian."

"Suppose I want to pay off some time?" Sax said warily.

"I'll pay you off any time you say, and pay your passage home. I got to do that anyhow under the old articles if I don't take the ship north."

Captain Halkett took another pull at his glass and sat back in the chair, fanning himself with a Kingston newspaper. The two men regarded each other. Sweat stood in small drops like a rash on their tanned faces and their shirts were wet. Sax had a whimsey that the sun had slipped down from the sky and lodged on the schooner's mastheads. He was surprised by Halkett's offer. He had shipped with the simple idea of dodging conscription in some island far to the south. But now he saw what a piece of luck this was. He had no affection for Halkett or *Albertine* but they offered a home for the duration of the war, at a good wage, and at a good safe distance from the Canadian army police. What more could he ask? Not a thing.

"All right," he said. "You talked me into it."

"Ah!" the skipper grinned and put a long bony hand across the table. "Shake on that, Nolan — Sax." They shook, and over the clasped hands Halkett added cheerfully, "You stick with me, Sax, and you'll get an education and put money in the bank besides. I'll show you things you never even dreamed of, and I don't mean scenery."

⌢ ⌢ Chapter 4

THE education of Sax Nolan, had Captain Halkett reflected a bit, was already well advanced. As for scenery, of which Sax saw a vast amount as time went by, the lush West Indian landscapes were like a scatter of picture post cards seen in the wavering air and steamy heat of a boiler room. The only thing real about them was the heat. He found the scenes monotonous: a jumble of hills or a lone peak reaching into the clouds, too lofty and too rich a green to be quite credible, and at their feet, like the folds of a dropped petticoat, a sprawl of undulating fields or a white town vibrating in the sunshine at the sea's edge. Some of the towns were cleaner than others. Some had trams and motorcars, some only mule carts or horse carriages. Some had tall hotels and office blocks gleaming like white cliffs above the docks, some were just a clutter of smelly shacks; and all swarmed with people of various shades and speaking outlandish tongues. Even the English sounded a bit queer.

The schooner wandered up and down the interminable chain of islands, loading cargo in odd little harbors and open roadsteads, and putting it ashore in places that looked exactly like them but where tramp steamers called to take the stuff abroad. At intervals she loaded a full cargo for the States; and from Key West or New Orleans or Galveston she returned with manufactured goods consigned to merchants all along the chain. At the end of six months the mate went home, and after a brief debate the bosun, the cook and Norris went with him. Sax moved his new sea chest to the mate's small cabin aft, and thenceforth the cook and foremast hands were Barbadian Negroes, good seamen all, and willing to work for half the Canadian wage.

The war's end came sooner than Sax and Halkett had expected. Halkett feared a sudden drop in freights but the shipping boom went on. Indeed all through 1919 and 1920 it gathered pace with the price of sugar and other staples of the West Indian trade. Even the girls in the Havana dolly shops were calling it the "dance of the millions," and *Albertine* prospered with the rest.

In Havana harbor in the spring of 1920 Mate Nolan walked into the captain's cabin with cool familiarity, dropped into a chair and announced, "Halkett, I want a better deal." The captain's eyes, somewhat bloodshot from a night ashore, met his mate's coldly.

"What d'you mean?"

"Just what I say. You're making all the money. I want some."

"What's wrong with your wages?"

32

"I'm not talking about wages, I'm talking about the freights — the profits."

The skipper put out a long jaw. "The ship's mine, Nolan."

"Sure! And she's getting rotten, so you aim to make your pile while the going's good. I don't blame you for that. But I'm not here for my health either. As a matter of fact I only planned to stay till the end of the war. Well, all that's blown over now and I might as well go home. I want a big piece of the ship from here on or I quit."

Halkett struck an injured tone. "Why, Sax, where's your gratitude? I took you green as grass and made a seaman out of you, paid you steamer wages ever since you come aft, treated you like a son. 'Cause why? 'Cause I like you, Sax. D'you think I couldn't ha' got another mate, feller with a proper ticket, any time the past two years?"

Sax grinned. "Stow it, Halkett. You haven't kept me in the mate's berth all this time because you like the way I part my hair. You like me because I run the ship while you sit under the awning aft sipping rum and stinking the wind with your damned cigars. You like me because you don't like arithmetic except for adding up the dollars, and I can shoot the sun and figure a position better than you ever could. You like me because I look after the charter parties and bills of lading and everything else that comes in writing — except the checks. You like me because I'm not just the mate, I'm the engineer and the rigger and sailmaker. You like me because I'm tough, because I can lay out a crazy 'Badian nigger and bluff it out with the dock police if I hit him a bit too hard. You like me because you couldn't get along without me now, not for a minute, in this trade or any other. And that's why you're going to give me a nice fat piece of the ship. You'll like that too."

Halkett closed his eyes. A flare of rage burned with the rum in his veins. An old desire to take this cocksure jackanapes down a peg or two came back to him fiercely. But he did not know how. Nolan had spoken the uncomfortable truth. Inch by inch he had slacked his grasp and let the running of *Albertine* pass into the broad palms and clever fingers of the mate, and it was too late to change now. Soon all this postwar dance would come to an end as suddenly as the war itself, and then would come small pickings for old schooners in the island trade. Then *Albertine* must be steered into other enterprises, mostly on the windy side of the law, where a man like Nolan would be worth almost any price, even a nice fat piece of the ship.

"Give me a day to think it over, Sax."

"I'll give you five minutes."

"How much d'you want?"

"Half."

"You're crazy."

"Half, and I want to see the freight checks myself, each trip." The captain reached slowly for the bottle on the table and poured himself a drink that came halfway up the tumbler. It was a long time before he spoke and when he did the words came mushily.

"All right. S'robbery but never mind. You win."

"I make a point of that," Sax said.

So they went halves on *Albertine,* and within twelve months the slump of 1921 struck the shipping trade like a hurricane, washing up ships and crews on the lee shores of the world. The partners in *Albertine* had to take freights or part freights wherever they could, and at any rate offered them by the sharp sallow businessmen of the islands. Sometimes by taking a freight at a loss they man-

34

aged to outbid a steamer line and make a voyage to one
of the Gulf ports in the States; and there certain unspeci-
fied goods were added to the return cargo and smuggled
ashore in Jamaica, Guadeloupe, Barbados or Trinidad, or
in stinking little towns along what used to be called the
Spanish Main. In these and other matters Sax Nolan
proved his worth.

There was a matter of getting certain firearms into Nic-
aragua, broached by three mysterious little brown men
who came aboard in Manzanillo, Cuba. One with quite
unnecessary dramatics remained outside the cabin door
with a small automatic pistol clutched in his jacket pocket.
The other two offered a good price in American dollars, half to be paid on shipment, half to be paid over the
rail by the consignees. Halkett at first refused. Too old a
game, that, he said. All the gun-running tricks were
known and a lot of smart blokes had been caught and
shot against a wall or in a ditch behind a banana patch.
It was Sax who insisted it could be done. Their New
Orleans agent had cabled an offer to freight eight-inch
iron waterpipe to Bluefields at a miserable rate and they
were on the point of refusing. But now they accepted,
and when they landed the pipe each length contained
three rifles firmly wedged inside and hidden by wads of
sacking.

There was the matter of ferrying Chinese and other
furtive immigrants into the States from Cuba, another old
game that Sax played with new finesse. There was the
common and always profitable game of selling American
cigarettes in the various European colonies of the Caribbean, duty unpaid. And there were the shadier enterprises, the packets of narcotics concealed in the laza-
ret, the brown girls from Cuba and Porto Rico consigned
to madams in New Orleans and Galveston, the criminals

fleeing from one island to another with good currency in their pockets. The partnership refused nothing that paid a profit, however slim, and as time went by *Albertine* gained a repute that smelled a bit queer from Tampa to Demerara.

They had their ups and downs, as Halkett said. There was an awkward business in St. Kitts, where they were caught with hundreds of cartons of illicit cigarettes. There was a disaster in Port Arthur, Texas, where in a small test of the new American prohibition laws they had to pay sharply for the presence of several dozen cases of whiskey concealed in the coral ballast. In Aruba, for a second offense, the unreasonable Dutchmen not only fined the ship but clapped the captain and mate in jail for thirty days without the option.

By the summer of 1925 they were literally at the end of *Albertine's* cable. Apart from her reputation in the islands the ship herself was rotten. By dint of new sails, much paint and some ingenious carpentry she had passed her last insurance classification, but the underwriters had raised their rate to a very stiff figure on the obvious grounds of age. One day Sax called Halkett into the forehold and drew a sheath knife from his belt. Without saying a word he stepped on a cask and made a light stab at the nearest deck beam. The blade went in two inches.

"Couldn't we give her a new toppin' in a yard somewheres?" Halkett said. "In Barbados, say. They'd do a good job there."

"You know better than that," Sax said, putting the knife back in his belt. "If you took her deck off she'd fall apart like a rotten basket. She's not fit to go from here to Barbados anyhow, not without frapping the hull with chains. She'd look pretty that way, wouldn't she, warping into the Canash under the eyes of a lot of nosy shore people?"

"Think we could sell her?"

"Only to the underwriters, if you get what I mean."

"Ha!"

They picked a shoal on the edge of the Caicos Bank and chose exactly the right weather, a falling barometer and a dull scud working up from the south. *Albertine* scraped twice on the coral before she fetched up hard. Sax himself was at the wheel and there was no one else on deck except Halkett and one of the Barbadian seamen, who was curled up and dozing in the shade of the main-sail. The rest of the crew ran out of the forecastle, looking more surprised than alarmed.

"She's a goner," Halkett told them calmly. "Current set us to loo'ard more'n I figured on." He jerked a thumb. "Pack your duds and lower the boat. We've just got nice time to make that island yonder afore the weather breaks."

They reached the shore without difficulty, and from the shelter of a salt raker's hut they watched *Albertine* perish. They had left all sail set, and under the first hard gust of the wind she heeled sharply, bringing her keel off the coral. She drifted a length or two farther onto the shoal before striking again. Then she was firmly wedged, and the next gust took the masts out of her. After that she was hidden in rain, a gray Niagara that filled the whole view between clouds and sea and hissed on towards the land. In the morning there was nothing to be seen but her forward end, flung up on a reef with the bowsprit pointing almost to the sky, and a scatter of planks, spars and rubbish bobbing in the surf beyond.

Three weeks later the informal partnership of Halkett

and Nolan dissolved informally in Nassau, where they divided the nine thousand dollar insurance money and shook hands for the last time.

"Going home, I suppose?" Sax murmured, wondering what he should do himself.

"No." A dreamy look came over Halkett's long tanned face. "Used to think I'd make a pile and then flake down in some little Nova Scotia town where there's nothin' much but a post office, a church and a cider mill, inland, y'understand, where I wouldn't have to look at the sea all day and hear it windy nights on the shore. Place where I could build a bit of a bungalow and have a nice garden at the back and maybe a few apple or cherry trees. But I dunno, I don't seem to see it that way any more, not after all this time away from ice and snow and those blasted long wet springs. I'm gettin' on, Sax, fifty-four, and this Bahama climate suits me to a *T*.

"Never told you, Sax, but I've had a woman Jamaica way the past fourteen years. Off-and-on affair, a week together maybe and then I'd be off on my travels for months or a year, maybe more. When the war broke out I left her and come north to Nova Scotia. Hankered to see the old place ag'in. Figured to get a job coastin' and stay awhile. But I got tired of it and bought *Albertine*. Got to hankerin' for some sunshine with a bite to it, and trees that ain't bare half the year, and all the good cheap rum."

"And the woman?"

"And her. Funny, ain't it? 'Cause she ain't young any more. She's over forty now. I've had others, north and south, you know me; but there never was any like her. So I've wrote her to pack her stuff and come up here to Nassau. I've got enough money salted away to build a little place on one o' the out-islands, away from all these blasted tourists, and to keep her and me nice and com-

38

fortable the rest of our time. Take my advice, Sax, and do the same here or somewheres afore you get as old as me. Ever wonder why you're so dam' restless? Like a cat on hot bricks all the time? I'll tell you. T'aint natural for a strong healthy man like you not to smoke nor drink nor ever take a shine to a woman. What's the use of everlastin' schemin' and workin' to make money if you wind up with nothin' to spend it on? Think that over, Sax. And so long!"

Sax tipped his straw hat forward to shade his eyes, turned away from the black rectangle thrown down by the shop arcade and walked into the blinding heat of the street. He did not share Halkett's liking for these latitudes. He hated the stinks, the glare, the poisonous green of the fertile islands, the harsh palmettos and scrub pine of the rest. And he despised the people, all of them. His inner demon jeered at that naïve confession of Halkett — Halkett of all people! — and the captain's notion of peace on earth. Rum, cigars, a Jamaica slut and a little place in the sun. None of that for Sax Nolan! He detested still the smell of tobacco and he had never been tempted to drink, for he had seen too often what happened to people who drank; they fell into the toils of people like himself.

As for women, his old obsession remained. He had never been able to forget the girls of Port Barron who laughed at him, and the promise he had made himself all that time ago. He could see no satisfaction of that promise in the women of the Caribbean ports, not the kind a sailor met anyhow, who peddled their flesh in fo'c'sles or in dim-lit rooms up reeking alleys by the docks. Not even the more difficult kind, the wives and daughters of poor whites in the islands, whose favorite word was "respectable," who had to be won over with smooth lies and compliments. He had seduced a few of these and

39

come away unrefreshed, despising them because they gave something for nothing, because they were not smart as he was smart.

As he walked along in the sunshine two women rode past on bicycles and stopped before him at the curb. They stepped off, laughing and chatting for a few moments before passing into a shop. People from the hotel. Mother and daughter probably, although they looked like sisters — you never could tell with these rich American types. Their thin white dresses fluttered in the hot wind along Bay Street and showed the sleek shaved legs and the lines of their tall figures. Their faces and arms were honey-tanned, and when they smiled their teeth made a clean flash in the sun. Sax gave them a bold stare and passed on.

Class! Now there was something! But of course you couldn't get near a woman like that unless you had Class yourself, or money, a lot of money. His notion of wealth was still the old notion of the cape, where fifty thousand dollars was a sum pronounced in widely separated syllables, each with emphasis, and where anything over that was associated with distant bodies like John D. Rockefeller or "guvment." After eight years of sweat and artful dodging his own fortune was less than fifteen thousand dollars. He told himself sourly, Here you are twenty-nine, and you'll probably end up like Halkett, settling for a quadroon woman and a shack amongst the conchs.

In this mood he reached the harbor and saw among the gaudy sponge boats and out-island sloops with their fantastic names a long gray motor craft sliding in towards the dock. She had an expensive but raffish look, for her paint was blistered and her deck unclean and all her brasswork had gone green with verdigris. About her deck lounged half a dozen men in grimy ducks, some with shirts and some without, three of them obviously mulattos, one plainly a Negro, and two apparent half-castes whom, on closer inspection, he saw to be white men deeply tanned. One of these he recognized. It was Norris.

~ ~ *Chapter 5*

IN a dockside bar, sipping at a planter's punch and jingling the ice in the glass, Norris told a tale; and Sax, over an iced lemonade, regarded him with interest.

"How long's this been going on?" he asked.

The former Grand Bank fisherman shrugged and grinned. "Ever since the States went dry. When I got home things were pretty flat, fish prices down, vessels laid up, fellas with empty pockets mooching about the wharves. Somebody got a hunch and took a schooner up to St. Pierre, you know, that French island up by Newfoundland. The Frenchmen don't hold with prohibition. They've got lots of booze to sell, and they can smell a dollar as far as the moon — with a fair wind they could smell a dime. A sprinkle of palm oil in the customhouse gets you two clearances, one to the Bahamas with a cargo of booze and the other to Nova Scotia in ballast — nothing more.

"See the game? If you don't you're blind. Inside six months a whole fleet of ships was playing it, everything from old cod hookers to swank steam yachts. You load the booze at St. Pierre and sail to what's called Rum Row, outside the three-mile limit off New York. There you sell the stuff over the side for cash, to a lot of blokes who come offshore in fast motorboats. If the U.S. Coast Guard gets nosy you sling your hook and head south. If they stop you, why, you show your clearance for Nassau with a load of liquor and what can they do? Not a blooming thing. A ship bound from St. Pierre to Nassau's got to sail right down the east coast of the U.S. to get there, ain't she? Soon as the C.G. boat's out of sight you circle back to the Row, or sell the stuff off Atlantic City or some other place."

"What's the clearance to Nova Scotia for — the one in ballast?"

"Figure it out, Sax. You got to refit somewhere, get water and provisions, have your engines checked over, a caulking job maybe, all that kind of thing. St. Pierre's no place for that. Nothing there but booze and codfish and five-centime coppers in the change. So on your way back empty from Rum Row you put into a Nova Scotia port somewhere, show the Canadian customs your clearance in ballast from St. Pierre, and there you are. You lay up alongside a ship-fitting wharf, snug as a bug, and all nice and legal."

"Then what are you doing here? I thought you said the clearance to Nassau was just a bluff."

"Sure it was. Still is, for fellas working Rum Row from St. Pierre. But listen to this. Last year I was in that game in a Lunenburg schooner that had a diesel aft for extra speed. We got overhauled off Rum Row by one of the new Coast Guard cutters, thing like a small warship, guns and all. Our skipper showed his papers for Nassau, the same old game, and started jogging south. But this time the cutter stuck to our wake like a shark. Couldn't shake him off. We dodged about, specially at night, but they kept a searchlight on us and stuck right with us. Finally we got so far south there wasn't anything for it but to go on to Nassau for grub and water and oil fuel. So in we came and showed our clearance with booze from St. Pierre. Funny thing when you stop to think of it. Like taking ice to Labrador. But all nice and legal as I said afore. The customs bloke didn't even crack a smile.

"Our owner had an agent here and everything was hunky-dory. It was nice to be going about in a shirt and trousers and taking it easy again, after all that knocking about high latitudes in every kind of weather, mostly cold. Next day, right here in this very bar, I met a bloke in the rum game out of Nassau, running the stuff across to Miami. In our old hooker the seamen got a hundred and fifty dollars a month and we thought we worked for Santa Clause. This bloke was getting double that just for working as a deck hand in a motor launch, and a bonus every three trips. I thought he was swinging the lead but it was gospel truth.

"Well, Sax, I got to figuring. Those new C.G. cutters ain't carrying guns for fun. Cannons, I mean, and machine guns besides. They must plan to use 'em sometime. We heard the U.S. government had passed a law that shoved the old three-mile limit out to 'one hour's sail,' whatever that means. What's more, if a C.G. boat spots you inside that she can chase you to hell-and-gone, anywhere on the high seas, and shoot besides. There's been a lot of talk about it here in Nassau. Some said if you flew the British flag they wouldn't dare. Some said the Yanks meant business and you might as well fly Maggie's drawers. Anyhow I could see one thing plain. The game was getting rough and I didn't fancy our old hooker for it any more. That kind of game, you want to be in something low and fast. So I got myself this job in the rumrunner at the dock. She don't look pretty but she can dam' near fly. We run the stuff right in to shore, no hanging about. She's one of a little fleet that belongs to a bootlegging gang in

Miami and they fix things so we don't have anything to worry about over there. We just chuck the stuff onto a beach or a wharf and beat it back to Nassau."

"Sounds like fun," Sax murmured.

"It sure beats jigging codfish on the Quero Bank."

"Any chance of a berth?"

"I'll speak to the big shot if you like. Not my skipper; he's a tough bloke and he'd give me hell for blowing the gaff, even to a friend. The Boss is more broad-minded, when it comes to picking up good seamen anyhow. You really mean it, about a berth? If you do, come with me."

The Boss lived in style, in an apartment on the airy side of a swank Nassau hotel. As they passed through the foyer, Sax in his coarse straw hat and soiled linen suit, Norris unshaven and clad in singlet and ducks, Sax fully expected to be stopped and ordered out. But they drew no attention at all. On the second floor Norris knocked at a door and called, "Norris, Boss!" There was a silence, then a petulant feminine voice saying something indistinct. A single blunt word in a man's voice. A sound of movement and a quick tic-tac of heels across a bare part of the floor. Then the man's voice sharply, saying "Okay, come in."

The two seamen entered, Sax taking off his hat politely. A large man was seated in a comfortable cane chair facing the door. A thin streak of cigarette smoke hung across the room, and there was that peculiar blend of perfume and woman flesh, always intriguing to Sax, which betrayed the recent presence of a lady. It was a sitting room with Venetian blinds tilted to shut out the afternoon glare, and the blinds were swaying and rattling with the puffs of the trade wind.

"Boss," Norris said, "this is Sax Nolan, looking for a job. I was shipmates with him in a Nova Scotia schooner, Ja-

44

maica way, some time back. Good sailor. Smart head on him. Do anything. Tell him, Sax."

Sax wondered what to tell. He knew the Boss must be a gangster of some kind and he was surprised to see one who looked so exactly like the boss gangsters in newspaper tales. A bullet head, half bald, half oiled black hair, a large round pale-cheese face smudged with the beard of a man who should shave twice a day (like a nor'west moon in a fog, thought Sax), a strong figure gone to fat and clad in well-cut pongees, white socks and shoes and a silk shirt open at the throat. Everything was there, even the gold rings on the fat fingers and the one big diamond.

He did not get up and he did not ask his visitors to sit down. He inspected Sax with a pair of black Sicilian eyes that would have looked better in a woman's face. "Well?" he said. Norris stood with feet stiffly apart and his hands tucked behind him, the proper attitude of a seaman in the owner's presence. But Sax met the black stare with one as bold, with a flickering impudent smile; and he slid into a chair, tossing his hat on the floor. In the silence the small plop of the hat was like an explosion.

"You heard what Norris said," he murmured in his light suave voice. "I guess there's not much else to say. I'm a seaman all right and I want a job. Been mate of a schooner in the island trade and now and then a run across the Gulf, carrying everything from sugar to Chinks. Carried whiskey once."

"Where?" snapped the Boss.

"Texas."

"Outside our beat. What makes you think I'd give you a job?"

"Nothing. I'm not here to beg a job from you or anybody else. I'm giving you a chance to take me on,

45

that's all. If you don't, somebody else will. In this rum game there must be . . ."

"Who said anything about the rum game?" The Boss shot a black glance at Norris.

"Everybody in Nassau — everyone I've met anyhow. It's all they talk about. If you don't know that, it's time you did. Don't keep looking at Norris, man, look at me. I'm something you won't often see, a man that don't give a damn for anyone this side of Fiddler's Green — including you. Seems to me you could use my kind of man. If you can't, say so quick. My time's worth money."

The Boss uttered a sound between a chuckle and a snort. The door into the bedroom was slightly ajar and Sax knew the woman must be listening there. Norris was shifting uneasily and breathing hard.

"You're quite a character," the Boss said, regarding Sax's clothes, which looked like something shot upon him from a soiled-laundry chute. "You got some queer pals, Norris, if they're all like this one. More gall than a canal horse. Jesus! Well, Nolan — that your name? — I guess I could use a man with that much gall if the rest of his guts are okay. I'll give you a chance to show me, anyhow. Go back to whatever hole you crawled out of and wait there till Friday morning, see? I got a boat coming in Thursday called the *Belle of Jumentos* and I'll put you in her for a trip or two. You report on board, Friday. Captain's a man named Figueroa, half Mex, half rattlesnake. Don't try any funny business with him. I'll notify him about you. Now get out."

They got out, Sax first putting on the cheap and grubby straw hat with the deliberation of a man who has all time at his disposal. In the street Norris turned upon him angrily.

46

"You bloody fool! What made you act like that?"

"He did," Sax replied casually. "The Boss. The Big Shot. Ha! He's just a sixteen bore trying to make a noise like a ten. Sized him up in a minute. You might have known, if you'd ever stopped to think, he's just the local agent, the bloke who looks after the shipping end of the business. The real boss must be in Miami, in a better apartment in a bigger hotel, with a more expensive woman."

"You didn't see no woman."

Sax let that pass. "This Figueroa, know him?"

"Yes. He's tough. Don't try . . ."

"I know. What's his weakness, booze?"

"I wouldn't know. What makes you think he's got one?"

"Your boss. He's no fool. He wants to see how I stack up with Figueroa. That means he's got a hunch I might be a better man at Figueroa's job."

Norris pulled a squashed packet of cigarettes from his pocket and stuck one in his mouth. He paused to strike a match on his shoe.

"You know your own weakness? You're too dam' cock-sure about Sax Nolan."

Sax laughed softly. "I find it pays. Stop blowing that foul smoke in my face. If you were half as sure of Jim Norris as I am of Sax Nolan you'd be skipper of that boat of yours. You might even be the Boss. You've been here long enough."

⌐ ⌐ Chapter 6

THE *Belle of Jumentos* was a lean gray craft so like the one Sax had seen first that they must have been spawned in the same boatyard in the States. After reporting on board and seeing the inside of her he realized how far the rum game had advanced since the early days that Norris had described. The *Belle* had a pair of expensive and powerful motors, the best of navigating instruments, a short-wave radio outfit, an ingenious device for making artificial smoke astern; and she could carry a large amount of cargo for her apparent size and shape.

Yet he was told that boats like the *Belle* were already out-of-date, that smart marine architects in the States were busy on designs for bigger and faster boats with a longer range. And boats were only a small part of what everyone here called the Racket. In the slangy chat of the bars and docks Sax learned of all-powerful bootlegging rings in American cities and towns, of police and politicians "fixed," of organized trucking between coast and customer, of a whole nation officially dry and apparently soaking wet.

In the past eight years he had seen very few newspapers and most of these in Spanish. The ones he could read were the dull little sheets of the British islands, full of local trifles. Even on *Albertine's* trips to Galveston and New Orleans the thirsty talk ashore had meant little because he did not drink. The experiment with whiskey in Port Arthur had been Halkett's idea and it had turned out badly. He could understand that prohibition had created a vast American thirst. But that the satisfying of this thirst could become in a few years a major industry, with millions of dollars involved, came to Sax as a shock. The petty coups in *Albertine* seemed suddenly a waste of time. This is where I should have been, he reflected glumly. Here, with all this going on. He looked past Hog Island to the hot blue glitter of the channel and seemed to see beyond the slowly sailing wool over Florida Strait a giant machine that sucked in bottles at one end and poured out money at the other.

The skipper of the *Belle,* known in formal moments as Cap'n and familiarly as Fig, was a dark intense person of thirty or thirty-five with the body of a tango dancer and a face ruined by smallpox. In this disfigured mask a pair of sunken black eyes looked forth with darting glances right and left and straight before him as if he suspected a continual menace somewhere within the compass of his gaze. When Sax introduced himself Figueroa cried, "So! You are the man! The Boss takes my best hand and gives him to Ashley and I must take you, a man I never saw before!" He followed this with a rapid recital of Mexican saints with long sonorous names, all the time glaring in Sax's eyes, then over his right shoulder, then the left.

"You can steer, what-is-your-name?"

"Name's Nolan. I can steer."

"You know something about engines? Radio?"

"Engines, yes. Radio, no."

"You are not an American."

"I'm a Nova Scotian."

Figueroa made a gesture of his hands as if Sax had said Eskimo or something else beyond the limit of Christian knowledge.

"You better be good, whatever you are. You drink?"

"No."

"You lie then. Everybody drinks but me. Nolan? Is that right?"

"Nolan. Right."

"We pull out in the morning. You be here, on board, sober, understand?"

The skipper went off towards the shops of Bay Street, a dapper figure in neatly pressed ducks with a yachting cap cocked over one eye. The other members of his crew, a mixture of whites and mulattos, lounged in the shade of the long cabin house. One of them arose lazily and addressed Sax in the drawl of a Florida cracker.

"So you're the new man?"

"Here we go again. Yes, and the name's Nolan."

"What do you think of Fig?"

"That a personal question or part of the routine?"

A disarming grin. "Take it any way you like."

"Ah! Well, so far I don't care much for Fig. Face like a nutmeg grater. Acts like a sick wolf. What's wrong with him, booze?"

"He don't drink. He told you that."

"Dope? Women?"

The cracker shook his head. "I wouldn't know." And with another grin, "Oh he ain't bad, Fig, if you do your job and let him do the talking."

"I aim to do just that," Sax said.

For two months Sax did his job, a variety of jobs — at the helm, in the hold stowing or unloading liquor, at the bow with a sounding pole in tricky passages among the Florida reefs in the dark, in the wilting heat of the engine room with Sands, the cracker, who was engineer. The boat made its runs from one of the outer Bahama cays. The cay was privately owned and the only buildings on it were a substantial house, the former winter residence of a Chicago plumbing contractor, a long capacious boathouse with a veranda running along the seaward side, and a stone quay. After the Chicago man's death it had been operated as a sea-anglers' club by a group from Miami, and the present owners maintained the fiction of the club.

Between the Bahamas and Florida lay the favorite

50

hunting ground of American sportsmen angling for tarpon and other large and energetic fish, and the Gulf Stream there was always dotted with expensive motor craft in that pursuit, operating from both sides. These made good cover for the Trident Cay Fishing Club and its busy boats, which could be seen in the afternoons moving at half speed in the Stream with the proper fishing poles outrigged and a fishing chair prominent in the stern. They slid in to the Florida shore after dark, at points given by short-wave radio in the seemingly innocent gibberish of ham operators on the American side. The points usually were close to Miami but they might be anywhere from Key Largo to the Hetzel Shoals. Sometimes the boat was unloaded at a dock, at what appeared to be a residence or a clubhouse like the one across the strait. Usually it was a beach with a huddle of cars at the head of it gleaming faintly in the starlight; and after the correct challenge by Figueroa and the proper answer from the shore a swarm of silent figures came down the beach to carry off the cargo.

Sometimes they found the beach empty, and after a long wait in the dark, with Figueroa cursing softly in English and Yucatán Spanish, the *Belle* slid out into the strait again until the puzzle could be solved by radio for the next night's run. Often they had to play hide-and-seek with Coast Guard patrols among the reefs and bars, and Sax became familiar with the *fit-fit-fit* of bullets passing in the dark. Once near Lauderdale they were, in Sands's phrase, jumped by highjackers, and the crew shoved off just in time while Sax and Figueroa sprayed the dark with pistol fire. It was all of great interest to Sax, and profitable, for he was getting in pay and bonuses three hundred dollars per month, paid promptly by the Boss and safely cached in a Nassau bank.

At the end of the second month Sax was called into Nassau to see the Boss. This time a woman remained in the room, a long blonde engrossed in dyeing and polishing her fingernails. Sax sniffed. A different woman. His keen scent for women told him that at once, some sharp animal instinct in him unspoiled by tobacco or alcohol. She was tanned and handsome and she used no cosmetics but lipstick, which made a bright scarlet slot in the tan — a little startling at first sight. She paid no attention to Sax and after that first quick summary of sight and scent he ignored her. Good-looking in a way but no Class. Without that they were just a lot of talking dummies. It brought the small twitch to his lips to perceive that the Boss changed his dummy from time to time. He dropped into a chair and threw his new and expensive Panama on the floor as he had thrown the cheap Bahamian straw on that first occasion, as a challenge. It said plainly, Here-I-am-speak-up. The Boss spoke up.

"Nolan, I been sizing you up."

"You mean Figueroa and Sands have been sizing me up and reporting back to you. Okay, what do they say?"

The Boss turned a hand on the chair arm and the big diamond glittered.

"That's none of your business. What I want's the lowdown on Figueroa now."

"Isn't Sands's opinion good enough?"

"I like two opinions when I'm sizing up a man. Let's hear yours."

"Okay. Fig's a good skipper. He's tough. He's loyal to the Boss. You said he was half Mex and half rattlesnake. Well, there you're wrong. He's all rattlesnake. And he rattles at the wrong end."

"What d'you mean? You mean he's nuts?"

"Of course I do. Sands must have told you that. It's been coming on some time, I guess."

"How d'you know? What way is he nuts?"

Sax crossed his white flannel knees with care for the creases, showing the silk socks above his fifteen-dollar shoes. On his new pay, and after a careful study of the visitors here in the Hollywood picture-set atmosphere of Nassau, he had discovered the pleasure of fine raiment.

"I'll give you a sample. That time up by Lauderdale. Fig got the shakes. He always does after a bit of excitement. But that time he pulled me aside and said he knew something bad was going to happen because the Devil had told him in a private chat the night before."

"Just kidding, don't you think?"

"It didn't sound funny to me. It seems Fig's pretty chummy with the Devil. You know he had a lot of birds from his part of Mexico, cardinals and green parakeets. Kept 'em in cages in the boathouse on the cay and paid the cook to look after 'em when he was away on business. After we got back that trip Fig went straight into the boathouse and after a minute there was a deuce of a row amongst the birds. They're a noisy lot, always whistling and squawking, but this time it sounded different. I went along the veranda and looked in a window, and there was Fig, swearing blue and taking the birds out of the cages, one by one, and wringing their necks. I yelled 'What's the idea?' He just gave me a nod and went on with the job, yelling over his shoulder that one of the birds, he didn't know which, had blown the gaff to the highjackers. *'Traidor! Traidor!'* he'd yell, and wring another one's neck. He went through the lot. It was something to watch. At the end he turned to me quite satisfied and said the

Devil had tipped him off. Maybe that was kidding, too. But a bit rough on the birds, eh?"

The big blonde went on painting her nails with undivided interest. The Boss sat with eyes closed, nodding slowly. His heavy white eyelids lifted.

"Okay, Nolan. What does Sands call you — Sax? So Figueroa's nuts. I been hearing things about Fig and what you say checks." He paused. "Heard a lot about you, too. Hear you're quite a man in a boat. Hear you don't scare easy. All that. Think you could handle the skipper's job?"

"I'm counting on it."

"Oh? Well, okay. So you're skipper from now on."

"What about Figueroa?"

"He's fired. I'll break the news to Fig myself."

"That's nice of you," Sax murmured, rising and picking up his hat. He closed the door behind him gently as he went. In the street the hot light exploded in his face but he went on through it with his quick gliding walk and reached the *Belle,* sweating and triumphant. Figueroa was ashore. Sands took one look at Sax's face and laughed.

"So you're cap'n for a spell."

"Yes. By the way, what did you tell the Boss about Fig?"

"Fig? Oh I just happened to mention Fig was getting a bit queer. All that stuff about the Devil when things went wrong. That jumpy look. You know. Fig was getting tough to get along with, one way or another. What he needs is a rest. Take a holiday somewhere. That's what I told the Boss. What did you say?"

Sax told him, with the faint smile, the monkey-imp gleam. Sands gave him a hard look and whistled.

"You know dam' well the cook got drunk and scragged

54

all Fig's birds while we were off, that trip. Fig wanted to kill the cook. He was fit to be tied."

"And fired," Sax said.

Sands was not smiling any more. "Fired? They don't just fire a guy that knows as much as Figueroa."

"Maybe they'll hand him over to the S.P.C.A. for cruelty to birds."

"Maybe. Quite a storyteller, Sax, ain't you?"

"Smart's the word," Sax said amiably. "Just smart."

◠ ◠ Chapter 7

AND so the affairs of Sax Nolan had entered upon a new and more profitable cycle. His pay now amounted to five hundred dollars per month. For a long time he was satisfied. In the course of four years the *Belle* was discarded for a faster thing called *Gloria B.*, and *Gloria* gave way to a succession of others that culminated in a floating torpedo named *Faquita III*. Sax saved his money carefully. His one indulgence was the taste for fine clothing that had come to him in Nassau. He kept a room there for a wardrobe, hung with suits of every stuff from pongee to Harris tweed; and there were shirts in a stack, silk underwear in another, and socks and hats, a parade of well-polished shoes, a tie rack that glowed like a flowering bush. All this was expensive in that place where money now was so flush, and shops and tailors set their prices to match the times. In the States the stock market and the Racket were booming along on their separate tracks, everyone was prosperous, and Nassau in the winter season was becoming a little Riviera in which the Cockney-Afro-Oxford accents of the inhabitants were overlaid by

American tones all the way from Harvard to the Chicago Loop and the plainer parts of Kansas.

Fine feathers may or may not make fine birds, but they require the birds to strut in fine places if they are to get their money's worth. On his spells ashore Sax began to lounge about the tourist hotels and the better bars, rubbing well-tailored shoulders with those of the well-to-do, easing himself into conversation and chatting pleasantly in his mild voice. By this time, like certain others in his trade, he was something of a character in Nassau. Residents and regular visitors pointed him out in the street as one of the most daring and successful skippers in the rum game. To newcomers the glamour of a twentieth-century buccaneer hung about him like a nimbus.

They relished his conversation and they would go out of their way to be seen with him. He met their curiosity about his current affairs with a grin and a shrug; but he would tell frank tales of his other adventures, the career of *Albertine* and the ports and places he had seen. He told witty little anecdotes and some of the best of them were repeated in the hotels, on the beach, at yachting parties, on the swank estates that lay outside the town. After a time he began to get invitations to lunch and dine, or to join a cocktail party, where his smiling refusal of drinks was regarded as the oddest thing about an oddly fascinating character. He wore his vivid reputation with indifference, as a tiger wears his stripes, and with very much the same careless grace.

He was smart about all this. In aping the clothes and manners of these rich and pleasant idlers he was careful to copy those with Class, and in all his associations he kept a sharp eye for the spurious, the second- and third-raters dressed in first-rate clothes, and the female dummies in their company. Moreover, he examined himself.

56

None of his clever schooling in Port Barron had been lost. He could talk easily and grammatically when he chose, and he furnished his mind for conversation with a careful reading of books and magazines. In the Nassau public library, a queer octagonal building formerly the jail, he made a study of Bahamian history, so that after a time he could take groups of his new friends for little tours of old Fort Charlotte and the other points of interest and amuse them with the proper tales.

In this capacity he encountered Ellen Carisfort. She was staying a month in Nassau with her parents and they had met Sax on one of the estates. They were Class, he knew at once. He was not surprised to learn that Carisfort was a senior partner in an old and prosperous law firm in Boston, that Ellen had gone the route of Miss Somebody's School, and Vassar, and a postgraduate course in social science, and that the family had a house in Back Bay and what they called a shack among the lakes of upper Maine. They did not mention a yacht; but wealth was not everything and all the rest chimed with Sax's carefully read and observed notions of Background, that essential part of Class. They dressed well but unobtrusively, they talked with intelligence and in quiet voices, their tastes were simple. They had Everything, even the right looks.

Ellen Carisfort was twenty-five, a slender girl of middle height with brown hair which she wore in a short bob. Her face was lightly tanned, the discreet tan of a woman who usually wears a hat when the sun is strong, and like everything else about her the cosmetics she used were moderate. She had clear gray eyes that looked at you with quick straight glances like a boy's, and she had a figure like a boy's, although when she put on bathing dress you had no doubt about her sex.

Mr. Carisfort was amused by Sax's tales and the rest of the family were curious about the man himself. They had heard all about him, he could see. When he offered to show them about the island the next day they accepted eagerly. In the course of the tour they came to the Nassau library and halted before a replica of the Nassau coat of arms. It showed a seaman in eighteenth-century dress brandishing a cutlass in one hand and holding in the other a scroll reading *Expulsis piratis commercia restituta.*

"I'm sorry I don't know what it means," Sax confessed.

Mr. Carisfort adjusted his glasses and cleared his throat. "Well, Captain Nolan, an old lawyer's Latin doesn't run to stuff like this, but offhand I'd say it meant 'We kick out pirates and, um, restore commerce.' Something like that anyhow." Ellen Carisfort turned a pair of lively eyes on Sax.

"Captain Nolan, aren't you scared sometimes?"

Her parents gave her amused but reproving looks. Sax laughed softly, seeing in Ellen's eyes a sudden interest that had not been there before, the interest of a healthy young woman in an intriguing male. From that moment he was lost. He was infatuated. It was an astonishing experience. He could think of nothing but Ellen Carisfort. To be hers and to possess her seemed the ordained and suddenly manifest object of his whole life. He demanded a fortnight's leave from the Boss so that he might spend every possible moment in her company. The Boss had changed three times since the fat Sicilian of his first acquaintance. The current one was a dry brown man, all bones and leather, with eyes of blue ice, who spoke with an English accent and carried himself like an army officer. He lived in a house in Bay Street and was known to the rum-boat crews as the Major. He was tough, but he knew how well Sax had served the mysterious syndicate which had its brains and bank account in Miami and he assented with a nod.

And so for two full weeks Sax basked in the Nassau sunshine and the light of Miss Carisfort's eyes. They were constantly together. If Mr. and Mrs. Carisfort had any qualms, they did not reveal them. Captain Nolan's manners were polite and he spoke remarkably well for a seaman. His very oddities were reassuring. His abstinence from drink and women, his positive hatred of tobacco, the fact that he seldom or never used profanity, were all well known and remarked in Nassau. To the Carisforts, therefore, the friendship was something to be accepted as they accepted the island, the sunshine and the sea, as a momentary phenomenon.

Ellen taught Sax to dance, in a corner of the jostling hotel ballroom, to the tunes of a famous American jazz band. He could never dance well but his natural step was a gliding one, and if he could never acquire a sense of rhythm he had at least plenty of agility and poise. Ellen did not drink herself and it annoyed her when people badgered Sax to drink as the trays were passed. But once or twice for a whim she induced him to smoke a cigarette in company with her, and the spectacle of what her mother called the Puritanical Pirate actually and grimly puffing at a Lucky Strike gave her an odd little triumph. In a quiet way she enjoyed the attention they drew at all times, the well-bred American girl and the tough daredevil seaman all Nassau was talking about. But her interest in Sax was real. She was drawn to him not by his adventurous career so much as his curiously repressed inner life, the feeling he gave her of an original male young enough to be companionable and ruffian enough to be dangerous, all chained and locked up by some whim of his own will. That she had a key to the lock and chain occurred to her sometimes in a puzzling and lightly amusing way, as if she had found a means of unlocking a cage in a zoo and did not know quite what to do about the tenant.

As the days slipped by Sax took her into his confidence. He was thirty-three, he said truthfully, and he had been knocking about the sea since he was twenty-one. He'd had enough of it. What he wanted now was to settle down. He'd made quite a lot of money and he had a notion to invest it in a coastal shipping business up north, in Nova Scotia, say, where he was born. A strictly legitimate business, he added with emphasis. He had thirty thousand dollars, and with that he could buy a decent share, enough to get him a job in the shore end of the business and give him a good cut of the profits. Then he could make a home. A home, he repeated with a wistful air. After twelve years of the sea a man got lonely. He wanted a natural kind of life, the sort of life other men enjoyed.

Ellen soon realized what all this was leading up to and she was embarrassed. Her acquaintance with this modern buccaneer had given the Bahama holiday an unexpected zest but it meant no more than that. She enjoyed the close-knit and affectionate Carisfort family life and she was keen about her social work in Boston. She supposed she would marry some day but her emotions were still intact and she was content. As for marriage with Captain Sax Nolan, the very idea was ridiculous. She was amazed that he could even dream of her consent. And so she warded off his sentimental trend, turning the conversation to other things. Sax found this maddening. When he persisted he found it more and more difficult to get her aside tête à tête. At length she refused even to dance with him.

At the end of his two weeks' leave he was baffled but

60

still polite, and he took a carefully casual farewell of the Carisforts on the evening of his return to Trident Cay. He resumed command of *Faquita* in a surly mood and for the next ten days his crew had a very unhappy life. He managed to run up to Nassau once in that time but the Carisforts were away visiting friends on another island. Their stay was getting near its end and he was desperate. He went to the Major and demanded four more days — "to settle some important business." This time he received a chilling stare.

"What's eating you, Sax?"

"Nothing — nothing that the next four days can't cure anyhow."

"I don't like the way you're acting. And don't give me any of that tough talk, I've heard it all before. I could put someone else in your job tomorrow for good."

"I know," Sax admitted with unaccustomed meekness.

"I am not blind and I'm not deaf, Sax. You've been hanging about an American girl at the hotel and she's had you jumping through hoops. I didn't think the woman lived who could do that to Sax Nolan. Well, it won't do, Sax. Not in this business. A bit of fluff now and then, yes, that's natural. But this girl's not fluff. Her father's a well-connected lawyer in the States. It's time you opened your eyes, my friend, not to mention shutting your mouth. Or am I too late with that advice?"

"You know me better than that, Major. Four days, that's all I ask."

"Very well, Sax. Four days, no more. And watch your step."

Sax haunted the Carisforts' hotel. They did not return until the day before they were due to sail, but when they found him in the foyer they greeted him cheerfully and invited him to lunch. At the table the conversation rambled all the way from deep-sea angling to New York plays and Ellen took a fluent part. Indeed, she was so talkative that her father and mother looked at her in some surprise; and when she was not talking she was gazing at her food, at the orchestra, at guests passing in and out of the dining room, often breaking into a bright smile at someone she knew and twiddling fingers aloft. When out of courtesy she turned to Sax and made a remark she did it with an evasive manner that galled him. As they discarded their napkins and drew back the chairs, however, Ellen turned and said diffidently, "We're joining the Telfords for a last afternoon on the beach. Over on Hog Island. We've dawdled so much over lunch that we won't dine till late, and we can all have a swim towards evening when it's best. Would you like to come?"

Would he like to breathe! Later on, changing to beach trunks in one of the dressing cubicles above the beach, he inspected himself in the mirror. He saw a face deeply tanned and smooth-shaven. He smiled two or three times and admired his teeth. And there was the glistening black hair, his particular care and pride, parted exactly in the middle and slicked back along the sides of his head, with a short ducktail at the back where the two wings met and combined. He looked down at his hands, at their broad tufted backs and the agile fingers which he kept so carefully manicured. He inspected his taut muscled legs, and the thick trunk with its jungle of black hair, the accepted mark of male virility on every beach in the world. An expensive wrist watch gleamed on one hairy wrist. He turned again to the glass, nodded, smiled, caught up the beach robe and stepped forth into the sunshine.

There were introductions. He approved of the Telfords. They had Class marked clearly upon them like

62

the Carisforts, although Telford was rather fat and Mrs. Telford too tall and thin. Their son Blaine was a good specimen of the young American of Class, tall like his mother and with his father's chest, a handsome blend. He spoke with a Harvard accent and was a junior executive in his father's business. He was about Ellen's age and apparently knew her well, for they sat together on the beach and chatted like old friends, with a frequent putting of heads together and murmured phrases and sharp little explosions of laughter.

Sax found himself in the company of the older people, sitting under a huge red parasol while Carisfort engaged him with leading questions for the benefit of the Telfords. They had been told about Captain Nolan and they gave him a curious attention that at any other time he would have relished. Mr. Carisfort would chuckle and say something like, "Captain, I'd like to hear that Havana story again, the one about your sailor and the bartender who stuttered in bad English and the girl with the silver bangles," and dutifully Sax would recite in the wooden voice of a boy at a Sunday school concert, and the story would fall flat in a little silence followed by four polite little laughs.

It was near the end of the winter season, and the beach was dotted with visitors like the Carisforts getting a last fill of sunshine before returning north. The island strand shimmered in the afternoon heat. Figures with brown skins and bright scraps of bathing costume danced in the wavering air, separating, merging in varicolored clots and dancing away again. An array of gaudy beach umbrellas swayed and flapped scalloped fringes in the trade wind like a bed of giant poppies. A scatter of brown children crawled and splashed at the edge of the water. Sax pictured *Faquita* far out in the Stream with Sands beside

63

the helmsman, getting ready for the nightly dash towards Miami. My God, he thought, how tired I am of all that.

Ellen was still engrossed with Blaine Telford, and when at last they all went down to bathe these two ran into the water together, holding hands and laughing. Sax took off his wrist watch and laid it aside with care. He walked down to the water inflating his chest, gripping his fists to make the muscles of his arms stand forth, and trying to make himself tall. For half an hour everybody swam and shouted. Then began the retreat towards the cubicles and the boats for the hotel, a straggle of wet figures up the beach. The older people already were pulling on their robes and leaving the beach, and young Telford trotted up to his mother and took her arm. It was Sax's chance. He met Ellen as she moved towards the red umbrella. The bathing dress clung to her slight body. Her skin was wet and gleaming. She appeared to him the most beautiful thing on earth. He cried in a choking voice, "Ellen, I've got to talk to you."

"All right," she said, still walking quickly.

"It's — uh — personal. D'you mind waiting a bit while the others go on?"

They had reached the parasol and Ellen picked up her robe.

"Please sit down," Sax begged. She sank down on the sand, catching the robe about her shoulders.

"I can't stay more than a minute, Sax. We'll be late for dinner as it is."

Sax murmured and gulped. She looked at him curiously. He swallowed again. Then the words came in a rush. "Ellen, I've wondered how to say this. Thought about it a long time. Still don't know how to put it right. All my life, ever since I was a kid out of school anyway, I've worked and saved money just for one thing. I wanted to marry a

64

girl like you. No, don't move. And don't say anything yet. You've got to hear this, Ellen."

With a quick movement he placed himself beside her and put a hand on her upper arm, that delicate miracle of bone and flesh. She sat facing the sea with her hands clasped about her knees. Her eyes were shut. Her whole attitude said, Oh Lord, how did I ever get into this? But she was calm. She felt that she was being very patient and she wanted to be kind.

"Ellen I've got thirty thousand dollars."

"Oh Sax, please!"

"All right. Money doesn't mean anything to you. Because you've always had it, see? It means a lot to me because I've had to work and save it so I could say this to a girl with Class. I mean a girl that's been used to having everything nice. Girl with education and looks and all that. Girl like you. As for me, I know you like me, Ellen. You like to be with me and hear me talk. You get a kick out of me, you've said it yourself. And why not? I'm a man that's been places and done things. I'm not like young Telford, who's never done anything but go to college and sit at a desk in his father's office. And I'm young — young! And strong, you see that. I've never poisoned myself with booze or tobacco or anything like that." He paused for breath.

Ellen spoke swiftly. "Sax — Captain Nolan — please don't say any more. It's impossible. It isn't that I don't like you. It's just that I don't want to marry you or anybody else. Now please let me go."

"Ellen! Ellen!"

"No! And you're hurting my arm."

She attempted to rise. Sax lost his head. He threw an arm about her waist and clutched at her breast with the other, dragging her towards him and thrusting his lips on

65

her mouth. Nothing of this was calculated. It was rooted perhaps in his few experiences with women, those shabby and unsatisfactory conquests of his early years in *Albertine,* the half-repelled, half-fascinated wives of planters and drunken dock officials, who had listened to his quiet voice and said No like Ellen Carisfort and then given in to a sudden embrace and the hot feel of his mouth. But he had too much respect for Ellen, for that aura of Class which she wore like a golden armor, to make a conscious blunder of this sort. What occurred was the instinctive act of a greedy urchin pawing at sweets on a passing plate.

Ellen's response was instinctive also, a quick swing of her palm at the swarthy face and a writhe that slipped her wet person out of his grasp. In the silence of the now deserted beach the slap was like a shot. She sprang away several steps, leaving him sprawled and clutching at the empty robe. He did not try to get up. He remained in that posture, astonished and dismayed, seeing his dream ruined in a stroke. He stared at her angry face with a piteous appeal. And then she crushed him.

"You — you ape!" she cried, and fled.

∽ ∽ Chapter 8

IT was no good, going over the past. It had been an uneasy night, pricking with all those memories. He had not slept. And when he walked out to Caraday House with the banker on the following afternoon he was in an irritable mood. The house stood a mile to the west of Port Barron, with a fine view of the sea and the distant

66

islands. It was at the end of the road. Beyond this point there was nothing but a sheep path wandering along the shore. Sax remembered a long trim lawn running down to the road, dotted with circular flower beds and screened from the salt winds off Fundy by a dense hedge of spruce trees. But now many of the spruces were dead, the lawn was a rank waste of unscythed grass gone brown in the winter frosts, and only the circles of conch shells grinning like the teeth of skulls betrayed where the flower beds had been.

They walked up one leg of a U-shaped carriage drive whose gravel had become overgrown with plantain weeds except for a worn footpath up the middle. The old mansion was a wooden one of the gingerbread-Gothic kind that sprang up in the eastern States and Canada during the opulent 1880's and 1890's. At each corner of its rectangular block arose tall oriels running up two stories and tapering off in spirelike roofs, each crowned with iron filigree. From the four delicately curved sides of each pinnacle peered four absurd little false dormers. Behind and within these like the keep of a fortress arose the main house roof, sweeping up in the same curves as the oriels to a captain's walk along the top, surrounded by an iron balustrade. Sax pictured old John C. up there scraping the horizon with a spyglass whenever one of his ships was due.

Along the front of the house ran a veranda with a wooden railing and pine balusters turned in rich feminine curves. From its eaves dripped an elaborate frieze of wooden fretwork. The windows were large, their upper sashes filled with stained glass in various hues; and there was stained glass in the upper half of the great front door, in the side lights running beside the door frame and in the fanlight above. The house had been painted brown

67

and its quaint candle-snuffer roofs a deep red; but the
paint had not been renewed in a long time, it had flaked
away in patches, some of which still hung by a shred, as if
the old shingles were nourishing a growth of lichen. There
were other signs of time and neglect — in the sagging floor
of the veranda, in the missing balusters here and there,
and in the broken sections of wooden gingerbread along
the eaves.

Someone had made a valiant attempt to keep trim a
part of the great lawn. A strip perhaps fifty feet wide had
been mowed with a small scythe or sickle, whose uneven
strokes still showed in the brown grass stubble. Within
this mowed strip were some shrubs of lilac, weigela and
deutzia, and three arched trellises covered with rambler
rose, all winter-bare and guarded from frost by a careful
layer of spruce boughs about the roots.

Sax noted these matters with a jaundiced eye as he
came up the carriageway, thinking of the times he had
dragged his little fish cart up there and around to the
back door. By God, he thought, I could put 'em into the
street now if I wanted to. He conjured a scene in which
the Caradays would beg him for mercy. He would let
them abase themselves to his satisfaction and then tell
them and MacIlraith coldly that he had no interest in
them or their bankrupt firm. And he would march down
that seedy and unkempt driveway and off to some other
town that pleased him better. As he crossed the wavering
floor of the veranda at the banker's side he knew the
very terms he would use and the way he would say them.
No rough stuff. Nothing crude. Just the cold polite manner,
the faint contemptuous smile, the bored look that would
leave them desolate.

The storm door that protected the main entrance from
winter gales had broken its rusty hinges and now leaned

useless against the shingles. MacIlraith hooked his walking stick over his left arm and rapped smartly on the inner door. A silence. Then the faint sound of a door opening at the end of the hall, and footsteps. The stained glass was of a purple tint and the low sun of a March afternoon shone under the veranda and poked a dyed beam into the hall. In this unearthly light Sax perceived a woman approaching the door and smiling at MacIlraith through the glass. At first he did not recognize her. She was of middle height, quite fat, and clad in an afternoon dress that might have been modish about seven years before. Her hair was mouse-gray and dressed in the high coiffure of Queen Alexandra's day. She wore pearl earrings and a black ribbon about her throat, and there was a small watch with a case of chased gold pinned to the breast of her dress. She opened the door and put out a hand to MacIlraith, who murmured at once, "Mrs. Caraday, may I present Captain Nolan?"

For a moment Sax gaped. He had thought this was the housekeeper. He searched his memory hastily. He had last seen the mistress of Caraday House as an elegant and somewhat petulant creature with a neat figure and brown hair, elaborately dressed and usually skimming between the house and town in the glittering Caraday carriage-and-pair. She must have been thirty-five or so, even then, but she had never looked more than a girl, and when you saw her with her seven-year-old daughter you had an impression that Roger Caraday must have married her out of boarding school.

Now after his long absence she must be fiftyish, as Bostwick had said, but she looked all of sixty. And a frump, a shapeless frump. He shook delicately the cool soft hand that was put in his and bowed slightly, wondering if she could know him after all this time. But she did not, he saw at once. To the elegant mistress of Caraday House he had never been more than a nondescript boy selling fish at the back door. It was just as well — he preferred to remain unknown — but even so he felt a further stab of resentment.

Inside, they hung their hats and overcoats on a rack by the door. There was a little armory on one wall, an array of guns, some ancient and some modern, including two very good English shotguns that must have cost a fortune even in John C.'s day. The two men followed Mrs. Caraday into a drawing room at the right. Sax gazed carefully about him. He had never seen more than the back door and a glimpse of the big kitchen, and now he felt the involuntary awe that smites any stranger who finds himself in a palace known to him only as a print in an old book.

But what might have impressed him in boyhood days now left him unmoved and even cynical. A lot of heavy mahogany furniture with the upholstery faded and worn. A carpet gone thin in the trodden places though originally "good." A tall case-clock in a corner. A grand piano with worn yellow keys. A Chinese screen. A mahogany *étagère,* whose shelves displayed a beautiful model of a brigantine in carved ivory, a bristle of white branch-coral, some curious West Indian and Mexican jars and an assortment of family photographs framed in gilt metal and plush.

A fire of split birch logs threw out a cheerful warmth from a brown-tiled fireplace at the end of the room. Above the mantel hung a portrait in oils, somewhat cracked, of a dignified man in middle age wearing a frock coat and beard. Old John C. without a doubt. The other pictures on the walls were a large English landscape with lush fields and trees and some horses drinking at a stream, three pen-and-wash drawings of West Indian scenes, and an-

70

other showing the Caraday wharf and a square-rigger loading fish. At Mrs. Caraday's suggestion they sat in chairs by the fire, for the room was distinctly cold. There followed some chat about today's fine weather, last week's storm, which had done so much damage to the coast, and the political news from Ottawa. The chat passed entirely between MacIlraith and the lady, but they regarded Captain Nolan as they talked and threw him a remark and a smile from time to time.

Mrs. Caraday spoke in an English accent undefiled by all her long years in Port Barron. It was the sort known derisively nowadays in England as "refained," and Sax had heard it before in Nassau and other West Indian places where a refained accent still passed for good British currency. He gave her a bored ear. She did not fit his notions of the Caradays at all. The big pinnacled house was right enough, and without seeing them he could picture very well the carriage house and barn and stables at the rear. It had been a thrill merely to walk in the front door instead of knocking, cap in hand, at the back and saying, "Any fresh lobsters today, please?"

He remembered the homes of other important folk in the Port Barron of his youth, where the lady of the house was always a stiffly corseted creature who peered at you over the housemaid's shoulder and called at once sharply for "Cook!" They were big women in his memory, with a put-on manner that he had resented even as a child because they spoke in the plain Nova Scotia accent of his parents and himself. The difference between them was entirely one of money, and now that he had money he was prepared to condescend in the same well-remembered tone.

He had never heard Mrs. Caraday speak before, and while there was a condescension in that English voice it did not belong here. She did not belong here. Her face was pale, with the sagged plumpness of a sail in a failing wind, much wrinkled about the clews. The eyes were a large pale blue. She might have been pretty in a dolly sort of way at some remote time but now she looked exactly what she was, a woman used to an easy life who has let her figure go and in recent years has had a lot to worry about.

The refained accent was not put on, it came from her in a tired and soft-voiced way as if she had clung to it as a sort of lifeline in the hurly-burly of circumstance. In some women, like those toothy and leathery dames in the islands, Sax would have called it swank. In this dumpy and beaten but I-must-be-brave creature it was rather pathetic. He found himself feeling sorry for her. The childish revenge he had promised himself as he came up the driveway vanished in a minute of this conversation by the fire, and all he wanted to do now was to bow out as soon as possible and take himself off to more promising scenes.

Mrs. Caraday turned to him with sudden animation. "Captain Nolan, Mr. MacIlraith tells me you're thinking of buying my late husband's firm. How splendid! I can't tell you how I've hated to see it without a strong hand at the helm — as poor Roger's father would have said. It means so much to everyone in Port Barron, and all it needs is someone like yourself, I'm sure." My God, thought Sax, she talks as if the thing were a going concern. His mischievous tongue ran along his cheek with a desire to tell her that the firm of J. C. Caraday & Son was not worth ten dollars to a man of common sense and he personally would not touch it with a ten-foot pole. He was aware of her china-blue eyes inspecting him as she spoke and he was glad that he had worn his best tweeds and his twenty-five-dollar shoes. He hitched his wrist a little to show the hundred-and-sixty-dollar watch.

The banker's voice intruded hastily. "Captain Nolan has seen the properties and talked a little with Bostwick, Mrs. Caraday. You realize of course that things aren't what they were when J.C. was alive. Times have changed a great deal, even since your husband's death. At the present time trade's in a very uncertain state." His hand went up in that nervous brushing gesture towards the dramatic silver hair. "I've made a proposition to Captain Nolan on your behalf and I hope that you and he will agree upon the terms."

"And what are they?" murmured the lady with the bright smile of one who owns a good thing and is not inclined to niggle over details.

MacIlraith coughed. "There's the bank loan as you know. And the accrued interest. All that must be paid off."

Mrs. Caraday smiled again as if all that were a matter of coppers.

"Once that is done," went on the banker carefully, "I propose that Captain Nolan take over the whole firm, giving you a quarter share in the business. I think I may say that the captain has a sum of eighty thousand dollars to invest in it."

Mrs. Caraday nodded. The figure sounded very large and comfortable.

"That would give you a twenty-thousand-dollar interest in the new firm, in other words. The entire control and management would remain in the hands of Captain Nolan. And you would retain this house of course."

"Of course," she said quickly, looking at Sax.

Sax thought ironically, They'll have me signing a check for it in a minute. Do they really take me for that much of a fool? He said bluntly, "Look here, ma'am, I'm no Rocke-

73

feller, I'm just a sea captain that's made a bit of money and wants to put it to work where he can keep an eye on it. I've looked over your properties and I may as well tell you the only parts worth any man's money are the store and this house. Granting you the house, as I see it MacIlraith wants me to pay twenty thousand dollars for the store and give you another twenty thousand besides. That doesn't make sense to me."

"But I don't understand," she exclaimed, turning a hurt and bewildered gaze on MacIlraith. "You say I'm only to get twenty thousand dollars or shares or something worth that. And Captain Nolan says you want him to pay twice that."

Patiently the banker explained again about the mortgage and the bank's loan. Mrs. Caraday pressed her lips together. Twenty thousand. Forty thousand. Eighty thousand. All these sums. What did they mean? What did Captain Nolan mean? Did he wish to take the roof over her head as well? She tested him with a suspicious feminine question.

"No," Sax answered, smiling.

"Ah!" She was relieved at once.

"Mind you," he added, with the monkey-imp peering from his eyes for a moment, "I'll probably marry one of these days. A man's got to have some sort of plan in life and that's always been mine. But right now I'm single and the thing is to find the kind of business I want and get going. I'm sorry. I can't see MacIlraith's proposition at all. Even if the price was right it's not what I want anyhow. Nothing like it. I told him that but he insisted on lugging me out here and wasting your time as well as mine. And now I guess I'd better get along."

He arose briskly. Mrs. Caraday looked alarmed. The banker spoke quickly.

"Do sit down, Captain. Suppose we forget about business for a bit. I'm sure Mrs. Caraday would like to give us a cup of tea."

"Tea!" she cried, and rose with a delighted smile, as if all her fears and perplexities could be dissolved in a little hot water and cream. Sax wanted to protest. He detested tea, he was a coffee man, and he had hoped to make a quick and careless exit. But the lady of Caraday House was on her way out of the room, calling gaily over her shoulder that they should smoke if they wished, and no doubt Captain Nolan would like to look about the drawing room and see poor Roger's sketches, and so on.

MacIlraith lighted a cigarette. Sax walked irritably away from its fumes and moved slowly about the room. The pictures on the walls meant nothing except that the West Indian scenes looked familiar. He halted at the *étagère* with its array of family photographs. He could identify most of the subjects. A very early one of John C. with a slight dark-eyed creature who must have been his wife. A more mature John C. with the full beard of the portrait over the mantel, and holding a boy of about twelve against his knee. A thin young man in college cap and gown who was certainly Roger Caraday. A stiff portrait of a lean side-whiskered man in the dress uniform of a British regiment, resting one white-gloved hand on the hilt of his sword and holding a pipe-clayed beehive helmet in the other — Mrs. Caraday's father for sure. Roger Caraday and his bride in their wedding clothes, the bride with a wasp waist, with a cloud of white stuff about her head and shoulders, and the train of her gown spread like a white pool on the floor before her. A charming thing she must have been. It was only by staring hard that Sax saw the slightest resemblance to the frump who had just left the room.

He turned to another shelf. Roger and his wife in tropical dress, his wife holding a parasol, with flowering hibiscus in the background and the name of a Kingston photographer on the frame. A snapshot of Mrs. Caraday lounging in a cane chair on the afterdeck of a sailing ship, with a brown barefoot seaman at the wheel behind her. Mrs. Caraday sitting on the veranda of Caraday House with a child on her lap and a vast Saint Bernard yawning at her feet. Mrs. Caraday in various other poses, sometimes with a spindle-shanked girl in the early teens. Roger's own photography probably, for he appeared in none of these. Sax ran an indifferent glance to the top shelf, and a small snapshot, unframed, caught his eye. A young woman in modern bathing dress, taken in an unattractive moment with her eyes squinted against the sun and her legs plastered with wet sand. One hand was dragging off her bathing cap and spilling a lot of dark hair.

He thought of Ellen Carisfort. He had seen her often in that awkward pose, but with Ellen there was always a clear suggestion of poise, of Class, no matter what she did. She wore it like an invisible garment. There were other differences. The girl in the snapshot was about Ellen's age but she was not so slender of leg and bust. And she was tall. A larger model so to speak. Figure like a — well, like a barmaid. Too big. Much too big.

There was a step on the carpet behind him and he found MacIlraith looking over his shoulder. "Who's that?" he asked, pointing.

"Eh? Oh, that one. That's Rena, Mrs. Caraday's daughter. Quiet girl, rather like her father. Roger took that picture four years ago, the summer he died."

"What's she do?"

"Rena planned to go in for teaching. But after her

father died Mrs. Caraday wouldn't hear of that. She's always had a notion that teaching in a country school wasn't the sort of thing she wanted her daughter to go in for. And of course since Roger died Mrs. Caraday's been terribly lonely and upset."

"Time she got over that, don't you think?"

"Frankly, yes. And she has to this extent — Rena's been away in Halifax since last fall taking a secretarial course."

"Is that more respectable?"

"It ought to pay more money, anyhow. And poor Mrs. Caraday's come to realize the importance of money, the past year or two. Apart from that I'm very glad for Rena's sake. Chance to get away and mingle with people of her own age and sort. Not good for a girl, cooped up in a place like this, you know. Last summer Rena worried us all. Used to see her outside, working about the garden and the grounds, mowing away at the lawn with a sickle — the mower went to pieces long ago and they couldn't afford another — or digging and hoeing in the kitchen garden like any fisherman's wife. Her mother complained that she was ruining her hands but Rena just stared past her in the rather sullen way she has at times and went on with it. You know, as if the whole support of Caraday House had suddenly fallen on her. The girl's like her father in many ways but now and then old John C.'s terrific energy crops out, and not a little of his temper."

They returned to the chairs in the glow of the fire. MacIlraith changed the subject and brought up the old one. "I've been thinking, Captain, about the house. Quite a valuable property in itself, don't you think? Especially on this splendid site. You couldn't build anything like it, even in these cheap times, for less than twenty-five thousand. Something a man could be proud to own. And live in, if he ever decided to marry, say. The local people have

77

always looked at this place the way feudal villagers used to regard the manor house. The seat of authority. The source of all good. You spoke of wishing to live in some kind of Class. If I understand you properly this house would fit your wish."

Sax lay back and pushed his fists deep in his tweed pockets. "Just what tack are you on now, MacIlraith?"

The banker lighted another cigarette and waved it in his long fingers. "I don't see why we shouldn't include the house with the other properties in the transfer. Mrs. Caraday could remain in occupation, couldn't she, until you wanted to move in? That mightn't be for some time."

"What makes you think Mrs. Caraday would agree?"

MacIlraith shrugged. "My dear Nolan, she'll have to, if it's any inducement to your purchase of the firm. For her own best interests, I mean. No doubt she'll hate to part with the full ownership of her home — you can scarcely blame her for that — but I'm taking the long view and so must she. Of course her share in the new firm will include a quarter interest in the house as one of the firm's assets, but she'll have to recognize your control of that, as she would in any decision you choose to make about the properties."

Sax looked about the room. "What about the contents? The house wouldn't be the same without all this stuff in it."

The banker sucked hard on the cigarette and blew out smoke slowly.

"You drive a hard bargain, don't you?"

"I want my money's worth, yes."

"You don't mean the entire contents of the house as it stands — the family silverware and china and all that?"

"Why not? It's all part of the setup. Suppose I swallow your proposition. And then suppose some day I marry.

78

If I brought a wife here I'd want to have everything just the way it is — the way the Caradays had it. Oh, Mrs. Caraday could take her photographs, the painting of the old boy, that kind of thing. I wouldn't want 'em anyway. But the furniture, pictures, silverware, these hangings at the windows, every bit of that kind of thing would have to stay. As you say, I might not want to move in for some time. But it would have to be laid down in the agreement that the house and everything in it belong to the firm and go in the deal just the same as the shop and wharf and so on. That means the house and contents are three parts mine like everything else, and I can buy out her part any time on the basis of her share in the whole thing."

MacIlraith turned to the fire and stared at the flames. He flicked his cigarette into their midst as if the taste of it were suddenly foul.

"Is this an absolute decision?"

Sax caught the ironical note in that. "When we walked out here my absolute decision was to say No to the whole thing," he replied coolly. "Now that I've seen this place it reminds me of certain things that happened when I was a kid. A kind of promise I made myself a long time ago. My common sense still tells me to say No and clear out of Port Barron as soon as I can catch a boat back to the railway line. But while I'm here in this house, in this room, I'm fool enough to feel a kind of sentiment about it. From here the whole thing has a rosy look it didn't have before, when I was wandering about that ramshackle wharf and shipyard. It's what the books call an illusion and if your client is smart she'll take me up before I have a chance to get outside and breathe some cold sea air. To tell you the honest truth I hope she lets me go."

The banker glanced at the portrait over the mantel and

then out of the window towards the sea. The afternoon light through the stained glass of the upper sash gave his spare figure a quaintly cloistered radiance. There was a silence relieved only by the flutter of the fire and distant sounds of movement in the kitchen. Sax watched the other's face. At last MacIlraith said in a chilled voice, "This is a thing I'll have to put to her alone, you understand. As delicately as I can. But firmly, of course. I suggest that after we've had a cup of tea you go on back to the hotel. I'll stay and talk to her."

You bet you will, thought Sax. You've got to get that loan paid off somehow or your number's up with the bank, my friend. He repressed a smile. It would be interesting to take old John C.'s place over the mantelpiece for half an hour and hear that conversation over the empty teacups. But now he heard the sound of slow returning footsteps, the rumble of a tea wagon and a faint tinkle of china and silver in the hall. His eyes met MacIlraith's. They gave each other a glance and turned with the silence of conspirators to the fire.

⌒ ⌒ Chapter 9

A LAWYER came from Eglinton to prepare the formal agreement, one Burrows, a tall man with cropped pepper-and-salt hair and a small mustache. He had thin black eyebrows that shot up and down as he talked, and this spasmodic movement drew the skin taut across his forehead and caused his ears to twitch, a trick that fascinated the juries he sometimes addressed in the courthouse in Eglinton. In a preliminary chat with MacIlraith he observed, "I'm only here to draw up the document of course, but you won't mind if I ask one or two questions. This agreement only protects Mrs. Caraday's interests as far as her capital share in the firm is concerned, right?"

"That's all she can expect," said the banker in an uneasy voice.

"What about the direction of the firm?"

"Entirely in the hands of Captain Nolan, naturally."

"And naturally he can pay her any sort of dividend he chooses or none at all. If Mrs. Caraday is to depend on her share for a living that puts her entirely in Nolan's hands, doesn't it? Does she fully understand that?"

"Oh yes. I think I made it clear at any rate. After all it's the risk anybody has to take with a minority share in a business. It's the risk you take when you buy a share of C.P.R. or anything else in the stock market."

"Ah, that's a painful subject nowadays. What do you know about Nolan?"

"Nothing," replied MacIlraith testily, "except that he's got a very keen head, knows the sea, and yesterday deposited in my bank three certified checks amounting to close on ninety thousand dollars. That should be enough for anybody. It satisfies me, anyhow. I don't mind telling you that if I hadn't evaded my instructions from Halifax the whole of the Caraday properties would have been sold under foreclosure before this, and Mrs. Caraday would have had nothing, not even a pillow for her head, as the saying goes. As it is, by judicious delay, and some careful persuasion, I've secured her a good deal more than that."

"And is she properly grateful?" asked the lawyer, shooting up the brows.

An unhappy smile appeared on the banker's face. "Women aren't properly grateful creatures. Mrs. Caraday didn't mind about the business properties but when it

81

came to including the house and all its contents she said the whole idea was 'monstrous.' She wept and showered me with reproaches as if I'd conspired with Nolan to defraud her of everything she'd got. I was shocked. I'd never seen her in such a state and I've known her nearly fifteen years. Finally I got her calmed down. In the end she was quite resigned. I pointed out how unlikely it was that Nolan would ever wish to occupy the house. He's a lone wolf of the money-making type and when that type gets to the age of thirty-five he's pretty safe as far as Cupid is concerned."

"Then why does he want the house and all its furniture and bric-a-brac set forth in the agreement?"

"He's just being canny, that's all. He's undertaking to pay off the bank loan and spend a further sixty thousand dollars on the business. That's quite a lot of money and quite a risk in the shipping game, these days. If Mrs. Caraday is to hold a quarter share in all that, he feels she should chuck in the house as a definite asset of the firm. It's worth twenty thousand, even in its present condition. Don't look so skeptical. Seems to me any well-to-do American would pay that for it, just for the sake of a summer home up here where it's cool and where he wouldn't be falling over a lot of week-end trippers every time he turned around."

"Umph. Well, on the whole Nolan's the one who's taking the gamble, as you say. The fishery, the shipping business, all that kind of thing — pretty sick since '29. And at the present time I'd say it's getting worse, not better. Business in the States is in a very shaky state and you know what that means to us in Canada. Of course Hoover's a good man and he talks of doing this and that."

"My dear Burrows," the banker said, and smiled with

a knowing air. "You're forgetting the one thing in the States that's flourishing. The national thirst."

The lawyer gave him a hard stare. "What d'you mean by that?"

"Just that I've been in the banking business for a long time and I know this coast and what its people do for a living. At the present time there's hardly a fishing port in Nova Scotia that isn't harboring at least a couple of vessels in the liquor trade to the U.S.A. It's quite legal. They use the home port for a refitting base, that's all. Their holds are always empty here, so there's no conflict with the Nova Scotia Temperance Act. Necessity's the mother of all kinds of things besides invention, Burrows. On this coast things have been dull ever since the war. The French at St. Pierre have liquor to sell, the Americans have a lot of thirsty money, and here we are between 'em with idle ships and men. What's that add up to? You know as well as I do. Well, now! I don't pretend to be any Sherlock Holmes, but when a sunburned man turns up here shivering in a fur coat on the tag end of winter, when he turns out to be a sea captain with a mind like a steel trap, when he reveals that he or his backers have got something like ninety thousand dollars in good bank deposits, when he picks Port Barron — Port Barron of all places! — to buy a practically defunct shipping business with a good old-fashioned name and reputation, and when I look at the map and see how nicely all this relates to the coast of New England over there — I draw my own conclusions, Burrows, I draw my own conclusions."

"Have you mentioned them to Mrs. Caraday?"

A wave of MacIlraith's hand. "Of course not. Why trouble her with my private suspicions? Even if I'm right, where's the harm? Shares in fishing and trading vessels are a very common form of investment in the Nova Scotia

83

ports. Merchants own 'em, fishermen put their savings in 'em; doctors, preachers, lawyers, politicians — even bank managers like myself — buy a share or two whenever a new vessel's launched. If Eglinton was a fishing town you'd probably own a few schooner shares yourself. In ordinary times a fishing schooner pays dividends up to fifteen per cent. But nowadays there's loss, nothing but loss — unless the directors put the ship in the wet-goods trade. So off she goes to St. Pierre. Of course it's all done strictly on the quiet. As far as the average shareholder knows — or cares to know — his investment is freighting lumber somewhere or catching codfish on the Banks."

"I'd call it pretty risky business for Mrs. Caraday. Eh?"

"Risk! In ships there's always risk, no matter what you put 'em at. As far as Mrs. Caraday is concerned she owns a share in the firm of J. C. Caraday & Son, a general shipping and trading business, and any dividends that come her way will be thankfully received. After all old John C. was a temperance crank but he never hesitated to swap his fish and lumber in the West Indies for rum or anything else he could sell here in the north. Business was business to him, and surely that goes for his successor?"

The lawyer stroked his long nose with thumb and forefinger. "You know, Mac, for a banker, sometimes you talk remarkably like the public's notion of a man in my profession." He was thinking that in John C.'s time rum was a legal import into Canada and the States, a recognized feature of the West Indies trade. But he said no more.

The signing of the document at Caraday House was a simple affair. Sax watched Mrs. Caraday curiously but her face and manner told him nothing of her thoughts. In her refained voice and with her air of faded and somewhat podgy elegance she talked to the three men about

84

everything under the gray March sky except the business at hand; and when it came to the point of signing she sat at her little escritoire in the small east drawing room and wrote her name in beautiful script, the kind that was taught in English schools for young ladies in the last years of Queen Victoria. To Sax her face was expressionless, but in her blue eyes when she looked up from the pen he seemed to detect a new and wary interest, as if she had not taken him carefully enough on their first meeting. As they parted she put out her hand, smiling faintly, and said she was sure all would turn out well for both of them.

Sax threw himself into the work with all the bottled-up energy of many idle days. The first job was to repair the wharf and warehouse and to get the shipyard in working order. He could not have struck a better time. In a place where every man was his own house carpenter and boat-wright there were skilled hands on every side, very eager to work for Sax at wages that would have set any building trades union screaming for his blood. The sawmills at Eglinton received his orders for timber and shingles with gratitude, and he was able to beat them down to prices that astonished even himself. He decided at once to haul out and repair the old schooner *Pamela Caraday* and to build a new auxiliary schooner for the coastal trade. And so the shipyard came to life very quickly, and with work on the schooners under way he sent for agents of the diesel manufacturers and went into the matter of engines.

The lobster fishermen were setting out their traps again now that the winter storms were past, and under the shrewd eye of Goodrich, a former fish buyer for the Caraday firm, Sax began to purchase their catch, shipping the crates to Barmouth, where they caught the steamer to Boston for the best American price. After a careful examination of the Caraday ledgers he wrote to their most recent connections in Cuba, Jamaica, Demerara, Trinidad, inviting offers for salt codfish, at the same time offering cargoes of pine lumber for delivery at any port north of Pará. In short, he neglected none of the former Caraday activities that might be revived with some of old John C.'s energy and longheadedness. The talk of hard times he heard with contempt, the babble of weaklings. Prosperity wasn't "just around the corner" either, as some of the optimists said. Prosperity, Sax said with his little grin, was something you dug up for yourself.

In May the daughter of Mrs. Caraday came home with a certificate from a Halifax business school, and through lawyer Burrows she got the chance of a job in an Eglinton timber firm. When old Bostwick mentioned this in his bumbling way, Sax went at once to the house and asked if she would care to take a job in his office. He couldn't offer much pay, he pointed out, but at least she could live at home and save the cost of board in Eglinton. Rena Caraday accepted, with a rather shy smile. Mrs. Caraday actually laughed. She was delighted and she said so. And Sax, politeness itself, murmured something about the good omen of having a member of the family engaged in the business again. The truth was that he needed a typist. The firm's new activities had brought a squall of correspondence beyond Bostwick's handling and he himself had been obliged to sit pecking the typewriter night after night in the office. And he got her for fifteen dollars a week, another bargain.

With his instinctive curiosity about women he watched the new secretary at her desk and as she moved about the office. She was too big to fit his notion of good looks, wedded to that elfin picture of Ellen Carisfort. She was actually taller than he, and resenting his own lack of stature he had always disliked taller people, especially women. The Caraday girl carried herself without a scrap of Ellen's nervous vivacity but with a certain slow grace in all her movements that probably went with the Caraday blood. There was little about her to suggest her mother. Her eyes were dark, her skin a healthy olive, and instead of that refained little mouth Rena's lips were long. She was calm and businesslike, and when she spoke her voice was low and her words went right to the point — a touch of old John C. She was better-looking than the snapshot, but of course that was not saying much. Her figure as far as Sax could judge was all right if you liked them big. Her one real beauty was her hair. She wore it long, a coiled mass of deep chestnut, glinting here and there with distinctly red hues when the sun fell on it. At such moments Sax found himself admiring it. The sort of hair you couldn't help looking at, and wondering how it would look with the pins out, falling over white shoulders and down that long arched back. But even that speculation was impersonal, for he always saw women without their clothes as a matter of habit, just as one woman might regard another and see nothing but a hat.

In a way it was awkward to have a member of the family sitting at the heart of the firm's affairs, for he had no doubt that Rena reported them to her mother and probably the banker. He imagined them discussing everything at those semiweekly bridge parties. But when he considered everything it suited him very well. If the world really was in the bankrupt state he heard mentioned on every side, there might come a time when he would have to dip beneath the surface of honest business. If that time came he could get rid of the girl on one pretext or another and do whatever had to be done. But all that seemed remote. He clung to his cherished ideal of respectability, of a solid position in some small community where people looked up to him and envied him as a capable man of means. He had always longed for that and here was the opportunity. The more Rena Caraday reported of his business affairs, the better. He was on the level and so was the firm of J. C. Caraday & Son, and he wanted that thoroughly understood not only in Port Barron but everywhere else along the coast.

After a time, when his footing was solid, he would make the acquaintance of people of Class, in Halifax for instance, the families of men who did business with him and respected him; and he nourished a dream of finding among them a young woman like Ellen Carisfort. A girl who would admire him for his brains and energy — and his fortune of course — and who (unlike Ellen) would marry him with the alacrity of any intelligent girl brought up with a proper regard for those things. He and she would live together happily, she would be wonderful in bed, and they would start a little dynasty of the sort you found in every old Nova Scotia town; and at the end he would go to the graveyard like old John C. himself, a man respected all the way from Port Barron to Montreal.

Wonderful fancies, these, and they could come true. But none of these rosy speculations blunted his sharp sense of business. He drove his workmen hard, he stalked like a hungry cat about the shop and warehouse, the wharf and shipyard; and people who tried to sell the firm anything from pine boards to typewriter ribbons found Captain R. Saxby Nolan a tough buyer. MacIlraith, perusing the checks drawn against Nolan's account and knowing the goods and services being delivered in exchange for them, was filled with admiration for the man. As time went on he confessed to his wife that his original suspicions were quite wrong. The man was sharp but honest and in his own way quite a gentleman. A pity he didn't play bridge.

The town of Port Barron perceived that Captain Nolan stayed quietly at the shabby little hotel and spent his days hard at work. He had no apparent vices. He was always in a front pew of the church on Sunday mornings and very attentive to the Reverend Mr. Bascombe's somewhat windy sermons. As an interested ratepayer he attended several meetings of the town council and gave a hundred dollars to their Poor Relief Fund, stating that it was to be anonymous. Personally and as manager of J. C. Caraday & Son he met all his bills and payrolls promptly. In fact he was an admirable character in every way and his sudden advent into Port Barron was a boon. The older people reminded each other that King Caraday himself had come to the cape from nowhere, just like Cap'n Nolan, and now history was just repeating itself.

Under Captain Nolan's instructions Goodrich was now outbidding the Barmouth lobster buyers for the cape catch, whatever they offered. And with Nolan's encouragement the fishermen were planning to fit out for the cod and pollack fishery as soon as the lobster season closed. Already, on their lee days, they had begun to restore the long files of drying-flakes along the shore, where all summer the boys and women and old men would "make" the catch. And now the Caraday wharf and shipyard rang once more with sounds of carpentry. Port Barron had a new life, not from Captain Nolan's money alone but from his confident example in spending it. Small savings came out of hiding to buy new fishing gear, to repair boats and homes, to buy fresh groceries after a long deadly diet of bread, molasses, fish and tea. New hats, new dresses, new shoes, appeared on women who had worn nothing new since 1929, some since the

89

postwar slump of 1921; and these things in their mysterious way brought a bigger crowd to the picture show and filled the church on Sunday morning. The Reverend Mr. Bascombe remarked on the new hope that had come upon his flock with the revival of "our good old firm" and directed a beaming smile at Captain Nolan, sitting with Mrs. and Miss Caraday in their pew towards the front. And Sax received the turning of heads with an embarrassed stare towards the ceiling, the picture of a modest Christian gentleman diligent in faith and works.

If there were some who grumbled about the wages Nolan paid, and the fact that only half was paid in cash and the rest in credit at the Caraday store, there were many others to cry them down. They liked Cap'n Nolan's easy manner, his decisive voice that was never lifted above a conversational tone, his quiet smile. They liked him because inside of a month he could call any man or boy by his nickname, because he never failed to inquire after a sick wife or child. They came to admire his almost soundless glide because for them it was the step of a man who always knew where he was going and exactly what he was going to do. They liked him because, as they said, he had no damned airs and got things done.

⌒ ⌒ Chapter 10

RENA Caraday walked the mile to the office each morning carrying her lunch in a basket, and she returned each evening with groceries for the next day's meals. On Saturday afternoons, when the office was closed, she worked vigorously in the garden or she roamed along the sheep path that led along the sea bank for a mile or two past the end of the road. There was a good view over the sea towards the islands, and close at hand were the bank, dropping forty or fifty feet to the water, the rough, wind-bitten spruce trees that clung to existence beside the path, and the sheep with the spring lambs pattering off into the barrens in their silly way at her approach.

From a rocky point she could look back and see the house with its four turrets and captain's walk, like a small brown castle on the slope of the cape, and beyond it the town — the waterfront bustling with lobster boats, the buildings of J. C. Caraday & Son glistening in fresh paint, the small floating pile driver from Barmouth thumping away at the Caraday wharf, the white plume rising from the long steam box in the shipyard, the clean ribs of the new schooner rising from one of the slips and the black hull of the *Pamela Caraday* now repaired and being painted on the other.

Sax had decided to keep the old ship's name. He informed Mrs. Caraday that she must come and officiate at a little relaunching ceremony. And on the appointed day she came, dressed in a smart gray costume, new hat, new gloves, new shoes and stockings (all purchased out of Rena's salary), and with a touch of rouge and lipstick in the modern manner. She looked very much younger and very much the lady of Caraday House as she sat on the platform erected by the shipwrights for the occasion; and at Sax's insistence her daughter sat beside her — Rena wearing a tweed costume made for her college graduation. With them sat the Reverend Mr. Bascombe, and Mr. Hilliard Cuff, M.P., the member for Eglinton County, and of course R. Saxby Nolan.

The town had taken a holiday and the yard was filled. From the platform Pamela swept a benign blue gaze over an acre of bobbing hats and faces. Just before her own nose the name *Pamela Caraday* glittered at the nose of the fresh black hull. High and dry like this, the schooner looked immense. The three masts rose towards the sky with bunting fluttering from stays and halyards, a very brave show. It was a sunny spring day with just enough wind to set the flags snapping. The tide was high, and across the water of the harbor the new grass on Big Sheep and Little Sheep islands had the fresh green shine of paint.

Sax uttered a few modest words to open the proceedings, and the children of the Port Barron school, grouped about the platform, then sang all the verses of "O Canada." The member of parliament followed with an eloquent speech recalling the days of Nova Scotia's glory, when her great windjammers sailed in every sea. The days of wooden ships and iron men — men like the late John C. Caraday, who had founded this fine old firm — and ships like the magnificent vessel before them, built and rebuilt right here in Port Barron. Good old Nova Scotia still had ships and men like that. Such men as Captain Nolan for example. (Cheers.) And such charming women as the lady for whom this ship was named, and who was right here on the platform beside him. (A patter of polite applause about the platform.) He was not going to mention politics (laughter) but he would be remiss in his duty if he did not point out that he had always kept the needs of Port Barron close at heart, and that he had been of some assistance to Captain Nolan in the matter of a new registry for the schooner, and certain other matters like insurance, which he was glad to say his position had enabled him to do.

He was happy to observe another vessel under construction. Moreover, he understood from Captain Nolan, who was too modest to mention the matter in public himself,

92

that the firm had in mind the purchase of a steamship, a steamship of some size, to round out its fleet. (Prolonged applause.) He need not add that all this would usher in a new era of prosperity for the town. (Cheers.) Mr. Cuff sat down amid these cheers. And now the Reverend Mr. Bascombe arose and gave a prayer for the town's people in these difficult but inspiring times, and another for this ship and all who sailed in her. The voices of the school children shrilled forth again, this time with all the verses and choruses of "The Maple Leaf Forever." Finally Mrs. Caraday stood to say a few refained words and to cut the ribbon which apparently fastened the schooner to the platform rail.

While she was speaking Sax went down to oversee the launching job. The small grin was on his face. He wore a smart gray suit and felt every bit the modest hero of the hour. The repair of the old schooner had been quite easy after all. She was very like *Albertine* and his experience in that ancient hooker had left him an exact knowledge of the way to repair the *Pamela Caraday* as cheaply as possible. It was wonderful what you could do with a derelict tern schooner and three thousand dollars if you knew how to go about it and stood over the shipwrights while they did the job. With an adroit approach to Hilliard Cuff, M.P., he had secured the right word from him and placed ten thousand dollars' insurance on the ship. He had every reason to feel proud of himself, and as the schooner slid down to the water he was able to look up at the little group seated on the platform with the calm confidence of a man who need not give another glance to the product of his handiwork.

His eyes came to rest on Rena Caraday. The costume made for her graduation from college three years before was cut on a brief pattern; and now, seated high above the staring fishermen and their families, she found the skirt embarrassing. The stuff seemed to shrink and her legs to grow. She gave a little sigh of relief when the thrilling spectacle of the moving ship turned every face towards the sea. Indeed, she was absorbed in the spectacle herself when Sax regarded her.

Somehow during the past few weeks the old troubling vision of Ellen Carisfort had undergone a subtle change. He saw her as clearly as ever but that once admirable figure of hers had become a meager thing. "Boyish," that finest compliment to young women of the 1920's with their lean hips and flat chests, now seemed all too accurate a term. Ellen had been boyish enough for any *Ladies' Home Journal* illustration of those days, but now when he thought of her she seemed puny and inadequate. It came to him suddenly that in Nassau he had fallen in love with a china figurine, not a living woman at all; and now while everyone else admired the long full lines of the moving schooner Sax regarded with interest those of the young woman on the platform.

It was only for a few moments. Other matters were pressing. He turned to shout orders for the mooring of the schooner now that she was water-borne; and his brow was still furrowed with the cares of the moment when Rena's mother appeared, advancing with hand outstretched and speaking in a high clear voice.

"Captain Nolan, what a pleasure this has been! It was so nice of you to keep my name on the ship and to ask me to cut the ribbon. I do appreciate that. But it wasn't just the compliment, it's knowing that you care so deeply for our old firm, just the way my poor Roger and his father did — how I wish they could have seen all this today. I'm so happy I want to cry. Absurd, of course."

Sax smiled past her at Rena, hesitating a few paces

away. "My dear lady, this is just a beginning, I assure you. The new schooner we're building on the other slip is to be called *Roger Caraday*. And the steamer — I hadn't intended to mention that yet but Mr. Cuff blew the gaff — she's to be named after the founder himself. This is the firm of J. C. Caraday & Son and I don't intend to lose sight of it for a minute. That's a promise."

He was surprised at the warmth and strength of the slender hand pressing his own. On their first meeting it had felt like a fillet of cold haddock.

"My dear Captain," Pamela cried, "I've been waiting to ask you something for weeks, but I see so little of you, absorbed in business as you are. I can't bear to think of you, the head of our firm, staying in that awful little hotel when we, Rena and I, have that great house all to ourselves. I can't help feeling that my poor husband and his father, dear old J.C., would be horrified if they knew we'd let you stay anywhere else. So come and stay with us at Caraday House. It's so awfully big and empty — we're lost in it. And it would be so wonderful to have a man in the house again after all this time. Two lone women, a mile from town — you surely know what that means. As a favor to Rena and me if nothing else, do come."

"Couldn't think of it," Sax murmured, wondering how long it would take to get his stuff packed and get out there. "An imposition."

Pamela closed her large white eyelids and opened wide her mouth. "Oh, Captain Nolan, what an absurd thing to say!"

For a moment she resembled a pale blind fish, gaping for unwary minnows in the depths of the sea and ready to swallow anything, even its own young. But only for a moment.

～ ～ *Chapter* 11

APRIL passed, and the warm breath of May rising off the land sucked in the heavy mists of Fundy. The foghorn far out on Gannet Head could be heard groaning through the dank chill nights. But frequently a west wind cleared the stuff away and then the sunshine fell hot on the cape. The fishermen's garden patches, plowed and hoed ready for the June planting, gave off little wisps like steam. Wild flowers began to bloom beside the shore road, and along the rough spine of the cape the rhodora bushes spread a magenta-colored fire. Swallows darted about the eaves of barns and sheds. Robins whistled from the pasture walls. Bobolinks sang in the bushes. Suddenly the cape was a pleasant place. Sax, offering his company to Rena in her walks along the shore, marveled at the change in so short a time.

So did the people of the town, whose season of spring had really begun on that bleak day early in March when Captain Nolan walked into Bostwick's office. Indeed, change was everywhere, and nowhere more than at Caraday House. The captain's quick eye and do-it-now energy had soon extended there. On the day he moved himself and his baggage Pamela had shown him over it from cellar to garret. She did it with a light mixture of humor and apology.

"Our poor little bathroom, Captain, the only one in the house. Don't compare it, please, with anything you've seen elsewhere. Those long, thin, curved things over the washbasin — like the awful thing the dentist hangs in your mouth — those are faucets. And this ridiculous bathtub on those hideous ball-and-claw feet — the last word, positively the last word, when poor J.C. built the house in the Nineties."

And: "Don't look too hard at my kitchen, please, the floor's so worn, and that sink, ugh! And that antiquated stove and water tank!"

And: "These quaint wooden ceilings in both drawing rooms, they make the rooms terribly dark, don't you think, with the maple paneling on the walls? Of course it's all beautiful woodwork, and parquetry's all right for a floor. On a ceiling it's absurd. When I came here as a bride I used to look up sometimes and wonder if I was standing on my head."

And: "The cellar's huge, isn't it? I've wondered so often why J.C. didn't put in a bigger furnace to heat this enormous house. I dare say it was all right in his day. And of course my poor Roger and I used to spend every winter in the West Indies, like the birds. Cold weather meant nothing to us then."

And: "We'll just peep into the attic. It's such a mess. I mean the roof leaks in several places, though not enough to damage the ceilings, thank goodness. Those narrow steps go up to the captain's walk on the roof. I can see poor J.C. tramping up there now with his telescope under his arm. The trap door — he called it the booby hatch — has been stuck shut for years, the hinges have rusted or something; and of course the iron railing outside is very insecure. But I don't suppose you'll ever want to go up there. Or will you?"

And: "Here's the dining room. Bird's-eye maple paneling and parquetry again. Mr. Caraday had a passion for woodwork and fine carpentry. Of course, you could get labor and all sorts of lovely wood cheaply here in his time, but I think it was a fad from his seafaring days. He built

97

the house as if he were building a West Indiaman. As a seafaring man I suppose you'll approve. I'd almost forgotten that, Captain Nolan; you seem so much a businessman. And here's some of the silver — you're interested in that of course. The big tea set belonged to my father's family in Somersetshire. The tea-and-coffee set was given us by the officers of his regiment. And here's the general's cruet stand. And of course there are the various silver trays and serving dishes and so on, and all those drawers are filled with the knives and forks and spoons and things that my father, Captain Charnsworth, got from England when Roger and I were married. In the glass cabinet over there is all the lovely chinaware that J.C. gave us, and some very rare things that my father got in Hong Kong when he was stationed there in the Eighties. That's where he got these cloisonné plates and jars and tea caddies, and those Chinese vases you saw in the east drawing room, where I have my little desk."

Pamela concealed nothing, not even the ramshackle stable and carriage house at the rear. She had the manner of a tenant turning over her home to a well-deserving stranger who is entitled to know the worst as well as the best about it, and Sax was duly appreciative. He was startled to find that all the household water had to be pumped by hand to a tank in the attic, and that this had been done for the past two years by Rena alone — just as she had tended that old coal furnace, wheeling out the ashes every winter morning, and just as she had done the gardening and every other chore about the place since they had parted with the last of the servants.

He suggested tactfully that some of these matters ought to be changed, and Pamela closed her eyes and opened her mouth and said she supposed they should. He asked if she would mind if he went ahead with repairs and some renovations, and Pamela murmured that after all the place was three fourths his and she supposed that as a businessman he ought to protect his investment. And so in the office Rena found herself typing letters to plumbing and heating firms in Eglinton. Carpenters arrived, and in due course the Eglinton plumbers and heaters; and all through the months of June and July the old mansion swarmed with men tearing things apart and putting other things together. Even the long lawn running down to the road was plowed up and harrowed and reseeded, the driveway weeded and covered with fresh gravel, the dead trees cut away from the windbreak and young spruce planted in their place.

The outbuildings were repaired and painted, and when the stable was finished Sax bought in Eglinton a new buggy, surrey and sleigh, with all the proper harness, and a beautiful young mare. The purchase of a large and impressive motorcar, which had long been one of his dreams, was given over to fact — the fact that the mile or two of road about Port Barron was quite unfit for cars — and to that memory of the smart Caraday carriage spinning along the town street in his boyhood days. Now in rainy weather he and Rena could get to the office with speed and comfort, and more important still, on Sundays he could drive in state with the Caraday ladies to church.

When his mind first sketched the necessary repairs and changes to Caraday House, Sax set the cost at about five thousand dollars, but he found that one thing led to another and before long his original estimate was out of sight. The renovation of the old bathroom and the creation of another formed a major point in all this. He wanted, and got, luxurious bathrooms in the best style of the magazine advertisements, gleaming with tile and plate mirrors and chromium, with cupboards and tiers of glass shelves, and fixtures enameled in delicate pastel shades. All this required a complete new system of water pipe, in brass for permanence; a sewer pipe deeply trenched beneath any possible frost and leading to the sea, instead of the primitive cesspool; an artesian well, a large new tank in the attic and an automatic pump to keep it filled.

And what was to drive the pump? The notion of a gasoline engine just for that led his mind to a large plant to supply the house with electricity, for there was the matter of modern lighting to be considered as well. And so electricians came from Eglinton and the whole house was wired and fitted, the water pump got an electric motor, and the shining new-tiled kitchen received, among other things, an electric stove and a refrigerator. To supply all this a powerful diesel-electric plant was installed in a special building far to the rear of the kitchen garden, where the noise and fumes of the exhaust would carry only faintly to the house.

Meanwhile, throughout the house the floors had a thorough scraping, sanding and varnishing. The old furnace, the tall gilded radiators and the ugly steam pipes from room to room were torn out and sold for junk in Eglinton; and in their place came a vast metal monster in the cellar, that burned pulverized coal with an automatic stoking device. From this, like the tentacles of a sheet-metal octopus, various conduits ran up between the walls; and through these and discreet gratings in every room the hidden monster sucked away cold air and breathed out hot.

All these matters required a drastic hacking and sawing at the old interior, which had to be smoothed over later by the carpenters and plasterers, and behind them the painters and paper hangers. Sax shared old J.C.'s liking for good joinery and he admired those wooden ceilings which Pamela so despised, so on his instructions they were simply scraped clean and revarnished. All other matters of interior decoration he left to her taste, and Pamela enjoyed herself choosing wallpapers, commanding paints to be mixed in various tints for her inspection, and keeping a firm blue eye on the work as it was done.

With all this going on inside, the outside of Caraday House had to be considered. And so the veranda was repaired, the roofs reshingled, the little iron balustrades cleaned of rust, painted, and set firmly in their places. The big chimneys had to have their mortar repointed and most of the top bricks replaced. Finally the whole exterior received two coats of paint. Adding up the cost, Sax found that in spite of low wages and sharp bargains with the Eglinton supply firms the five thousand dollar job had turned out to be something like eighteen thousand dollars, with much work still to be done on the grounds. Apart from this capital expense there was now a small house staff consisting of a cook-housemaid and a handy man.

But more surprising than the cost was his own indifference to it. The thing had begun modestly, but there had come a stage when he threw all his thrifty habits and instincts out of the window. Now that it was done he walked about the place with pride. A swell home at last, by God! His one faint regret was that his parents, those feckless wandering creatures, wherever they were, could not see him now, standing in his library, say, among tier on tier of Roger Caraday's books, bookcases crowned with models of old-time Caraday ships, and windows facing the superb sea view. The squire, he thought, grinning and mouthing the word. The squire of Port Barron!

Strictly speaking, the swell home was not quite his, but Mrs. Caraday had turned out to be a very sensible person — she obviously realized her position and she made it plain that she was grateful for his tact and generosity. He was treated like one of the family. When the MacIlraiths and Doctor Bannister came to play bridge Pamela always invited Captain Nolan to join them; and when he declined politely, saying with truth that he knew very little about cards, Mrs. Caraday commanded her daughter to entertain the captain at backgammon or some other simple parlor sport. And dutifully Rena got out the backgammon board, or she fetched old snapshot and post-card albums and went over them with him page by page, wondering why he was not bored to death.

But on other evenings, the evenings he preferred, Sax sat in a cosy family intimacy with the two women on the veranda, watching the sea tints changing as the sun went down, and seeing far across that shimmering expanse the silhouettes of Topsail, Frigate and other more distant islands standing black against the sunset flare. At such times Pamela was fond of talking about things past, not the Port Barron past but the days of her youth in Halifax. Her mind went back to those days whenever she had an audience, as if all that had happened to the world and herself since 1897 were just so much killed time. Leaning back in her basket chair and regarding Sax and Rena sitting by the rail in silence, she went on and on in her soft refained voice, like a phonograph that refused to run down.

Ah, that lovely year Ninety-seven. Queen Victoria's diamond jubilee, and all the wonderful army and navy displays at Halifax. Sailors and marines of the naval squadron marching up from the dockyard. The Regiment coming up from Wellington Barracks, my-father-Captain-Charnsworth at the head of his company, red coats, belts and helmets white as snow, band playing, all so lovely with the sun on the rifles and bayonets. Guns booming on York Redoubt and the Citadel. Lovely weather that summer. Afternoons at the yacht club. Warm evenings at Northwest

Arm, band playing waltzes on the roof of the clubhouse, water simply covered with skiffs and canoes and paper lanterns and strings of little colored lampions, all so lovely in the dark, and all the girls and young men laughing and singing. Jolly trips in the old *Dufferin* to see the camp on McNab's Island. Went there once with my-father-Captain-Charnsworth and a handsome young officer named Herries. Just seventeen and had on a new mauve dress and carried a parasol and felt awfully grown up. They let me shoot the Maxim gun. You sat down and held two brass handles and did something with your thumbs. Gun went brrr and I shrieked and pulled my hands away. Oil on my nice new gloves. All the men laughing. Poor chaps, half of them dead in South Africa inside three years, including my father-Captain-Charnsworth. Those wretched Boers. Lieutenant Herries such a nice boy, too, and in love with me. My father and mother liked him very much but of course I was too young and he had no money.

Reception at Admiralty House. All those nice young officers. Wonderful time. My first taste of sherry. Hated to go home. Dance on board the flagship, lovely refreshments, ship's band, waltzing on the quarter-deck under an awning of flags, lights on the water, wearing rose-pink, hair up for the first time, young lieutenant named Carson, awfully nice, mad about me. Kissed me under the Chinese lanterns. Mama there of course. Never saw him again.

The voice went on dreamily. Sax wondered what Rena thought of it. She must have heard the whole spiel a thousand times before. She sat with her head back, with eyes half closed, looking across the sea. Sax wondered if she had ever been in love. Probably not. No chance. Her story was apparent in those bulging albums filled with faded photographs. An unattractive somber child dragged back and forth on those seasonal trips between Port Barron and

Jamaica like an inconvenient piece of baggage. Then a shapeless creature in middy blouses and dark pleated skirts at that school where young Anglican ladies were prepared for college. And finally a tall young woman at Dalhousie, unsmiling, even a little anxious, as if she were keenly aware of the cost of keeping her there after her father died.

He regarded her, giving Pamela's monologue a polite attention, hearing the refained voice in disjointed phrases as his mind flicked back and forth. And one evening an odd thing happened. He seemed to see Rena's profile against a background of scarlet uniforms and bare white shoulders, of sword knots and parasols, and her mother's light drone became a sound of drums and bugles and elegant English voices. He was half asleep, of course. But as he jerked himself awake he was searching his mind for a word. After a minute it came to him. By God, yes. Rena Caraday hadn't inherited much in terms of dollars and cents, but she'd got the one thing that counted more than all the rest. She had Class.

⌒ ⌒ Chapter 12

On a warm afternoon in August, with the sea breeze blowing in the office windows, Rena turned to her employer and asked, "Captain, may I have the day off tomorrow?"

Sax looked across from his desk and smiled. "I wish you'd call me Sax. Of course you may take a day off. What a question to ask. If you're going up to Eglinton for a bit of shopping let me run you up there in the new motor launch."

She shook her head, "I was thinking of a day at Gannet Head. It's such a long time since I've been out there — it's years. I suppose you know that's where my grandfather started his career. Even after he built Caraday House he used to move the whole family out there for the warm weather. The old house is still there with all its furniture and I think I ought to go out and see that it's all right."

"Fine! Mind if I come along?"

"Not at all. Perhaps I can persuade Mama to come, and we could take a picnic lunch and make a nice long day of it."

When Rena broached this to her mother that evening, Pamela brightened and said Yes, she would love to go.

"Captain Nolan . . ." Rena went on.

"Sax!" he insisted.

"All right. Sax, then. Sax is going to take us out in his new motorboat, Mama. We'll take a lunch and stay all day."

"Lovely, darling. And how kind of you, Captain."

"Sax," he said again cheerfully.

"Too familiar," Pamela said with a grave little smile. "But it seems absurd to go on calling you Captain in that formal way. I'd rather call you Saxby if I may. What time do you leave in the morning?"

"Would seven be too early?"

"It is a bit. But never mind. You'd better put up the luncheon tonight, dear, and then Bertha won't have to bother about it in the morning."

When morning came and they met at breakfast Pamela wore a dressing gown and a thoughtful look. She confessed a headache. "But don't mind me, go along and have your holiday. A nice change for both of you after all these weeks in that poky office. Please give my regards to the Torbys —the foghorn-keeper and his wife, Saxby — dear old couple, they've been running that thing ever since J.C.'s day. Don't know how they stand it, really. Frightful noise. Bring me back a full report on the old house, Rena, and the dear little church, and that new radio compass or beacon, whatever it is. And now make haste, do, both of you, or you'll miss the lovely early morning light on the sea."

The launch was a sleek thing, built in the Caraday yard and equipped with a marine engine that pushed it along at ten knots. Sax had built it for errands to Eglinton and the outer islands, and for docking the firm's schooners when the wind failed to serve. The sky was clear, the morning sun blinding, as they swung around Big Sheep and turned towards the Head. A fitful breeze out of Fundy ruffled the sea in patches and left others smooth. There was just enough chop on the tide to give the boat a lively motion. Far to seaward they could make out the specks of fishing boats rising and falling, and occasionally they caught the flash of sun on glass.

Close on their left the cape unrolled its length. A high gravel bank with sea-washed boulders at its feet, along the bank top a fringe of grass and dwarf juniper, and behind these the barren bushland with its scatter of great rocks. After an hour's run this monotony of bush and stone gave way to the dark wood of gnarled spruce that marked the Head itself. When they turned the Head and met the long swell rolling in from the Atlantic, the boat rose and swooped dizzily. Rena stood braced against the cabin house with the wind dragging at her chestnut hair. She loved this, Sax could see, and his heart warmed. She had Class all right. Thoroughbred to the fingertips. No thanks to Pamela, either, really. A clear skip from King Caraday and my-father-Captain-Charnsworth. She stretched a hand, smiling, pointing out the gray foghorn building with its trumpet aimed seaward, the keeper's house shining white in the sun, and some distance away the small gray shack and twin masts of the radio beacon.

More scrub woods. They were turning up the seaward face of the cape now. And in another minute the launch was gliding into a cove that opened in the rock face like the cut of a giant ax. It was lined with weather-beaten shacks and rotting boat slips. Behind these stood a small church with its steeple a little askew, and in the woods beyond the church Sax caught a glimpse of a roof that must be the old Caraday home. He steered the boat in to the least decrepit of the slips, cut the engine and sprang out nimbly to fasten the painter. He was dressed in a blue jacket and white flannels, with a silk sport shirt open at the throat, every inch the gentleman on holiday. He put out a hand to help Rena ashore and kept the hand on her arm lightly as they moved along the stony lane between the slips and the abandoned huts.

"It's eerie," Rena said, and was silent. And it was. There is always something eerie about a village abandoned, even by daylight, perhaps more by daylight; for in the warm pour of sunshine it is natural to expect voices, to see smoke rising from the chimneys and children playing and women peering from the doors.

Caraday's Cove had no life at all, not even a rat slinking about the crazy sheds. There had been none for at least thirteen years. Old J.C. himself had given it the sting of death when he installed the first gasoline engine in a fishing boat as far back as 1904. Within five or six years every fisherman had one, and with these it was no longer necessary to live in the isolation of the Head. A man could run out from Port Barron at any stage of the tide and in any wind, overhaul his traps and nets, and be safely home by nightfall. By 1918 the last lone lobsterman had vanished from the cove.

Grass grew now between the smooth stones of the lane, about the old doorsteps, the decayed lobster traps, the worn wooden capstan at the head of each slip, and among the rusty tins, the old corks and killicks, the heaps of rotten net and cordage that mark a fishing settlement given back to the wilderness. The huts were simple frame affairs of two or three rooms, covered with warped gray shingles. The stovepipes were red with rust. Some had blown down. Here and there a rusty padlock still fastened a door, as if the owner intended to come back some day and never had. Others had mere wooden latches and some stood open, swinging in the breeze. Except for an occasional bench or a crude pine table, all the furniture was gone. In one shack a rusty tin dipper still hung above the bucket shelf. In another the head of a child's doll, scalped and blind, stared emptily from a window ledge.

When they came to the church, on the grassy slope at the head of the cove, Rena lifted the latch and they walked in on tiptoe as if not to disturb its ghosts. Here everything had been left as it was at the last service. The pine pews stood in orderly rows amid the dust. The morning sun streamed through the narrow east windows, carefully Gothic and filled with colored glass. A rack on the wall behind the dais still held the last hymn numbers. The little American organ was still in its place; and when Sax worked the bellows lever and Rena pulled out a few stops and pressed the keys, it uttered a wheezing chord, a whisper that died away at once, as if the faithful thing had saved one diapason for this moment and now gave up the ghost. Rena drew open gently the door of a small cupboard behind the choir benches, and there was the pewter Communion set, gone black with time and neglect.

The bell rope still dangled in the porch beneath that rakish steeple and Sax gave it a cautious pull with his free hand as he and Rena left. Overhead a single clang shattered the silence, and then a dry squeaking as the old ship's bell swayed slowly to a stop. Behind the church were a number of graves marked with beach stones, and here and there a rotten wooden cross on which the epitaph, burned with a hot iron, was now too faint to read. Beyond these stood the tangled mass of cat-spruce trees with their dangling rags of old-man's-beard.

Rena led the way along a path through the trees to the Caraday cottage, a plain wooden thing in the old story-and-a-half style, with two dormers peering from the forward slope of the roof. John Caraday had built his first home here in the heart of the wood for the sake of shelter from the winter gales, and apart from a small grassy space before it the trees enclosed the house like walls. A green gloom hung there, and a scent of warm spruce gum.

There was a storm door, propped shut with a stout chunk of driftwood. Sax threw the log aside and opened it. Rena drew a large brass key from her pocket. The lock of the main door turned with a dry scrape. She paused for a moment as the door swung open. Sax's hand on her arm was reassuring. She was glad now that he had come and not her mother. Pamela had never liked those bygone summer removals to the old house at the Head and she had always heaved a gust of relief when J.C. packed the family off to Port Barron again. And now, here, Rena could imagine her mother's reaction all too clearly. The little cry as the door crept open, the sniff of musty air, the click of tongue and the half-amused, half-indignant, "Rena darling, it's like a tomb, why on earth did you want to come out here?"

Like the church, the house and its contents had remained untouched since J.C.'s day, for Roger and Pamela had never made that summer flitting after the old man died. From time to time Roger had come out to see the place, taking along the child for company, but that was all. The furniture was of the very simplest kind, fashioned of maple and pine wood by fishermen-carpenters when the house was built; indeed some had been made by J.C. himself, and the old man had treasured it always for its reminder of early happiness and his first success. Sax and Rena wandered through the rooms arm in arm, leaving twin tracks in the dust. Upstairs, in the small bedrooms of the half-story, where they had to stoop, the old mattresses with their sheep-wool stuffing and rotten striped ticking remained on the plain wooden beds; but sheets and blankets together with such things as table cloths and all other household draperies were stored away in big chests in the lumber room. There, too, lay the carpets, tightly rolled and bound in sailcloth coverings. The old seaman had laid up his cottage each fall as if he were laying up a ship for winter.

Rena was silent and Sax followed her mood. Curtains of spider web, thick with dust, hung in the window casings, in the corners of the rooms, stretching sometimes from floor to ceiling in the less drafty parts and wavering gently as they passed. They moved about the rooms like comrades on a pilgrimage, Rena with an absorbed, almost devout air, and Sax watching her. He liked the way she moved at his side, the mute and graceful gestures of her free hand pointing out this or that, or thrown out suddenly with the long fingers curved as if to touch or catch something precious floating in the air. He admired her profile in the half-light through the dusty windows. She wore a walking skirt of pleated tartan that swung kiltlike at her knees and he admired her legs. A well-built girl. She was all right. She was really a fine piece.

At last she had seen enough. They locked the door and in the drowned green light of the clearing took another path that led through the trees towards the point. It brought them to the back door of the foghorn-keeper's dwelling, and Mrs. Torby, seeing them from her kitchen window, jerked open the door and cried a welcome. She was a little gray woman with black button eyes and a tongue that wagged delightedly, as if it had been wound up for months awaiting just this moment. Rena kissed her affectionately. She never kissed her mother like that, and Sax, whose eyes missed nothing, reflected once more on the influences of her childhood.

↶ ↶ Chapter 13

THEY found Sam Torby in the foghorn building, and again there was a happy greeting. He was a big, slow-moving man in the sixties, with a voice enlarged by constant competition with the powerful diaphone horn and eyes bright and round and unwinking, like the eyes of a gull. His massive nose had a squashed look, the mark of some bare-fisted argument long ago, but his face was mild, the benign weathered face of a seaman long past the heat of his youth and now gone a little to fat. The top of his head was bald, and about this expanse of shining pink ran a fringe of long white hair.

The old sailor shook Sax's hand politely and showed the visitors about his engine room with pride. It was as clean as a ship. The government-gray paint on the walls and the concrete floor gleamed as if polished. Two big single-cylinder gasoline engines worked the air compressor and Sam insisted on starting one of them to show how well the thing went. The engine sneezed and chugged, the great flywheel spun and became a blur, the long belt swayed and

111

flapped. In a few moments the horn outside uttered a tremendous bray and the whole building vibrated. Rena put her fingers in her ears. As the engine wheezed to a stop Sam wagged his head at her. "You didn't use to mind it, Rena, when you was small. What a fine big girl you've growed."

"Don't say that." She threw a laughing glance at Sax. "You make me feel like an elephant, Sam. I feel as old as one anyhow, after looking at the church and the houses by the cove and remembering what they used to be. They made me sad."

"Ah! It's too bad, all that. You know, Rena, after all the people left we used to tidy up the church, Jennie and me. Didn't seem right to let that go. But after four or five years we give it up. Time, you can't hold off time with swabs and dusters. It's sad all right. I well remember those Sundays when J.C. would read the Bible out loud, and young Mr. Roger in the summertime would play the organ whilst I pumped the bellers, and there'd be pretty nigh a hundred men, women and youngsters singin' in the pews. The old times. The good old times. I was just a young man then, mate in one of Caraday's vessels, but I was courtin' Jennie here and I wanted to settle ashore. So J.C. got me this job when the gov'ment built the first horn on the Head. Old steam thing, that was. Minister come out from Port Barron and marrit us in the church. T'was the same summer Mr. Roger got marrit himself, and the next year he fetched his bride out here, your mother, Rena. Pretty li'l thing she was too, one o' those pink-and-white-complected English gals, and dressed stylish the way we'd never seen a woman dressed, even up to Eglinton. And by-and-by that summer her father and mother came, English people, very polite, and stayed a week or two. He was a soger, very tall and straight, and could bring down a pair o' ducks with a quick right-and-left as good as the best gunner on the cape. But I guess you know all that."

"Doesn't anyone ever come here now?" Rena asked.

"Oh, a fisherman sometimes puts into the cove for shelter or maybe to tinker his engine a bit or to get a jug o' fresh water from the spring. They never stay long enough to walk through the wood and say How-do. Every few months the gov'ment steamer comes with supplies for the foghorn and the radio beacon. Lands 'em in the cove by boat, and I hitch up my old horse and haul the stuff out here. For all the people we see here we might be at the world's end."

"But you have some company," Sax observed, pointing towards the radio hut.

"Oh, yes. The radioman. Name o' Pascoe. Stays with us. Don't talk much. Been up North a lot. They lose their tongues up there, seems like. Knows his work though. Oftentimes gives me a hand with one o' my engines when she breaks down. 'Course he's got these fancy new ones like a motorcar engine that starts automatic and all that. Gov' ment built the thing here two years back. Uncanny, I call it. I mean here's my horn, a good loud noise that the fishermen can hear ten mile, wind favorin'. And there's that outfit o' Pascoe's, makes no more sound than Jennie's cat purrin' and mewlin' by the stove, but ships pick it up a hundred mile or more. Feller aboard ship twists a dial and he's got a bearin' on Gannet Head as good's if he could see it over a compass bowl. Dark, rain, fog, snow — none o' that signifies. Often wonder what J.C. would ha' thought to see a thing like that, right here where he was shipwrecked as a young man and come ashore on a gratin' with nothin' to his name but a pair o' canvas trousers — and all along o' thick weather and a lee shore and nothin' to warn ships off."

"I wonder what he'd think of the place now anyway," Rena said. "It's haunted."

"You ain't afraid?" Sam said smiling.

"Oh no. I like ghosts — that kind. You know how I loved it here when I was small. I was always unhappy when I had to go back to Port Barron, and I hated those winters in the West Indies. Do you suppose the radioman would mind if we peeped at his box of tricks?"

Sam led the way. The point was low, a shelf of turf barely ten feet above the tide and strewn with sea-urchin shells broken by foraging gulls. Below they could see the naked ledges of the shore with their crannies full of cobblestones. Beyond marched the Atlantic, moving in long orderly ranks out of the east. They followed a narrow path worn in the turf and passed between the short steel masts and aerials. Sam gave a stout knock on the door and threw it open. The hut was a single chamber that seemed full of strange apparatus. There were two radio transmitters, each coupled to a separate gasoline motor, each with a tall black panel studded with dials and switches. Between them sat a small desk with a box of receiving apparatus, a telegraph key and a loud-speaker in a gray metal frame. At the moment the loud-speaker was crying dots and dashes on a shrill note, and listening to it was a man in a Mackinaw shirt, a pair of faded blue dungarees and a pair of oil-tanned moccasins badly worn and with the leather laces untied and dangling. He sat in a swivel chair, with one foot on the desk. A blond stubble covered his jaws. His hair needed cutting as well, but what it needed most at the moment was a comb. His gray eyes seemed very light in the tanned skin. He sprang up as they entered, with Sam shouting introductions, but he did not seem disconcerted by these smartly dressed visitors or even conscious of his own appearance. He took the hands they offered one after another, murmured "How d'you do?" politely and stood with the patient air of a poet disturbed in his garret by a slumming party. He was quite tall. Sax had to tip his head back a little to look him in the face.

"Owen," Sam Torby roared, "tell 'em all about this stuff." Obediently the man began, moving about the room and explaining matters in a mild slow voice. Sax, always interested in gadgetry, especially gadgetry that had to do with the sea, followed his words and gestures intently. Torby beamed on them both. Rena found herself ignored. She looked about the hut. It was bone-clean like Sam's own establishment and the walls and floor shone with the same government-issue paint. All the visible brasswork on the radio gear was highly polished. Not a speck of dust could be seen, not even a mote in the dazzling sunbeam that crossed the room from the window facing the sea. There was a smell of paint, of gasoline and oil, and the peculiar smell of electrical apparatus warm from recent use. She looked at the operator whimsically. The contrast between his care for the equipment and his own slovenly appearance seemed to her very droll. A log sheet lay beside the telegraph key, covered with scrawled pencil jottings, and there was a portable typewriter and an untidy heap of typed sheets beside it. Above the desk hung a framed certificate with the name Owen John Hercourt Pascoe written in ink among a lot of official print.

"Now," came Pascoe's voice, moving back towards the desk, "the beacon signal will come on again in half a minute. Watch the relays here and you'll see the switches close." Sax came to Rena's side, slipping an arm through hers. They watched. As the clock hand reached the minute the maze of wires and delicate apparatus came suddenly to life. Something clicked here, something else there, slender blades of copper fell into place, and one of the engines be-

115

gan to purr behind the panel, like an idling motorcar. From the hidden bowels of all these things came a faint high whine sounding dots and dashes.

"You hear?" Pascoe said, addressing himself to Sax. "First a long dash, then *G* three times, then the long dash again. The *G's* for Gannet Head of course."

The machine repeated this monotonous refrain. Finally another series of small clicks, another vision of delicate bits of metal moving here and there, and the whole uncanny thing went back to sleep.

"And you mean to tell me that's all you have to do?" said Sax with a clear note of scorn. "Oh I know you have to keep the thing in running order—but it's all automatic, I mean?"

"Oh yes. Of course I have to keep a listening watch on the air at certain hours of the day, and twice a day I have to call up the station at Barmouth just to show I'm alive and on the job." He smiled, oblivious of the other's contempt.

"They also serve," put in Rena diplomatically.

Pascoe seemed to notice her at last. He turned that diffident smile and murmured, "That's nice of you. It's the only excuse for people like me, and there are quite a lot of us between here and Hudson Strait. Only we don't stand and wait. We sit, or sprawl."

Rena heard Sax snort and she drew him outside hastily, calling thanks over her shoulder. "Let's have our picnic," she said. "I'm starved." There was some argument with Torby, who bellowed that Jennie would be expecting them for dinner, but they got away towards the cove, where Sax picked up the rug and lunch basket. Rena led on, taking an old sheep path that led along the shore. There were a few clumps of cat spruce dwarfed by the poor soil and the winds, but chiefly the common bushes of the

116

barrens brushed against them as they passed. Once in a stretch of open sand dunes the path vanished, but Rena went on confidently. She stopped to point out something almost buried in the sand, and Sax had to stare for some moments before he recognized the thing. It was an old-fashioned mowing machine of the horse-drawn kind.

"My grandfather's," Rena said. "In his young days this used to be a sort of meadow where he cut wild hay for his cattle. The dunes have moved in since."

On the farther side of this sandy place they picked up the path again. Rena halted at last where it skirted a sea-worn ledge. The shore and the endless barrens ran on towards the left. To the right they could see the spire of the church and the tips of Pascoe's radio masts above the dark mass of the wood. Rena spread the rug on a patch of turf at the head of the ledge and took the lunch out of the basket. They ate with appetite and sipped hot coffee from the Thermos. It was pleasant there on the shore. The bushes screened them from the northwest wind. The clear sky of the morning was littered now with drifting clouds, whose shadows made moving gray patches on the sea. Between each passage of cloud overhead the sunshine poured, bringing out the summer blue and sparkle of the water. In the immediate lee of the ledge each wave had a slick skin that vanished in foam as it broke on the rocks, but farther out the surface was ruffled and whitecaps flashed and danced all the way to the horizon. The gannet colony for which the Head was named had vanished long ago, when the people settled at the cove, but the more companionable herring gulls remained, and the terns, the petrels and the shags. Now and then a pair of eider ducks flitted in towards the shore, saw the two humans sitting there and sheered off quickly.

Sax talked lazily about West Indian days, telling his most

respectable stories with effect, as he had learned to tell them long ago to the Carisforts and their friends. It was a very different sort of West Indian life from the one Rena had known as a child. At the droll climax of each yarn, sprung suddenly after an adroit approach, she threw back her head and laughed until her eyes were wet. She was naïve, of course. She had not seen much of life, for all those childish travels of hers. It pleased him to see in this educated young woman an almost pathetic ignorance of the things that really made the world go round, and his own wisdom in those very things gave him a delightful feeling of superiority. He set himself to show her, suavely and humorously, how much he knew and how little she. And Rena made the best of listeners. For the first time since her father's death she found herself in close companionship with a man. There was a difference that she did not trouble to examine; she was aware of nothing but that he interested her and that he had in him some quality of her grandfather, that rugged adventurer who had come to the cape so long ago and opened its windows on the world.

As the afternoon drew on, the clouds became white masses piled high in the sky and with pregnant gray bellies, all moving ponderously out to sea. There distant rumbles of thunder. Far out over the sea one heavy-bellied mass let down a dark curtain of rain. To one side of it appeared the faint trace of a rainbow, the end of the arc, no more, curving from cloud to sea. Seeing how closely now the clouds were pressing together, Rena said reluctantly, "I suppose we'd better go." They packed up the luncheon things and shook out the rug. On the way back to Port Barron the boat ran into heavy thundershowers that sent Rena to the shelter of the cabin. Sax was at the wheel, a stocky confident figure with the rain beating on his face. His smart clothes were drenched but he did not care. He felt the gaze of the girl looking out past the cabin slide and seeing a stalwart male in his element. He would never dare, of course, but he hankered to tell her the more exciting tales of his career, the tough encounters and smart tricks of his way to fortune. He itched to have her admire him, not as a jester but for what he really was, a man of immense courage and resource, the kind of fellow who made the heroes in books look pale and soft. And what tales he could tell! His mind dwelt especially on the big one, the coup of his career, the final adventure by which he had beaten the sea and the Racket and made a fortune in one stroke. That was something, really something. As he looked at the girl and licked the spray from his lips, he smiled. He could almost hear himself saying Listen to this.

ᔎ ᔎ Chapter 14

IT had begun soon after that painful episode in Nassau with Ellen Carisfort. The Major had sent for him. Sax, still brooding on the affair, went up to the Major's house with a set face, ignoring the greetings of people in the street. As he sat down the Major lighted a cigarette and blew out a long jet of smoke that offended his visitor at once.

"Sax, I've got news for you. I've been over to Miami talking to the bigwigs. Have to do that from time to time. Make a report and see what's cooking across the water. Well, the firm's branching out. There's some new tie-up with a mob in New Orleans and we're to run the stuff."

Sax looked up and frowned. "That's a long run. Must be

all of a thousand miles. Do they know that?" He had a low opinion of the brains in Miami.

"Of course. You'd be surprised how much I know myself, Sax."

"I'll be surprised to know how you're going to do it. Not with boats like ours, that's sure."

"That's right, not with boats like ours. With schooners."

Sax looked at the man scornfully. "Out of Nassau? That means sailing right around the heel of Florida with a chance of being picked up anywhere between Miami and the Tortugas. D'you think the Coast Guard's blind?"

The Major smiled indulgently. "Not out of Nassau, Sax. Out of British Honduras. Get it? A nice clear run up the Gulf of Mexico and nothing to worry about till you get inside Trinity Shoals."

"I see." And with sudden concern, "You're not picking me for this? What?"

"I am," said the Major, flicking ash. "You've been in schooners before. You've been to New Orleans before."

"Not in this game."

"What's the difference? Listen, we've got an agent in Belize. I'll give you his name later. You load the stuff there and he'll see that you get any stores you want. Now get this. Ever take a close look at one of your Canadian dollar bills? The serial number's printed in two places, one each side of the King's head. Tear one of those bills right down through His Majesty and you've got a serial number on each half, see? All right. The agent will give you some Canuck half dollars torn like that, and you'll take the schooner to a certain position on the other side of the Gulf."

"In U.S. waters," Sax said glumly.

"Outside, Sax, well outside. We're playing this thing safe, see? In fact it's foolproof any way you look at it. Wait till you've heard it all. You get there on a certain date. You may have to hang about there a day or two if the weather's rough. Let on you're fishing, maybe. Have some nets about the deck, that sort of thing. Towards dark with any decent sea a motorboat will come out to you — boat something like *Faquita*. When she comes alongside you'll let one man come aboard. Just one, see? Keep a gun handy and don't let anyone else over the side till you know what's what. If it's the right crowd this chap will show you the other half of one of your Canuck dollar bills. Make sure. Check the number. And keep that other half — it's your receipt. We'll expect you to turn over each complete bill to the agent when you return to Belize. That accounts for your cargo, see? Keeps everybody honest, including the New Orleans mob. The actual payment's all arranged in banks ashore. Now get this and you'll understand what I mean. For every one of those Canuck bills complete, you let a shore boat have six hundred cases, no more, no less. Now there it is. Foolproof, as I say."

Sax stared at a spot past the Major's shoulder. "Where are you going to find the schooners for this little game?"

"We've got one for a start," returned the Major briskly. "One of those Nova Scotia hookers that used to work Rum Row. Maybe you saw her lying among the sponge boats along the docks a bit from the steamer wharf. A two-master called *Jill Be Civil* — where do they get these names? — and she's got a pair of big diesels for extra speed and a gasoline deck winch for hoisting sails and working cargo. You'll like her, Sax. I can see you having a dam' fine time in her up and down the Gulf."

"All this," Sax said carefully, "is orders, I suppose?"

"Right, Sax."

"What's the pay?"

"Five hundred a month, the same as you're getting now.

121

It's a cushy job compared with this Miami run, where you're apt to get knocked off any night at all. And, Sax, you need a change."

"Ah!" Sax made a mouth and nodded slowly. "So I need a change."

The Major turned his cold gaze to the ceiling. "Sax, it's a tough show, this little run across the Stream. Gets a man after a time — and you've had four years of it. You haven't been quite your old self, Sax, the past couple of months. I've been chatting with Sands . . ."

"Ah! Sure! And Sands, he gets *Faquita*, hey?"

The Major shrugged. He was still engrossed in the ceiling when Sax left. As he emerged from the house into Bay Street Sax uttered a dry laugh. He was thinking of Figueroa. It had taken Sands quite a long time to get smart.

Sax had been in Belize before in summer, when, as Halkett used to say, it was like Hell's own engine room with the hatch nailed fast. As the schooner came in from the sea, she met the massive wet heat of Honduras like a wall. The town was the same straggle of roofs and verandas along both banks of the river, most of the houses built on piles because the land was barely above sea level, and all apparently drowning in a green flood of coconut and cabbage palms. In the distance, past miles of swamp, a thunderstorm was booming and flashing over the Manatee hills.

On the broad veranda of the agent's house, where a hot wind rattled the slats of the blinds and clashed the ragged leaves of the palms outside, Sax reclined in a cane chair fanning himself with his hat. The agent was a small desiccated man of fifty with a gaunt malarial face. He was full of business.

"Well, Captain Nolan, as I understand it you've got a full cargo of liquor from Nassau but after this you load here. Let me know what else you want — provisions, fuel, water, anything for the ship at all, the owners have given me a free hand. I'm ready to serve you, sir, in any way. You have only to name it."

"Get me a glass of water for a start," Sax said, dripping sweat.

"Did you say — water?"

"With ice in it."

Sax took a long slow drink of water and resumed the fanning motions of his hat. "I'll let you know what I want in the way of stores. If you've got a sailmaker in this place, send him down in the morning. I've got a fair suit of sails except the foresail. That's so rotten you could poke your finger through. You know the game we're up to, I suppose?"

The agent cackled and showed the jaundiced whites of his eyes. "Ah yes, Captain. And a pretty little game it seems to be."

"What makes you say that?"

"I suppose I must be careful what I say. Well, f'rinstance there's a Canadian schooner very much like yours operating out of here. Called *I'm Alone*. She's nothing to do with your crowd. Operated by a Canadian crowd, I believe. Anyhow, she's made several trips from Belize, discharging off New Orleans somewhere, and everything's gone as smooth as glass. Making money faster than the mint. Well, I take it that your crowd's heard of her success. I take it further that your crowd intends to — how do you say — get in on the Racket? And why not? New Orleans — a jolly big market, that. Must be a lot of good people thirsty in those parts if the climate's anything like ours, eh?" He cackled again.

"If it's one degree hotter, mister, they must be a thirsty lot of sinners."

123

For several moments the agent looked blank. Then he laughed all over his meager flesh and bones. He rattled in the chair as if the endemic fever of Honduras had come upon him in a moment.

"Aha! See it now! Priceless! Thirsty lot of sinners —oho, that's good, that's very good, Captain Nolan. I must tell my wife. If it's one degree hotter . . ."

The cackle was still going on and on as Sax went down the steps.

The first trip was ominously easy. On the appointed day *Jill Be Civil* reached the appointed spot off Trinity Shoals, far to the west of the Mississippi passes, after a spanking run of four days with sails and engine from Belize. Promptly at dusk the shore boat appeared, a fast gray thing coming out of the north like a purposeful ghost. A thin dark man in rumpled seersucker came aboard with a proper half dollar, and six hundred cases went over the side. In four successive nights the cargo was discharged, and Sax returned to Belize. The second trip went as well, although they were hung up by a gale off the Shoals for twenty-four hours. Eventually the shore boat turned up with the same precision, as if the rendezvous were a street corner in New Orleans instead of a chart spot fifty miles off the Louisiana coast.

On his second return to Belize, Sax found the agent wearing a look of concern on his yellow face. The man said at once, "Captain, I've got news."

"That doesn't mean good news. Well, let's have it."

"That other schooner I told you about, the *I'm Alone*. She's been chased by a pair of American cutters away out into the Gulf — chased and sunk, Captain! By gunfire. Two days ago."

124

Sax considered this. "Phew! Looks like they're not fooling any more. Sure she was outside U.S. waters?"

"When they sank her she was a good two hundred miles southeast of the Trinity Shoals light buoy. That's according to the wireless news. There's the deuce of a row. Firing on the British flag. Ship sunk on the high seas. Crew put in irons. One man dead. Nasty business, Captain. The Yanks, you know, they can't do that."

Sax smiled sourly. "They've done it, haven't they? They're just getting smart, that's all."

As he watched the third cargo being loaded Sax was thoughtful. He looked over his men. Three of his original crew of Nassau toughs were down with fever in the local hospital, and in their place the agent had supplied two zambos and a Hindu boy named Eustace, all from Belize. Of the four remaining Nassau men, two were mulatto and two white. The whites were in charge of the diesels. All of them boozed in the sweltering bars ashore except Eustace and the zambos and the Nassau mate. A scummy lot. He wondered how they would act if *Jill Be Civil* ran afoul of the U.S. Coast Guard, like *I'm Alone*. He wondered what he would do himself. With the engines going and all sail set in a howling gale, the schooner could not outrun the new Yankee cutters. That night in his rattan chair under the awning on the half deck he sat and brooded long.

In the morning he picked a quarrel with the engineers. It was easy. They had been drinking thirstily ever since the schooner reached Belize, and they were in a surly morning mood when he tackled them about the filthy state of the engine room. The younger one flared up at once. Sax poured oil on this flame. Standing with his feet apart, with hands in his jacket pockets and wearing the monkey-imp smile, he began with "A couple of lousy no-good

Nassau conchs" and went on from there. The conchs had some excellent phrases of their own concerning the captain, accompanied by a brandishing of fists. Inevitably one of them aimed a blow at that faintly smiling mouth.

An interested crowd on the wharf, including the dock policeman, attracted by the sound of argument, had the best view of what followed. The stocky figure in the white ducks became for a few moments a flickering blur. There were sounds like a stick swung hard against a sugar sack. When the blur steadied it became the skipper once more, breathing somewhat heavily but with the same smile on his lips and his hands back in his pockets. One of the engineers lay on his back, with arms flung out and a knee drawn up. The other lay some distance away, curled up as if asleep. They moaned a little. There was quite a lot of blood.

Sax turned to the policeman on the wharf. "Get these men up to the calaboose. I'll lay drunk-and-disorderly charges later." He sent Eustace for the agent, who came hurrying down just in time to see the mate and the policeman carrying the second engineer ashore. In the cabin Sax snapped, "I'm paying those men off. I won't have scum like that in my ship. Not any more."

The agent gave him a fascinated stare. "My God! What happened? Their faces were cut to pieces. I never saw anything like it."

Sax drew a hand from his pocket and showed him the grooved and twin-edged metal ring through which the fingers were thrust.

"What's that?"

"A thimble. The kind they fit in the cringles of square sails. I've carried one in each jacket pocket for years. They make handy knuckle-dusters I find."

The agent whistled. "What next!"

126

"Ah! That's just what I want to talk to you about. I want you to hustle those stevedores and the warehouse people. After that get me a couple of diesel men. You can pick 'em up from some of these trading schooners here. The pay's two hundred fifty dollars a month — and U.S., not B.H. — they'll jump at it. I want to clear the ship for sea by to-morrow noon, no later."

And the *Jill* sailed at noon, with the sun's heat coming straight down in pulsations like hammer strokes and a small breeze off the land chafing the leaves of the palm trees in uneasy puffs. The sky clouded over as she drew past Ambergris Cay and she went on up the coast in a thunderstorm that hid the long fringe of cays and low mangrove islands in rain. Sax shifted the course to get a safer offing. It was a tricky coast at the best of times and he was never easy until he had cleared Cape Catoche and entered the great Gulf itself.

Then followed the long monotony of the run across the Gulf: the sickly gleam of seas gliding by like waves of molten grease, the sails pressed hard by the hot wind, the seamen sprawled on the deck, talking in languid voices and shifting with the shadow of the sails, the sweat dripping on the chart as Sax pricked off each noon reckoning. He followed the usual course most of the way, but after crossing latitude 28° he ordered the ship swung to the northwest. At the same time he told the mate to check over the boat's sail and oars and then have it towed astern "to let the seams take up." The mate obeyed but he looked surprised. He was a Nassau mulatto named Brackley, an intelligent fellow with good features and a sleek black mustache that the hybrid girls of Belize found delightful. He had a great love for flashy clothes, for rings and wrist watches and fancy walking sticks; and these and the girls and a weakness for dice took all his pay. But he was a good

127

seaman and he admired the *Jill's* skipper to the point of awe.

Sax drew him aft with a look and a jerk of his head. There was no one in earshot but the helmsman, part Negro, part Mayan Indian, who knew no more English than a few nautical phrases and a carefully memorized boxing of the compass.

"Brackley," Sax said carefully, "we're a long way from Nassau, eh?"

"Yes, Cap'n."

"You like this trade?"

"Oh yes, Cap'n. Fine."

"You like money, eh?"

The man smiled broadly. "You bet, Cap'n. That's why I like this trade."

"Um! But did it ever strike you our pay's damned small for what we do, for the risks we take? Ever strike you the owners make a fortune every trip, while we get a handful of dollars? That's true, isn't it?"

Something in the captain's tone frightened Brackley a little. He looked away uneasily, staring first at the back of the helmsman's head and then off to sea.

"Why you talkin' this way, Cap'n?"

"Listen — you know what happened to that other schooner, don't you — the *I'm Alone?* You heard the talk in Belize? D'you hanker to get your head knocked off by a cannon? Look pretty that way, wouldn't you? A swell sight for those girls in Belize — only they wouldn't see you any more. You'd be shark meat somewhere off Trinity Shoals."

"Don't talk like that, Cap'n. Please, Cap'n."

"Ah! Gripes you, that, don't it? Well, it gripes me too. We might get away with it again this trip, maybe half a dozen trips, but sooner or later the Americans'll catch up with us. Then if we try to run, bang-bang, and down we go.

128

If we stop and chuck in we get a nice long stretch in a Louisiana jail. Know anything about Louisiana jails?"

"Yes, Cap'n. A li'l knife fight in N'Orleans once."

"Ah! Well, I hear they're not so good. So if it came to a choice I'd head the ship down the Gulf like that other bloke and let 'em shoot. What d'you think of that?"

The mate gulped. He glanced at Sax and away again.

"You don't believe I would," Sax said.

"Oh yes, Cap'n. You would. I know that."

"Okay! Now listen to this. I don't intend to die at my age and I've never thought it smart to land in jail. You can't make a dollar either way. And money's what I'm interested in, the same as you. Now I see a chance to make a lot of money in a hurry, and no more slogging up and down the Gulf for ha'pence. It means taking a chance for ourselves, that's all, instead of the owners. Look here, I'll give it to you straight. Remember those engineers, the white men from Nassau? The owners always put one man in each crew to watch the captain and report everything he does. I knew it was one of those two but I didn't know which. So I scuppered 'em both to make sure. That gave me a free hand with the *Jill* for this one voyage anyhow.

"Now here's the lay. The U.S. Coast Guard's got its dander up about all this booze coming into the New Orleans area by the schoonerload. They're watching all round there like a bunch of pelicans about a half-tide shoal. They've even pulled in their patrol boats from other places. I got a tip in Belize that right now Galveston's wide open. So the deuce with the owners and their mob in New Orleans. We take the booze to Galveston — strictly on our own hook, see? Don't look so nervous. We'll stay well off the land. I'll go ashore in the boat and find a customer. We've got to get rid of the cargo quick and we want cash, so we'll sell it cheap. We'll sell the stuff at cost. We ought to get fifty or sixty thousand dollars, cash over the rail, with any luck at all. Then we head back for Belize."

"How you goin' to 'count for the cargo to the agent, Cap'n? And what the Major goin' to say, back home in Nassau? I'm 'fraid, sir. No, sir."

"You scare too easy, Brackley. Listen to this. Somewhere off Ambergris the ship catches afire. Never mind how, I'll explain all that later. Next day we turn up in Belize in the boat. I report to the agent that we got chased and shelled half across the Gulf before we got away, and on the way back to Belize she caught afire and sank with the full cargo still aboard. Too bad. And what can they say? Not a damned thing. See what I mean? All the agent can do is pay our wages and sign us off. Now these Belize men aboard, they won't know what it's all about, they'll take their pay and go. The only man we'll have to fix is the cook — he's a Nassau man like you. So we'll slip him five thousand to keep his mouth shut and split the rest between us fifty-fifty. And there we are, set up for life. Think what you could do with twenty-five thousand dollars, Brackley. And nothing anyone could put a finger on."

The mate's eyes still wandered nervously from Sax to the stolid zambo at the wheel, but there was a gleam in them, and now a hand crept up to the black mustache, caressing and twisting the tips. Sax smiled.

∽∽ Chapter 15

SAX'S faith in his luck and his own bold abilities was never more justified than in that final adventure in the Gulf of Mexico. The boat's crew had landed him in the dark on an empty stretch of the Texas coast and then returned to the *Jill* — a little epic in itself, for under the watchful Brackley the schooner was hovering fifty miles south of the Galveston lightship. Sax set off in the first gleam of sunrise, found a road, thumbed a ride in a passing truck, and reached Galveston that afternoon. He made for the waterfront at once, calling himself a seaman on the beach, which was quite true, and he soon found a place where seamen of any sort could buy a drink. A brief chat with the proprietor passed him on to a restaurant three blocks away, and in a room behind the kitchen he found awaiting him a fat man in an expensive cowboy hat.

"I hear," said the fat man in a ten-gallon drawl, "you got a proposition. I ain't sayin' I'm interested but spill it anyhow."

Sax spilled it and it did not take him long.

"How much you got aboard, and what kind?"

"There's three thousand cases of rye, one hundred ten-gallon demijohns of Bacardi, two hundred and fifty cases of Scotch, and a hundred and fifty cases of various champagnes and liqueurs. We shipped it out of bond at Belize. That means bottom prices: eighteen dollars a case for the whiskey, eight a gallon for the rum, an average of twenty a case for the other stuff. And all good stuff, the real Mc-Coy. For quick discharge you can have the lot at what it cost in Belize — say sixty thousand dollars, cash over the rail."

"Why all the hurry?"

"I told you. I got chased off Trinity Shoals, slipped the cutters in a rain squall and dodged this way. They'll be searching for me further down the Gulf. I can't afford to have a single case aboard if they fetch up with me. Do you want the stuff or not?"

"Where's the ship?"

"I'm not saying, except you've got to have boats that can make a round trip of anything up to a hundred and fifty miles and do it fast."

"Yow! How do we find her?"

"I'll go along in one of your boats and you can put me aboard. Can you do it tonight?"

"How d'you want the money?"

"Hundred-dollar bills."

"That's a lot o' dough to get in a hurry. Besides, there's the boats to round up. Make it tomorra night. Tell me this much, which way's the nearest place to land the stuff outside Galveston?"

Sax jerked his head towards the west. "Got a nice long island, haven't you?"

"Ah! That's good. That's very good. Cap, you've made a deal."

"Just one more thing," Sax murmured.

"What's that?"

"My crew's a touchy lot. And handy with shotguns and Winchesters — in the way of the trade, you understand. Just thought I'd mention it."

A few days later *Jill Be Civil* turned Cape Catoche and swung down the coast of Yucatán. A strong northeast wind and the thrust of the engines brought her up with Ambergris Cay in another twenty-four hours. As in most Nova Scotia schooners the galley was in the forecastle, and at noon all hands but the helmsman and the engineer on duty went forward to eat dinner. On this occasion, however, the mate said carelessly to the helmsman, "Go for'ard and eat. I'll take her."

At the same time Captain Nolan went into the stifling heat of the engine room. To the sweating zambo on watch he declared, "I smell oil. Too much. You smell oil?" The fellow sniffed right and left and shook his head.

"You go eat, savvy?" the captain said. "I want to find. Smell oil too much. No good, savvy? You go."

The man went cheerfully and Sax wasted not a moment. There was a drum of gasoline for the deck winch, formerly kept on deck. On this trip Sax had ordered it stowed in a corner of the engine room, where it would be safer in bad weather. He unscrewed the plug, cut the lashing and threw the drum on its side. A stream of gasoline belched forth. He leaped to the ladder, struck a match, ignited a handful of oily waste and dropped it. In another moment he was on deck. Brackley stood at the helm, watching the engine-room skylight with a sickly smile. They could hear gulping noises from the drum below. Then another sound, a swish and a snap very like the sound of a jib filling out on a new tack. A puff of greasy smoke came up through the skylight, followed by a feather of white flame with a bright blue tip that reached up to the main boom and began to scorch the canvas.

The mate could hold his fear no longer. His tea-colored features had gone a strange mottled hue. He spun the wheel to bring the schooner across the wind, at the same time uttering falsetto cries of "Fire! All hands! Fire!"

A rush of astonished faces, black and tan, appeared in the forecastle doorway one after another and made at once for the boat. It was stowed beside the forehatch on the starboard side and they launched it in four minutes, a record. Getting into it and away was an awkward business, for the *Jill's* engines were still running faithfully in the midst of the flames, all sail was set, and she was making close to nine knots. For a moment Sax wished he had ordered it towed and ready. He had thought of it and rejected it in case the crew became suspicious. The mate was the first man into the boat. Sax was last. He was quite calm. He passed a suitcase down before cutting the painter and jumping in. It contained his sextant and chronometer, a clean suit of ducks, three shirts, a pistol and fifty-eight thousand six hundred dollars in American currency. For security he had wound three fathoms of log line around it, tied with intricate knots, and for the past hour it had been standing just inside the companionway.

They ran out the oars and pulled clear, and the schooner moved rapidly away. Under the mate's last set of the helm she steered a wide circular course, with the whole afterpart of her burning like a matchbox. The mainsail had gone to a black sheet and then blown away in sooty tatters on the wind. When she came around, with the wind astern, the whole flame blew forward, and in a few moments the jibs and foresail flared and vanished as well. There was something uncanny about the way she traveled on, pouring black smoke down the wind and at last heading back towards the boat as if determined to join her company once more. The men began to row violently, shouting in all the tongues of Belize, while Brackley prayed aloud in his Nassau-Cockney accent.

But now came the thing they had been expecting all this time, thinking of her fuel tanks in the heat, and the drum of gasoline.

The explosion made a dull *pom* and blew out the oakum between the sun-dried planks of her topsides aft, so that for an instant she breathed smoke from every seam. In the same moment the engine-room skylight sailed up past the mainmast head, followed by a tall spout of flame and smoke. The long-enduring engines perished with that, and *Jill Be Civil* abandoned her course and drifted slowly down the wind, a floating bonfire. Her crew drifted also, watching the spectacle. When the schooner sank they could see the surf breaking white on a reef and beyond that a line of mangroves. The *Jill's* spars remained standing and she went down until their caps showed above the water, that was all.

It was almost dark. In the last of the light Sax steered the boat through a gap in the reef. They spent an uncomfortable night slapping mosquitoes in the lee of a small mangrove island off the main shore of Ambergris. On the next afternoon, after a parched voyage with sail and oars in the full blast of the sun, they reached Belize and told their tale. It surprised nobody. After the *I'm Alone* affair everyone in Belize had predicted a bad end for the *Jill,* and there it was.

After a bath and shave and a change into clean shirt and ducks at the agent's house, Sax relaxed in one of the veranda chairs. The sun was getting low, there was now an air from the sea, and the big slatted blinds had been drawn up to admit every breath of it. At the other end of the veranda the agent's wife and daughters were amusing themselves with a .22 rifle, sniping at land crabs on the lawn. The agent was engaged in a long recital of trading schooners burned like the *Jill:* the oil that collected in the bilges, the carelessness of native engineers, the tinder-dry hulls that went up in a flash. His droning voice, the flutter of the tall cabbage palms, the recurring pop of the rifle and the laughter of the girls all came to Sax as if from afar. The whole affair had gone so well that it seemed more like a dream than anything else. He had to resist an urge to run to his bedroom and make sure that the suitcase was still there and that the money itself was real.

There was just one thing wrong. The attitude of Brackley and the cook. He had seen their heads together outside the agent's store, soon after the boat got into the river.

When he emerged from the store and told the crew to come back for their pay in the morning, the two Nassau men drew him aside. One look at their faces was enough. He heard the ultimatum with the air of a man enduring a twice-told tale.

"Cap'n," Brackley said boldly, "we know how much money you got for the cargo. When Americans pay over the side it's always fifty dollars a case."

"But I tell you . . ."

"Can't fool us, Cap'n. We can figure. We're not like these ignorant Belize men. Fifty dollars a case. You got more'n a hundred and fifty thousand dollars in that suitcase and we say share and share alike. Only fair, Cap'n. You know that."

Sax had a swift urge to fall upon them both and knock them into the river. The insolence in their greedy faces made his hands twitch. For a full minute he looked his hate at them, thinking of his own risks and labors and how soft it was for them. Then his cooler self took charge. He jerked his head and laughed.

"Okay. You're to windward of me, I admit, though you don't deserve a cent, the pair of you. Well, I can't haul open the suitcase right here and count out all that money, you must know that. Besides, in a couple of minutes the agent's taking me up to his house to eat and stay the night. I'll see you in the morning."

"Where?"

"Right here. I'll have all three shares done up in paper parcels and you can take your pick. That should be fair, eh?"

"How do we know you'll be here?" Brackley said, with a droll glance at the cook.

"Figure it out for yourself — you're good at figuring. There's no steamer out of here for another five or six days, not even a trading schooner. I asked the agent. You can

136

check with him if you like. Till then I've got to stick around Belize the same as you."

They looked at each other and nodded. But he heard them question the agent before his departure for the house. The agent chuckled as they left.

"Why are you people so anxious to get away from Belize? Our town's not so bad as all that, is it?"

"My friend," Sax replied with a humor he did not feel, "I can only speak for myself. I could mention the heat and the mosquitoes, of course, but you'd only go on like a tourist booklet about the refreshing sea breezes and all that. So put it down to plain superstition. I just don't like to stick around a town where the main road leads straight to the graveyard."

The familiar cackle rasped his nerves all the way to the house. After the evening meal he pleaded weariness and went to his room. He was weary enough, his tough body yearned for rest, but his nimble mind was at full race.

He waited an hour after the last movement in the house had ceased and the drowsy voices of the servants had trailed away towards the rear. Fortunately the windows had no covering of mosquito wire. The agent was a frugal man who clung to the old-fashioned netting over the beds. Sax unwound the length of the *Jill's* old log line to lower the suitcase to the ground. It was not far, in spite of the piling on which the bungalow stood. He swung himself out and dropped. The sea breeze had gone and now a humid draft off the inland swamps blew down the river and through the town. A few people were still abroad, moving in chattering twos and threes. He kept to the deeper shadows and reached the waterfront, with sweat running down his flanks and into his shoes. The *Jill's* boat was still where they had left it, tied up among the crazy native craft. He lowered the suitcase into it, cast off the painter and stepped onto the stern sheets. An oar sculled over the stern took him into the stream, flowing with a slow and massive current out of the heart of the land and darkly shining like the flow of hot molasses from a vat. He stepped the mast and set the lugsail and steered for the sea.

There was curiously little to remember after the boat slid out of the river. He recalled one or two squalid fishing villages where he put in for food and water; and calms when he labored at the oars, counting the strokes to a hundred, resting a few minutes, and taking up the labor and count again; and languid airs that barely filled the sail, and sudden gusts that nearly snapped the flimsy mast, and then the good steady thrust of the trade wind settling down. But there were long gaps born of thirst and exhaustion and the unmerciful clubbing of the sun; and there was one afternoon in the long passage across the Gulf of Amatique when he thought he was back in Nassau, drifting over the sea gardens in a pleasure boat with Ellen Carisfort and hearing that charming voice exclaiming, "Look! Look down there, Sax! On the bottom. Isn't that lovely? Isn't that simply marvelous?"

Five nights and not quite five days after quitting Belize, he tottered ashore at Puerto Cortés in the Honduran Republic, an obscene object with a black face and disgraceful clothes, clutching a rope-bound suitcase and asking directions in bad Spanish, with a voice like the scrape of a match. For months he lay ill there in a filthy lodging, with the pistol under his pillow and the suitcase under the bed, like a sick but wary beast from the Honduran jungle itself, awaiting full strength before venturing forth. And it was there, thinking wistfully of the Canadian snows and the clean coast and the cold smack of the sea, that it seemed to him the time had come for his return. With his savings and this last rich scoop, he had a fortune beyond that old dream of

138

his youth, and now he could take up not so much a new life as the one he had intended all that time ago.

He had given himself a month in New York to buy a wardrobe, to eat fancy food and see shows and, in general, to sort himself out. Then he had come to Port Barron intending to thumb his nose at the place, and instead met MacIlraith and the Caradays. Seeing Rena's face in the cabin now, and reflecting on all this, he felt how ironical it was to become a gentleman. You could tell little jokes but you could never breathe a word about the best parts of your life.

∽ ∽ Chapter 16

ON a day in September 1931 Rena Caraday came to her mother in the garden, where she was trimming the last withered blossoms from one of the rose arbors. The new lawn ran like a roll of green plush spilled towards the road, with a pattern of flower beds neatly stitched down the middle. A breeze with a cool hint of fall carried up to them the purr of a gasoline mower on the lower slope.

"Mama," Rena said.

"Yes, dear?"

"Sax wants me to marry him."

Pamela drew in a quick breath and released it slowly. "Oh?"

"You don't seem surprised."

A small silence. Then, crisply, "Well, darling, I'm not. The fact is, Saxby came to me the evening after you got back from that picnic at the Head and said he admired you very much. He went on to say — your ears must have burned, dear — that you had the qualities he'd always looked for in a woman, that you'd come to mean a great deal to him, that you seemed to like him, and would I mind if he asked you to marry him. That surprised me, of course. Apart from anything else, one doesn't expect that touch of old-fashioned manners in anybody nowadays."

Rena frowned. "I wish he hadn't done that. As if I were a child. What did you say?"

"Oh," with a wave of the clippers, "just that I was surprised to hear it" (snip) "that I knew nothing of your feelings — you never confided in me" (snip) "which was the truth" (snip) "and that it was a matter entirely between yourselves. He's been very attentive to you since. And now he's popped the question. What did you say, darling?"

"I didn't know what to say. He's nice but, well, for one thing he's so much older than I am — eleven years."

"Ah! That makes him ancient, of course." Pamela lowered the clippers and sat on the bench within the arbor, laughing. "Poor Saxby, doddering at thirty-five!"

"I wish you wouldn't laugh."

"I wish you knew how funny you sound, Rena. After all you're no ingénue, darling. You're twenty-four, almost twenty-five. I married at nineteen."

"I don't see what that's got to do with it."

"Nothing, dear, except that by nineteen a woman's older emotionally than any man twice that age. Men never quite grow up, you know. At thirty your father was as naïve as a boy, and he remained absurdly in love with me all his life. It was touching, really."

"But I hardly know Sax at all. And marriage seems such an intimate thing."

"Of course it is. What else could marriage be? My dear Rena, prudishness is something you have to drop with your maiden name. After a time the intimacy becomes a habit and you don't even think of a word for it. How absurd it seems to be telling you all this. But you were always closer to your father than you were to me somehow and I suppose that's why we've never had a cosy mother-and-daughter relationship of the kind one reads about. It's worried me sometimes. Do sit down."

"I'd rather stand," Rena said.

"You say you don't know Saxby at all, after working with him and living in the same house with him all this time! What a strange creature you are. Haven't you ever wanted to be loved?"

"Yes, I've always wanted that."

Pamela gave her a sharp glance and was silent a moment. "Well, you can't dream forever. You know, you read too much, Rena. Time goes by and men do, too. At least they don't pop up out of novels, not here in Port Barron anyway. Tell me, how did you answer him?"

"I said it was awfully sudden and he must give me time to think."

"How banal!"

"It was true, Mama. I simply hadn't thought of him in that way, not in the least. I don't dislike Sax. I admire the way he gets things done. There's something vital about him. And of course he's been very kind and thoughtful, he's done so much for both of us."

"Of course he has."

Rena sank down on the grass and plucked at a dead rose in her lap, gazing towards the sea. "You seem quite willing to be rid of me."

"Nonsense! If you marry Saxby we can all be very happy here together. And comfortable, too. I suppose that sounds a bit smug. But smug or not I'm thinking of you, darling. I'm not young any more and I want to see you settled with a husband who can provide for you decently. Money — you mustn't turn up your nose at money, Rena, it's too dreadfully important. Heaven knows I found that out. Your father was a charming man but so impractical. In a man with family responsibilities that's a kind of selfishness. And I'm thinking of your grandfather and his firm, he had such pride in it; and how it would have galled him to see it go out of the family's hands. For it has, you know. We've nothing but a minor interest. As things stand, I mean."

"I think I see exactly what you mean," the girl said in a chilled voice. "But apart from my own feelings — is it fair to a man to marry him when I don't love him?"

"You know nothing about men or marriage," Pamela retorted. "I do. And I can tell you it makes a much better marriage when the infatuation's on one side — the man's. I don't mind telling you I didn't love your father when I married him. I was never in love with Roger in the silly romantic sense. I liked him and I admired old J.C. in spite of his puritanical ways and we all got along very well. Roger and I had no children for years. I think old J.C. felt I wasn't doing my duty. But then you came, quite unexpectedly I may say, and your father and the old man were delighted. It was a very successful marriage except that the money gave out at the end and you and I were placed in such an embarrassing position."

"But at least you didn't marry Dad for his money," Rena persisted.

"I married your father because I wanted to be married, because none of the young English officers I met at the garrison hops had a penny outside their pay, because Roger adored me and his father had money. All very good reasons, I think. My parents didn't approve Roger at first — a student, a mere civilian, and what my father called a 'colonial,' not in a snobbish sense but in the way all the garrison officers at Halifax regarded anyone who didn't come

142

from 'Home.' But they made inquiries and found out that Roger's father was well off and of course that changed their minds. I don't blame them a bit. Father himself had nothing but his pay, and in the British army in those days an officer without a good private income couldn't even get into a decent regiment. So you see. No matter how refined you are, when you've been pinched for years you take a practical view of things. That's what I'm doing now."

She paused. Rena was still staring at the sea. On the lawn slope Jim Ferrand, the handy man, tramped back and forth behind the mowing machine. The wind stirred the brown rags of the roses and fluttered the skirts of the two women under the arbor. There was a smell of kelp from the shore.

"Consider Saxby," Pamela said. "He's told me something of his life, how he went to sea as a youth and so on. He was hard-working and ambitious, he was determined to lift himself out of the common rut. And now at thirty-five he's moderately rich and able to leave the sea and find an outlet for his energies here. That's admirable, don't you think? As a woman you ought to find it so, especially when you consider that he must have kept his — his natural instincts — under lock and key all that time. Why, he doesn't even drink — good heavens, he doesn't even smoke — imagine the will power! A most remarkable man. And now that he can permit himself to marry he's found what he'd always dreamed about, a charming girl of good breeding and intelligence. He told me in those exact words. You should feel flattered, girl, although it's quite the truth."

"There must be others he could find," Rena said.

"Ah! There you put your finger on the very point, Rena. Others. Others, of course. The world's full of women looking for rich husbands. And a lot of them can put on the charm, the air of breeding and the rest. Every woman's an actress from the time she's out of pinafores, and a man who's put off marriage till the age of thirty-five makes a very susceptible audience. Rena, have you ever thought what would happen if by any chance Saxby brought a creature of that kind here? I have. There's not room for three women in a house, even a house as big as ours, when one's the wife and the others are people like you and me. She'd be jealous of you, and as for me she'd know I could see right through her the moment she stepped inside the door. And you know what she'd do about it. Tcha! It makes me sick and furious just to think of such a thing. Your poor father would turn over in his grave, and think of old J.C.!"

"But suppose Sax married someone nice? Why must you take such a gloomy view of things?"

"Because I'm not young any more and because I know the world."

"It seems so selfish to marry a man just because . . ."

"Selfish! Selfish because Saxby's in love with you and wants you very badly? How absurd. Think of Saxby, darling. And after all he's not bad-looking, he's such a virile man, and really very clever. He'd make you a good husband, of that you may be sure. He's not a gentleman born, one can see that, but he's mingled with nice people somewhere and learned their ways, and after all that's what counts."

Rena's eyes remained upon the sea. The tide was at full ebb out of Fundy now and streaming through the islands. Far in the distance where the dark woods of Topsail showed above the sea the whitecaps must be dancing in the Race, the tidal overfall that flowed between Dutchman and Topsail and the Whales. The fishermen were full of tales about the Race. If you got caught in it on the ebb or the flow it was useless to fight the tide. You had to go with it and hope for the best, putting all your trust in a stout

144

heart and the boat. If all went well, it was an adventure that carried you through powerful eddies and strangely tossing waves towards the open sea, something to look back on for the rest of your life.

"You want me to accept — you want that very much, don't you?" she said. Her lips were trembling and the words were blurred.

"You must make up your own mind, Rena."

"But that's your wish?"

Pamela turned and clipped another withered rag from the ramblers. "I really don't see what else you can do, Rena," she said in her most refained tone. "For your own sake, for Saxby's and for mine."

⌒ ⌒ Chapter 17

AT Rena's request the wedding was a quiet one, performed in the west drawing room by the Reverend Mr. Bascombe in the presence of Pamela, the MacIlraiths, Doctor Bannister, the servants and old Bostwick, and with the happy couple standing by the mantel under the shrewd gaze of John C. When it was over everyone kissed the bride in good cheer except Pamela, who was tearful and sobbing softly, and the whole affair passed quickly and well. Sax had proposed to combine his honeymoon with a business tour of Europe, where he could look about for a steamer for his coasting trade. There were ships to burn these days. Shipping brokers reported almost incredible bargains in places like Antwerp and Hamburg and he proposed to see for himself. A very sensible idea, as Pamela observed, and how lovely for Rena, too.

They left in the mailboat for Eglinton, where they took a hired car and chauffeur off towards Halifax at once instead of staying overnight and taking the slow morning train along the coast. In the car Rena was silent but Sax was gay, chatting in his liveliest fashion. The car rushed and swayed on the gravel highway, and behind them a cloud of dust arose as if to shut off all that was past. Miles of woods and barrens flew by with swift glimpses of the sea and of small towns huddled over wharves, all revealed and shut off with an almost audible click like the snap of a camera shutter.

It was late when they reached their Halifax hotel, and Sax wrote a dashing "Capt. R. Saxby Nolan and wife, Port Barron" in the register. And later still, in the suite that Sax had reserved by wire, the best in the house ("Nothing's too good for you and me, sweetheart") Rena faced the crisis which comes to every bride with joy or fear or merely distaste, according to her inclinations, and which all survive. So she too survived. When Sax took her into his embrace it turned out to be strangely like her first swim as a child, when she had found herself gripped and borne down by the sea, and panting, a little frightened, even a little sick, yet finding in her own spirit something comforting because it was unconquerable. And if her feeling towards her bridegroom thus was one of submission rather than rapture, the bridegroom did not seem to mind. Indeed Sax, made free of that splendid flesh at last, had ardor enough for both and he indulged it with all the stored hunger of long abstinence. And with triumph. It seemed to him now, in the midst of these fierce pleasures so long deferred, that he had covered finally the long journey that led from the kitchen door to the bedroom of Caraday House.

In Britain for the first two weeks they went about seeing the usual things: London and the Tower, Saint Paul's,

Westminster Abbey, Madame Tussaud's, and King George in a tremendous busby riding past the Guards; and then Edinburgh and the Trossachs, and then the Shakespeare country, and Cornwall, and finally Kent, where Rena searched out the grave of her grandmother Charnsworth at Tunbridge Wells. Then Sax plunged into business, and this pursuit took them to various docks about the Thames, and Liverpool and Glasgow and Belfast, and then across the Channel to Rouen, and on to Antwerp, Rotterdam, Hamburg, Bremen and Stettin.

Thus Rena came to see a curious view of the Continent, composed largely of waterfront hotels and miles of dreary docks, where it seemed to be raining all the time. But here Sax was at home as he had never been at Claridge's, or walking the streets of Stratford or peering at portraits in the National Gallery. On the Continent there were ships to burn indeed. He found them tied up everywhere, in various stages of neglect. And there were knots of unemployed seamen hovering outside every dockside tavern and accosting any stranger like himself who had some appearance of a man about to put a ship in motion. With his instinct for a bargain, with a sheer joy in challenging the sharp-eyed and crafty men who, in every kind of foreigners' English, offered ships for sale, he went from broker to broker and from port to port, gliding about the endless wharves and under the lines of idle cranes like a savage on the warpath and asking questions in the curt tough voice of his West Indian days, which had been silent for so long.

The chance remarks of an English captain in the Saint Pauli docks at Hamburg sent him finally to his goal. "Nova Scotia? Ah, I know that coast — rough place in winter. What you want's a ship built to stand ice, with good wide hatches and proper winches and derricks for handling logs and that kind of cargo. You'll find 'em up the Baltic, lots of 'em. Stockholm, Helsingfors, umpteen little ports between. Mind you, they're tough at a bargain, the Swedes and Finns. They know how to run a ship on a bosun's blessing and sixpence and how to lay it up for nothing. If I was you I'd try the German side of the Baltic first. Stettin, say, for a start. Everything there's built to stand ice, and not too deep a draft, so they can get above the Haff. Then have a go at Danzig."

At Stettin he found exactly what he wanted lying in one of the Lastadie basins on the east side of the river, a thousand-ton steamer with heavy winches, big hatch coamings and wide-reaching cargo booms. Her paint had been knocked and scraped badly in the Baltic timber trade and there were rusty patches everywhere. In faded letters on the stern he found the name *Nachtigall*. By good luck and some diligence among the taverns he found and hired her former chief engineer, a cynical blond man in the thirties named Dahl, who spoke English fluently with a strong Pomeranian accent. He informed Sax that the ship had been designed for the German army's use, ferrying artillery up the coast in the campaigns toward Petrograd, but it was still on the ways when everything collapsed in 1918. Later a shipping firm in Stettin had completed it for the Baltic and North Sea timber trade, but rates and cargoes had been lean since the war and finally they had gone bankrupt in 1928.

Sax came back to the hotel in triumph. "Done it! Done it, Rena! The one I told you about. The creditors wanted a lot of this German funny-money for her but I had Dahl beside me to point out all the faults and neglect of the ship and he did it with bells on. Those long German statements that take a whole lungful of wind and chuck the big punch at the end — one final word sort of snarled out and bitten off. He hit 'em right between the eyes. You should have seen 'em flinch and mutter. In the end I got her for twenty-eight thousand five hundred, Canadian — peanuts for a ship like that. I couldn't help grinning in their faces."

He went up and down the room with his peculiar step, snapping his fingers excitedly, while Rena watched him from the bed. After the first two or three ports she had withdrawn from his dockside travels, partly because the round became monotonous but chiefly because she saw that she cramped his style in dealing with shipkeepers and brokers. She amused herself in exploring the various towns alone or with a paid guide from the hotel. Stettin seemed huge, sprawling over its hills beside the busy Oder. It was odd, this great port so far from the sea, and here in the Pomeranian landscape the sun produced a baking heat that had no salt breeze to temper it. Her college German was hopeless here, and the constant clamor of harsh voices with their rolling phrases and explosive verbs seemed to exhaust the very oxygen from the air.

After another wandering afternoon she had been glad to slip off her dress and shoes and lie down; and here she reclined while Sax prowled between the door and the open window like an excited animal dancing up and down a cage.

"Of course," he went on, talking mostly to himself, "there's the deuce of a lot of work to be done on her. Needs a boiler job. Dynamo's no good. Winches worn. Whole ship needs cleaning. Like a pigsty. Get some of the work done here. Not too much though. How these foreign ship-fitting sharks would love to get their teeth into me or anyone else with dollars to spend! Patch her up for the trip across and do the rest at Port Barron. Dahl knows what's what, and his engine-room hands can do what has to be done."

Rena drowsed as he went on. The hot air of the room debilitated her as it seemed to stimulate Sax. She was almost asleep when she heard his voice saying "Rena, darling." She sat up at once and he dropped on the bed beside her, throwing an arm about her waist. For a moment she thought he was in one of his sudden and frequent amorous moods. Her tongue moved to protest that it was too hot, that she was tired, and that in any case she disliked being tousled on the bed in the broad afternoon, like the women the German commercial travelers brought to the hotel. But he surprised her with a very different proposal.

"Look here, darling, all this is very dull for you, I know. I'll have to spend all my time for the next week or two getting the kind of crew I want and standing over 'em while they put the ship to rights. I've got an English skipper, the one I booked in London and told to stand by. He's on his way now, but I feel I ought to sail in the ship myself to keep an eye on things."

"You?" she said dully, with a mind still lost in fatigue.

"The ship's been idle three years or more. It'll take some hustling to get her in any sort of shape for the trip across. And the trip'll be a close thing itself, she can't carry enough bunkers for a voyage of that kind. I'll take her north-about, around the tip of Scotland. Top off the bunkers again at Kirkwall, say. Should make it from there to Newfoundland all right if Dahl watches his firing properly. Bunker at St. John's for the run to Nova Scotia. Taking a chance of course. A lot of head weather could put us in a pretty fix. But it's the only way to get her over there."

"But why hire a captain if you're taking the ship your-self?"

Sax paused. "You see," he said carefully, "I served my time in sail. I haven't got a steam ticket. As a matter of fact I haven't got any sort of ticket. Never bothered to go up for one so long as I could get a job without it — and I always could." And then in his old quick tone, "I'll be master, though, don't make any mistake about that. I had to sign on a qualified master to satisfy the authorities and the in-surance people. I bet I've forgotten more about the sea than that brass-bound old boozer I hired in London will ever know, but there it is. The point is, I've got to know all about this ship if I'm to operate her properly on our coast. How she steers, how she behaves in a seaway, how much coal she eats, how small a crew can handle her. I've got to find out what she can do and what she can't. And I don't know a better way to learn."

Rena thought on the thousands of miles of sea, so stormy in the autumn months, and pictured the *Nachtigall* out of coal and helpless in the midst of it.

"It sounds rather dangerous."

He laughed. "Don't give it a thought. If it was some old wooden tub of a windjammer now! You won't mind going home alone?"

She had not thought of that. "Oh no. For that matter I wouldn't mind going with you in your precious *Nightin-gale*. After all I've sailed a lot — in windjammers mind you — and in some very rough weather, too."

"Good girl! There speaks a granddaughter of old John C. But she's not going home in my steamer for all that. No, Rena, the accommodation's poor and there's no refrigerator and the water tanks are small. We'll be short of everything before we get across. And besides, what kind of honeymoon is that. You ought to see a bit of Paris while you're over here. Stop off there and shop, get yourself some swank clothes and a lot of fancy underwear and perfume and all that kind of thing. Enjoy yourself and do me proud when I get back. I'll book your passage in one of those big liners via Cherbourg and you can see a bit of New York on the other end as well."

"I'll probably be the first bride to come home from a honeymoon alone."

"That's right." Sax chuckled. "I wonder what Port Barron will think of that?"

"You'd better turn up eventually or I'll never live it down."

He ran his free hand lightly along her thigh, warm and smooth under the taut silk of the slip.

ᔆ ᔆ Chapter 18

PAMELA was on the stairs when she heard the door open and recognized the step. She uttered a little cry and came running down with surprising agility on the small feet of which she was so vain. She held out her arms and gave Rena a long moist kiss. "There! Now let me look at you — what lovely clothes! Darling, you do look well. Do come and sit down and tell me all about your trip — I've had absolutely nothing from you but that post card from London and the wire from New York. But first, how is Saxby? It's so like him, bringing the ship back himself. Duty before pleasure always. That's what I said to myself the moment I read your wire. I hope you've been very good to him, Rena."

"Yes. Will you ask Jim to bring my trunks upstairs and

leave them on the landing? I think I'll run up now and have a bath and change."

"Oh. You'll find all your things in Saxby's room, dear. I thought it best, it's so nice and large for those new twin beds and there's plenty of wardrobe space for both of you, and such a nice view from the oriel."

Rena paused on the stair. "My own room had all that, of course. I thought . . ."

"I've moved my things in there, dear. Before, with the old furnace, that room was simply frigid in fall and winter —all that window space and those awful winds from the west. That's why long ago I chose a back bedroom, though it had no view. Everything's different now, thank good- ness."

"Yes," Rena said slowly, "It is, isn't it?"

When she came down she was wearing her old walking dress and shoes.

"I'm going outdoors for a while, along the shore."

"Now? Why you've just got back, and there's so much I want to hear."

"There'll be plenty of time for that, Mama."

The china-blue eyes searched her face. "Rena, you're quite happy, aren't you?"

"Of course I am. It's wonderful to get back." She moved away towards the door.

"You sound," Pamela exclaimed in an accusing voice, "exactly like your father."

It was October and all along the railway from New York the hardwood trees had been a hanging fire of gaudy leaves. In Nova Scotia the maple leaves were a little past their best, and falling, with a sharp north wind whirling them against the windows of the train. Here on the cape itself the solitary poplars and apples of the town were turn- ing yellow and their leaves hissed in the wind. Along the

153

shore path the huckleberry leaves had gone scarlet already, and the bushes along the sea bank, stung by the salt spray flung up on the first of the autumn gales, were showing a fringe of brown.

The birds that summered on the cape had gone to the south, but now there were flocks of robins and curlews resting on their way from the more distant north; and once in an alder thicket, as she passed, a covey of woodcock exploded through the leaves and went away over the sea. Cranberries hung red in the boggy spots. On stretches of turf above the sea bank her step turned the air alive with small grasshoppers, leaping waist-high before her and blowing away on the wind. Below, the tide rattled the cobbles of the foreshore. The whole view to the west was a sweep of hurrying waves with a strong sun-dazzle on them, so that she had to gaze with narrowed eyes before she could make out the distant white spouts of the Whales. These marked the exit of the Race on an ebb tide and its entrance on the flow. She gave them a pensive stare.

At the end of her walk, where the sheep path halted abruptly at a bold wall of naked rock, she climbed the ledges and stood for a time with the wind lashing her skirt about her legs, gazing towards the distant Head with its crown of shaggy woods. How wonderful to be out there now, with the wild geese flocking out of the north and honking about the cove and Gun Hole; the shags, the coots and eiders flitting low over the sea; the gulls perched like gargoyles on the roofs of the deserted huts and sheds; the crows cawing in the wood at sunset. And that lovely lonely silence in the twilight, when the tip of the church steeple caught the last gleam of light above the trees, and the shadow of night slid out of the wood and covered the graves. She had called up that scene often in the too plushy bedrooms of Continental hotels, weary of foreign voices

154

and the hoots and clangs of insane street traffic, awaiting Sax's return from the docks. She had been able to shut her eyes and see it in every detail, and if she kept her eyes closed and thought on it long enough she had seemed to smell this air. She filled her lungs with it now as if to drive out the last cloying reek of that other atmosphere; and beneath the dress her breasts strained at the impudent Paris brassière as if eager to be free of that too, and of everything that had to do with the world into which she had been carried by Sax Nolan.

Heralded by cables from Kirkwall and Newfoundland, the ship turned up safely in Port Barron. It was a dull day with a cold rain falling. There was no wind and the bunting that Captain Nolan had ordered hoisted to her single stub mast and derrick gantries hung limp and sodden in the downpour. Jim Ferrand, oilskin-clad and with the old Caraday telescope, had been watching from the captain's walk on the roof for several hours, and it did not take him long to run down bellowing his news or to hitch up the mare and drive Rena to the wharf. Bostwick had spread the word that the new steamer was due, and now every man, woman and child in Port Barron who could throw on a coat and run appeared promptly at the dock.

There was a halt in the rain. A thin unbroken rope of greasy smoke traced the ship's path around the Head and hung low and unmoving along the sky. As she swung between the grassy humps of Big and Little Sheep, a series of white plumes sprang from the steampipe behind the funnel, and the sheds and warehouses echoed with a sudden noise of war whoops. This was the final note of Captain Nolan's triumph and the people were impressed. Here it was, the promised steamer — not so big as they had expected, but important-looking enough with its shining

155

black hull and green funnel and the letters *JC* in a white circle painted near the funnel top — giving forth smoke and steam and now sound, the authentic voice of the machine.

As the ship eased in to the dock Rena could read the name *John C. Caraday* in white letters on the bow, and she could make out the head and shoulders of Sax on the bridge, wearing oilskins and a nautical cap, and calling orders to the seamen at the mooring lines. His quick brown eyes searched the crowd for Rena's face but could not find it. It was not until the gangway had been lowered and Sax appeared at the head of it, and Rena found herself being thrust forward with everyone shouting "Here's Mrs. Nolan, make way there!" that he saw her at last. The white teeth flashed in his swarthy face. He ran down the gangway and swept her into his arms and everybody cheered. It was absurd but touching. The general air of excitement infected Rena herself. She met his lips with warmth, and when they walked up the wharf with his arm about her shoulders she was proud of him. It was really a splendid and daring thing to take that rusty derelict in the Lastadie basin and patch it up and bring it across the North Atlantic in the windy season of the year. The sort of thing that her grandfather might have done in his struggling days, and with as little hesitation or fuss.

Pamela was effusive when she met them at the door, kissing Saxby with a fine maternal affection and calling out to Bertha, the cook-maid, to come and take the captain's coat and cap. And later on, when Sax described the voyage, brushing over dangers and difficulties with whimsical phrases, mother and daughter hung on every word. But they were not content with that. On the following evening when he brought his captain and the blond German engineer to tea they insisted on having the tale again, calling on Eckles and Dahl for details that Sax swept past.

At a time when Sax was out of the room the elderly cockney, Eckles, turned to Rena with a sigh, and said in his high tremulous voice, "I wouldn't want to do it again, ma'am, not at my time of life, not in a ship like that, meant for short runs about the Baltic, and the shape she's in. Your husband's a very remarkable man, ma'am. A driver, no mistake. I never met anyone like Captain Nolan. He don't ever seem to rest, like. On the go all the time, day and night, on the bridge, about the deck, into the fo'c'sle, down the engine room, into the stokehold — before we was halfway across he knew more about the ship and the crew than me and Dahl put together. That's a fact. And nothing scared him. Nothing. Though I don't mind telling you I was scared a good many times. Everything happened. Dynamo broke down in the North Sea but we kept right on, with no lights but a few oil lanterns all the rest of the way. Engines broke down three times, always in a nasty place. Steering gear went adrift before we cleared the Cattegat and never did work proper-like, spite of all we could do. Good thing we went north-about where there was lots of room and not by Kiel and the Channel. The coal we got in Stettin was some cheap dusty stuff, a lot of pit-head scrapings by the look of it. Dahl had to stand over his firemen all the way, cursing 'em in German and English and a bit o' Swedish and Finnish here and there; and it was shovel-and-slice, shovel-and-slice the whole blessed way. Barely made Newfoundland — the firemen were fairly scraping the bunker plates when we got inside St. John's.

"Ran low on water long before that and had to drink condenser water till we got there. And the grub ran low, of course. And then there was the weather. Gales, gales,

gales. First from the east and then from the west, then a bit of a breather and around the compass to the east again. One good thing about the easterlies, they shoved us on our way, or we'd never have made St. John's. And there was rains fit to blind us sometimes, hours on end. And fogs off the Banks, among all those fishing craft blowing little horns, like barging along Sauchiehall Street in Glasgow on New Year's Eve with a wet coat over your head. Oh no, I wouldn't want to go through it again, ma'am. But your husband, he didn't mind. There was times when everything was going wrong that upon my soul he seemed to enjoy it, as if the whole thing was some kind of tough game that he'd find a way to win."

"Yes," murmured Rena smiling, "that sounds like Sax." She had met Dahl briefly in Stettin but she had not seen Eckles before. She remembered what Sax had said of him and wondered why, of all the shipmasters out of a berth in Britain, Sax had chosen this old thin man with the bloodshot blue eyes, the shock of white hair and the face of a worried ghost. Because he came cheap, she supposed; but she knew what Sax thought of men who drank, even at cheap wages.

On going to bed that night she asked him. She was brushing her hair before the dressing-table mirror and Sax came behind her, slipping down the top of her nightdress and running his lips over her shoulders. He delighted in that, and in seeing the fall of dark hair with its coppery glints that made her skin so white by contrast, and watching in the mirror her absorbed face and the superb breasts that rose and sank with her breathing and the movements of her arm. She met his possessive eyes in the glass.

"Sax, why on earth did you engage that funny old man to command the *John C.?*"

"What's wrong with him?"

158

"Oh, he's nice, you know; he goes in great awe of you."

"Well, that's why." Sax smiled.

"But is he competent? You said he drank, or words to that effect."

"He drinks like the well-known fish, or words to that effect. But he knows his job. Long experience. Got a British master's ticket in steam, deep-sea, which satisfies the underwriters — I've managed to slap thirty-five thousand dollars' insurance on the ship. And he's got a wife in an English lunatic asylum and a daughter with three half-grown kids and a husband out of work. What's that add up to?"

She swept the brush down her hair again and paused. "You know, Sax, sometimes I think you have a heart."

"Can't you smile when you say that?"

She smiled.

ᜪ ᜪ Chapter 19

ALL through November and December the *John C. Caraday* lay at the Port Barron wharf undergoing a course of homemade repair and overhaul. Throughout these frigid weeks the townsfolk heard mysterious clangs and knocks in the ship's bowels, where Dahl and his second engineer and donkeyman labored. Her fires were drawn, there was no heat of any kind except the incidental warmth of a blowtorch flaring in that cold little hell, and Dahl and his men came ashore each night to the food and warmth of the hotel with faces blue under the dirt. But they were not alone in their tribulations. Captain Nolan in a suit of greasy dungarees spent most of each day with them, watching, suggesting, arguing with Dahl, often crawling into some cold foul place to tackle the worst of jobs himself. The others cursed the work, the ship, the Canadian winter, and behind his back they cursed Sax; but they did not ask why they had to earn their wages in this rugged way. They knew. It was to save J. C. Caraday & Son the long bill of a ship fitter's job in Halifax.

January came, the bitter genesis of 1932, with its winds cracking out of the northwest and its snows flung in from the sea. In the second week of January, with the last nut wrenched down tight, Sax got the ship a charter freighting coal from Cape Breton to Newfoundland. It was a rough and uncomfortable trade at a meager rate, but it was the best, indeed the only, business that Sax could find for her in these winterbound months. Off she went for Louisburg with the white-haired Eckles on the bridge, wearing his shabby British merchant-service uniform with its tarnished sleeve rings, and a hooded lammy coat over that, and wearing too the bleared and vaguely frightened look that never left his old blue eyes.

Sax watched the ship pass outside Big Sheep and then walked back to the office, where Bostwick pored over his ledgers and Rena sat at her desk. After their return from Europe he had suggested that she give up her job now that she was a wife, but she had refused with vigor.

"I'd rather be here doing something useful than mooning about the house, Sax."

"Yes, but look here, you can't keep on with it indefinitely. I mean, you're planning to have a baby, aren't you?"

She flushed. "There will be plenty of time to get another typist if that happens." A pause. "You want a child very much, don't you, Sax?"

"Yes," he said bluntly. It was true. He was eager to have an heir, to have heirs, a family of his own, that necessary part of his dream. But even more than that he lusted to see

160

her pregnant, a living proof of his virility — feeling that he must beget in Rena's flesh to seal his possession of her and to mark the full rise of his tide, he the poor boy from Herring Point and she the woman of Class. His notion of biology was that of the fo'c'sle, where every man cherished his male prowess and believed that given any woman of clean health and the important natural instincts he could beget at will. With this in mind Sax had enjoyed the full possession of Rena and after the first month awaited confidently the result. But it had not come. Months had gone by and still his ardor had no effect.

The failure puzzled and irritated him. He felt himself ridiculous in the eyes of men. It was like those boyhood crises when he had felt impelled to run, jump, fight or swindle better than anyone else in the crowd. And he suspected, indeed he was certain, that the fault was Rena's own. He had never been able to arouse in her the passion that he felt was his due. She was submissive enough, she complied without a murmur whenever he claimed her but the passion was all his. It was a damned shame. There were fo'c'sle terms for women like that. And there was a polite one, "frigid," that somehow implied the worst that could happen to a man. His wife was frigid to him — the phrase was like a slap in the face whenever he thought of it. He could almost hear the taunting voices of the crowd. He tried to put the thought from his mind but it kept coming back to anger him. It stung his ego where it was most sensitive.

The thought crossed his mind now as he entered the office and saw her sitting at her typewriter with that good erect back and shoulders and that fine curve at the hips. She looked up from her work and smiled. What was she smiling at? Was she thinking the same thing? Did it please her to play the fraud? For a moment the bull-ape peered

161

suspiciously from his eyes, but she had turned back to her work at once. He dropped into a chair beside her, grunting "Take a letter," and dictated a formal notice to the *John C.'s* charterers.

Bostwick lumbered to his feet and passed him a slip of paper.

"You asked for just the rough figures, sir. Here they are."

Sax studied the slip and a wry twist came to his lips.

Bank loan pd.	$20,000
House reps. etc.	19,000
Reps. to wharf, warehouse etc.	7,500
Reps. to schooner Pamela	3,000
New schooner	8,000
Steamer purchase	28,500
Steamer reps. wages etc	4,000
Trip to Europe Mr. & Mrs.	3,500
Misc. incl. bank loan int.	2,000
	$95,500

"They're rough all right," he said with a short laugh. "Tell me more."

"We've got a lot of outstandin' bills, sir. The machinery parts for the steamer and all that. Of course there's been some profit from the lobsters and the fish we shipped, but not much, the margin's very small on all that nowadays."

"What about the ships' freights so far?"

"Well, sir, the *Pamela's* barely earned her keep so far. She's on that voyage to Florida now with the pine lumber from Eglinton that you bought on credit, but money's pretty tight down there accordin' to the agents and we won't know if she's made or lost money till we get the final account o' the consignment sales. The new schooner,

162

the *Roger*—well, you know that story, Captain. Coastin' trade's pretty thin these times, what with the other coasters and competition from the railroads and these motor trucks they're usin' more and more on the shore highways nowadays. 'Course, coastin' business ain't somethin' you can pick up in a hurry anyhow; you've got to run the vessel reg'lar from port to port whether there's full or half cargo or nothin' but a wheelbarrowload o' turnips in one o' the holds. Matter o' takin' a loss for a time and buildin' up a trade. And then there's the steamer, the *John*. She's been all expense so far and just goin' off now to earn a few dollars. On the whole . . ."

"On the whole we're in the hole."

" 'Fraid so, yes, Captain. I didn't mention the store. Store's doin' quite well, considerin'. Money's loosened up a bit since you came here. Store's doin' more trade, takin' in more cash, but a lot o' the local business is on credit still. Fishermen, you have to carry fishermen. Fishin's all ups and downs."

Sax dismissed him with a jerk of his head. He crumpled the scrap of paper in his fist and tossed it into a wastepaper basket. Rena turned to him, saying in a low voice, "I couldn't help hearing that, Sax. What does it mean? You paid Mama a thousand dollars at the year end and said it was a dividend. But how could there be dividends when . . ."

"My dear," Sax said ironically, "your mama has such a charming belief in me that I hated to rob her of an illusion. And I'm sure she can use the money much better than our creditors right now. Besides, the firm's all right. I'm just getting things started and trade happens to be in a bit of a slump. It'll take some time before the business really begins to pay. All that's happened is that I've tied up my money without thinking enough about working cap-

163

ital. I'll just get a loan from MacIlraith. That's what banks are for."

But when he told MacIlraith what he wanted the banker's mouth went grim. He looked the counterpart of at least three of the portraits on his office walls.

"Twenty thousand dollars," he repeated slowly.

"That's not much, Mac. You lent that much to the Caradays before I put a fortune into the business. You'll have all that extra collateral."

"I know, but it's awkward, Nolan, damned awkward. To my district office the firm is still the firm of J. C. Caraday & Son, who borrowed twenty thousand dollars years ago and were the deuce of a time getting it paid off. Now, within twelve months, the firm wants to borrow the very same sum again. I can tell them about the new ships and the improvements to the properties and all that, but you can surely see the letter I'm going to get."

"Sure! And I can see the letter you ought to write 'em back. Stick to your guns, man. That's the only way to get business done nowadays. People in head offices can't see what's stirring in the country towns and villages. That's why they have branch managers. Why, on the strength of my firm's assets you ought to give me fifty thousand dollars if I asked for it. Without batting an eye."

MacIlraith was silent. He admired the plunge Nolan had taken at a time when all the bank reports indicated a world about to fall flat on its face, and from the moment he had succeeded in getting the old loan paid off he had been curious to see what a man of Nolan's force and brains and brash self-confidence could do with such a world. But he had no illusion about the firm's assets. His memory of J. C. Caraday & Son was all too clear. Business history, like other kinds, had a nasty way of repeating itself, and every time it did the price went up. Still, he thought, a bank has a definite function to perform. If you suspend all loans whenever business begins to look bad, you might as well go out of business.

He said at last, "I'll tell you what I'll do. I can't give you the loan now, off my own bat. I'll write to the district office and recommend it, pointing out the present state of the properties, the whole investment you've made. I think you'll get the money all right. I'll send off a letter by the first boat up to Eglinton."

"Fine!"

"There's just one point, Nolan. Promotion's one thing, operation's quite another. You've done a first-rate job of putting new works in the old business. Now let's see you make it tick. This loan is for operating purposes only. No more capital expenditures, no more goods bought on credit and sold on consignment, none of that at all. From here on you keep things on a sound liquid basis. Agreed?"

"Agreed. But what made you say that?"

"You're a bit too much of a gambler."

Sax grinned sourly. "From a man who plays cards to one who never does, that's the funniest thing I've heard this year."

It was MacIlraith's turn to smile. He could not help liking Nolan. He had often noticed the force that prickled the air of a quiet room when Nolan walked in. He amused himself sometimes with speculations on the past of this man, still young and obviously sprung from ordinary beginnings, who had been able to make money in big chunks in these tough postwar years and did not hesitate to risk it in the same way. And he thought on his own drab life spent in small branch banks, much of it in Port Barron, a nice careful groove that led to a pension and retirement, with not a single splash of color to look back on. At times he envied Nolan.

"The year's young yet," he answered cheerfully. "It's only January. Have patience, old man. A lot of funny things can happen in twelve months."

❧ ❧ Chapter 20

THE new year brought forth a succession of stiff white weeks like the Monday-morning bed sheets of Port Barron, washed and hung out one by one and promptly frozen on the lines. The fishery was at a standstill in this time of ice and storm. The shipyard lay silent under snow. The *Pamela* had returned from her Florida voyage and gone off again, this time with a cargo of salt fish for Porto Rico. The *John* was making her rough and dirty passages to Newfoundland in the service of the charterers. The *Roger* made her steady round of the coastal ports with the paltry cargo of wintertime. Even business in the store was dull, for at this time of year the fishermen nursed their savings and were frugal with their credit. In fact, like any small port in this latitude, Port Barron had gone into semihibernation, peering through frosty panes towards the street, venturing out now and then to shovel a path through the drifts, or for a walk to the post office, a yarn by the stove in the Caraday store, a game of bowls in the alley over the Odd Fellows' Hall, or to church on Sunday morning.

From Christmas until mid-March Pamela would not set foot outdoors except for the Sabbath trip to church, when she and the Nolans drove in state by horse and sleigh and well wrapped in carriage robes. Sometimes on bright afternoons Sax and Rena took this equipage and jingled up and down the road that ran from Caraday House through Port Barron and ended at Herring Point on the other side.

166

Sometimes after a blizzard they strapped on snowshoes and tramped over the buried fields, coming back with tingling toes to the warmth of the new furnace and the rich smell of Bertha's food. But it was an idle time, even though they went daily to the office for an hour or two to deal with the mail and to pick up groceries from the store. Rena frankly enjoyed the weather and the isolation that it brought. The sweep and rattle of the sea wind about the house, the boom of it in the chimney flues, the hard flick of snow on the panes, and in frosty calms the queer hush of the tide, the crackle of cold woodwork, the gaudy sunsets over Fundy, the blaze of stars — in all such things she took what seemed to Sax a childish and somewhat stupid pleasure.

Often when he had sunk into one of his bored reveries and sat deep in his chair by the fire, refusing to move, she put on her snowshoes and went alone along the shore. The big tides of Fundy, rising and falling in these bitter temperatures, formed a glaze of ice about the islands and the cape. Every sea bank became a precipice of glass. It was dangerous to go near the edge, for if you slipped and fell to the foreshore there was no way of getting back. In Port Barron there were many grim tales of such mishaps. If you fell at high tide, you drowned at once among the grinding ice trash. If you fell at low water, that meant death too, but death slow and miserable as the tide rose.

Rena kept her webbed tracks well away from that fatal edge and paused now and then to look across the sea towards the islands and the Race. The distant ice walls loomed and shone in the thin winter sun, even the Whales had turned a glistening white, like three Moby Dicks just rising from the deep. On days of that unnatural calm which goes before a spell of easterly weather, and when the sun was at noon, casting an illusion of warmth on the air, the uncanny freaks of the mirage appeared, and then in the distance the ice walls of Topsail and Frigate arose and shimmered like enormous floating bergs.

One day in early March Sax joined her moodily. There was no scope for his natural restlessness in this winter landscape. There was nothing real to do and he hated walking just for walking's sake. Rena could move gracefully on snowshoes, but on his short legs they forced him to a waddling gait that made him feel ridiculous. Rena led the way to the ledge at the end of the buried sheep walk and they saw the spectacle of the mirage. With the blink of sunshine and the vagaries of air currents over the sea, the islands swelled and shrank, dwindling sometimes to a white dot on the horizon and then rising swiftly, towering, shining, with every fold of their ice walls magnified; now Frigate, now Topsail, now the Whales, and other white ghosts beyond, where Dutchman and Goat and Inner Bald and Outer Bald stretched on to the northwest.

Rena pointed. "The islands — terrible places, Sax, in the old days before there was a light on Frigate. Ships would strike there on a winter night, or in snowstorms or an ice fog. A big sea running after a gale, perhaps, and the ship smashed to pieces in an hour. The sailors would take to the boats and make for one island or another, and find themselves dashed against the ice walls. Nothing to grasp, not a foothold anywhere. My dad used to tell me the tales. In the olden time people went out every spring to Frigate and Topsail and Dutchman just to gather up the winter's dead and bury them — bodies flung into the edge of the woods sometimes, by a big sea running up the wall. And one poor creature they found crouched over a little heap of sticks with a tinderbox in his hands, frozen to death of course — after getting ashore alive. Once long ago Dad

168

took me out to Topsail and showed me mounds in the woods where some poor fellows had been buried. I never forgot them. I suppose that's why I feel a special affection for old Sam at the Head and all the others who spend their lives staving off that kind of thing. It must be rather wonderful to live a life like that."

Sax looked at her in a mixture of curiosity and contempt. "You really love this place — the cape and the islands, don't you?"

"Yes, Sax, I do. After all it's been my life — this place."

He snorted. "It's all right in summer maybe. But you can have it this time of year. This damned feeling of being shut in, away from where things are really going on. I'm not used to it like you. I like action, something doing all the time. Right now I feel as if I'd been buried alive in a snowbank for the past four months."

"I'm sorry you've found it dull, Sax. There's one comfort, you're saving money, living quietly like this. That's something, with times the way they are, and the money you owe the bank and so on."

"Who the hell said anything about the bank?"

"Don't be angry, Sax. I'm sorry I mentioned it."

But he preferred to be angry. He was in a mood to vent his boredom and frustration in a black old-fashioned rage, and as they tramped in silence back to the house the chafe of a snowshoe strap rubbed his toe raw under the moccasin and sharpened his mood.

He was curt and sullen at the table that evening, and Pamela swept an inquisitive gaze from one to another, sensing a quarrel and giving Rena to understand, with the swift telegraphy of women, that it was probably her fault. In the bedroom later Sax paused in undressing and stood in trousers and undershirt with his fists on his hips.

"I didn't like that crack of yours about the bank and so on. What's the matter? Worried about the way I'm doing things — you and your mother?"

She was slipping on her nightgown, and as her head and arms emerged she saw on his face an expression new to her. His lips were tightly pressed, so tightly that a white line showed in the dark blue-shaven skin about them; and under the frowning black brows his eyes peered at her with a beady suspicion that seemed very close to hate. Even the thick hair on his arms and chest seemed to bristle.

"Of course not, Sax. It was just . . ."

"Just that you're afraid I'll make an unholy mess of things the way your father did. Isn't that it? That's the way you all think, all you cape people, from MacIlraith on down. You've had to pinch pennies so long yourselves that you just can't savvy a man willing to stick his neck out for dollars."

"Oh Sax, that's not fair."

"I bet that's the way they looked at old John Caraday, right up to the day he died. Like a lot of gulls hanging about a steamer's wake, all very ready to snap up the galley scraps but telling 'emselves the damned thing's bound to sink because it's got neither feathers nor fins. Bah! So I owe the bank. Sure I owe the bank. What business is that of yours?"

"It's none and I'm not going to quarrel with you, Sax."

Rena slipped into her bed and faced the farther wall, with the covers drawn about her neck. Sax went on talking in the low quick voice which in this mood was so much more formidable than a shout.

"I'm running this show. Me, Sax Nolan. It was my money put the thing on its feet and I'll do what I like about it. You worry a lot about my money, don't you — you and the rest of 'em. Wonder how I got it, I suppose, seeing the way I spend it with both hands. And now I've borrowed from the bank. Well, that's my business. You know, Rena, my big mistake was having you in the office at all. I see that now. Your place was here, minding a woman's own business. You're not much good at that."

She said to the wall, "What do you mean by 'that'?" And Sax told her, in a hot rush of words, in phrases that would have had more meaning in a sailors' brothel. But the gist of it was clear. Rena turned slowly with a face the color of the sheets. She gave him a wide stare. The look in her eyes was one of sheer astonishment but there were tears as well, and he saw her lips trembling. It pleased his mood for a moment to see that he could arouse her passion in one respect at least. But now, as if someone had struck softly a deep and resonant gong in the room, a warning sense in his brain began to vibrate. With sudden alarm he perceived that he had let the fret of these idle weeks, his worry about the business, his touchiness about the source of his money and his deep and constant suspicion of what others might be thinking or saying about it, and, beneath all this, the queer frustration of his self-love and his love for Rena — he had let all these things gather and plunge him into something dangerous, a blind betrayal of Sax Nolan, and to the one person whose opinion mattered more than all the rest. His inner demon jeered at him for a fool, a three-masted, copper-bottomed fool with too much canvas and no helm. And now he saw something else in her eyes, a sort of sea change, as if that coarse explosion of his had brought up another and more ominous kind of weather behind the rain. He took in sail hastily.

"I'm sorry, Rena, forgive me, darling. I didn't mean to say anything like that. I don't know what made me say it. Forget it like a good girl. It was just nerves. Nerves, nothing else. My mind's been a bit ratty lately. I'm not used to being idle, 'specially when things aren't going right. The business — all business is a headache nowadays. I guess I'm just too impatient about everything I want. Can't get satisfied with anything. And this shut-in feeling gets me down. I'll feel better when the winter's gone. In fact I'm off for Halifax in the morning — some business there and a chance to sort myself out a bit."

He went on in this way, gabbling the phrases as they came to his tongue, in a frantic eagerness to make good his apology and to prevent Rena from saying anything until she too had cooled down. But she made no attempt to speak. She had turned to the wall again. The two thick bronze braids in which she had twisted her hair for the night were drawn forward over her shoulders, and he had a strong impression that one of them was caught between her teeth as if to keep her from crying out. She seemed to hear nothing of what he was saying now. It was as if those other things he had said were still making obscene echoes in the room.

Cautiously, almost timidly, he came to the edge of her bed and put a hand on her shoulder. At once the white skin shivered under his touch. He drew back quickly. Was she afraid of him? Rena? Impossible. Rena wasn't afraid of anything on earth. If there was one thing she had it was courage. So what? Anger? That must be it. He had never seen her angry but he recalled MacIlraith's saying once that she had more than a bit of old J.C.'s red-haired temper. So she was lying there in a rage. Shaking with it. And no wonder, after being insulted in that fashion. But why didn't she let her temper fly and get it over with? He moved to his own bed and turned out the light. But he could not sleep. His mind went over every word and moment of the episode, and he was filled with an angry wonder that he could have made such a fool of himself so quickly, and over nothing. And there was no solution, except to take himself out of her sight for a few days and give her a chance to simmer down. What a pity she had no sense of humor. She was always so damned serious about everything.

When he left in the morning he paused in the hall to say good-by. Under the wary gaze of her mother Rena said calmly, "Good-by, Sax." She had got a grip on her feelings, then, whatever they were. But she did not offer to kiss him, she met his eyes firmly and he saw that he was not forgiven. And on the train from Eglinton, as he stared out at the flitting winter landscape, the touch of that shuddering flesh last night came back to haunt and puzzle him. Suddenly he felt a pang, so sharp that he uttered a cry. It stabbed him to the heart. His eyes were on the passing forest and snow but what he saw there was the warm beach in the Bahamas, the deserted umbrellas and the scornful face of Ellen Carisfort.

⟋ ⟋ Chapter 21

HE was away from Port Barron most of the spring on one errand after another, driven by the devil of unrest that always had been so large a part of him and which now took entire charge. He made several trips up and down the coast in the *Roger Caraday*, a thickset dynamic figure harrying the captain and crew, stirring a smart activity in longshoremen, calling on merchants in the scattered little ports to solicit cargo of whatever sort and however small, dropping his rates below all competition. His motto now, and he made it clear to everyone in the employ of J. C.

Caraday & Son, was *Never mind the profit get the business.* By underbidding every other yard on the coast, he secured a contract to build a large wooden schooner for a company trading in Labrador. When the *John C. Caraday* came off charter in the coal trade, he fixed a new one to carry pulpwood logs to the big paper mill at Ridgeport from the mouths of rivers and half a dozen small ports about the coast.

At the paper mill he met his match, a marine superintendent who knew ships and men and the present buying power of a dollar to the fraction of a cent. Moreover, the mill had a steamer of its own for freighting wood, and what its own ship could not handle was let out on contract to various small and hungry schooners in the coastal trade. By the exercise of his motto and an aphorism of his own ("What's the good of having a steamer if you can't get to windward of a flock of schooners?") Sax got a season's charter to carry the wood at a dollar and a half to two dollars per cord, according to the distance from the mill and the difference between loading slowly from a river boom and taking a quick freight from a town with a good wharf and a fleet of motor trucks rolling down from the forest. The season would hold until December, when ice in the rivers and snow on the hauling roads would put a stop to it. Thus he settled the employment of the *John* for the most of that year, and he had the promise of another year's contract at the same rates if the ship proved satisfactory.

Figuring with care and allowing for bad weather and other unbusinesslike acts of God, he found that by driving old Eckles hard he could make a profit, though it was not large. By cutting all maintenance costs, together with the wages and provision scale of the crew, he could make a better one. He cut them savagely. The foreign hands in the steamer he had shipped home long ago, a thing forced on him by the immigration laws. He had managed to retain Dahl, for whom he had got naturalization papers through that useful man Cuff, M.P. Eckles, of course, was a British subject, shipped under Board of Trade regulations. Their wages were not touched. The rest of the crew, all Port Barron men, were reduced to a scale of food and pay that had not been known thereabouts since the days of the frugal square-riggers.

The men were first astounded and then enraged. When, at the first chance, they trooped up to the Caraday office, muttering and nudging each other to speak, Sax confronted them with soft words about hard times. When they began to shout he snapped, "You're fired, the lot of you." The look of monkey glee was in his eyes. In their place he shipped a crew of seedy strangers from the Devil knew where, as old Eckles said, and ready to shovel coals in Hell for ha'pence.

The *Roger's* crew were more tractable. The schooner's smart new lines and powerful auxiliary engines, and her short runs with almost every night in a port or anchorage, all had a charm rarely to be found in the shipping trade. They grumbled but clung to their jobs. The big three-master, *Pamela*, engaged on long foreign runs to the south, had no such charms. Her crew protested loudly. Sax promptly discharged them all. Indeed he seemed quite eager to get rid of them, and when the skipper and mate, with the dignity of honest men, reminded him of their wives and families, he answered, "I'm running a shipping business, not a soup kitchen. You're through." Again he went away to hire a shabby crew of nondescripts, and he sent them off to Trinidad in *Pamela* with a full cargo of salt codfish and barreled herring for sale by commission agents there.

The wage economies applied to everyone, the shipyard

hands, the warehousemen, the two sad-eyed spinsters in the shop, the servants at Caraday House. Even old Bostwick's thirty dollars a week, paid without question by the Caradays for years, went down to twenty-four. Cash, Captain Nolan said, was scarce and they could co-operate or else. He carried his economies further. In the beginning, by paying the Port Barron men a cent more per pound, he had discouraged the Barmouth fish and lobster buyers. Their collecting smack had ceased to call. Now he cut his buying price a cent below the Barmouth rate and kept it there. He did something else. He had from the first obliged the fishermen to take half their payment in goods from his store. Now they must take all.

For the salt fish he bought at small outports up the coast, chiefly to make freights for the *Roger,* he had formerly paid cash. Now he demanded credit at ninety days. The outport merchants looked surprised, but fish were hard to sell and the old revered name of J. C. Caraday & Son had a kind of magic on a piece of paper still. For the timber he had shipped to Florida he was getting a small dribble of cash from the consignees, but he passed none of it on to the sawmill people at Eglinton, telling them coldly they must wait. With all these measures, as he said to Bostwick, he got things scraped down to the wood. And as he told himself, it was a damned good thing to get tough again anyhow. He had been soft long enough. Make the thing tick, MacIlraith had said. Well, it was ticking now after a fashion and it would tick better as time went on. People could grouse all they liked. They'd respect a tough man anyhow, and in the long run they'd admire him.

Rena went to the office every day. There was much more to do now, with the fish and lobsters coming in, the payrolls to be typed and met, and letters and documents to be prepared from Sax's hasty notes sent in by mail from various ports about the coast. When he turned up in Port Barron on one of his hurricane visits the work redoubled and she worked in the evening as well. Their attitudes were those of boss and typist, moving about each other with a casual impersonal air. Even in the house Sax kept his distance; there was no more laying on of hands, and they went to their separate beds in the manner of strangers in a crowded country hotel, compelled to sleep in the same room and making a polite best of it.

They were aware of Pamela's vigilant eyes whenever they were together in her presence. One day she tackled her daughter alone. Sax had come and gone in his sudden way, this time in the *John* to watch the loading of pulpwood at a port up Fundy and to see it discharged at the paper mill. It was a rare day for the cape in spring, that time of east winds and rain. There was a hot sun and a calm atmosphere that turned the islands and the far wooded hills of the mainland a smoky blue, as if bush fires were burning there. Jim Ferrand was raking the carriageway towards the road, and a distant rattle of dishes told Pamela that the cook-maid was out of earshot as well. She sat with Rena on the veranda, in the warmth drifting up from the sunny lawn, and suddenly she said, "Rena, there's a question I want to ask you. What's wrong?"

"I don't know what you mean."

"Oh yes you do, Rena. I mean between you and Saxby."

"Why do you ask?"

"You seem strange when you're together."

"In what way?"

Pamela gave an unrefained snort. "I couldn't say. But I can see something's wrong. Is it the business? I noticed the strangeness between you first about the time Saxby cut all the wages and started rushing about the province in this tiresome way. I've been talking to Bertha. I get all my news of the town from her. After Saxby cut her wages she was sulky for a time and wouldn't gossip, but now she seems resigned. I dare say you know everybody in Port Barron's talking about the firm. They can't understand these sudden economies when everything seemed to be going so well. And they've lost their liking for Saxby. He was too hard with them, Rena, much too hard."

"These are hard times," Rena said.

"Ah, yes. But it seems to me Saxby didn't use much discretion about it. Bertha's and Jim's wages, you know, they're not much. And poor Mr. Bostwick's. And then there's the way he sacked all the Port Barron men in the ships. He was actually rude when Doctor Bannister tried to say a word on behalf of one or two of them. It's all so queer — not like Saxby at all. Are you sure you haven't done something to upset him? Because he loves you very much, Rena. I've never seen a man so devoted as he's been to you. A man like that might take it very hard."

Rena turned her face away. She folded her arms and crossed her knees tightly, an attitude of defense. Her mouth was as firmly set. Pamela went on another tack.

"Mr. Mac told me over the bridge table last Saturday night, in a casual way, of course, that Saxby had borrowed twenty thousand dollars from the bank. That's a lot, isn't it?"

"No more than the firm owed before."

"You don't seem at all worried."

"I'm not. Sax is quite competent to do that."

"Rena, I can't help thinking it was the bank loan that ruined us before. If it hadn't been for Mr. Mac we'd have lost everything."

Rena shrugged.

178

"You don't seem to care. Tell me, are you angry with Saxby?"

"No. If I were merely angry with Sax there might be some point in what you're thinking, Mama. If you must know, he revolts me."

Pamela's eyes, the exact tint of Jim Ferrand's washed-out blue overalls, went very bright. She folded her beringed hands over her stomach and smiled her most indulgent smile.

"So you *have* squabbled. I knew it. And of course you're furious with him. One always is. And you despise him. One always does. But, my poor Rena, people have been falling in love and marrying and squabbling and getting revolted and falling in love again ever since Adam and Eve. Every woman knows Adam was a cad; but after all Eve was no better than she should have been, and if you come down to the fine point I dare say the serpent was the most respectable of the lot. Do smile, Rena, there's a good girl, and stop all this silly emotional nonsense."

Rena closed her eyes. She knew exactly what to say. She had gone over the thing in her mind so much that every phrase was ready for her tongue. Mama, she would say, you've always treated me like a half-witted child and no doubt this will strike you as quite in keeping. I don't love Sax. I never did. I married him because I was weak enough and blind enough to let you push me into his arms. Have you ever noticed Sax's arms, Mama? His hands? Anything about his person at all? Probably not. But, you see, as his wife I had to notice everything. When Sax proposed to me and I hesitated, you thought I was merely being squeamish. Well, I'm not squeamish any more. I got over that. I had to. But something he said to me in March let me see inside Sax for the first time, and what I saw there matched his outside. It was like seeing two twos, one be-

179

low the other, and suddenly realizing that they make a sum. And four was what my instinct had been trying to tell me from the start.

Do you want to know the truth, Mama? I'll tell you. Sax Nolan isn't any ordinary man. He's not really a man at all. He's an animal. Oh, a very clever animal, very pleasant when he wants to be, full of energy and courage in his own way, but still an animal. I know what you're going to say. You're going to tell me that all men are primitive creatures, really, and a woman's job is to put up with them and make them nice. Well, I refuse to believe that all men — that any man's like Sax. It just can't be. It isn't just the physical side of him, you understand. It's his mind — his instincts. Something crafty and cynical about him. Something too restless about him. Something cruel. Something without conscience. Something terrible and insatiable about his lust for money or me or anything else that affords him pleasure. There's even something animal about the way he shies away from alcohol and tobacco — as if he had to keep his sense of taste and smell for catching prey.

He can't help any of this, you understand. He couldn't do anything about it — not really anything — even if he wished. He tries to conceal it but it comes out in all sorts of ways and after a time you add them up. It's the way he is, the way he's made. In some ways I feel sorry for him. As I'd feel sorry for — well, for instance, as I'd feel sorry for an ape that had wandered out of the jungle and learned some rather clever tricks inside a cage. I'd want to let him out. I'd want to let him go back. But, you see, I'm shut up in the cage with Sax. That makes a frightful difference. . . .

But Rena uttered none of these things. She pressed her lips and held herself in that feminine attitude of defense, as if she were sitting in the cage at that moment and as if

180

Pamela were Sax himself. She gazed at the sea. The islands loomed like vague blue phantoms in the haze. When she glanced down at the foreshore, she saw that the tide was high and on the slack. There would be no deep eddies and leaping waves in the Race just now, only an ominous calm, awaiting the next turn of the great salt stream. She murmured at last in a low set voice, "I've said all I'm going to say."

Pamela studied her face and attitude carefully. She told herself again that the girl was a bit hysterical over some silly bedroom squabble. But Rena did not look a bit hysterical. She had in fact the calm and scornful look of old J.C. when in his forthright seaman's voice he condemned some sinner at the Head. Pamela peered again at the handy man, working in the shade of the spruces now, and listened for further kitchen sounds. With privacy still assured, she spoke.

"Whatever's happened, you don't seem afraid of him."

"I'm not. I told you what it was. It's disgust. He revolts me. He said something rotten but it isn't just that. It isn't any one thing he's ever said or done. It's the sum. It's what I realize he is."

"What are you going to do?"

Rena considered that for several minutes. "I'm not sure. Go away for a time perhaps. If I could go and live among other people a few months, I might be able to throw off this feeling that I have for him."

"You ought to try here," Pamela said primly.

Rena merely shrugged. She was struggling again with that impulse to speak her mind fully. Oh yes, Mama, it's strange how well I see Sax now. And now I can't help wondering about the other things we all accepted without question when he came. Where did he come from? He says Halifax, but I know Halifax very well and I've found he doesn't. What sort of life had he lived before he came here? He talks amusingly about some parts of it, but knowing him as I do, I can't help feeling there's a lot more, something dark, something not funny at all. Where did he get all that money? Speculating in ships, he says. But what ships, and where? Whenever I've asked him questions like that he's turned me off with a joke as if it were none of my business—a favorite phrase of his. Why did he come to Port Barron, so far out of the way, to invest his precious money? And why did he marry me? Of all the women he must have met in the world, why me?

In the stress of emotions held in for so long the last two words escaped from her tongue. They came as a cry. Pamela was startled. She glanced away and stirred uneasily. But Rena's gaze was still towards the sea.

ᔑ ᔑ *Chapter 22*

SAX returned to Port Barron in the steamer, having watched her load another cargo of pulpwood in a Fundy creek. It pleased him to play the skipper on these voyages, even to taking over the captain's cabin and obliging Eckles to take the spare bunk in the mate's room. Eckles was inclined to be cautious in his navigation, keeping well outside the reefs and islands, running at half speed in the Fundy fogs, slipping inside for shelter when a gale came up and the ship was light, protesting against the berths up Fundy, where the tide dropped thirty or forty feet and left the ship sitting on the mud beside the wharf. Sax changed all that when he was on the bridge. His monkey humor delighted in the look on Eckles's face whenever he took a hardy chance with the weather or a short cut among the islands, or a berth in some winding creek where at low tide the sea vanished completely and left the ship in a sailor's nightmare, sitting dry between the red-mud buttocks of the creek and apparently lost among hillsides covered with forest.

He found a companion in Dahl. The cynical German disliked Eckles as a coward, a fool and an Englishman, and he admired Sax for being all the things that Eckles was not. Dahl had the maniac restless streak of the German who sees no prospect of advancement in his profession, who has exhausted the pleasures of women and drink and now craves some other excitement. In Sax's ventures with the ship he found it. The course for Ridgeport took the ship around Gannet Head as she came out of Fundy, and it was only twenty miles out of her way to set down Sax at Port Barron. Eckles's usual course for the Head took him outside the islands altogether, and it was Dahl's suggestion that the ship take the inside passage and save the wide tour around Topsail and Frigate.

"You mean run the Race?" Sax said, and grinned.

"The tide . . ." muttered Eckles.

"As it happens the tide's just right," Sax said. And to the man at the wheel, "Stand away, there. I'm taking the helm myself."

The tide was just on the ebb, the Race was not at its worst, and at this stage there was plenty of water over the shoals, even for a deep ship. The *John C. Caraday* was carrying a tremendous load of pulpwood, soggy from a river boom, that filled the holds and was piled and lashed high on the decks. She resembled a floating woodpile fitted with a bridge and funnel. In the tidal overfalls she dipped and swayed and rose like a galloping truck horse. Eckles stood by Sax at the helm, with his old slack mouth moving as if in prayer. The ragged men of the crew frowned or

183

grinned, according to their sporting instincts. But it was Dahl who got most out of it. He had just come from the engine room, wiping his sharply cut cameo face with a sweat rag, and now from the bridge he watched the ship's passage, shouting aloud in German from time to time and laughing like a fool.

In the eddies just forming at this early stage of the ebb, but already powerful, the burdened ship swung clumsily, now heading to port, now to starboard. At the wheel Sax had a continual quick labor on the spokes. The steering engine clamored, the ship's plates groaned under the shifting stresses, the deck logs strained at their lashings. Below, in the bowels of an apparently insane iron box, the duty engineer and fireman clung and swore. Dahl was laughing wildly long after Sax brought the ship safely out of the passage between Topsail and the Whales and swung up inside the cape towards Port Barron. The exploit had given old Eckles the shivers. It left Sax unperturbed. When he stepped on the wharf at last in his smart shore clothes, hatless as always, with his black hair combed and glistening, there was nothing but the little smile to betray a satisfying experience, a smart trick done and over with.

In the office he found a heap of unopened mail. Bostwick said, "There's a telegram, sir. Came out from Eglinton in Jameson's boat. I didn't open it."

"Why not?" Sax said, looking for the yellow envelope.

"Mrs. Nolan always sees to the mail and all that."

"And where's she?"

"I don't know, sir."

Sax opened the telegram and read it. He walked across the street to the bank and stepped into MacIlraith's private office with the assurance of a favored customer. The banker looked up with his wise eyes in the inflamed lids, wondering what new demand was coming and what he should say.

"I've had a bit of bad news, Mac. Thought I'd better tell you right away because it concerns one of the firm's assets — you know, your collateral."

"Well?" MacIlraith said grimly.

Sax waved the telegram. "From the agent in Trinidad. The *Pamela's* aground on a shoal somewhere about the Dragon's Mouth, the strait between Trinidad and the mainland. The crew got off all right but the ship's a total loss. So's the cargo."

"What was the cargo — fish, wasn't it?"

"Right. Salt codfish in barrels — drum fish as we say — and herring ditto. Fish that I'd picked up along the coast on ninety-day credits. All that trouble for nothing. Fortunately it was insured."

"And what about the ship itself?"

"Fortunately that was insured too."

"For how much?"

"Ten thousand." Sax tucked the wire in his pocket and moved away towards the door. "It's a queer wind that blows no grief for the underwriters, eh? But the point is, now I can pay off half your blessed loan. I knew you'd be happy to hear that."

He closed the bank door with a cheerful slam and passed with his quick gliding step up the road to the Caraday House. When he gave his news to Pamela her bland smile of greeting was completely wrecked, like the schooner itself.

"Oh Saxby, how awful! My lovely ship, the one with my name. And the last of my poor husband's vessels." She paused. "That's very bad for the firm, isn't it?" She watched her son-in-law's face anxiously.

"Yes, it is. The ship had been doing fairly well, considering the way freights are nowadays, and she was just the right size for the southern trade. She was old though — as ships go, I mean, of course. That's to be considered. She couldn't have stood up to much more North Atlantic weather, 'specially winter weather. And as it happens she was fully insured."

"Oh!"

"So in a way she's no loss at all, you see. That's nice, isn't it? You forgot to ask about the crew. They got ashore all right. Where's Rena?"

Pamela flushed and stared past him fixedly. "Rena's gone away, Saxby."

"You mean for a visit? Where?"

"I don't know, Saxby. She simply said she was going to stay with friends."

"For how long?"

"I got an impression that she planned to stay some time."

"Friends!" Sax muttered in a dazed way. "Where's Rena got friends 'away'? She's lived here all her life."

"You seem to forget," Pamela returned sharply, "that Rena went to Ridgeview — that's a school for young ladies near Windsor — and then she was four years at Dalhousie. Young women at college go and stay with each other on holidays, they love to visit back and forth, and they keep up their friendships afterward with a card at Christmas, and so on. It's all rather silly, but you know how young women are. Or do you?" She gave him a shrewd look.

He was puzzled and angry and he shook his head. "She never said anything to me about that kind of thing. And why this sudden notion? Didn't you try to talk her out of it?"

"As a matter of fact I did. But Rena's headstrong when her mind's set."

"Didn't she leave any message? Didn't she say anything about me?"

"No," Pamela said with a tight mouth. She looked away. Sax caught the false note in that and frowned. He wondered how much Rena's mother really knew, not only about this sudden flitting but of the quarrel that went before. Women weren't like men, they held no secrets from each other. Pamela's eyes returned and met his somber gaze. For several moments they stared at each other in silence. They had the quaint air of a stern father and a doting mother considering the action of a wayward child.

"Look here," Sax exclaimed. "You must know we had a tiff last March, Rena and me. I won't beat about the bush. The fact is I lost my temper over nothing and said something crude. It happened to be the truth but I put it in a pretty nasty way, I admit. I shouldn't have said it at all and I was sorry as soon as I did. I told her so, but Rena was insulted and she's been touchy ever since. I've been careful not to touch her since—in any way, you understand. I figured the best thing to do was to shut up and wait for the ice to thaw. That's been going on for the past three months. And now it looks as if the freeze is on harder than ever."

He paused and prowled along the carpet under Pamela's careful gaze. He halted before her again, and cried in a tone of sudden anguish, "I'm no angel, I know that. I'm not even a gentleman the way you'd reckon it. But I love Rena, see? I'm mad about her. And I want her. It's torture to me — torture, you understand? — being stood off like this. Rena knows that of course. Perhaps she just wants to punish me. If I thought it was just that I could stick it. But look here, suppose it's more than that? Suppose she's got some notion in her head that she's really through with me?"

187

Pamela did not answer. He looked and sounded rather wild. But now he steadied himself. He regarded her. And he went on in a more patient tone, "Now, Rena's your daughter and it's natural for you to side with her. I can't expect you to see my side of it. But it seems to me you've got a stake in this. We three got along very nicely here together till this thing happened, we had a good life of it and you don't want to see that chucked overboard any more than I do. I've got a hunch you know where Rena's gone and you don't know what to do about it. I'll tell you what you ought to do about it. For the sake of us all — not just for me, see? — you've got to get in touch with her and try to talk her out of this sulky fit she's in. Otherwise, if she broods on it long enough, it may turn into something worse."

He paused, waiting for Pamela to speak. She was silent.

"You realize that, don't you?"

"Quite," Pamela said.

"I don't know what Rena's told you but I do know she's got a fanciful mind. She lives in a world of her own that I just couldn't get inside. That's what caused the row, really. I felt I was entitled to something more than she was giving me. But let that go. The point is, with a mind like that Rena might look at a man one minute and see a prince, or at any rate a good fellow, and then look at him in some other mood and see a bogeyman of some kind — if you get what I mean."

"I think so, yes," Pamela said. Her fingers toyed with the antique watch on her bosom. "Saxby, I'm afraid you've been stupid. You should have known you couldn't treat a proud creature like Rena as you might treat one of your sailors. As you say, she lives a lot to herself. Her mind's mysterious. I never knew what went on inside, from the time she was a child. It made me rather sad —

188

her mother — as if I were a stranger like everybody else."

She glanced about the long room, at J.C.'s portrait, at the rich new carpet, at the expensive new piano from New York, and finally came back to Saxby's blue-shaven face, his small anxious eyes, his black hair neatly parted and shining like the folded wing cases of a beetle.

"At the same time, Saxby, Rena's a woman like any other. A fine healthy girl, as I've always said. I don't know what passed between you of course but I suspect Rena's pride is hurt more than anything else. And that being the case, she's in no mood to be approached, even by me. I think you'd better resign yourself to not seeing her for quite some time. I have an idea where she went — a mere notion, no more — and I feel quite sure she won't attempt to communicate with me in case I should tell you. You've got to give her a chance to get over this state of mind she's in, and time to get homesick for Port Barron and this house and her garden and you and me. That can't happen in a month or even a summer, Saxby. Rena's too stubborn for that. A winter — if she's where I think she is, a winter would do it. Even with friends that can be very long."

"A winter!" he cried, as if this calm creature had just sentenced him to solitary confinement for life. And with this last yelp of protest an astonishing change came over him. In a gush of self-pity and fear his pride vanished. He broke down completely. The habitual self-confidence of thirty-five years had gone from his face in that moment when Pamela told him of Rena's flight, and now in its place came the doleful grimace of a small boy whipped for some petty crime and about to howl. Tears bubbled from his eyes, the first tears of his life. He fell on his knees before Rena's mother, clutching at her skirts and crying that he had been a fool but he loved Rena, he loved her, that he

189

was no good without her now, and that he was afraid. He cried that repeatedly. "I'm afraid! I'm afraid!" as if Rena held the symbol of his whole life's purpose and he saw her in a fit of cruel anger snatching it away. He sobbed miserably. He said he would do anything — anything to get her back. He shook and gibbered, a wretched object.

Pamela, standing rigidly over this groveling penitent, was first alarmed, then interested, and finally amused. She could not trust herself to speak for fear she would laugh. She permitted herself a faintly contemptuous smile. So this was Rena's bogeyman! This object! How absurd! He was so completely the fool, the naïve human male in love and thwarted and sick and sorry for himself. How weak they were after all! Bumptious, stubborn, domineering, selfish — and then in a moment whimpering at some woman's knees. And she felt a little blaze of satisfaction that Saxby was now at hers. It established her importance in this little human comedy. It made her indispensable. She could not help feeling that their quarrel, whatever its earthly roots, was in some measure heaven-sent.

After a pause to let him thoroughly humiliate himself she spoke crisply and in her most refained accent, the firm but kindly gentlewoman dealing with a weaker vessel of the common clay.

"Get up, Saxby, please. And do try to control yourself."

He arose obediently, sobbing still, and slumped into a chair before her, with his hands clenched between his knees. He stared at Pamela's toes. Standing over him in this way Pamela felt at least ten feet high. It was an odd sensation.

"I'm glad you've opened your heart to me, Saxby," she said softly. "The best thing you could have done. If Rena had been half as frank with me I might know exactly what to do. As it is, let us consider things calmly. Naturally I

190

want to see my daughter happy, and happy here, in this house. And naturally you want your wife. I think we can work from that basis very well."

Sax looked up with an expression of relief. "Then you will hunt her up, wherever she is? You'll talk to her?"

"I shan't do anything of the sort," she answered composedly. "It would be too obvious, and with Rena one can't afford to be that. No, as I said before, it will take time and patience, Saxby. With some careful letting alone Rena's bound to find herself lonely and anxious to come back. When that happens she'll probably communicate with me, in an offhand sort of way you understand, as if coming home were the last thing in her mind. I know my Rena. Stubborn, stubborn, stubborn. Well, then I'll correspond. I'll write her chatty little notes about the house and garden and the people she knows and likes — including you, of course. In an unobtrusive way I'll let her see that the world goes round in its usual fashion whether she's here or not, and that if she's gone off to sulk she's only punishing herself."

"And what do I do all this time?" he asked resentfully.

"You'll go about your business like a sensible man and forget this little tempest as much as you can. I feel I can promise you this: with proper management, and in the proper time, Rena will come home, and then you shall make your peace with her. Just how you'll do that is a matter for you to decide. All I can say is that by next spring the silly girl should be — what shall I say — tractable?" She was going to say ripe.

⌇ ⌇ Chapter 23

THE Torbys were charmed to have Rena under their
roof and horrified at her notion of moving alone into what
Jennie called "that old dead house in the wood." They
tried to talk her out of it and had no success. And so on the
morning after her arrival they went with her along the
shady path, armed with buckets, brooms, mops and cloths.
As on that other visit Rena was glad to have company when
she opened the door, in spite of her determined air. Life
flowed into the house with Sam's great voice roaring
through the rooms and up the stairs, and with Jennie's
chatter, the sounds of furniture being moved, the hearty
swish of brooms, the trickle and slap of mops. A hot fire of
driftwood crackled (and smoked painfully) in the rusty
kitchen stove. Every window had to be pried open. But
when that was done, with a fresh blend of salt air and
warm spruce needles blowing through the house, the last
damp taint departed; and with it went the faint melan-
choly that gathers always in a house where people have
been happy and then shut the door and gone.

On the second day Jennie commandeered Pascoe as well,
and that bemused young man came unshaven and shabby
in his Mackinaw shirt and dungarees and labored hard
with Sam, dragging bundles of carpets and curtains and
bedding from the attic. Opened and spread on the patch
of grass before the house, all these made a sorry spectacle.
Old John Caraday's wrappings had saved them from
moths but not corruption; the years of damp and mildew
had ruined them all.

"Oh dear," Rena said, dismayed. "I should have come

out every summer and stayed long enough to open everything and put it out to air." But she put her chin up. "It
doesn't matter, though."

"I've got a spare mattress you can have," Jennie said.
"And sheets and blankets, everything like that. But what
about them rusty cooking things? You can't use them."

"I'll get Sam to buy me some the next time he goes up
to Port Barron."

"Looks like you plan to stay awhile."

"I do."

"Ain't that fine! Husband coming later, I suppose?"

"No, Jennie. He's much too busy nowadays. He doesn't
even know I'm here. Nor does Mother. It's a sort of private holiday, so please don't mention it to anyone." Jennie looked surprised. Rena smiled and said, "Don't you
ever want to get away from everything sometimes — even
Sam?"

Sam roared at that, and Jennie looked at him and
sniffed.

On the third day all was ready inside. The floors were
bare, but the old paint shone and smelled of soap and water. The wallpaper, faded and hanging away from the wall
in great blisters, was nevertheless clean. The last dusty
cobweb had been swept away. The small square panes of
the old-fashioned windows now let in all the light that
found its way into the clearing. The stove had been
scrubbed with emery paper and then blacked, and Sam
had fitted a new length of pipe into the chimney. The
chimney itself had been cleared of a multitude of swallows'
nests by passing a rope down the flue and dragging a bundle of spruce branches back and forth. The windows,
well soaped, moved freely at last, and all the door handles
and hinges now turned silently on oil.

With all this accomplished Sam and Pascoe turned their

energies outdoors. They bailed out the well and daubed a coat of limewash on the inner stones. They hacked away the growth of spruce that had crept about the sides and back of the house.

"Roof seems tight," Sam observed. "You can't beat cedar shingles, I always say. What about a radio — you bring a radio? You'll want one for company, nights. We better rig a wire up there."

"Oh no, I haven't got one, Sam."

"Better take our'n. Belongs to Pascoe really but he won't mind."

"No."

Pascoe overheard. He dumped outside the kitchen door a wheelbarrow load of driftwood for the stove and turned a blond-stubbled face to Rena.

"You ought to have one, Mrs. Nolan. If you're worried about taking something from Sam and Jennie I can fix one for you. I've got the parts and it's quite a simple matter."

Rena did not want a radio. She wanted to hear nothing of the world outside. But they were so concerned, they seemed to think music and voices from distant cities such a necessary part of life nowadays, that she had not the heart to refuse.

"Well, all right, if it really won't be much trouble. You must let me pay for whatever you have to use."

Pascoe smiled. "As I said, I've got the parts, and some spare batteries and all that; and I guess the Department won't miss a few yards of aerial wire. There's nothing to pay for. You'll realize that when you see it. The thing won't look pretty, but it'll work."

So in the end she had a house with a tight roof, a clean well, a woodpile, a bed, a pair of kerosene lamps, a stove, a chimney that drew properly, food in the cupboard, some simple furniture and a radio, the chief requisites of life

194

anywhere on the cape from Eglinton to Gannet Head. And she was content. She had no fear at night. If the house had ghosts they were a friendly kind, a sentimental kind; the old moss-hung trees outside made a good fence against the world, the wind in their tops was old-familiar and so was the pungent air through her bedroom window. If she wanted other friendly reassurances they were there in the boom of Sam's horn in foggy weather, in the intermittent day-long, night-long purring of Pascoe's gasoline exhaust, and the music and chatter of Pascoe's gift whenever she chose to turn the switch. She had brought a few books from her father's library, tales of travel, of the sea, but nothing whatever of romance between man and woman.

She accepted with an amused patience the Torbys' concern for her loneliness. To please them she went sometimes to have a meal and spend the evening at their home; and in turn she would invite them to tea, their lodger and all, and go to much pains over the stove with cake and pie and the various disguises of tinned meat and vegetables. And she was happy — happier indeed than at any time since she was small and running about the Head in a short frock and bare feet in those old vanished summers when Caraday's Cove was still a living village. In the mornings, getting breakfast and washing up afterwards, running a broom about the floor and dusting the ancient furniture, she hummed and sang. In the afternoons she explored the abandoned sheep paths along the shore, where every bit of the stark view recalled some tale of her father's. At times she could almost hear his quiet laugh and see the gaunt dreamy figure moving beside her, talking of the things that always bored Pamela so and that always seemed to Rena so important and delightful.

Occasionally, inevitably, the dark brooding face of Sax intruded and she could not put it away. Then all these delightful things lost their pleasure. The very sunshine went flat and cold, or a fog in the spruces dripped from their moss beards with a dismal sound; the sad and charming cries of the gulls became a mere squalling over fish, the silent church had a cynical air, as if to remind her of her marriage vows, and all the wonderful sense of privacy was gone.

For this there was a single cure, a prompt visit to the Torbys or a call on Pascoe, sitting at the narrow desk among his mechanical mysteries and smoking absurd little handmade cigarettes. Jennie Torby was one of those housebound creatures, common about Port Barron, who preferred spending their lives indoors or at best taking the sunshine in a chair set just outdoors. The church and the old houses at the cove gave her the creeps, she said. As for roaming the shore, that was all right for menfolks gunning for ducks but not for a sensible woman.

Thus Rena made her walks alone, but sometimes for variety she joined Sam and Pascoe on one of their gunning expeditions, chiefly because she liked to watch the dog. For Sam had a bird dog, a clever old red setter named Bosun, trained in the art of tolling ducks. The hunting process was always the same and always interesting. It was so naïve and yet so sure. The gunners crept through the bushes to a small cove where the ducks were feeding. At a soft command from Sam the dog stepped into the open and began to gambol easily along the stretch of shore just in front of the gunners, rolling on his back, waving his paws in air, puppy-fashion, or chasing his tail with unwearying zest, or merely standing looking off into space and slowly waving that long gleaming brush.

It was a game that required patience. At the first the ducks quietly watched the dog's antics from afar. Then slowly, with a little chorus of soft quacks, they began

196

swimming back and forth with heads up and eyes alert, moving in a long arc that closed gradually towards the distant dog. At last they came within gunshot, still swimming slowly and still quacking as if in comment upon the phenomenon ashore. The rest was quick and deadly. At Sam's hoarse "Now!" the gunners sprang up, and as the ducks began to fly the guns cracked. The game never failed, and that night Jennie would serve duck stew.

Once Pascoe remarked to Rena, "You know, this tolling stunt's got to be seen to be believed. When Sam first told me about it I thought he was kidding. How the deuce did anyone think of it?"

"It's quite simple," she said. "Our ancestors here learned it from the Indians and the Indians learned it from the fox. Foxes toll ducks whenever they get a chance. That's why our people always choose red dogs to train for tolling."

"And where did you learn all this?" he asked, smiling. Sam had gone with the dog along the shore to retrieve a shot duck.

"From my dad. He wasn't much of a gunner but he liked to study wild things. He used to tease me when I was small and my hair was a bright red. He said he'd rent me out to the duck hunters for a toller. All I'd have to do was to get down on all fours and shake my head." Pascoe glanced at her hair and they both laughed.

"It wouldn't do now," he observed.

"No, it got darker as I grew up, thank goodness."

"I've heard the Torbys talk about your father. But mostly they talk about your grandfather. He seems to have been a remarkable man."

"Oh he was!" she exclaimed with enthusiasm. "He was wonderful. I suppose you know how he came to the Head in the first place, and built up a big business in Port Barron and all that. But money wasn't his main interest, ever. I think at heart he was always a little sorry to leave the Head. He loved this place, the village and the church. I'm so glad he didn't live to see it all abandoned and tumble-down the way it is now. After he died the fishing boys molested the birds in their nesting places and drove a lot of them away. Grandfather always kept it as a sort of sanctuary while he lived. My dad used to come out here with me once or twice a summer, just for the day. He saw what was going on but he was too gentle a man to be able to put any fear into the boys and young men, and after a time he stopped coming. He couldn't bear to see the place any more."

"Some of the birds seem to have survived," Pascoe said, feeling guilty with the shotgun in his hands.

"Oh yes. You know where they nest, I suppose?"

"Only the terns. I've seen their eggs among the grass tufts on the dunes back there."

"If you're interested in birds — apart from shooting them I mean — I'll show you where the herring gulls nest, any afternoon you like. Most of the chicks are hatched now, but you'll see a few eggs if you're curious. And later on I'll show you where the shags nest, and a few pairs of egrets. And I know a place on the west side of the Head, a turfy spot above a high bank, where the Mother Carey's chickens still make their burrows."

Pascoe smiled sheepishly. "I've been here eighteen months and you know more about Gannet Head than I do."

"That's because you spend most of your time in that stuffy radio hut. What on earth do you do with yourself? When you're not on watch I mean, or shooting ducks?"

"Oh, I fiddle at the typewriter. Reports, that kind of thing."

198

Sam returned with a draggled duck, Bosun at his heels. He held up the bird.

"Now there," he announced in his diaphone tones, "is one o' them purty li'l teal, a loner. Ain't seen a teal for years. What's she doin' out here, I wonder, so far from the rivers and lakes where she belongs, and all by her lone?"

Rena put out a hand and stroked the wet breast. The bird's small bright eyes still had the clarity of life.

"Poor thing! Maybe she was just like me, Sam, a wife on a holiday, and see what happened to her! Aren't you ashamed?"

The old seaman looked at her ruefully. She might have been old John C.

ᔐ ᔐ Chapter 24

THERE!" Rena said. The place was a shallow fold bristling with cat-spruce trees. Spreading in a broad V, it ran down to the sea on the west side of the Head, where the outer fringe of the clump was exposed to the whole rake of the Fundy winds. On the edge of the sea bank the trees were dwarfed, rising no more than a foot or two, and with their stems and branches bent close to the earth and away from the west. In the lee of these the next rank gained another foot or so in height, but with their thin trunks gnarled and creeping and their branches intertwined as if for mutual support. Behind these again the growth stood taller, with thicker trunks and branches and a little more upright. In this gradual way the thicket rose until a stone's toss back from the sea edge there were trees straight upright, some with butts twelve inches through, although none reached a height of more than twenty feet.

The whole wood leaned sharply from the Fundy side, like a penthouse roof. It was a little weird in the calm summer afternoon. The trees seemed to cower away from a cold and ghostly gale while elsewhere not a breath of air stirred the grass. Just as strange was the clutter of brown reed nests on their flattened tops, and the snow crust of birds. As Rena raised her arm they spread their wings and went up in a sudden white storm, hovering over the wood and the intruders and chuckling in almost human voices.

"They don't cry and squall when you disturb them at their nests," Rena remarked. "They just keep flying overhead and saying ha-ha-ha, like that, but they're like Queen Victoria, they're not amused. The brownish-looking ones are this year's young. They can fly quite well already, although you'll see some still resting on the nests. The lighter ones are the second-year birds. Gulls' breasts don't get pure white till the third year, but I suppose you know that. I dare say we could find a few eggs if we went down into the wood, but I'd rather not. The fishing people at the cove used to gather eggs for a change of diet. Grandfather didn't like it but so long as they didn't molest the hatched birds he let it pass. It always seemed cruel to me. The bird usually lays three eggs. If you take those she lays two more. If you take those she lays one. Then she gives up."

"And no wonder," Pascoe said. "Where do the shags nest?"

"Farther back in the wood. I'll take you there late in July or early August, when the young shags are about ready to leave the nests. It's a special experience — like something out of a nightmare."

"Why?"

"You'll see."

200

"And what about the egrets — you promised to show me those. I didn't know egrets nested this far north."

"Oh they nest with the shags. They're very chummy, heaven knows why. The young egrets are such funny charming things. The shags are horrible."

"And what's that I see down there on the edge of the wood — this side — those rotten poles, like a bit of old fence all thrown together?"

"One of Grandfather's old shearing pens. You'll see two or three others between here and the cove, all falling down now. He had two Scotch shepherd dogs, clever things, and at shearing time he'd go out with the dogs and half a dozen men to round up the sheep in the barrens."

"That must have been a job," he said, looking over the bushy waste of the barrens. His hair hung in lank blond locks about his temples and the back of his neck. He needs a shearing himself, Rena thought impishly, but at least he's shaved today. Aloud she said, "Some of the sheep escaped the roundup and ran wild all winter. During storms they'd shelter in the wood. After the first heavy snow had matted on that awful tangle of branches overhead, it was just as snug as a shed. But don't ask me what they lived on. They couldn't even get kelp after the cold weather set in, because of course the ice wall formed along the shore. I've heard Dad say the eagles and ravens got a lot of them."

They made their way back along the old sheep track above the western bank, pausing to examine bits of ship wreckage flung up in ancient storms and now rotten and interlaced with bushes and long grass. The sea ran on the shore in long slow swells, glittering in the warm light.

"Fundy," Rena murmured. "There's nothing like this in the world."

"Except Hudson Strait," Pascoe said.

"Oh come! I know our cape's barren and rather bleak in

the wintertime but it can't be like anything up there. After all Nova Scotia's only halfway between the equator and the pole."

"Hudson Strait's a long way from the pole too, but it's pretty chilly just the same. Anyhow I didn't mean your cape. I meant the sea — the tide. You people always talk as if Fundy had the only big tides in the world. Well, you're quite wrong. Up in Hudson Strait you get tides as big as the Fundy kind, and in several places you get a strong tidal overfall like the Race. When you've seen pack ice shoved along by a gale and caught in one of those tide rips in the Strait, you've really seen something."

"I'd rather see this, thank you. The North's always seemed a terrible place to me, seeing what our winters are like here."

"Oh you're quite mistaken about that. I spent eight years up there — three on stations along the Labrador and five on Hudson Strait, and I liked it. I'm going back there the first chance I get."

They were walking slowly along the path, Pascoe ahead, with the stunted laurels brushing against their legs. Rena said to the back of his head, "How old are you?"

"Twenty-eight next fall, why?"

"Let's see, you've been here eighteen months or so and before that you were in the North eight years. Anywhere else?"

"No. Except home and going to school of course."

"Then you've been living that kind of life since you were eighteen? What on earth for?"

"Oh, just that I was born and brought up in a city and I was crazy to see the North. Anyhow, I quit high school to take a radio course and went up to the Labrador when I was eighteen. Then they opened the new stations along Hudson Strait and I got myself shifted up there. It's rugged along the Strait but kind of wonderful, all that rock and ice and sky, and that terrific feeling of challenge you get when you first touch the fringe of the North — the real North, I mean. Like your first taste of rum. It puckers up your mouth and stings your throat and makes your stomach flop, you wonder why anybody drinks the stuff; and then you get that wonderful feeling inside and you know why. After you've been a few months up there your face keeps turning towards the pole like a compass needle— only your face points true, not magnetic. You know you're only on the fringe of it and the rest is a mystery. You hanker to get further up and find out what it's all about, what's behind the next hill or the other island — what's behind the northern lights."

Pascoe tossed these remarks over his shoulder, smiling as if confessing a childish folly. "Of course some fellows hate it, and they're glad to get away. I didn't and I wasn't."

"Why did you leave?"

"Because I had to. Because I was transferred here. I think they have a theory that after a certain number of years in the North without a break a man's apt to get bitten by the ice worms."

"What on earth do you mean?"

"Loony. Wacky. You know."

"What were your symptoms?"

"I don't know, unless it was that I was always talking about getting further north, and going on long hunts with the Eskimos and all that. I was always saying that a white man could move about and survive anywhere in the arctic if he set his mind to it." He chuckled. "Maybe it was just the book."

"What book?"

"I started to write a book up there — a sure sign of the ice worms, according to the others on the post. They used

203

to kid me a lot about it — the other radio ops, and the weather bloke, the Mountie corporal and the H.B.C. trader. They used to call me the Genius and they'd suggest pen names like Frozen Owen. They had a name for the book, too — *Pascoe's Fiasco*. But I went on with it."

She saw a light. "Is that the heap of paper I saw on your desk?"

"Yes."

"What's it about?"

"Oh, the North. I'll show you sometime if you like. It's just a mess, you understand. I can't really write. I see the things all right but I can't put 'em on paper. It's just a way of passing time. I find it interesting by spells. Then I get fed up with it and stuff the whole thing away in a drawer for months. Then sometime when I've got nothing better to do I drag the thing out and have another go at it. Most of the time I just sit over it, scratching my head and wishing I had brains in there instead of fishbones and sawdust."

"You've got the brains," Rena said. "What you lack is the energy."

"You really think so? You think I'm lazy?" He stopped in the path and turned with a rueful expression. "That's what your husband thought, wasn't it, the day you came with him to see my outfit?"

She regarded him frankly. "I don't mean lazy bodily. You do your job well — because it's routine and you don't have to make any mental effort — and you're always ready to pitch in and help Sam or Jennie or me with our chores. It's not that, Pascoe. I think you're a mental lazybones. You're a dreamer. You remind me very much of someone I knew very well. He was quite a nice person, mind you; he was gentle and easygoing, he had brains and he meant well. But he didn't accomplish a thing in his life.

204

He just drifted along like you. It was a pleasant life, I suppose, but it disappointed his father and friends, and underneath I think he was unhappy himself without ever knowing why."

"Did he ever try to write a book?" Pascoe asked whimsically.

"No, he just read other people's books. And he made little sketches and water colors and collected butterflies."

"That sounds like a darned fine life to me."

Her tongue coiled on something tart. "Well, we won't argue about that."

Pascoe plucked a handful of bayberry leaves, crushing them in his palm, and put his head down to sniff their fragrance.

"Would you like to see that stuff of mine?"

"Yes. I'll come over some day when it rains and there's no chance of a walk. Or you can drop it at my house if you like, sometime when you're passing. I warn you I'm no soft critic."

He laughed. "You can't say anything worse about it than I've said myself."

He opened his fingers to let the pungent green shreds sift away to the ground and watched them musingly. Rena itched to say Wake up, do, and why don't you let Jennie cut your hair? But she announced briskly, "We'll have to run if you're to catch your radio watch on time. Aren't you supposed to call Barmouth at four sharp?"

His tanned face reddened. He had forgotten that completely.

~ ~ Chapter 25

ONE morning when Rena was sitting down to breakfast in dressing gown and braids, Pascoe brought the untidy bundle to her door.

"Here's the great work. I'm just on my way to Sam's boat. Jennie wants fish for dinner."

He might have picked a better time to call. But when she murmured with a forbidding politeness, "Will you come in?" he seemed quite heedless of the hour and her appearance and the tone of her voice.

"Thanks. Just for a minute. I'll dump this on your sideboard. I suppose I'd better tell you what it's all about before you tackle it, otherwise you won't make head or tail of it. My typing's pretty wild and my composition's worse." Her breakfast was getting cold. He saw her straying gaze and said, "Oh, I'm sorry."

"Will you have a cup of coffee?" Rena said quickly.

"Yes, if you've got lots."

He stirred sugar and tinned milk into the coffee thoughtfully. "I got the idea when I was at Nottingham. That's an island, a thundering big heap of rock at the west end of Hudson Strait. The wireless station was on a small harbor at the southern end. Some kindly souls in Montreal sent up two or three barrels of old books to the outposts and the supply steamer dropped off one for us. It was like one of those ten-cent grabs at a church rummage sale. You shut your eyes and stick in your hand and you pull out anything from *Tom the Bootblack* to a Presbyterian hymn book. The thing that took my fancy was one ragged old volume of *Purchas His Pilgrims*. Do you know it?

Well, I didn't either. But I found in it Abacuk Pricket's account of the last voyage of Henry Hudson. Right down my alley, so to speak. At first it just amused me, going through that quaint spelling and trying to identify the places Hudson saw. Some he'd named and some he just let go. But I could pick out our island all right, because Pricket went ashore in charge of the boat, and he and his men climbed up high enough to get a good view of it. And of course they found themselves looking at what's now known as Hudson Bay."

Pascoe paused and sipped his coffee. "Well, you must know Hudson's story — it's in all the schoolbooks. He was looking for the Northwest Passage, and when he struck the big strait he thought he'd found it. When he came to the Bay he assumed it was the China Sea — the chilly end of it. So he sailed in and headed south. He'd found a sea all right, as big as the Mediterranean. But it came to a dead end in James Bay, of course, and he had to winter there. That's a pretty frosty latitude and they had a tough time of it. In the following summer he wanted to go on with the search, but his crew weren't having any more. He was a tough old nut. He hadn't shown much common sense in handling his officers and men, or in dishing out the stores or anything like that. I suppose he was a bit mad with his one idea, right from the start. Anyhow, the crew mutinied. They turned Hudson adrift in a small boat with his boy and most of the sick and lame, and off they went to England — a callous lot of beggars any way you look at 'em."

He drank again and put his cup down sharply. Enthusiasm lighted his face.

"Now that's one of the great mysteries of the North. What became of Hudson? He wasn't the type to sit there in a perfectly good boat and wait for death, and he knew it was hopeless to try the passage back by sea. So where did he make for? And where did he end? The more I thought of that, the more fascinating it got. And the more I read of Pricket's account, the more clearly I could see the ship, that little fifty-five ton thing, and Hudson and his men. Prickett described 'em very well in one way or another. I could match most of 'em with men I'd known myself. Like Henry Green the clerk, the young man 'born of worshipful parents but by his lewd conversation' and so forth. I'd lived with that man or his counterpart in a station on the Labrador. I even knew Hudson himself — a tough old Newfoundlander, full of the North and quarrelsome with his men, who took me in a stinking little schooner once from Chimo to St. John's. Oh yes, I could see 'em all right. I could see the whole lot of 'em. And there was the actual scene, you might say, right before my eyes. And there was the tale of the Mountie corporal, who'd spent several years around James Bay and one time found some queer old relics up the Rupert River and didn't know what they were.

"So I began to put it on paper, or try to. The idea was to tell the whole story of the voyage, and the winter they spent, and the mutiny and all that; and then the sequel — what Hudson did and what became of him. I've got it all worked out in my mind — my lazy mind. I see the pictures all right. The trouble is to get 'em on the paper. You might read the thing as far as I've got, unless it bores you, and tell me what you think of it."

Pascoe said all this in a rapid voice, with an eager light in his gray eyes, as if those pictures he talked about were actually visible by some sort of magic lantern in his head. She was amused at the sudden change in him — like a sleepwalker coming awake and bursting with things to say — but she had a suspicion that it might be an act put on through pique at her remark about his laziness. Well, if so, he had at least some pride. She felt the satisfaction of a school ma'am who has found a sign of intelligence in a rather appealing dunce. Pascoe arose, pulling on the long-peaked cap that all the fishermen wore in summer, and with a nod was gone. She stepped to the window and saw the last of his rubber-booted figure vanishing into the trees towards the cove. He's thin, she observed. She pictured him eating out of tins all those years in the North, and now living more or less on fish, as Sam and Jennie did.

She washed the dishes and dressed, putting on old shoes, a pair of dungarees and a tartan shirt bought originally for snowshoe jaunts with Sax. She tied a bandanna over her hair, caught up her house-cleaning gear and walked down the path to the old church. She pushed open the door and gazed once more on that scene of neglect. The morning sun, through the slender east windows with their cheap little tinted panes, cast a bright pattern of reds and blues and yellows in stripes across the pews and floor. She set to work at once, sweeping vigorously. The dust of years arose in clouds, writhing like painted smoke in the sunbeams and pouring through the doorway into the clean sea air. She was there long after midday, sweeping like a youthful Dame Partington, when the big form of old Sam appeared in the porch beneath the bell rope. He sneezed, and roared, "Hold hard, there! Just a minute. Phew!"

Rena paused obediently, leaning on the broom.

"What's goin' on here?"

"Just what you see. I'm cleaning up the church. It's time."

Sam moved inside. "Time! Don't ye plan to stop and eat? D'ye know what time 'tis? It's after one — purty nigh ha' past."

"I forgot my watch. Anyway, I'm not hungry, Sam. What's on your mind? And don't say you'll round up Jennie and Pascoe for another cleaning bee. This job's all mine. I haven't a thing to do today or any day and I might as well do this."

"Anyone'd think you planned to hold a meetin'. What?" He looked about him incredulously. Rena burst into laughter.

"Oh Sam! You have such wonderful ideas. But I'm not planning anything at all. I just hated to see it in this state. After all, it's my grandfather's monument, really. He wanted to be buried out here, did you know that? A grave with the others behind the church, beside Grandmother's, and a little wooden headboard with his name burned on, like all the rest. Mama wouldn't have it though. She thought everyone in Port Barron would say J.C.'s heirs were burying him on the cheap, so she had him buried in Port Barron cemetery and ordered that monstrous marble pillar and urn from the stonecutter in Eglinton. How he must hate it."

"Um. Always wondered why he was burrit there when his wife was here. D'ye know, Rena, I was steppin' down to the cove, not thinkin' of anythin' p'tic'lar, when I see all this dust flyin' out o' the church door. Give me quite a turn. Larf if you like. For a moment I thought 'twas old J.C. back in one o' his tantrums, givin' the sinners hell."

⌣ ⌣ Chapter 26

To Sax in these restless days his brief returns home were a mockery. Each time he walked up the gravel of the familiar carriageway he felt the queer dread of a man lost in the woods who comes upon the ashes of last night's fire. In the bedroom, where his avid nostrils caught the lingering aroma of Rena the moment he opened the door, there was always the quick wild hope that she had come back. And when that perished and, like any lonely child, he thrust his face into the wardrobe where her Paris fripperies still hung, it was as if she were there, hiding among the silks, but still not to be touched.

The rest of the house was alien. It did not need the chattering presence of Rena's mother to confirm the impression of a stranger's home where for a moment, for a day or a week end, he was a tolerated guest. The gingerbread castle of which Pamela had been chatelaine so long had been changed very little by his expensive renovations after all. Somehow in less than a year she had reestablished that air of immutable ownership which he had met when he first walked into the house with MacIlraith. The very walls and carpets gave it off like a proprietary scent. The dull red bloom of the heavy mahogany furniture was Pamela's bloom. The gleam of the polished silverware that winked at him from all sides in the dining room was Pamela's gleam. When in a listless way he lifted the lid of the new piano and struck a key with a tentative finger the note twanged through the room with somehow the timbre of Pamela's voice. There were times when the portrait of J.C., gazing down upon Sax from the mantel, seemed to ask in a mute sympathy what either of them was doing there.

When he questioned Pamela about her daughter, the answer was always the same. The silly girl had written nothing. The silly girl seemed quite resolved to stay away. In far hotels, in trains, in the master's cabin of the *John* or the *Roger,* alone for an hour or a night with his sharp wife-hunger, he resolved again and again to have done

211

with Pamela's waiting game and demand to know where Rena was. But when he entered the house and came under that formidable spell once more, the bold plan perished. His spirit seemed bound to those knees at which he had wept and implored. He feared and admired Mrs. Caraday's adroitness. He felt that through her and her alone he might win Rena back and abolish the nightmare that haunted him, a nightmare in which again and again his wife uttered the words that Ellen Carisfort had flung in his face.

It was different in the office, the shop, the warehouse or the shipyard, where he was supreme. But there he encountered something else. Behind the ready obedience, the quiet "Yes, Cap'n Nolan — very good, Cap'n Nolan," even behind the faint smiles that greeted his occasional effort at a joke, he sensed an attitude that hovered between mere dislike and actual hostility. In the town itself he felt himself the object of a thinly veiled contempt. And when he looked within himself and consulted his familiar devil he was told that all these people were laughing at him for a fool, the greedy fool who had sunk his money in a rotten concern and married a wife as barren as the firm — a wife who would not even live with him any more.

Sometimes in the west drawing room, gazing at the pen-and-wash drawings of West Indian scenes, which, like everything Roger Caraday had done, were quite good but not quite good enough, Sax cursed himself for leaving those scenes and a trade in which at least he had been sure of himself. All that time in the West Indies he had been under that boyhood illusion of making good and coming back to play the Big Shot, country style, in the manner of 1914. Planning to take up a life that didn't exist any more! If he had taken a careful look at any of the provincial towns on his return, he would have seen that. What had deceived him was Port Barron, the poor community isolated on the cape, where the tradition of the old time remained untouched, with nothing new for contrast. And there he had fallen victim to his own dream and Rena Caraday.

Rena! He repeated her name to himself now as a phenomenon. It seemed to explain everything that had happened since he came north with his hard-won fortune and his antiquated dream. He could not put aside a conviction that Rena, his fortune and his dream were all bound up together now for better or worse. He saw her as one of those splendid female figures on the back of bank notes, who sit flimsily clad and gazing with a sensuous calm from a welter of grain sheaves, boughs of fruit, sawmills, ships and locomotives, as if the whole thing were the natural result of going to bed with the right man.

The person foremost in Captain Sax Nolan's thoughts was herself quite unconcerned with sheaves or men, except perhaps the dog-eared and badly typed sheaf of Pascoe's "great work." The tidying of the church took several days, ending with a careful polishing of the Communion set. In the evenings she was tired. When she tried to read a little before going to bed she found herself nodding over the page. It was not until a fine morning at the end of the week that she took her rug and some sandwiches to the bank where the petrels nested and sat down with the determination of reading Pascoe's typescript through.

On the next day she went over it again, this time studying certain parts and calling up half-forgotten precepts of English composition learned at school and college. She had got good marks in English, and at college she had won a rather important prize with a piece describing a voyage to Jamaica in a square-rigged ship. That had been easy, really. From the time she could walk she had known ships and the sea and it was simply a matter of putting them down. All through her childhood, on those biannual flittings between Port Barron and the West Indies, she had run about the deck and rigging with the men; and she had learned the name of every rope and sail, and every command that had to do with them, and why those commands were made and what happened when they were carried out. She remembered the sailors laughing and saying she was a chip off old J.C.'s block, no mistake, and a pity she wasn't a boy. She had never mentioned these things to her classmates at Ridgeview and Dalhousie, feeling that they were not the sort of things young ladies were supposed to know. And she had received with a guilty silence her Engglish professor's praise for her nautical research and the unusual scope of her imagination.

Armed with all this, she examined Pascoe's tale. She had fancied him laboring over it in lonely shacks during the interminable subarctic winters, making the picture piece by piece in his mind and then fitting it together on paper, as a man bored with solitude might complete a jigsaw puzzle and then transfer it bit by bit to another part of the room. What she saw now however, and with increasing dismay, was that he had spoken the truth when he said in his careless way that something happened between his mind and fingers. His grammar was quite good, but he had not the slightest idea of form and arrangement — his phrases were stilted and awkward, his choice of words inept.

There were parts that were rather good. It was like being in the Caraday store when the shopboy had rubbed scouring powder over the big plate glass but missed a spot here and there. The scene in the street was in general obscured, but as you moved about inside you caught a glimpse of a passing face, a bit of the house across the street, a horse's head, a pair of oars tipped over an invisible shoulder, all in sharp detail and lighted to throw the proper shadows and bring out the proper tints. But on the whole it was as he had admitted, just a mess. It was hopeless. She saw with vexation that he had lacked the fortitude to work it over, even to prepare himself for the task of writing it, and that he would never have the fortitude. His view of this was like his view of life, a thing to be dreamed, not to be nailed down hard and fast. And again she had that memory of her father, that amiable futile man, seeing him not with the contempt of her mother but with the sorrowful dismay of old J.C.

She ran her slender fingers over the piled edges of that appalling jumble, and thought, The proper place for it is in the sea. In honesty she ought to tell him that. But she could see him laughing and walking down that bit of salty turf before the radio hut and tossing the whole thing into the Fundy tide. The picture offended her frugal mind, not because it was a waste of paper or merely of the time he had, out of sheer boredom, put on it, but because somehow it embodied the waste of a young man. This bundle of bad typing and worse composition was, for all its faults, the one attempt he had ever made to get outside the pleasant mental fog in which he lived. In a few more months he would be able to get a transfer back to the North; and eventually up there in that stupefying emptiness he would go mad or perish in some vague foolhardy attempt to solve those remote mysteries towards the pole.

From all she had read and all he had told her about those frosty posts she had a clear idea of what they meant in terms of mortal humanity. There were practical men who could take the North or leave it, and most of them left it sooner or later for straw hats and tramcars and a daily newspaper; but Pascoe was not one of these. She saw

215

Pascoe as a kind of youthful Hudson, not yet bearded, not yet tired and old and mad, but doomed to end in some Northern adventure wonderfully dreamed and miserably bungled, and all because some charitable soul had not steered him into a safer thought-climate before it was too late.

At intervals she looked up from Pascoe's sheets to rest her eyes on the scene. The day had begun with a fine morning, the sea sparkling everywhere, especially in the bright path towards the sun, where the glitter was almost painful. The robin's-egg blue of the sky was streaked with cirrus and beneath it the water was not blue at all but a fine pearl-gray, wimpling in the first stirs of a breeze from the west. It was almost calm. The tide barely whispered on the rocks below her bank. On the reef beyond, exposed at low water, the dark masses of bladder wrack lifted and fell lazily on the light swell. Even the gulls were quietly sunning themselves on the foreshore.

By noon the breeze had shifted to the south. A pale gray scud, mackerel-mottled in patches, crept across the sky and blotted out the high cirrus of the morning. The change of wind made a dead lee under her bank, but farther out the shadows of cats'-paws played over the surface, and beyond these again the wide sweep towards Topsail and Frigate was ruffled with small waves hurrying in towards Port Barron. By three o'clock the clouds became a pattern of pale and dark gray bars, the dark ones sagging like ragged udders charged with rain that could not fall. The fishing boats came in one after another, each trailing a snow squall of gulls fluttering and diving to catch the offal flung out from the gutting knives. From the foreshore of the cape the gulls flew off to join this feast. But below Rena's bank one remained, a bird of the second year, not yet pure gray-and-white, that stood poised on a rock and drowsing, as if it did not know what hunger was.

He's like Pascoe, thought Rena. He simply doesn't care, he wants to dream. In a stir of vexation she picked up a pebble, but she put it down. No, my dear. And you can't throw a stone at Pascoe, either. You can't wake up anybody like that, really. You can only hope to shift his dreaming into a sensible channel and try to keep it there. And how do you do that?

ꜱ ꜱ Chapter 27

On the day they went to see the nesting place of the shags the sky was again overcast, this time with a dank air moving in from the east. Exactly the right weather for it, Rena observed.

"When we go down into the wood, Owen, you must imagine you're ten years old and seeing it for the first time, as I was when my dad took me there."

"Why?"

"To get the whole effect. Of course I was an impressionable child. My mother always hated the sound of the wind in the spruce tops about the house — said it was like the hissing of snakes; and for a long time I thought snakes lived in trees."

They crossed the barrens at some distance from the shore and entered the wood from the rear of the hollow, where the trees were straight and fairly tall. They stepped into a green gloom at once, for the cat-spruce tops were close and interwoven and clotted with old-man's-beard, a living roof. Starved for light, all the lower branches had perished and gone to harsh stubs or fallen, and there was no undergrowth at all. They moved silently on a mat of brown needles and rotten twigs. The dense green ceiling came lower as the trees dwindled in height towards the sea, and at every step the gloom increased. The absence of sunshine in the sky itself made the shade of the wood darker still. After a time Pascoe became aware of a faint but disgusting smell. It became more emphatic the farther they went. Eventually they reached a place where it hung under the trees like a foul and almost visible fog. Looking about him, Pascoe saw the ground on all sides littered with decaying fish, some gone entirely to bones, some almost whole. There were fetid lumps of fish flesh that looked as if it had been chewed and then spat forth by a berserk grinding machine. The whole of this noisome carpet had a white pattern of spattered guano.

The tree boles here had a thin furry covering, in color the bright poisonous green of verdigris. In the queer twilight they looked wet and slimy but when Pascoe put out a hand he found the stuff dry, a thin moss of some strange sort, nourished perhaps by this putrid air. Rena had stopped some distance away with a handkerchief held over her mouth and nose. She was watching him. There was not a sound. In the heart of the wood nothing moved, not even a breath of air. The stillness, the gloom, the foul reek, the poisonous green pillars standing about him, all conveyed a sense of something mysterious and abominable. He did not have to imagine himself a boy of ten. It was eerie enough at twenty-eight.

"Look up," Rena called.

He looked up and was startled. The ceiling of moss-hung branches here was not more than five feet above his head. Through it, on wavering black necks, peered three snake heads regarding him with bright malicious eyes. Instinctively he crouched. Staring upward to right and left, he saw the heads of other snakes thrust below the roof a foot or so and wavering and peering like those above him. Then it came to him. He grinned and straightened himself, seeing now the hooked beaks, the naked orange patches below the eyes, and the strange scalloped feathers on the necks, that looked so exactly like scales. Rena's voice came muffled by the handkerchief. "Aren't they horrible?"

"They certainly don't look any better than they smell."

"They're almost full-grown. In another day or two they'll fly.

"In another minute so shall I. Phew! But where are the egrets, I want to see those. You said they nested with the shags."

"They do. If you want to climb one of those trees and push your head out through the roof you'll find yourself looking over the whole colony. There should be at least two or three egret nests amongst them."

He climbed, with some repugnance, and thrust head and shoulders into the open air and light. The top of the wood sloped sharply towards the sea, and on the flat crown of every tree about him sat a crude nest of sticks and reeds. Most were inhabited by young shags, whose scaly necks and naked faces were now pulled up and staring at him, all in utter silence. They were well grown, apparently three feet long from tail to beak, much of which was neck. Farther away he saw the nests of the egrets and the young with their tall white crests, all sitting erect and staring at the intruder. He smiled. They looked absurdly like old Percival Hawthorn, the dignified town clerk of Port Barron, in a moment of indignation and with his white cowlick a lit-

219

tle wild. Beyond these lay a stretch of vacant treetops, and then began the nests of the herring gulls, which he had seen before from the seaward side.

He climbed down into the gloom and the smell. "Wish I'd brought my camera — what a picture! No sign of the old birds. All off fishing somewhere, I suppose. Must keep 'em busy, Rena, all those greedy characters to feed, and all that waste between producer and consumer. Phew!"

"The old ones are probably drying themselves after fishing. You must have seen the shags doing that. They sit on rocks by the shore, with their wings opened and hanging down like a lot of old broken umbrellas. Shall we go?"

"Let's!"

When they got into the open again and cleansed their lungs with deep breaths of sea air, Pascoe chuckled, "I see what you meant now, about seeing it at ten years old. They look like those nightmare flying reptiles you used to see in school geographies, in the dawn-of-the-world chapter, only shrunk to the size of a small goose. You must have got a fright."

"I was petrified. My poor dad was so distressed. He was so interested in the birds that he climbed up as you did, and when he came down I was crouched at the foot of the tree, in that awful mess, with my hair pulled down over my face — scared stiff. I didn't go back again till I was sixteen or seventeen. Even then — even now it makes my skin crawl. The whole wood's like a witches' cave somehow, and when the shags poke those snaky heads down at you — ugh! Of course they can't help it, poor things. There are some things in nature that you just can't love."

As she said this her mind went instinctively to Sax, and she was silent all the way back to the cove. Outside the church she paused to take leave of her companion before turning into the home wood, and Pascoe said, "Oh, by the way, you haven't said anything about that stuff I wrote. Have you found the strength to read it — any of it?"

"I've read it all, Owen. Two or three times."

"Oh?" He puckered his forehead. "And you didn't chuck it in the stove?"

"No. Let's sit down here a minute."

Pascoe dropped his lean person onto the church step beside her. He grinned. "Frankly I don't think that stuff would even burn well."

"I do wish you'd be serious about it," she answered straitly. She drew in a deep breath and plunged. "The fact is, I think it's wonderful."

"What!"

"Well," she went on hastily, "the idea's wonderful to begin with. It's such a great story in itself. Everybody's read about Hudson's last voyage in school history, but nobody's ever taken the trouble to set forth the whole thing and make it interesting. You know, as if it were a tale. Owen, a really good book along those lines could make your fortune."

He grinned again. "Now I know you're kidding me. Anyway, who wants a fortune?"

"It could make you famous, then. I suppose you don't care about that either. What do you care about? Suppose I put it this way. If you did this thing properly thousands of people who never saw the North might be able to get the feeling of it. You know, the feel of a land made for giants, not just men, and cold and cruel and yet inspiring — that spirit you found up there yourself. And the beauty of it — because it must have some beauty, surely, or men wouldn't be so fascinated with it. Well, all that. And remember this. If you did write such a book, no matter what you did or didn't do after that, no matter what luck you had in life, there would always be that one fine thing you pulled

221

out of your mind and put down for the world to see. One thing that everyone found good."

"Phew! You scare me already. I can see the world peering at me from the treetops like a lot of hungry shags."

"Oh do stop talking nonsense," she said crossly. "I'm serious, Owen, and it's time you came down from the clouds if you're ever going to make anything of life. What I see in what you've written isn't just what's on the paper, it's what it could be if you went about it in the right way."

"And what way's that? For instance?"

"For instance you've got to write to England and find out everything you can about the ship *Discovery*, her sail plan and all that. You write about the working of the ship as if she were entirely fore-and-aft rigged, because you've sailed in schooners and that's that. But Hudson's ship must have carried square sails of some kind. Schooner rig wasn't invented then. Don't look so hopeless. I've sailed in square-riggers a good many times and I know how they're handled. So does old Sam. We can help you in a lot of this, once we get the facts."

"You seem really keen on it," Pascoe said in a bewildered voice.

"Of course I am. You — we — have got to study Purchas thoroughly, and anything else on Hudson and his times that we can get through the book dealers. Apart from anything else we've got to write the way they talked then, and we've got to know the world as they knew it back in sixteen-hundred-and-whatever-it-was. We've got to get good charts of Hudson Strait and the Bay, and maps of that region around James Bay and from there to the Saguenay — all that area you mention in your account. Oh, a hundred things we've got to know."

"But all this would take months!"

"Well, why not? Suppose it took years? To make an

honest job of it you should take years. Listen to me, Owen. You've got to set your mind on this book and keep it there. You've got to think about it all the time and work a bit on it every day, summer and winter, rain or shine. That's the only way you'll ever get it done. And you can do it. Because you've dreamed of the North ever since you were a boy, and because you've lived in it and been a part of it. You've seen and heard it. You've felt it. And you can't just waste all that."

One of the Port Barron boats had put in to the cove for fresh water. Pascoe watched a fisherman walk up to the spring with a brown jug.

"You make it sound quite possible," he said, as if that were a phenomenon. He turned and regarded her with interest. "Old Sam always said you were a chip off J.C.'s block, now I see what he meant. It's funny in a way. You knowing about square-riggers, I mean, and all that."

"What's funny about it?" Rena demanded. "Some of the best poetry ever written about the windjammers was written by a woman. Any sailor could tell you that."

"I know, but I've always pictured her as one of those females with whiskers on her chin. You, I can't imagine anyone more feminine than you."

"It's very good of you to say so. For my part I couldn't imagine C. Fox Smith with whiskers. But I'm not writing this book, you are. This is the story of Pascoe His Pilgrim and don't you forget it for a minute. I'm just going to help you any way I can. So long as I'm here I'll work with you every day. You'll just talk, and I'll try to see what's in your mind and put it down on the typewriter. We'll start tomorrow if you like."

"Before we get the books from England or wherever?"

"We can work on the chapters about his passage through Hudson Strait and into the Bay, because you

know that part best. We can fill in the Elizabethan talk
and nautical details later — and anyhow you've still got
your copy of Purchas. I saw it on your desk. You're not
going to sit about all summer waiting for books."

"How long will you be here?" he asked cautiously.
Rena regarded him.

"As long as you like," she said.

~ ~ Chapter 28

MACILRAITH heard the gossip first. In the small
fir-wainscoted office where he sat with a sensitive finger
on Port Barron's pulse he received all kinds of visitors and
heard all kinds of tales. He repeated this one to his wife at
lunch. She was a small energetic woman and she gave a
small energetic snort.

"That's ridiculous."

"Of course it is."

"I didn't even know Rena had been out there all this
time. Pamela merely said she'd gone away for a holiday.
How on earth did it start, do you suppose?"

MacIlraith broke a fresh roll and buttered it.

"Apparently from Jennie Torby."

"But she's such a nice old thing, and she worships
Rena. So does Sam. If you ask me I think the whole thing's
been cooked up here in town. Some woman who doesn't
like Pamela probably. Pam's never been popular here, you
know, the people have always considered her a snob."

"But everyone likes Rena," he objected.

"Nevertheless, a little malice goes a long way, Jim.
Maybe it's Nolan they're after. You know how they all
feel about him — and I'm with them there. There's

224

something about that man — ugh! I've never been able to understand what Rena saw in that busy little tyrant. Of course he was very smooth when he came here first, and he's still very nice to you and me and Pamela — and Rena, I hope. It's a bit odd when you stop to think of it, though — Rena going out there without saying a word to anybody and staying all this time. Never coming up to town, even to shop. And Pamela keeping so mum." She paused and looked at her husband with narrowed eyes. "And there's Nolan. Very busy, it's true, but you'd think he'd run out to the Head to see her sometimes if all was well between them. Do you suppose they've had a row? I bet that's what everybody thinks. I bet that's where this silly gossip got its start. I wonder if Pamela's heard. No use hinting to her of course, she'd just put on that Lady Vere de Vere look and shut up like a clam. This man Pascoe — what do you know about him?"

"I've only seen him a few times. He gets his pay checks by mail, and about once in four months he comes up to town and cashes one and deposits the rest. Nothing remarkable about him. Thin, blond, bit taller than average maybe. Dresses like a fisherman. Twenty-five or thirty. Speaks well. Rather shy. Moves about like a sleepwalker. One of those vacuous characters who might be anything from a secret boozer to a runaway divinity student. A misfit of some kind, that's sure. I can't see Rena going off her head about a chap like that."

He took up his fork and attacked the fried butterfish, a dish of which he was very fond. They were small and plump, and cooked like this they were delicious, but they were not a commercially important fish. The mackerel traps usually caught a few butterfish in the general haul and MacIlraith had a standing order at the wharf that brought him enough for a meal twice a week. After a time he noticed his wife's silence. She had not touched her food. She was staring across the table with a bright air of interest but he knew she was not seeing him at all.

"Jim, you're quite wrong."

"Eh? About what?"

"About Rena."

"What? You don't really think there could be anything between a fine healthy redhead like Rena and a washout of that type? Pooh."

"That's just it. Just the sort of man a girl like Rena might go absolutely mad about. Now don't put on that smug male look. A woman's passions aren't necessarily satisfied or even aroused by a tough human bull like R. Saxby Nolan, much as that may upset all the accepted male notions of the subject. If Nolan were as handsome as all the gods it mightn't make any difference. I don't know this Pascoe but I know my Rena. She's got a father complex."

"What the deuce is that?"

"Never mind. All I'm saying is that it could very well happen. Not that I believe that preposterous story of course."

MacIlraith smiled and helped himself to more butterfish.

"You mean you've begun to see a point in it. Kitty, there are times when the feminine imagination is just a bit shocking to the simple male. Before you turn yours loose altogether let me recite the facts as far as I was able to ferret 'em." He spoke in his precise banker tone, as if she were a client trying to borrow money on poor security; and Kitty put down her fork, rolling her eyes towards the ceiling and tapping her fingers on the table, Patience on the monument.

"It's typical of the way these small-town rumors start,"

226

he went on, articulating every word clearly, as if she were slightly deaf or not quite literate. "Rena apparently went out to the Head for the summer, a thing the Caradays used to do every year in J.C.'s time. Then she decided to stay the fall. After all, her husband's tearing up and down the seaboard on business and she might as well be there as here. What happens next? Jennie Torby comes up to town with Sam for a bit of shopping and a chat with her sister here, and in the course of conversation she drops some innocent remark about Rena and her friendship with the radio man. The sister's a good soul but her tongue's hung in the middle and wags at both ends, so the little remark passes on.

"A week or two later one of the Port Barron men rounding the Head close inshore happens to see Pascoe and Mrs. Nolan strolling along the bank, absorbed in conversation and Mrs. Nolan's hand tucked in Pascoe's arm. Just that, mark you, no more. A fortnight or so after that a government inspector making the rounds hires a Port Barron boat to take him out to the Head for the annual checkup on the foghorn and radio beacon. The boatman is young Medcalf, an unpleasant lout, the one who got the Barnett girl in trouble last year. They walk into the radio hut and find the operator and Mrs. Nolan sitting with their heads together over a map of some sort. Again just that, no more.

"Some time before or after that, one of the fishermen, that Carpon character, puts into the cove on a hot afternoon to get some drinking water at the spring. He happens to see Pascoe and Mrs. Nolan talking together on the steps of Caraday's old chapel. He goes back again on a warm day in September — to repair his engine, he says, but probably just snooping — and comes upon them swimming in the cove, Pascoe in trunks and Rena in one of

227

those one-piece things that all young women wear bathing nowadays. They were just laughing and splashing about and after a time they climbed out on one of the old boat slips and lay in the sun, watching that oaf tinkering with his engine.

"Now that's all, Kitty, that's absolutely all. The rest is moonshine brewed right here about the wharves and the bowling alley and the barber's shop and, I suppose, half the kitchens of Port Barron. This stuff about Pascoe and Rena living as man and wife, and bathing together in the raw and all the rest of that damned nonsense. Why, you ought to recognize it for exactly what it is, it's so hackneyed, the lot of it — it's just the sort of stuff they read in those cheap drugstore magazines and booklets that come out in the boat from Eglinton."

Kitty retained her musing air. "Some of it's original, though. That bit about Rena redding up the old church before she and Pascoe went through some sort of handfast rite there, eh? That doesn't sound like the barber's shop. In fact the more I think of it, the more it sounds like Rena."

MacIlraith put down his knife and fork with a rattle. "Now that," he retorted with some violence, "is just the way these damned things grow. Rena tidied up her grandfather's old chapel. Why? Some dark and sinful purpose surely. No young woman on a holiday would do such a chore for nothing. Can't you see the gossips working over that one? And finally some senile brain comes up with that old practice of handfast rites back in times when there wasn't a preacher to be had for marrying. Right away, that's the answer. It doesn't make sense — Rena happens to be married to someone else — but then nothing does in their whole nasty contraption."

"Hm. Well, at least it shows imagination. I like that bit. I think it's quite ingenious."

"You're as bad as all the rest."

Kitty arose to serve the coffee and dessert. With her hands busy on the sideboard she declared, "I'm nothing like the rest. They're just taking out their malice towards Pam and her son-in-law, and Rena happens to be the victim. I'm looking at it in quite another light altogether. Call it moonshine if you like. There may be nothing to it, but if there's any truth I don't blame Rena a bit. I think it's very courageous and rather beautiful."

For several moments he was speechless. Kitty served the plates and moved around to her place to pour the coffee, receiving his outraged look with the serenity of a wife married twenty years to a man she likes.

"Where's your sense of morality?" he burst out at last.

"Buried, darling, buried with your sense of humor. In death they were not divided."

ᔐ ᔐ Chapter 29

RENA heard the gossip from the lips of the person who had so innocently started it. On a day in September Jennie Torby returned from a trip to Port Barron and came running under the spruces like a frightened partridge. When the door opened Rena was at the stove preparing tea. She glanced up and saw the old woman in her worn mail-catalogue coat and hat, and looked back to the brown pot into which she was measuring spoons of tea.

"Welcome home! What's new in Port Barron?"

Silence. Rena looked up again, surprised. "Jennie, is anything the matter?" Poor Mrs. Torby put her hands over her face and burst into tears. She dropped into a chair and wept broken-heartedly, rocking back and forth. Alarmed, Rena went to her at once. "What is it, Jennie? Is it Sam? Something's happened to Sam! I'll get Owen."

She began a swift rush to the door but Jennie stayed her.

"It's you, Rena. You and Owen."

Rena came slowly back to her. She dropped on her knees beside the small doleful figure and put her head on its lap.

"All right, Jennie, tell me."

Jennie told her, in long incoherent phrases, each begun on a high note, coming down the scale in an increasing gabble and ending in a wail and another burst of tears. It took Rena some time to get it all. She said from time to time "What else?" and "There's more, I can tell," and "Go on, darling," and "Are you sure that's all?"

At first she was astonished and even a little amused at the minds that had contrived so much from so little, but as the tale unfolded she was bitterly angry. Not at Jennie. Poor Jennie's "All I said to my sister was . . ." absolved her. It was stupid to be angry of course. You might as well be angry at the rain that drenched you in a sudden summer shower. The Port Barron gossips didn't mean to be cruel any more than their boys who caught sculpins at the wharf ends and beat the soft bellies with sticks to make them bloat, and then tossed the bruised fish back into the tide, to float and struggle and eventually to die. They were simply bored and curious and they had no other sport.

With her head still in Jennie's lap she murmured, "It's all right, darling, don't cry. It's silly to cry. I'm not hurt.

230

I'm not even angry now — it's all so fantastic. Like one of those dreams you have when you're small, where you see yourself sliding down a banister rail and having fun, and suddenly it lands you right in the middle of the Sunday school, flannel nightshirt and all. And all the time it was just mince pie."

She felt Jennie's thin hand touching her hair. The old woman sniffed.

"Your ma," she said solemnly, "will she think it's just mince pie? And your husband, Rena. What about him?"

Rena lifted her head and stared at the table, where the supper things were spread. Suddenly the thought of food was nauseous. On the stove the kettle steamed insistently. She arose and set the thing aside. Looking down at the stove, she said slowly, "Jennie, I may as well tell you. What Mama thinks is a matter of indifference to me — I'm not a child any more. As for my husband, I don't love him, I never did. I came out here because I was sick of marriage, because I couldn't stand it any longer and I had to go somewhere and be by myself. Whether my husband understands that or not, I don't know. Surely he must. In any case he knows I'm not at all likely to put myself into the arms of a man again. In fact he told me as much. I won't tell you what he said. The point was that as a woman I'm absolutely lacking in — in what it takes to indulge in the sort of thing they're talking about in Port Barron. That makes me perfectly safe."

She moved towards Jennie briskly. "That's all over your head, you poor good darling, of course, so don't give it a thought. You go on home and get supper for your Sam, he must be famished. And don't say anything about that silly tale to him or Owen. Not that they'd understand a word anyway."

Jennie arose, fumbling for a handkerchief. She stood

very small and erect and she blew her nose as if it were a trumpet before judgment. "Rena," she snapped, "you're a nice girl, always was, but I don't know what to make of you. If I was you, knowing what they're saying about me, I'd be in a tantrum the finest kind. But you — you don't even cry. You stand there cool and calm as a dipper o' spring water and tell me it don't signify." She was so outraged that Rena had to smile, and the smile brought another blast.

"My head's set a lot higher'n you seem to think, Rena. I ain't much surprised about you and your husband — never liked the man. What surprises me is what you say about yourself. If you really believe that, Rena, you're about as safe as a child with a box of matches — and so is Owen Pascoe."

The door slammed.

ᔑ ᔑ *Chapter* 30

Pamela heard the tale from Bertha Kendrick. She was probably the last to hear it of all the people in Port Barron. The cook-maid was a block of a woman with square shoulders, a bosom, thick legs and large splayed feet. Sax had once remarked that she looked like a bosun treading a deck in a bad cross sea, a simile unspoiled by the bushy brows and the black hair drawn back and tightly bunned. However, she was a good cook and a strong though somewhat sulky maker of beds and wielder of brooms. Her former experience in a well-to-do merchant's house in Eglinton, in a domestic staff of four, convinced her that under Pamela's cool authority she was doing at least two jobs for the wage of one; and when

Captain Nolan cut that wage still lower in his general raz-
ing of last spring she had said nothing but she was enraged.

On her Sundays off she went to morning service in Port
Barron and spent the rest of the day and evening chatting
with her friends and relatives in town. They were glad to
see her, not least because she always had a budget of
small news about the inmates of Caraday House, concerning whom Port Barron had an abiding curiosity; and
in turn she was stocked with all that had happened in the
town during the week. This she carried to her mistress,
who was just as curious about the little world a mile
away, especially its more interesting level, the fishwife
level, of which her friends the MacIlraiths and Doctor
Bannister so seldom spoke. This exchange gave Bertha
a certain importance at both ends and she enjoyed it
thoroughly in her dark unsmiling way.

The whispers about the guilty lovers at the Head gave
her a peculiar satisfaction and she nursed the tale for
months before revealing it to her mistress. Her reasons for
this were deep and involved and they included her
hatred of Captain Nolan and a very great fear of him as
well. She did not like the way he prowled about the
house, or the way he looked and spoke to her — "Like I
was dirt under his boots." She was always glad when he
went away, and glum whenever he made one of his jack-
in-the-box reappearances. When he departed in the autumn for a long business trip to the States and the West
Indies she was delighted, and when the trip extended
through the winter months she felt, as she told her
friends, that every day was Christmas.

Several times she was tempted to tell that juicy tale for
the pleasure of watching her mistress's face as it unfolded
and of hearing what she had to say. Each time she put it

away, as a child might put away a nice red apple, to save the flavor a little longer. When, therefore, Mrs. Caraday told her one day in March that Captain Nolan was on his way home, she saw a crisis. The man was bound to find out about Rena now, the scandal was everywhere, and there would be a tremendous row. She looked forward to that with excitement. Just what the results would be she could not guess. But one thing was sure, she must have the pleasure of telling Mrs. Caraday now, before the explosion.

She made the most of it. This was not a tale to be poured out in twenty minutes over the breakfast cups. She first dropped a hint, no more. Pamela saw at once that something of great importance was astir. She liked to pretend an indifference to Port Barron gossip even when she was avid for Bertha's slightest word. It salved a guilty feeling that backstairs chatter with a servant was not the sort of thing a gentlewoman went in for. The cruel creature in the kitchen made her put aside this haughty pretense and beg for what she had to tell; and Bertha spun it out, a thread at a time, adding to that web of ribald inventions a shrewd thread or two of her own, so that it was not until a cold evening shortly before Nolan was due to arrive in Port Barron that Pamela heard the final touch.

She heard it in the dining room, where she sat at her solitary meal. Bertha in cap and apron loomed between table and sideboard like a slowly perambulating oracle, speaking in her deep hoarse voice and yielding every phrase with the false reluctance of the gossip triumphant. Pamela pushed away her plate and stared long and hard at a still life of pheasants, rabbits and fruit that hung over the silver display at the end of the room.

"And is that all?" she asked with frosty dignity.

234

"That's every last word, ma'am. I wouldn't have said anything only you was bound to have it out of me."

"And do you believe it, any of it?"

Bertha put on her sullen look. "I don't want to believe it, any more than you."

"Can't you see the whole thing's false?"

"The whole town says it's true. There's even witnesses."

"Then they lie!" Pamela cried. She arose, pushing back her chair. "I shan't want anything to eat tonight." She passed a trembling hand over her brow and moved towards the door. Her usually firm step faltered and she caught at the table edge for support. For a moment Bertha thought her mistress was about to faint. But Mrs. Caraday drew herself together and walked firmly out of the room.

Pamela spent most of the night sitting in a chair in her bedroom, the chamber that had been Rena's until her marriage. With a shawl about her shoulders she stared out of the dark room upon the sea. The day had been zero-cold and now a faint haze lay on the water, not enough to obscure the horizon, which was clearly marked between the dark mass of the sea and the somewhat lighter mass of the sky, but enough to give the white shore of the cape a ghostly look. Out of this haze the moon appeared, almost full, rising over the cape like a luminous tangerine with a small slice gone from one side. The moonshine on the water had an orange tint as well, and the waves gave it a mysterious life, a series of shimmering movements that ended each in a low long wall rising blackly just before the shore and falling in orange froth among the rocks.

On nights like this old J.C. had loved to sit well muffled on his captain's walk with the big telescope mounted on its tripod, staring at the moon. A good thing he wasn't here now! What a storm the fanatical old puritan would have raised over this affair at his precious Gannet Head! Pamela went over the story again and again in a kind of sick storm herself. For all the disdain she had shown to that malicious woman below, she felt the tale to be true. Not all, of course. She could see how it must have grown in the winter's telling about Port Barron. That bathing episode, for example — bah! A daughter of mine, the granddaughter of J.C. and my-father-Captain-Charnsworth, behaving like a silly tart with some hobbledehoy picked up at the seashore — absurd! But one thing's sure. Rena's having an affair with a man. Deliberately. Out of spite for Saxby.

How utterly selfish of the girl, how inconsiderate — and how immoral! Not the slightest regard for appearances. Witnesses, actually witnesses! Was the girl daft? As the night went on and the moon rode up the sky towards Fundy there were times when she trembled with rage, times when she dropped on the bed and wept wretchedly, times when she arose and marched the carpet thinking feverishly of the outcome of all this. It occurred to her that no one in Port Barron liked Saxby well enough to tell him of his wife's misdemeanors or even tell him where she was; for they all suspected the quarrel now. And probably nobody hated him bitterly enough to risk a beating by flinging the tale in his face. There was a pale comfort in that. But you couldn't count on it. There were too many other ways — anonymous notes in the postbox, a calculated whisper here or there — oh yes indeed. He was bound to learn. Bound to! Bound to! And now he was on his way home — due in another day or two according to his wire to Bostwick. Such a little time!

On the following morning Bostwick looked up to see Mrs. Caraday coming into the office a few minutes after he had opened it for the day. She was dressed in a thick tweed costume and fur coat; she had a pair of Rena's warm snow boots on her feet and a woolen scarf bound about her head. She looked as if she were going for a sleigh ride, and he was astounded when she informed him she was going out to Gannet Head and he must order the firm's motorboat to take her there at once. Mrs. Caraday's well-known aversion to the Head was equaled only by her aversion to small boats in choppy weather. But he murmured obediently and trundled his old bulk down to the wharf to make the arrangements.

When Mrs. Caraday stepped carefully into the boat from the slippery wharf ladder Bostwick quavered down to her a warning, "Pretty thick outside I'm afraid, ma'am. One o' these ice mists. I hear the horn." But she was not to be discouraged.

"The sun," she remarked with something of J.C.'s manner, "will burn that all off the Head by noon. In any case the boatman can steer by the foghorn, Bostwick." The sea had an uncomfortable lop kicked up by a wind against the ebb tide. Within ten minutes Pamela was lying on a cushioned locker in the cabin, dismally sick. A little later the boat ran into freezing fog, which penetrated every crevice of the cabin and every fiber of her clothing. The inner chill that comes with seasickness added itself to the clammy cold of this vapor from the Banks. Pamela's teeth were rattling when at last the boat nosed into the cove and the boatman helped her ashore.

With an effort she forced herself into a semblance of the imperious Mrs. Caraday. "I shall probably stay until late afternoon, Martin, but I may return sooner. You had better stay by the boat. If you get hungry run over to the Torby house and Jennie will give you something to eat."

237

It was more than twenty years since last she had set her small fastidious feet on the rough lane that ran between the fishermen's cottages and the shore of the cove, and although all were deserted and the slips had lost their last smell of fish offal, she felt her old loathing of the place as if it were yesterday. When the church loomed out of the mist she noted that the snow had been shoveled away from the door. She opened it and peered in curiously. Everything clean. Everything in order. Even a set of numbers in the hymn racks. A bunch of withered goldenrod in a jar on the preacher's desk. Her breath hung in visible wisps before her face and she could almost see John Caraday standing there, with one great fist on the Bible and the other smiting the air in the course of one of his denunciatory sermons. She threw a musing glance at the Caraday pew and saw herself sitting primly there again with Roger, and taking Communion on those occasions in the early motorboat era when the parson came out from Port Barron. But what she saw chiefly was the bunch of goldenrod, obviously gathered and placed there last August or September, when the stuff bloomed all about the Head. She thought contemptuously, They might as well have chalked the date on the wall.

She closed the door and walked up the narrow, hard-beaten snow path under the trees towards the cottage. She had never seen it in winter but there it was, familiar enough, and she knocked on the familiar door. No answer. She opened it carefully and called, "Rena! Rena darling, are you there?" Rena did not seem to be there. She was tempted to go upstairs and peep into the bedrooms, but after some hesitation and a cautious look about the kitchen she went outside and took the path towards the point. The mist seemed thicker there, and at regular intervals the foghorn stunned her ears with a long blast, ending in that animal grunt which the fishermen swore they could hear farther than the tone.

She avoided the Torby house and followed the shoveled path towards the radio hut, where she could hear the purring exhaust of a gasoline engine, very different from the staccato chug of Torby's machine. But suppose Rena wasn't there either? Well, then she would introduce herself to Rena's lover and chat in an impersonal way, but with a few adroit questions, to see what she could make of him. She was curious to inspect the man for whom her daughter had thrown her cap over the moon. She could hear the sea thrashing on the icy rocks nearby, and now the small gray building swam out of the fog. A window was open and she paused beside it, hearing Rena's clear voice within.

"Well, go on," she was saying animatedly. "The look of the shore and the ice — you can't just say 'The sun went down' and let it go at that. You've got to give the reader some sort of picture, otherwise these men of yours are just moving about in a vacuum. Come on, darling, shut your eyes and tell me what you see, so I can put it down."

Silence, and then a man's voice saying slowly, "Well, there are cliffs quite close by. They're a dark gray really but they look black in that light. They go up pretty sheer. Full of deep crevices and folds. The evening light touches all the bold parts but there's shadow in the seams. A few birds fluttering about the face of 'em, white you know — gulls and swans — but they look sort of pink in the sunset. You know, as if someone was chucking pink flower petals down from the cliff top somewhere — don't put that down."

There was an expert rattling of a typewriter, and Rena said, "Oh yes I will. That's what I want. Go on. What about the sea — the water of the Strait?"

"That's black where you see it in the shadow of the headlands, but just on the edge of the light it's sort of lead-colored, and outside that it's all pink."

"What sort of pink?"

"Well, it's like a sheet of pink silk that's got wet and crinkled, if you know what I mean. Only in this case the wrinkles are moving, they're alive. Just in ripples, mind. There's still a lot of drift ice about and that keeps the sea down."

"You mean icebergs? The kind in that painting — there's a copy of it in one of the books — that painting of old Hudson adrift in the boat with the boy and the others?"

"Pooh no. That artist was adrift in his own palette. You don't get that kind of ice in that part of the Bay. Not those tremendous bergs. It's all floe ice out of James Bay and some from around Churchill probably, because the winds at that time of year are mostly westerly."

"All right. Go on. You're still up in the Strait and you're looking at the ice."

"Well, there are patches of open water between the floes, what we call leads, and near at hand they take up about as much space as the ice. But as you lift your eyes towards the west, the floes seem closer together — that's perspective, of course — and in the distance they look like a solid sheet."

"Don't forget the sunset."

"Ah! Well, that makes a pretty fine show. Few strips of black cloud in the west and the sun glowing red between 'em — like a coal fire in a grate. Huge red splash over that part of the sky of course. Among the old floes you can see patches of new ice, thin stuff, frozen the night before — it's still quite sharp at night. The light's different on the new ice and the old. For a time everything's pink. Then the

240

new ice turns a kind of green, very pale and delicate, and you can see the sky to the north and along the south showing that same green. But the old floes go from pink to a sort of violet, and then they go red, red as blood, till the flare goes out of the sky. The new ice doesn't do that. It goes from that pale green to a sort of gold — no, bronze — it's like old bronze that you've rubbed a bit with a cloth — that dull shine. The moment the sun dips, all the colors begin to darken, because of course the night's shoving up the sky then from the east. Finally the night's over everything. There are stars of course; and up over the cliffs you see the first flicker of the northern lights sort of warming up for the main show later on. And the water's black and the land's black and the ice floes just make a sort of pale shadow on the sea."

He paused while the typewriter clattered, and then chuckled. "Frankly, Rena, I think you're on a wrong tack, taking down all this stuff. I mean, old Hudson wouldn't care a hoot about the sky or the sunset or anything else of that kind. All he wanted to see was the face of a Chinaman, down over the skyline somewhere towards the sou'west. And Pricket and the rest of 'em, those tough English seamen, they wouldn't see birds as pink flowers, not by a long shot. After eating salt junk all the way from the Thames river they'd just be drooling for a mouthful of roast fowl."

∽ ∽ Chapter 31

PAMELA pushed open the door boldly and saw Rena sitting at a desk before a small typewriter and surrounded by electrical apparatus. At the moment she was resting her head against the lean young man sitting beside her. His hair was a bleached yellow and it appeared to have been clipped lately by an unskilled hand. He seemed oblivious of Rena's bronze head at his shoulder. He was staring at the black radio panel before him as if he could still see there the pink birds and ice he had been talking about.

"Hello!" Pamela cried with a cordiality she did not feel. They sprang up together as if someone had thrown a bomb into the room. Pamela stepped inside and put out a hand to the man. "I'm Rena's mother," she explained brightly, "and I've just run out to see how she's getting along in this lonely, lonely place." He took the hand politely for a moment and dropped it without a word.

"You must be Mr. Pascoe," she pursued, fixing him with a pale blue stare.

Rena spoke sharply. "Mama, what on earth are you doing here?"

Pamela turned the stare to her daughter, a pair of blue signal lamps that said in a code invisible to Pascoe, You know very well what I've come for, Rena darling, so do let's get away from this young man and discuss it. Openly she murmured, "I must admit I didn't pick a very good day for it. The sea was a bit — you know — and it upset me rather, but I'm sure I'd feel better for a good cup of tea." And flicking her attention back to Pascoe, "Do you mind?"

The man shook his head like the clod he undoubtedly was. He seemed dazed, as if the recall from arctic sunsets had left his mind somewhere in mid-air. Pamela examined him ironically. Stupid. Not even good-looking. Whatever was Rena thinking about to compromise herself with such a creature? Not even the saving grace of manners, dropping her hand as if it were a wet fish, and star-

242

ing over her shoulder in that dull, dull way. Not a word to say for himself. Like — like Roger Caraday in one of his more irritating moments. Rena glanced from one to the other, and then to the desk and the sheet of paper in the typewriter. At last she said with evident reluctance, "I'm afraid that's all for today, Owen. We'll take it up again tomorrow." And to Pamela — with a flash of dark eyes that said, All right let's get it over with — she declared aloud, "A cup of tea you shall have, dear, and some of my own biscuits. Come!"

She drew on a parka swiftly and led the way back along the snow path to the house in the wood. The mist was still thick, the horn still brayed. Inside, Pamela took off her scarf and loosened her coat while Rena put wood on the sunken coals of her morning fire. A peculiar silence was upon them. Like Pascoe's twin radio machines, their minds were tuned to a single wave, each vibrating a message that said in effect Here I Am Beware. With a blaze of driftwood snapping under the kettle, Rena moved between cupboard and table, setting out the tea things. Pamela watched her face relentlessly. At last she said, "I suppose you know what I really came for?"

"I think so, yes."

"Then you've heard the scandal they're talking in Port Barron?"

"Oh yes."

Pamela swallowed hard. "And are you really as indifferent as you seem, Rena?" Rena paused by the cupboard with one hand on a shelf. "Of course I am. You know very well that sooner or later somebody will appear in church a bit the worse for drink, or the postmaster will change his politics or beat his wife, and right away everybody will forget me and rattle off on another track." She gave her mother a whimsical glance. "Do you mean to say you've

243

come away out here on a winter day to worry me about anything as frivolous as that?"

Pamela felt a glow at the heart. It was anger and its warmth was comforting. It drove away the last qualms of seasickness and it braced her for the duel that she had longed for ever since she heard Bertha Kendrick's tale.

"You admit it, then. I thought as much."

"I admit nothing, Mama, whatever you may think."

"Then just what are your relations with this man?"

"For one thing, as you saw, I'm helping him to write a book."

Pamela laughed, a small dry chuckle, an unpleasant sound. "A book! Surely you don't expect me to believe you've spent all this time with a man in this lonely place merely discussing nouns and adjectives? Come, Rena, do give me credit for a little brains and at least some knowledge of the world. A young man with time on his hands and a married woman bored with her husband? — oh no, dear, the book won't do. I shouldn't insist on that if I were you. I can imagine only too well what the humorists of Port Barron would do with that — from title to illustrations."

Rena said disdainfully, "You seem terribly concerned with what Port Barron thinks. I'm not." They surveyed each other in open hostility. After a minute Pamela said, "Rena, I want you to think of Saxby for a moment. Please! Possibly he failed to live up to your romantic notions of a husband. No doubt his ways were crude at times. After all, he'd spent the best part of his life at sea before he came here and met you. You couldn't expect too much polish or finesse about a man like that. Remember your own grandfather Caraday was such a man and everyone respected him — no one more than I, who came

244

from a cultured home. There are more important things in life than polish and romance, Rena. There's generosity, for example. And there's love. Whatever else Saxby may have been to you, he was always generous and he wanted nothing but your love. You must know that. If only you could have seen him, as I saw him, the day he found you'd gone!"

"I can imagine," Rena said. "Like a greedy imp robbed of a toy."

"Oh come!"

"That's all our marriage was. An imp and his plaything. His doll that could never dance quite the way he liked. And I couldn't stand it any more. That's why I put an end to it."

"Nonsense, Rena. You can't throw off your marriage as easily as that."

"I have!" Rena said vehemently. "There wasn't anything legal or holy about a thing that tied me to a creature like Sax. At best the marriage was degrading and at worst it was impossible. So I ran away from it. I scrubbed myself clean of it. I declared myself free."

"Oh?" Pamela murmured. "Precisely how does one do that?"

Rena shrugged. "It's something you do in your mind. It came to me when I got here. You wouldn't understand — you always hated this place. But from the time I was a child I've always felt more at peace here than anywhere else. When I made up my mind to leave Sax I thought at once of the old house here in the wood. So I came out in Sam Torby's boat and told him not to mention it to anyone. After I'd been here a month I began to feel myself again. It was wonderful after that nightmare with Sax. And I thought it could go on. I felt secure, somehow. I had the money I'd saved out of my salary, I didn't need much, and Sam bought groceries for me whenever he went up to town. Then something happened that I hadn't foreseen. I found a friend in Owen Pascoe."

"Who made the most of his opportunity!"

"Who was a dreamer and decent, the way dreamers are — the way Dad was, as you should know. For a long time we didn't realize what was happening to us, though I knew first. It was long before he knew. We were together a lot. We didn't do those stupid things they're talking about in Port Barron but we were good companions and we worked together on his book."

"Ha! From what I overheard I should say it was your book, not his. I doubt if the man could even write a post-card. But never mind that. You suggest that something happened. What did happen, eventually?"

Rena tipped her head back. Her eyes were warm. "Eventually we were lovers. It came about very naturally and it's been sweet and wonderful, not like that filthy gossip in the town — and nothing at all like my marriage with Sax."

Pamela cried indignantly, "You seem — you seem actually proud of it!"

"I am."

"I should have thought," her mother said coldly, "this — this decent man of yours would have had at least the decency to ask Saxby to divorce you before things went so far. But I dare say on that score he had no more courage than morals. He was satisfied to take you on the sly, as if you were any common slut of a fish-girl he might have picked up in Port Barron."

"That's not true! I had to beg him not to go up to Port Barron and have it out with Sax. I knew what that would mean."

"Ah! And so you eased his conscience by inducing him

246

to go through some ridiculous ceremony in the old chapel at the cove. That much of the gossip's true, isn't it?"

"That much, yes. But not quite in the way you think. I'd heard the gossip of course. It started from poor Jennie's prattle and she'd mentioned me cleaning the old church. But it was the gossip that put the idea in my head. I remembered Dad talking about the handfast rite in old colonial times and it had always seemed to me very simple and beautiful — the way a marriage ought to be. So we all went together to the church. I asked Sam and Jennie to be the witnesses. I stood with Owen before the little table where the Bible is. We recited the Lord's Prayer together . . ."

"Including 'forgive us our trespasses,' I hope?"

"Yes, and 'deliver us from evil.' Please don't be so cynical. I tell you we were absolutely sincere and our hearts were at peace. I felt as I never felt for a moment during that travesty in the drawing room with Sax."

"Well, what then?"

"After that I took Owen's hand in mine and declared myself his true wife in the sight of God."

A silence. And then Pamela cried in a high thin voice, "And you actually think that silly bit of make-believe made everything all right? In this day and age? You could impose on those ignorant Torbys because they knew no better, because they had some tradition of handfasting in lonely parts like this, because no doubt they and half Port Barron are descended from such marriages back in times when there was no other way. And of course that dreamer of yours was quite willing to believe the moon was made of cheese. But you? Oh come now, you're much too intelligent to deceive yourself with anything as preposterous as that. As a child, of course you used to play alone a good deal and you were always up to some mummery or other — it used to amuse your father and me to see how earnestly you went about it. But you're anything but a child now, Rena. You know the difference between fact and fancy and you know right from wrong. In the eyes of God indeed! In the eyes of God it was a frightful piece of sacrilege. And in your grandfather's chapel, too. Poor old man, he's dead, but whatever would he think?"

"Stop it!" Rena turned her back and tucked her hands into the parka sleeves as if her mother were a cold wind of some kind. "I won't hear any more."

The fire snapped in the stove. Outside the foghorn boomed. The house was so still that a fall of soot in the chimney had the sound of a great flutter of wings, as if the swallows had come back. Pamela sat rigidly in the chair, regarding her daughter's back. When she spoke again it was in another tone, the tone of one woman of the world to another who has been caught in an indiscretion.

"Rena, I came out here in this bitter weather hoping to appeal to your natural good sense. I thought you were having a little affair out of pique with your husband, nothing more. That I could understand. Please remember that I've been your age and married, and piqued very often too. I've never mentioned this of course, it's not the sort of thing one talks about, but since we're speaking candidly as woman to woman I don't mind telling you that several times in those Jamaican winters when you were small and Roger was wrapped up in his stupid drawings and moths and butterflies I had little love affairs myself. That surprises you, doesn't it? But don't look round at me like that. What right have you to be shocked? At least my lovers were gentlemen. They belonged to the army and I never saw them again. I didn't even want to.

248

That's the difference between you and me. You've let yourself get infatuated with this man and now you don't care a fig about your own good name, or mine, or for anything you've been taught about what's done and isn't done in our kind of life. So I must appeal to the one thing you do recognize. Your love — I'll call it that — your love for that dull creature in the radio hut."

She bent forward with her normal putty complexion gone scarlet. The refained voice was harsh. "Rena, you fool! Saxby's been away ever since the autumn but he's on his way home now. I shan't tell him anything, you may be sure, but the gossip in Port Barron's not a whisper any more. The whole town's talking about you and this man. The story's being yelled in the streets, with a whole winter's imagination in the details, absolutely disgusting. Saxby can't fail to hear something, and he'll have the rest if he has to choke it out of someone with his hands — you know that very well. And you know very well what will happen next. He'll come out here like a — like a tiger. I'm not afraid for you, of course. Whatever else he does he won't hurt you, he loves you far too much. And don't make a hard mouth at that. He does. The man's daft about you, now more than ever. I tell you I've had him groveling at my feet, weeping, begging me to get you back — that tough creature who has everybody about the wharves jumping when he speaks. Oh no, Rena, it won't be you. It's your precious Pascoe who will have to pay the piper for this little dance. I shouldn't like to be your lover then. I can only hope Saxby will stop short of killing him, poor clown. Do you think I'm saying this just to frighten you? If you give yourself one minute's thought free of this vulgar passion of yours, you'll see that it's just as certain as tomorrow's tide. And that's why I came. That's why I'm here. To try and save this indecent farce from becoming something frightful and tragic to us all. To us all, you hear?"

She stopped, gasping, exhausted by her own violence. Rena had moved over to the window. She leaned against the frame, gazing at the cold vapor eddying in slow wisps in the pit of the trees. The sound of Pascoe's engines came faintly, dulled by the mist and the snow-laden trees, and drowned at exact periods by the blare of Sam's faithful horn. But what she seemed to hear and see was Sax. Sax in one of his bestial rages. The rest was nightmare. In the silence of the room she could hear her mother's bronchial gasps subsiding gradually in the chair beside the stove. At last Pamela began again, and now it was the old matter-of-fact voice, brisk, assured, even a little amused.

"You may as well face it, Rena. You must have known all along that this idyl of yours would come to an end the day Saxby found out where you were and what was going on. Well, here it is, or the next thing to it. And now for this man's sake — if not your own — you've got to give him up. You've got to put aside all this nonsense and come back with me now, today, and be a sensible wife to your husband again. Then all this nasty scandal's lost the ground it started from, and if Saxby hears a word of it you can induce him to laugh it off, if you're any woman at all. Good heavens, don't look so tragic and put-upon. No woman outside of a play ever died of a hopeless love affair, my dear — we're much more durable than that. Sooner or later your wonderful Pascoe will find another fatuous creature — his kind always attract them — and you'll be quite forgotten. As for you, Rena, you've got a lot of life to live yet, and a position to maintain and a husband who can give you all the love you need. Come, be sensible. You see all this as well as I do. Come back with me and take up your life with Saxby as if nothing had ever happened. He's learned his lesson. You'll find him quite understanding now. After a time you'll be able to look back on this little affair as a prank that lasted just long enough and came to an end before it became a bore. And thank your stars you came so well out of it."

Pamela arose with energy. She had said all the things she had wanted to say, all the arguments, the denunciations and persuasions that had occurred to her in the anxious hours of the night, and she felt that she had said them very well. She glanced about her now as a general might glance about a camp before giving the order to strike tents.

"Now what have you got to pack?"

⁓ ⁓ Chapter 32

CAPTAIN Nolan arose from the thwart of the mail boat from Eglinton, cramped from long sitting in the cold, for characteristically he had refused the stuffy comfort of the cabin. He swarmed up the icy ladder of the wharf, grasping the iron rungs and swinging himself from one to another with quick powerful movements of his long arms. In the office he found Bostwick pecking at a typewriter. The old man arose in his elephantine way.

"Good day, sir. Nice to see you back after all this time. You look well, sir. Easy to see you've been where the sun goes in the wintertime. Come a bit sooner'n we expected. Your wire said Sat'day."

"I got a better train connection."

"How did you make out, sir? Well, I hope?"

Sax unbuttoned his overcoat and threw his fur cap on the desk. He dropped into a chair and scowled at a calendar on the farther wall.

"I didn't make out. Anywhere. For almost three months I trapesed up and down the eastern states trying to drum up business in fish and lumber. And there was nothing doing. Might as well have tried to drum up George Washington's army. Business in the States is as dead as that."

"Even for barreled mackerel, sir? You can usually sell . . ."

"Not so much as a pickled herring. The American tariff makes it tough to compete with their own fish people at the best of times, and now the market's flat. So's the timber market. Nobody over there's building anything bigger than a doghouse. At last I went on down to Florida to try my hand at bill collecting — you know, on that lumber we shipped there in the *Pamela* last year. The consignees have been stalling right along and for the past six months they haven't even answered letters, as you know. Well, I might have guessed what the answer was. The consignees have gone bust along with most of their customers. This depression over there's really getting to be something. D'you know where most of that good spruce and pine lumber is, the stuff we bought on credit from the sawmills at Eglinton? It's part of a bloody big hotel standing half-built in a palmetto swamp along the shore — some promoter's dream that didn't click. We took on all that debt in Eglinton just to build a fancy roost for birds in Florida."

He chuckled, a dreary metallic sound like the rattle of chain links in a hawse.

"I hung about Tampa for a time, talking to lawyers and collection sharks, but they didn't give me a hope. So I shoved off for the West Indies. I steered clear of one or two places that I'd known before and didn't like, but I went to Cuba and from there to Jamaica, and then to Haiti, Porto Rico, Trinidad, God knows where I didn't go — even Demerara, and that's the last place God made. Finally I thought of the old salt-fish trade to Brazil and I took a boat for Rio. It was the same story everywhere I went — no business. Oh, there were lots of people ready to take all the fish and lumber I should ship, you understand, but when I went to the banks and popped the question I found they were all bad risks. Well, we've had a bellyful of those. So I caught a boat for New York and came on home. There's only one thing to say for the whole bloody trip. It's a nice warm way to spend a winter if you've got the money and the time."

He poked a finger moodily at a pile of letters opened and spread on his desk.

"What's new up here?"

"Nothing very good, sir, I'm afraid. I had to stop buyin' fish. The warehouse is chock full of salt fish now, sir, stuff we picked up from merchants around the coast. Had to refuse their drafts, o' course. Now they're threatenin' to collect through the courts. So's the sawmill people up to Eglinton."

"No doubt. What's wrong with the *Roger?* I see she's laid up in the harbor."

"Engine trouble, sir. She's laid up, waitin' parts, and the diesel people want cash down. Anyhow she lost money all summer and fall, sir, so I paid off the crew and let 'em go."

"What about the steamer? She's making money anyhow."

"When it comes to the steamer, sir, she made some money durin' the pulpwood season, yes. She's been takin' loads that shoved her marks clean out o' sight, just like

253

you told Eckles to do. She's back in the coal trade now, unloadin' a cargo o' furnace slack at St. John, New Brunswick. She ain't in very good shape, I'm sorry to say. That pulpwood trade's a killer, sir, for ships. All that layin' in mud berths up Fundy with the tide clean out o' sight, and the heavy deckloads and so on. Strained her frames and started several bottom plates. Dahl has to keep his bilge pumps goin' the whole time. Cap'n Eckles says she's got to have a dry-dock job and a proper refit up to Hal'fax afore another pulpwood season starts. She ain't had a refit, not a proper one, since you bought her, sir."

"Ah, tell me something I don't know."

Bostwick coughed and examined a scrap of note paper on his desk. "There's one or two messages for you, sir. Mr. MacIlraith wants to see you, soon as you get back. Urgent, he says."

"That's what he always says. What else?"

"There's — um — let's see, there's a man stayin' at the hotel, wants to see you social-like, he says. Name of Halkett."

"Don't know the man — wait a minute." Sax gave the old man a sudden stare.

"Did he call here?"

"Yes sir."

"Tall man, oldish, with gray eyes and a face like a horse?"

"Yes sir."

"Drawls when he talks?"

"That's the man, sir. Is anything the matter, sir?"

Sax withdrew the stare. He licked his lips. "Why?"

"You look a bit queer, sir."

Sax arose and with great care straightened the heap of papers on his desk.

"Indigestion. How long's this man been staying there?"

254

"About a week, sir. Said he could wait. Minds the cold. Don't stir out much."

"I see."

Halkett was sitting close to the stove in the hotel parlor, with a pair of cheap spectacles perched far down his long nose, and reading, of all things, last week's copy of the Eglinton *Weekly Chronicle*. The familiar gaunt face had the purple-mottled look that comes of years in the tropics and then a quick trip north at the frosty time of year. A thin cigar was fastened in his teeth.

"Hello," Sax said, without cheer. But Halkett had cheer enough for two. He cast the paper to the floor and sprang up shouting, throwing out a hand, switching the cigar to the far corner of his smile with expert movements of tongue and teeth.

"Sax! Sax, you old son of a gun. Togged out in a fur hat and coat like a bloomin' millionaire! Put it there!"

They shook hands, and again the warmth was Halkett's.

"What are you doing here?" Sax said, with a careful glance at the hotel maid sweeping the floor.

"Just on a trip," Halkett said blandly. "Got a bit tired o' that everlastin' sunshine and come north for another look at snow. And seein' I was up here in good old Nova Scotia, why, I said to myself I'll just run over to Port Barron for a gam with my old friend Sax. And here I am and there you are. Been on a trip yourself I hear. Bless my soul it's good to see you again after all this time."

Sax put his hands in his coat pockets. "We can't have a proper gam here. Let's go to my place, eh? It isn't far."

"Why now that's nice of you, Sax, and just like you, too. But they tell me your place is a mile outside the town and lonely-like, and all that snow. I ain't so young as I used to be, Sax, and I find I mind the cold. Let's you and me go up to my room where we can gam away chummy-like and nice and warm. It's just up the stair and nigh enough to the management that a shout'll get us anything we want. Take off your coat and leave it in the hall. Here, let me hang it for you. There. Now step this way and foller me." It proved to be Sax's old room, one of the pair available to transients, a comfortless chamber with a rag of carpet, a hard bed, a washstand and a battered chest of drawers. Sax thought of his nights here, when he first returned from the Caribbean, turning restlessly in the bed and hearing all night long the mysterious creaks and shuffles of the elderly folk who were the hotel's chief guests and who seemed never to sleep.

Halkett waved him to the only chair and sat himself on the bed, fumbling underneath. He produced a bottle of rum, gave Sax a nod and sucked down a long dram. "Ah! That's better. You don't know what you're missin', Sax, up here in this blasted cold and you not a drinkin' man. It's bottled sunshine, that's what it is, right off o' the Jamaica sugar fields."

"Okay," Sax said. "Now let's have it. How did you know I was here? And after that you can tell me what you really came for."

Halkett smacked his lips and put the bottle on the floor. "Same old Sax. Always to the point and no dam' beatin' up the wind. Well, it's quite a story, Sax, and again a pity you don't drink, for with a good swaller under that fancy vest o' your'n you could appreciate it proper. As you'll recollect me and Ada — that's my woman I told you about — me and Ada took a bit of a cottage on one o' the Bahama out-islands, clear o' Nassau town. Still there, matter o' fact. Nice place. Y'ought to see it. Calabash tree in the front yard, hibiscus all in blossom round the side, hammick on the veranda where the sea wind blows — do your heart good, that's fact."

"Shove it along a bit," Sax said.

"Ah! Well, Sax, I'm a man that's easy satisfied and likes things quiet, but now and then I get a hankerin' for a yarn and a bottle in good company. Then I tell Ada to be good and I hop aboard a sponge boat goin' up to Nassau and I make for that bar in Bay Street where the seamen come. Often sat there thinkin' of you, Sax, and wonderin' where you was. Everyone about the Nassau waterfront said you'd pulled out in a schooner for British Honduras and never come back. Well, Sax, it's funny how things go. Can't be more'n a month ago I got into a gam with a feller on his way north. Said he'd been in a Nova Scotia schooner called *Pamela* somethin'-or-other that got lost last summer down by Trinidad. He was dry and broke, with nothin' but a D.B.S. passage in a steamer that called in Nassau to pick up a bit o' freight for New York. So I bought his drinks and he give me a yarn. Seems this *Pamela* was a scuttlin' job and they done it very neat."

Halkett paused, gave Sax a shrewd and comical glance, and with a shout of laughter threw himself back on the bed.

"Go on," Sax said.

"It was dam' good," Halkett said, still chuckling. He came upright on the bed with a bounce. "Soon as he finished I said to him, I says, 'That sounds like a job I pulled off once in the Caicos with a feller named Nolan, Sax Nolan. Smart a feller as ever you see.' And the feller looks mighty surprised and says, 'Why that's the bloke who owned the *Pam*.' You could'a knocked me down with a feather. 'You mean to say old Sax was aboard this hooker o' your'n?' I says. 'Oh no,' says he, 'Nolan don't go to sea no more. He runs a shippin' company up north in Nova Scotia.' So I asked him where at, and he says Port Barron. And with that he thanks me kindly for the drinks and he's off to board the steamer for New York. Well, there you are. And here I am. And mighty glad to see you lookin' so well and doin' so well too, Sax. They tell me you're quite a swell, married a lady, live in a big house, everything hunky-dory. I might'a known you'd fetch up in a berth like that. You had what it took. Ambition's the word. You had it, Sax. No drinkin', no smokin', no women to speak of, no nothin' till you'd stowed away a good-sized bank account. Smart. That's what you were. You used to say it yourself. 'I'm smart.' Remember that?"

"Yes," Sax said.

"I've always said the same, talkin' about old times down there. 'Smart's the word for Nolan.' I never found a man wouldn't say the same that knew you half an hour."

"Okay," Sax said. "Now chuck that damned cigar out of the window and get down to why you're here. You haven't come fourteen or fifteen hundred miles in winter just to tell me how smart I used to be. What's the game?"

Halkett regarded him shrewdly. He tried to put on an expression of wounded dignity but his features were not meant for such a task and they dissolved in a sly laugh.

"Strictly business, eh? That's like you, Sax. You're a caution, always was." He walked to the window, opened it a reluctant inch or two, flicked the cigar butt down to the snow, and closed the window with a hurried bang as if the winter air were poisonous. He resumed his seat on the bed, shivering after that brief moment in the cold draft from the sea, and reached down and took another long pull at the rum.

"Well now, it's like this, Sax. Things ain't gone well with me, in a way o' speakin', since I come to moorin's

258

down there in the Bahamas. I had some money as you know. Fact is, I had twenty-odd thousand dollars, enough I reckoned to keep me and my woman till kingdom come. Down there, I mean. You can live cheap down there if you pick the right place and ain't fussy about what you eat or wear so long as it's fillin' and comfortable. So there I was without a thing to worry about. But y'know a man's never satisfied with what he's got, and I got a hankerin' to put that money some place where it'd earn more than just the interest they pay in a Nassau bank. So I met a bloke, a tourist at the hotel, that owned shares in an oil well, Texas way, and was willin', when he found out what I'd got, to sell me twenty thousand dollars' worth. As a favor, see? As a favor to a friend."

Halkett sank back on the bed again, and again his laughter shook the rusty springs. "You see, Sax? After all my time at sea I fell afoul of a shark in a Nassau bar. Ah, I never was smart like you. I give you credit there, Sax. No shark had a chance with you, afloat or ashore — not you!"

"Well?"

"There ain't any well. That's the joke, see? That's the catch. Why don't you laugh? It caught me neat. Inside a few weeks I found I hadn't got a cent. Broke! And me at this time o' life, with a woman to keep and not a soul to care a damn. I could'a kicked myself all over the island round by the east."

"So you thought of me."

"That's right, Sax. So after a time I thought o' my old friend, up there in the north with a nice little shippin' business and a heart as big as all outdoors."

Sax regarded the lank figure on the bed. "I see. And you figured you'd run up here and twist my ear for a bit of hush money, seeing what you knew about the *Pam*. Ha!

259

You make me laugh all right, Halkett. That insurance case is closed and written off the underwriters' books. It's deader than Julius Caesar. And all you've got is some boozy tale you heard from a sailor in a bar. Hell, if it came to telling tales like that I could tell a pretty one myself, a sober one, too, about a schooner called *Albertine*. Her registered owner was a man name of Halkett, remember that? He had some kind of deal with his mate but that was a private affair and didn't show in the ship's papers. If you want to stir up old bones I can shove in a long oar myself."

Halkett shook his head sorrowfully. It was odd to see him wearing spectacles. They gave him a quaint air of age and respectability. He looked like a Sunday school superintendent gone a little yellow in the tooth and just now considering a bit of blasphemy chalked on the classroom wall.

"Aw now, Sax, what a thing to say! I wasn't figgering no such thing about the *Pamela* what's-her-name. That's old bones, like you say. Nothin' anybody could do about it now — and good luck to you. I just thought I'd mention it, that's all, as a compliment like. Just to show I know a smart trick when I see one. But that ain't here nor there. What I got to thinkin' was like I told you. There's my old friend Sax up there in Nova Scotia, a shipowner, married respectable, fixed up snug; and here's me down here with my poor woman and not a cent to bless ourselves. Not a bloody Bahamas ha'penny, Sax. And you and me old friends that's been through thick and thin."

"Oh stow it," Sax said wearily. "I'm not as well off as you seem to think. In fact right now things are getting pretty thick with me and I'm hard up. There's a depression, or didn't you know? You ought to know one thing anyhow; when times get dull in this part of the world the first thing that takes a wallop is the shipping business. The next one's fish. The one after that's lumber. And I'm in all three. Up to here." Sax drew an emphatic hand across his chin. "That means I can't afford luxuries like old chums down on their luck. Just the same, for old times' sake I tell you what I'll do. I'll give you a thousand dollars and buy you a passage home first-class in one of the Canadian National liners out of Halifax. That's all. And don't ever show up here again."

Halkett received this with a long cool stare. And holding this enigmatic gaze he put a hand to his breast pocket, drew forth another of his thin Cuban cigars, bit it, struck a match, lighted it and blew out a deliberate challenge in smoke.

"Sax, it ain't enough. Not by a dam' long shot."

"Oh? And what would you call enough? — just as a matter of curiosity."

"Well, as a matter o' curiosity, and havin' regard to what you got and I ain't, I'd say quite a lot, Sax. I'd go as high as twenty-five thousand dollars. That'd just give me back what I lost in the Lone Star Drillin' and Land Development Corporation and pay me for my expense and trouble comin' all this way north at the cold time o' year."

"You're crazy," Sax said, half angered, half amused.

"Ha!" Halkett took another puff at the cigar and removed it from his thin lips with a gesture. "Now that sounds familiar. Ain't that just exactly what I said to you the time you asked me for half of *Albertine?* In Havana harbor that time, remember? And what happened? You got your half. And she was everything I owned in God's world. Now I ain't askin' you for half of all that" — he waved the cigar towards the frosty sign of J. C. Caraday

& Son across the street. "I'm a reasonable man, Sax. Seein' it's hard times, I'll say twenty grand. Twenty grand and I buy my own passage home. What d'you say?"

Sax came to his feet and moved towards the door. "I say you can go to hell and work your passage any way you like."

"Hold on," Halkett said amiably. "T'ain't as easy as all that, Sax. Nassau's warm enough for me. A grand place any way you look at it. A man livin' on one o' the out-islands can come up to town and sit in a bar and hear all kinds o' things besides a yarn about some little ol' schooner beached for the insurance money. F'rinstance a year or two ago there was a colored bloke named Brack-ley turned up from Belize with a mighty queer yarn about a rum hooker called *Jill Be Civil*. Ever hear of her?"

Sax spun about and came slowly to the patch of carpet before Halkett.

"So that's it."

"That's it, Sax. Now ain't you lucky it was me found out where you'd fetched up, and not a certain party called the Major or any o' his chums Miami way? Ain't it a piece o' luck I'm here and none o' them? And you tell me to go to hell — a man that never used to swear. Why, for your address those blokes would give me anything I'd a mind to ask — they want to know that bad. It's been common talk in Nassau for two years. Now just you sit down, Sax, and put them two fists back in your pockets and take that look off o' your face. The landlord's just down the stair. This ain't the deck of *Albertine*. It ain't even a room in that lonesome ark of a house you've got a mile outside the town — the place where you wanted me to come for a gam, begod. That would 'a been a pretty do, now wouldn't it? 'Cause there's my woman, Ada, lyin' in the hammick back home with a note I give her just afore I left. It's addressed to the Major by his right name — ever know what that was, Sax? — and if anything happens to me up north she's to put it in his hand. Ah, there's times when I'm smart myself, Sax. As I get older like. Well, set yourself in that chair again and think it over. You gave me five minutes in Havana. I'm generous. I'll give you ten."

Sax glanced at the chair and rejected it. His fingers were twitching for a grip on that scrawny throat with its Adam's apple moving slowly up and down. For two of the minutes he stood in silence, glaring at the man on the bed and feeding his mind a picture of the struggle there, and the bulging slate eyes, the gaping mouth, the silly jerking hands and legs. Halkett watched him carefully. Sax put the temptation away at last and stepped to the window, looking moodily at the snow in the street.

"They wouldn't dare," he said. "This is Canada. They couldn't pull off any rough stuff here."

"No? What's to stop 'em, Sax? Who's to question 'em? There ain't a policeman handier'n Eglinton, ten or twelve miles away. Remember him? The fat bloke that use to disappear up the back street somewhere on Saturday nights when the sawmill hands were fightin' drunk? Ha! Nobody knows better'n you that every rumrunner workin' out o' St. Pierre comes past this cape on the way to Rum Row, and half of 'em's owned by characters like the Major's lot and all tied in with each other. What's to stop any one of 'em, any night, slippin' inside the cape and out again afore mornin'? Where d'you think the Eglinton bootleggers get their rum from anyhow? Santy Claus? Ho, the Major'd dare all right. You can bet your life on that. There ain't anything the Major wouldn't dare to have a word with you about the *Jill*."

Sax gazed forth at the white street, the shoveled paths, the breaths of passers-by trailing out behind them in the cold. Winter — winter can't last forever. This hard snap of zero weather may be the final bite of it. There's one good thing about a rugged March, it makes the spring feel that much better. The worst of the weather always comes before the thaw. That must be how it is with tough times too. All you have to do is suffer it out and watch for the break.

He turned to the alert man on the bed. "I haven't got twenty grand or anything like it. Right now I doubt if I could raise two. Go down and ask the banker if you like, or anyone in town. All I've got is what you see, some buildings and a couple of ships that don't even pay their way. You put your money in a phony oil well and I put mine in this, and what's the difference? Well, there's this, if you're interested. I've got a business that'll turn out okay if I can hang on till things pick up a bit. All I want is time. You'll have to give me that if you want a cent. Now listen to this. You clear out of here and go on home and keep your mouth shut. I'll send you a bit of money now and then, whatever I can afford. As things get better I'll send more. And that's all I can do. Take it or leave it. Don't think I'm scared of the Major or any of those rats in Miami, either. I can take care of myself, I always could. But I'll admit I can't afford that kind of brawl up here where I've got a business and a reputation — name and good will, as the saying goes."

"Which I could bust with a ten-word telegram," Halkett said lazily.

"There's another old saying, Halkett — sue a beggar and catch a louse. You bust me and you know what you'll get out of it."

Halkett turned the cigar in his fingers as if inspecting it for flaws.

"All this about your business," he murmured. "I knew all that, tell you the truth. Heard it all here in the hotel. This feller Nolan — they don't seem to like you, Sax. Nolan bit off more'n he could chew. Hard luck. Tough times. Debts. Ships in bad shape. Wife run off to a younger man. All that. Still they all say you got money's worth in property. I reckon you could raise some money on it if you tried. Tell you what I'll do, seein' how things are. I'll take five thousand cash and the rest by installments like. You could put me on the payroll o' the firm. As your agent in the Bahamas, say, 'case you ever want to do a bit o' business down that way. I'll make it easy, too. Say a hundred and fifty dollars Canadian, cabled to the bank in Nassau the first of every month — on the dot, mind. I'll settle for that."

"You mean you want a pension for life. That makes it easy, doesn't it? — for you. And where would I get five thousand cash?"

"That's for you to figger out. All I got to say is, that's final, Sax. That's bottom price. I ain't goin' back and shut my mouth without five grand stowed in my pocket. I could get that from the Major just for givin' him your latitood."

"You'll have to wait — you'll have to give me time."

"How much?"

"A day — a week — it depends on the bank — on a number of things."

"I'll give you a week at the outside."

Sax nodded, twisted his lips, and walked to the door.

"On your way out," Halkett called, "you can tell the bloke downstairs to charge my bill to you."

The door closed with a bang. He heard Nolan's footsteps going down the stairs. A pause, and then Nolan's voice calling for the proprietor. Halkett grinned. His long fingers groped for the bottle and took it up almost with a caress.

◡ ◡ *Chapter* 33

IN the thick weather at the Head, where so much depended on their oddly contrasted machines, Sam Torby and Pascoe kept close to their jobs. Pascoe was just completing another check of his instruments when he heard the door open and shut, and then a soft rush of moccasins across the floor. Rena came to him with her skirt snow-dabbled and the parka hood drawn about her head. Turning, he saw in the hood's shadow a dead-white face in which the eyes looked black and glittering and strange. She was breathless from her run through the snow, and as he put his arms about her he felt her trembling. She stood for a time panting, with her own arms clutched about his waist. He raised a hand and put back the hood.

"Something's the matter, darling. What is it?"

She murmured something indistinct against his chest.

"Please tell me." He stroked her hair. "Is it — is it Nolan? Is he here?"

She turned her face aside. "What made you ask that?"

"Just that I've always felt he'd come, sooner or later."

"He's not here," Rena said.

"Then what's the trouble? You seem afraid."

She turned that deathly face up to him and burst out, "It's you and me, Owen. They've been talking about us in Port Barron. Rotten things — cruel things. How awful people are!"

266

Pascoe tightened his mouth. "I suppose we should have expected that. But it hurts, I know. I'm sorry, darling. I wish I could have spared you that."

"Oh it's not the hurt, Owen, I don't mind that, I could put up with that. I know our love's not something obscene the way they say it is. But don't you see what all those tongues have been doing to us? Mother believes them — that's why she came. And Sax is sure to hear them too."

"Ah!" Pascoe gazed into the eyes that stared at him with such a strange intensity. She was trembling still and breathing quickly, but not from the running any more. "Rena, there's just one thing to do. The thing I've wanted to do all this time only you'd have none of it. I'll go to Nolan and face it out with him. If he's any man at all, if he's got any regard for your feelings he must see . . ."

She interrupted him with an impatient click of tongue. "No he won't. You don't know Sax. He's never been able to see a thing in this world but his own devices and desires. Owen, I know his mind. He's so greedy about everything. The house, the business, the ships and me — everything he thinks he's bought and paid for. He'd rave like a beast. Even when I took myself away he felt robbed. He begged my mother to tell him where I'd gone. He wept and raged. He begged her on his knees to get me back." She shuddered violently. "You know, in my life with Sax I came to loathe him but I never was afraid of him. Never. But now I am, I am!" Again she clasped him in that fierce convulsive way. He felt her fingertips pressing into the flesh behind his shoulders as if she expected to be torn away by some brute force at any moment.

"You think he'll come," he said quietly.

"Yes."

"Don't be alarmed, darling. It's a relief in a way. I expected him long before this. He must have suspected you were here."

"Oh no, I don't think it ever occurred to him. So near. And so bleak a place. His mind's too devious to think of anything as simple as that. His own life's always taken him over long distances, and I suppose if he ever thought of refuge it would be some place far away, where things were comfortable. He's always hated life anywhere on the cape. He was always restless, even in the big house at Port Barron. His mind always seemed to be somewhere else."

"But surely you didn't think you could hide yourself here forever?"

She shook her head. "Owen, when I came, I didn't think or care about anything. I just wanted to get away from him for a time, a few days, a week, anything. When I'd had a month alone it seemed a miracle. And after we fell in love I could only pray for the miracle to go on. I was blind, I suppose. I thought it was quite possible. I might have cautioned Jennie more perhaps. But that wouldn't have made any difference in the end. They found out in other ways — those people at Port Barron. It's not fair," she exclaimed, looking up with tears in her eyes. "Why couldn't they have kept my poor little secret? What harm was it? It wasn't as if they'd any regard for Sax — they hate him. I don't understand! I just don't understand!"

Pascoe kissed her gently and smiled. "Why try?"

Again those agitated fingers at his back. "Owen, I'm frightened — frightened to death. He's been away ever since the autumn. That's why we've had these wonderful months in peace together. But now he's on his way back — back to Port Barron, where everyone's chattering scan-

268

dal about you and me. You don't seem to realize yet what it means. You can't, of course. Not everything. Sax — Sax isn't any ordinary man. Apart from everything else about him his mind is strange. It's always seemed to me that in his eyes I wasn't just a woman he'd married. I was that and something more, a token of some kind, something to do with his old life, whatever it was. Something he had to have whenever the mood was on him to satisfy an old lust or a spite or some queer ambition, I never could tell, it depended on the mood. Perhaps it was all three. Sometimes when he had me in his arms I felt quite sure that was the case."

"Don't speak of that," Pascoe said sharply. "Don't even think of it."

"I've got to, Owen. Because you've got to understand what I have to say. You talk of facing Sax as if he were someone like yourself. I tell you he isn't. Even at his best he isn't. And at his worst he's a beast, cunning and strong — frightfully strong — and without a scrap of reason or mercy or anything civilized as we understand such things. So you see? We must go away. Now. Before he has a chance to come back and find out everything."

She felt Pascoe stiffen in her clasp. "We couldn't do that, Rena."

"Why?"

"Run away? No!"

"But why? Why?"

"Look here, darling, you've always kidded me about being a dreamer and maybe I am. But even dreamers are awake some of the time. I've thought about this, ever since we came together. I knew there'd have to be a showdown sometime. Frankly, I'm glad it's come. You say he's bound to turn up here, and you're frightened, naturally. Well, I'm not. Let him come."

Rena wrenched herself out of his arms. "Oh now you're being very male and stupid and talking like a schoolboy in a squabble over nothing. You — you idiot, Owen. You simply don't know what you're talking about. Do you think for one minute I'm frightened for myself? I'm frightened for you. You don't realize what he'd do to you."

He ruffled her anger further with a deliberate grin. "Punch me on the nose, I suppose. But two can play at that. Do I really seem so helpless, Rena? I might surprise you."

She backed away to the desk and sat against it, with her hands beside her, gripping the edge. For a full minute she regarded him with exasperated eyes. Eventually she said, with a forced calm and in a voice low and shaking, "Owen, you can't deceive me with that silly pose. I suppose inside you feel very proud and heroic and you've got a fine notion that you're doing the honorable thing. Well you're not. You're just being deliberately blind and stubborn. If you only knew how horrible that seems to me when there's so little time and I know what will happen if you stay. You're no match for Sax. And he'll stop at nothing. He'll kill you!"

"He could try."

She sprang up and thrust her hands about his neck. "Owen! Owen! Please come with me — please take me somewhere, anywhere away from here. Now. Please!"

"No, darling."

"If you love me you'll come. I'm begging you."

"I love you and I'm not running off with you like a thief with someone else's purse." He paused, and added reasonably, "Besides, I've got a duty here. You forget that. I couldn't clear out and leave the radio beacon unattended. Ships depend on it in this weather."

"Duty!" She broke into a frantic weeping. "I'm nearly

mad with fear for you and all you can think about is this machine. Haven't you any duty to me?"

He set his mouth firmly. "Rena, we're not running away from Nolan. That's flat."

She drew herself away and walked slowly across the room. Near the door she turned and faced him, biting her lip in an effort to stop the sobs that were shaking her. "Can't you guess why Mother really came? She didn't come just to warn me. She wants me to go back with her to Port Barron — back to Sax. Don't you understand? She says that will stop the gossip and settle everything. And she's pointed out what will happen to you if I don't — as if I didn't know." She struggled again with the sobbing and added in a trembling voice, "She's packing my things now."

Pascoe jerked his head up sharply at that. "She surely doesn't think for a moment that you'd really go? Back to that man?"

"You leave me no choice."

"What! You can't!"

"I can!" she cried passionately. "I could do anything, Owen, if it meant as much as this. If you can't swallow your stupid pride at least I can do what I choose with mine." She saw his frown and misreading it she went on quickly, "I'm not making a silly threat to induce you. I mean it. Sax may be back tomorrow. The boat's waiting and there isn't time to argue any more. Either you come with me now or I leave with Mother now. For the last time, will you come?"

She drew the door open, and after the first outrush of warm air the fog entered like a cold white smoke, swimming about her and past her into the room. Suddenly in its uncanny way the beacon apparatus began to click and purr, and then to make its high, thin signal note. The

271

irony of it pierced her to the heart, this reminder of his duty in that moment. She uttered a single cry and plunged into the mist. Pascoe sprang to the doorway with hands outstretched as if he could catch and hold the frantic ghost that was not there any more. He followed blindly along the path in the snow. It was a strange chase. Running desperately, slithering on the icy footing, staggering drunkenly at every bend, he could not overtake or even catch sight of the swift hooded figure. It was as if she had dissolved in the vapor drifting thickly about the scattered buildings, the woods and the cove. From time to time the foghorn bellowed into the murk, the voice of a bereft and angry bull. It might have been the voice of Nolan himself.

At the crosspath by the corner of the wood Pascoe checked himself, wondering swiftly which way to take. To the house? Mrs. Caraday must still be there surely, packing Rena's things. Or to the boat? It would be more like Rena to make straight for the boat. He ran down to the cove and found the big motorboat still moored to the slip and the boatman peering from the cabin slide.

"Rena?" the fellow said. "Ain't seen her, no. Ain't seen the old woman since the forenoon neither. Hey! You see Miz Caraday, you tell her we got to get away pretty soon. I don't like goin' up to Port Barron in the dark, not thick-o'-fog like this, and the tide runnin'."

Pascoe trotted through the wood to the house. The front door was open and he passed inside, calling Rena's name. There was no answer. There seemed to be no one in the lower rooms, but after a few moments he heard sounds above and presently a slow step on the stairs. Mrs. Caraday appeared, dragging a large suitcase. She regarded Pascoe with a prompt and bright hostility.

"What are you doing here?"

272

"Rena — where is she?"

"Why should I tell you? I don't know why I should even speak to you — you've done everything you could to ruin her."

"Where is she?" he persisted.

Pamela shrugged. "Very well, if you must know she left the house rather suddenly. She didn't even stop to shut the door. I was afraid she'd gone to see you." And she went on tartly, "I may as well tell you that Rena's going back to her husband like a sensible girl and there's an end to all this nonsense. If you've a scrap of good sense in your whole wretched body you'll not try to see her again."

"You waste time," Pascoe snapped. "Rena did come to see me. She was in a hysterical state and suddenly she left me, ran off into the fog, just the way she left you. I thought she'd gone down to the boat but she wasn't there. And you say she's not here?" In a flash of suspicion he strode to the foot of the stair and shouted Rena's name. No answer. Nothing but an echo of his own voice in emptiness.

"Are you satisfied?" Pamela asked in a voice lofty and suddenly serene. It had occurred to her that Rena must have gone on to say good-by to the Torbys, and it gave her a gleaming satisfaction to know that the girl had taken leave of her lover in so short a fashion. Clearly her mind was made up. And now nothing remained but to get rid of this anxious lout before she returned.

"If you are," she went on majestically, "I suggest that you leave. Now, please. The very sight of you makes me ill."

Pascoe gave her a bleak look and went out. The dense vapor drawn from the naked sea by this sub-zero temperature was freezing on the trees and coating them with hoar, so that they swam on either hand like icebergs in the mist. The snow in the path had been beaten hard by their simple daily traffic and now was crusted by the sea rime, freezing wherever it touched. On that not even a heeled boot could leave a mark, let alone Rena's moccasins. He walked on quickly, taking the path to Sam's house. At the door Jennie greeted his question with a look of mild surprise.

"Rena? Ain't seen Rena today at all. She ain't to the house? Nor your place? You don't suppose she's gone down to the whistle-house for a chat with Sam?"

She saw the concern in Pascoe's face and followed him, clutching the stuff of her dress about her throat against the cold. But Sam knew no more than she.

"What's wrong?" the old man shouted.

"Everything!" Pascoe snapped. "My poor girl's gone — vanished." He was shaking with anxiety. "She was talking to me for a few minutes in the radio shack. There was something on her mind — she was very upset — and suddenly she ran out. You must help me find her. Quick!"

He set off towards the cove again, calling out to them to search the path towards the point and then towards the old house. Again he found nothing at the cove but the boat and its gloomy keeper, who now joined in the search. When they all came together in the wood before the house they saw Mrs. Caraday in the doorway, looking vaguely alarmed. She caught the infection of fear in all their faces now, and as they turned for another search she came behind, screaming Rena's name in a high voice through the trees.

Chapter 34

THE tall mahogany case-clock was sounding three soft notes when the mistress of Caraday House re-entered the hall and closed the doors on the cold and the dark. After the long day and the night with its frantic emotions and exertions, the return boat journey in the dark and against the ebb, and finally her trudge alone through the snow from Port Barron, she was tottering with fatigue, and a little amazed that she could have endured so much. The hall was dark but there was a light in the west drawing room. She entered slowly, dragging the heavy snow boots across the floor and fumbling at the buttons of her coat. The warmth of the house was stupefying after the sharp air of the night. She wanted nothing now but to fall on the divan and sleep, just as she was, for the notion of bed was involved with climbing the stairs, an impossible feat.

She had taken several steps into the room before she observed the still figure below the portrait of John C. It was Sax, in his favorite chair, in the familiar moody attitude, staring into a fire that had gone dead long ago. She halted, plucking at her numb wits now. He must have heard her come in, for he arose and gave her a nod.

"Good morning — it must be morning, isn't it?"

"Yes," she whispered, not moving.

"Pleasant trip?"

Her wits were stirring a little now. "I don't know quite what you mean."

"Sit down," Sax said. She moved across the room and dropped without elegance on the divan, a shapeless bun-

275

dle of black fur and scarf and boots and wavering mittened hands.

"I mean of course your trip out to Gannet Head," he said suavely. "You know, to see Rena."

"What makes you think . . ."

"You can drop all that," Sax said. "I know the whole game."

"Game?" she muttered in the same dazed voice.

Sax moved a few steps towards her and halted, clasping his hands behind and with little springing motions raising his heels off the carpet and letting them down again. "Oh no doubt I'm short a few details here and there, but I think I've got the story pretty well. It took a bit of digging, of course. You knew she was there all the time, didn't you? And you knew what was going on out there too. You fooled me nicely, you and Rena. I've got to hand it to you both. It was smart, the whole damned trick."

Pamela stared. Saxby seemed at ease. There was a light in his small eyes that might even have been pleasure.

"What have you heard?" she asked carefully. The heat of the room came at her in waves and engulfed her, a sensation delicious and dangerous. She felt stupid and disarmed.

"You don't really want me to repeat it? After all, you know the tale a lot better than me, you must, you've been in on it all this time. Funny thing, I never suspected Rena of anything like that. She didn't seem the type to begin with, and besides she was a lady. Ladies aren't supposed to romp with characters of the sort you find around the cape. It isn't in the book. Maybe I didn't read it right. Would you like to know how I found out? In the hotel this morning — yesterday morning now — a man talking to me let fall a remark about my wife running off to a younger man. He seemed to think I knew all about it so I let it pass. But that put me on the track, of course. In a flash I knew what a numskull I'd been all this time. I came out here right away. When I asked for you, Bertha said you were away for the day. When I asked her where, she gave me a look and a sniff and said it wasn't for her to say. I began to smell the whole rat then. I've often heard you pumping her for the local chatter in that delicate way you have. Well, my way's not so delicate. I had to slap her about a bit before I got what I wanted. Finally I slapped her a bit too hard and she went down — sprawling. She let me have it then."

He chuckled. "First she told me what she thought of me. With a pretty mucky choice of language, I may say. I gathered she didn't like me and never had. Then she spat out the whole thing, lying right where she was on the floor and glaring up at me — chucking it in my face. Rena and her lover and all those high jinks at the Head, and what a fool they'd made of me, the whole town laughing its head off, and serve me damned well right. Now and then she'd stop for breath and I'd have a chance to ask a question. She'd snap right back with the answer, screaming and laughing and bawling all at the same time. When she couldn't think of anything more to say, she'd go right back to the start like a crazy parrot and reel it off again. I could see she wasn't making it up. The whole thing came too pat."

"Where is Bertha now?" Pamela demanded hoarsely. "What have you done to her?"

"My dear lady, don't sound so alarmed. She's probably a bit bruised about the gills but I fancy I hurt her feelings more than anything else. When her spring ran down after all that rigmarole I told her to get up and clear out. She didn't waste any time. She went and packed her stuff and got Ferrand to drive her into town. You'll have to

277

hunt up a new cook tomorrow, that's all. Too bad, isn't it?"

He remained before the weary creature on the couch, giving her his monkey-imp look, dancing his heels up and down, thinking of that other scene here in this room and what a booby he had made of himself, slobbering at her feet; and of Pamela's triumph then, and the hold she had kept on him ever since. Ah, she had been clever, clever! But now the boot was on the other foot. It was her turn to lick. He wondered how she would go about it.

But the lady disappointed him. No weeping, no imploring, no gabble of excuses for Rena, nothing. Only that fixed stare. Abruptly he put off his air of expectant triumph. He dragged up a chair and sat in it, facing her.

"Okay, now let's hear your tale. You must have one. You went out there to tip off Rena and this sweetheart of hers, the radio bloke, that the talk was getting dangerous and I was coming back. Bertha guessed that much anyhow. So you can go on from there. What happened? What did Rena say? After all, I'm her husband and I'm curious."

"I'm tired," Mrs. Caraday said drearily. "I've had a frightful day — frightful. Please let me rest, let me sleep. Ask your questions in the morning."

"It's morning now," Sax said. "I've had a long day and night myself, and I've got another big day or two ahead. I've got all kinds of hot business on my hands — you'd be surprised. Now let's get this bit straight. You might as well come out with it and then we'll all know where we stand. What happened at the Head?"

Rena's mother drew herself erect with an effort, sitting with her hands clasped tightly in her lap. She had drawn off the mittens. The rings hurt and she went on twisting the fingers cruelly to keep herself awake.

"Very well. I went out there to warn her as you say. And to beg her to come home — to come back to you. You may believe that or not as you wish. I said you were sorry for whatever happened between you a year ago and that you'd be happy to have her back. That was true, wasn't it?"

"Suppose it was. Get on with it. What did Rena say? And what about this man, this Pascoe — was he there when you said all this?"

"Rena was alone in the old cottage. I talked to her there for quite a long time. She didn't say much. But at the end I felt sure I'd persuaded her. She went out, to say good-by to Pascoe I supposed, and I began to gather and pack her things."

"Well, what are you stopping for? What then?"

"Then something happened. From what he said afterwards — Pascoe — she talked to him for a while, not long, and then ran off. There was an ice mist all about the Head. It was very thick, impossible to see far anywhere. Pascoe ran after her but she'd gone and he couldn't find her. None of us could find her. We searched everywhere, shouting her name. We even looked in the church and the old fish houses at the cove. There wasn't a sign. It was terrible — terrible. Knowing the state of mind she was in, knowing she must be out of doors somewhere in this bitter weather, and night coming on."

Pamela halted again. The long hours in the cold had given her cheeks a pinched look, and now there were tears dripping down the sharp folds past her nose.

Sax sprang up crying, "Go on! Stop sniveling. What happened?" His voice filled the long room and echoed strangely in the empty hall and staircase.

"When it got dark," Pamela faltered, dropping her voice to a whisper, "we decided she must be in the sea. That was the awful moment. The worst moment of my life." She looked at Sax with her washed-out blue eyes.

"She never loved me — Rena. She gave all her love to her father. And when he died she locked up her heart, she shut me out. I've been wicked — wicked. I know that. But I loved her, you understand? She was my daughter and I loved her."

Sax regarded her with rage and contempt, a selfish old woman gone maudlin and wasting time. "For God's sake go on!"

"So we began to search along the shore. We began by the radio hut, where she disappeared. The sea is very close there. It was difficult in the dark. All the rocks covered with ice. Nothing to hold. The tide running and making that awful chuckling sound it does in the dark. Hours. Miles, it seemed. And nothing. Then Pascoe thought of Bosun."

"Who's that?"

"The dog. The dog he and old Sam used for duck hunting. Bosun was very fond of Rena. They should have thought of him before. Sam let him out and said, 'Rena, find Rena.' And the dog ran back and forth a bit and disappeared. They'd forgotten to put him on a leash of some kind. The mist had begun to blow away by then. There was a cold wind through the trees out of the north. But the night was very black and we were just as badly off. We called to the dog but he didn't answer. There wasn't a sound but the tide along the shore and the wind clashing all those icy branches together in the wood. It was horrible. Then, after a long time, we heard the dog barking somewhere towards the cove. We went that way along the path. Pascoe reached her first, running like mad. The dog had found her lying in the snow just off the path at the corner of the wood, where you turn to go down to the cove. We must have passed her a dozen times — more."

280

"She was alive? Quick, tell me that!"

"She was alive."

Sax let forth a long breath. His jaw worked visibly. "Okay, go on."

"Apparently she'd been running down towards the boat. The footing was icy in the path — even the snow under the trees had a crust like glass — and she must have slipped on the turn. She was thrown into a hollow under one of the cat-spruce trees where there was very little snow. The trees are low and stunted there at the edge of the wood and their branches hang down to the ground. She was underneath, quite concealed. And there were rocks."

Pamela shuddered. Her lips parted and quivered but for a time no words came. She looked shrunken and old. To Sax in his impatience she seemed to have gone senile in a moment, as if these strange matters coming suddenly into a life lived at ease for so many years had shriveled her plumpness and capsized her mind in one stroke. But now she drew her lips together. She seemed to catch at a point that had flickered into her thoughts demanding a supreme effort, and it steadied her. She spoke with a new energy.

"She must have lain there eight or nine hours in this freezing weather, with her left leg broken and her head badly cut. She was unconscious still. The blood had run down over her face and frozen. When Pascoe parted the branches and struck a match — when I saw her face and how still she lay, and that one foot in the moccasin turned back in that awful way, I thought she was dead. I screamed and screamed."

"Go on, go on."

"Pascoe . . ."

"Talk about Rena."

"Pascoe was there," Pamela said with some dignity. "He seemed to know what to do. He bound up her leg very carefully with sticks and cord, and he and Sam carried her to the Torby house on an old fish-barrow from the cove. Her clothes were frozen stiff, we had to cut them off before we could put her in bed. Jennie washed the blood off her poor face and bandaged the cut in her scalp. And Pascoe made proper splints out of a piece of board and bound them on with medical tape."

"A very handy man, eh? Where Rena's concerned I mean."

"He was skillful and gentle, if that's what you mean. And he'd been in the North, he knew what to do for exposure and shock and all that. Whatever you may think or feel about him, Saxby, the man loves her very much. That was plain."

"You seem impressed," Sax said. She did not answer. "I must get hold of Bannister right away."

"I've done that," Pamela said. "I went to the doctor's house as soon as the boat reached the wharf. It took me twenty minutes' banging on the door before anybody came. He's going out there at daylight."

"Good! I'll go with him."

Pamela licked her chapped lips, glancing away and back to Sax again.

"I beg you not to do that." Sax raised his brows.

"Why not? Rena's my wife."

"That's not the point."

"You're thinking of Pascoe again. That skillful man of hers. Well, so am I. Has it struck you that none of this would have happened if he'd kept his skillful hands off Rena in the first place? He's had his fun, why shouldn't he pay for it?"

Mrs. Caraday twisted her lips in distaste. But she said

282

quietly, "I'm thinking of my girl. Rena's badly hurt and ill, you understand? When I left she was delirious, crying out your name — in fear. Fear! If you've any sense or pity you'll stay away from the Head until she's got over the state of shock she's in. She can't be moved. In any case it's impossible in a boat in winter weather, you must know that. The best the doctor can do is to set her leg and leave her in Jennie's care."

"And Pascoe's. That's what I call a charming setup. And you want me to let 'em get away with it? In spite of the fact that Rena's mine? With all Port Barron still laughing its head off? What kind of man do you think I am?"

"Sometimes I wonder," Pamela said strangely. She gave him a long stare. "Who are you? Where did you come from? Sometimes I have a weird feeling that I've seen you before somewhere, long ago. But that's impossible, of course. When you married Rena I was delighted. I'd wanted to see her married and settled in comfort. Oh, I had a selfish interest, I admit. In another year or two we'd have been paupers, both of us. And we were grateful, you know that. Then about a year ago you quarreled, you and Rena. You've told me something of that and so has she, but not enough to show me what was at the bottom of it. One thing Rena said keeps coming back into my mind. Because of the word she chose. She said you revolted her. And that it wasn't just a few words you'd said in a fit of temper, it was everything about you from the time you married her. What did she mean? Tell me that."

Sax felt the skin of his face going tight and cold over the bones. His fingers flickered uneasily on the chair arms. He cleared his throat but his voice was husky. "She was angry at the time, whatever she said. I'd insulted her and what could you expect? But Rena loves me, always has.

Even after this affair at the Head she was ready to leave that man and come back to me. You've admitted that. She was actually running away from him when she got hurt. She was heading for the boat — and me. That proves it, doesn't it?"

"It proves something but it isn't what you think. You'd better hear the truth. It proves she was anxious to protect her lover, nothing more. To shield him, you understand? She knew if she delayed you'd come out there and kill him. So did I. We both knew you too well to believe anything else. And I was just as desperate as she. I thought — and I told her — that if she became your wife again she could stave off all that. She could induce you to think that she'd just gone away to sulk alone for a few months and now it was all over and she wanted you again. What I didn't know until a few hours ago was that Rena couldn't have deceived you, and she wouldn't have tried in any case. Nothing was farther from her mind."

"Just what d'you mean by that?" he muttered.

"She had a wild notion that you'd be satisfied to take out your spite on her for — for everything. You see? She wanted to be the scapegoat — to offer herself to whatever frightful mood you might be in when you found out the final truth."

"You tie your talk in knots. What final truth? What are you driving at?"

Unexpectedly Mrs. Caraday arose and made a firm step or two towards him. The movement was so abrupt, her whole manner so changed, that Sax was startled. The faded blue eyes had a sudden hot sincerity. There was a peculiar vigor in the gesture of her thin hands thrust down and clenched at her sides, an air of defiance, as if she had cast off all the fatigues of the past twenty-four hours and a life's pretenses with them. She might have been my-father-Captain-Charnsworth himself, facing the Boers in that last fatal moment on the Tugela.

"I mean the fact that changes everything. The fact that Rena's pregnant."

He was still so astonished at her manner that the words for a moment had no meaning. Then he whispered incredulously, "Since when?"

"Since about four months ago."

A chill sweat covered him in a moment. He had a desire to scream. His toes crawled in his shoes. When he spoke at last it was in a high, thin nasal tone that did not sound like him at all.

"Why do you tell me this? To torture me?"

"Because whoever you are, whatever sort of man, there must be in you some scrap of decency, some hope to be respected, even a little, by a woman you've loved. I wonder if that isn't what you've always craved in your strange way — to be respected, to be looked up to, not only by Rena but by everyone. And you've never got what you wanted, in that or any other way, because your self stood in the way. Something about you that repelled everyone. And nothing you could do about it. That's the pitiful thing about you, Saxby. You can't help being what you are. You have the power to do many things but not that. You could go out to the Head tomorrow and behave like a beast. You could go to Rena's lover, the man whose child she's carrying, and do whatever you like. He has no fear of you and that should make it easy for anyone as quick and strong as you. You could kill him with your bare hands. You know that, so does Rena, so do I. And what would that get you? Rena's love? You know better. Respect from anyone? There isn't a man in Port Barron who wouldn't help throw you into the sea or drag you to the court in Eglinton. And that would be the end of everything, your career, your ambitions whatever they are, all you've got out of the world. And for what? For a bit of savage revenge. Nothing more."

"What do you want me to do?" Sax said, staring at the floor.

"Divorce Rena."

"I'll never do that."

"Then at least let them go. You must have humanity enough for that."

Sax refused to look up. The phrase rang in his head and made it ache. The thick palms, the clever hairy fingers were clenched on the knobs of the chair, the bent dark head swayed to and fro as if in contemplation of the pattern on the carpet at his feet. He was at a disadvantage with the imperious woman looking down. His skin felt that blue stare, which seemed to search for a crevice through which to inspect his secret heart. He muttered and arose, shambling away towards the hall. The woman watched him in silence. She heard him move across the hall and then the sound of his slow footsteps on the stairs, a creak of the upper floor, and at last the soft closing of his bedroom door. She turned towards the divan then but she did not reach it. Her bones refused to hold up the tired flesh any more. She sank to the floor and lay there shaking.

⌁ ⌁ Chapter 35

THE *John C. Caraday* lay at a wharf, discharging coal. The air was thick with coal dust, and a light fall of snow during the morning had made a thin black slush about the decks that passing feet picked up and carried to every part of the ship. The steamer looked what it was, a battered and grimy tramp that had suffered eighteen months of the most bruising charters known to the coast, a picture of hard times in the shipping trade. The Fundy tide was in and the ship rode high at the dock. The gangway went up like a fire escape. As Sax climbed the black and slippery thing, setting his toes firmly on the cleats and pulling himself up by the manropes, he looked over the side and noted that the bilge-pump discharge was going steadily.

Eckles greeted him without pleasure. The old man's unshaven face, his untidy white hair, his old faded uniform, his skinny hands, all were soiled with the creeping dust of slack coal, and not from this voyage alone. A winter's tale was written there. When Sax announced that he was making the return voyage as far as Port Barron, the captain received the news glumly and removed his sorry wardrobe and possessions to the mate's room. Dahl greeted him more heartily. They clasped hands and slapped shoulders with the gusto of companions long separated and eager for each other's news.

And that night, when the crew had clattered off to the nocturnal delights of St. John, the three forgathered in the captain's cabin. Sax sat in the armchair, Eckles sank wearily upon the small settee against the bulkhead and Dahl perched himself on the berth. Sax dived a hand into his bag and passed a bottle of rum to the skipper.

"Take a couple of good hookers, my friend. You'll need 'em."

He passed a bottle of schnapps to Dahl. "You won't need a thing, you German lunatic, but here's your pet tipple anyhow." Dahl looked at the label, drew the cork, sniffed, grinned in appreciation, and took a swig. Eckles got himself a glass from the rack overhead and took down the water carafe. He poured three fingers of rum into the glass and drank it at a gulp. He poured a little water into the glass and drank that to take the sting of the cheap Demerara from his throat. Nobody spoke. After a few minutes the captain and engineer drank again. They had the devout air of pilgrims performing a rite at some singularly blessed spring.

When Eckles reached for the bottle to pour a third drink Sax lifted a forbidding finger. The captain looked plaintively at him and at the rum, sighed, and relapsed into a huddle on the couch.

"You take your drinks too big and too fast, Eckles. I don't want you drunk till I've had my little say. After that you can drink yourself blind. How about you, Dahl?"

"All right."

Sax danced his fingers on the chair arms, smiling faintly, watching the two men.

"I'm about to sell the ship."

They were astounded. After a silence Dahl laughed and exclaimed in his rich accent, "Who in hell is going to buy this thing? If I stopped my bilge pumps for six hours she would sink here at the dock."

"Ay, who?" muttered Eckles in a wondering voice.

"The underwriters."

Dahl raised his blond eyebrows and whistled. Eckles seemed to shrink against the corner of the settee. His eyes were frightened. He trembled and cast a longing glance at the rum.

"Okay," Sax said contemptuously. "Pour yourself another."

The bottle in Eckles's hand rattled against the glass. He drank and coughed.

"Captain Nolan, I'm afraid I . . . I can't go through

288

with it . . . I . . . I stand to lose my ticket . . . and I have some principles . . ."

"No you don't," Sax said brutally. "This is what I hired you for, remember? There were men with masters' tickets out of a berth all the way from Glasgow to the London river, and I picked you, and I told you why. Ticket! What good's your ticket anyhow — a poor old character like you that couldn't stay sober long enough to hold any job he's had the past ten years, excepting this one. Oh, I know all about you, my friend. I made damned sure of that. And what did I tell you? I said I was buying a small tramp for the Canadian coastal trade. I said the chances were good for a steady job if things turned out as well as I expected, but if they didn't I might want to sell her to the underwriters. In that case when the job was done I'd pay you a bonus of five hundred quid and ship you home, first class, like a gentleman. You didn't yammer about your ticket or your principles then. You begged me for the chance. And you got it. All right. Now you're going through with it. I'm not asking you to put her on the beach. I'm doing that myself."

"Where?" demanded Dahl, leaning over with interest.

"Where?" Sax kept his hard gaze on the captain's face. "I'll tell you where. There's dozens of places where it could be done and ways to do it. But I've got to be careful. When I lost that old schooner, the *Pamela*, down Trinidad way, I made sure the crew was like this one, a lot of characters from nowhere. When the job was done they rowed ashore and got paid off in Port of Spain with a passage to anywhere they liked — and they had some wide ideas. And that was that. Just the same there was a yarn got about Port Barron for a time that she'd been scuppered for the insurance. I suppose one or two of the crew must have stuck around Port of Spain, drinking up their pay and passage money and wagging their tongues a bit, and some passing seaman from Port Barron overheard. I don't think it got back to the underwriters; if it did there was nothing they could prove and they paid up in full. But that's why I've got to be canny about this one. Well, in the first place I've got Eckles for master. A captain with a British master's ticket in steam, deep sea — they can't quibble about 'incompetent navigation' in the face of that. Okay. Now consider the time of year. A wreck in soft weather's all right down south where you don't get anything but soft weather anyhow; but up here it'd look suspicious. So now's the time; winter weather, snow blowing, ice about the shores, gales and heavy seas — every excuse in the book. Finally there's the place. It's got to be a place where we can do a nice job of it and get away in the boat and make the land all right. It's got to be a place where the first storm will finish her before any snooping underwriters' man or the Commissioner of Wrecks can get out and take a look. And it's got to be done in the course of a normal voyage, in other words on the ship's regular beat. Now what's all that add up to?"

"What?" cried Dahl, with the bright smile of a boy fascinated with a tale.

"Ever hear of Dutchman?"

"Ah!"

"Dutchman?" stammered Eckles. "Why Dutchman?"

"Why Dutchman, he says. Eckles, if you had half an eye for my interests and the brain of a sheep you'd know why — you've sailed past it often enough. It used to be called the Dutchman's Breeches, I'm told, because that's the way it's shaped. There's the two stubby legs, and the seat, and a pond in the middle makes the patch. It's low

— most of it's barely above the tide on the springs — so there's no ice wall to bother us if we want to get ashore there. The other islands are all steep-to; and this time of year, what with the tides and zero weather and the spray chucked up by the westerlies, they've got ice walls around 'em a fly couldn't climb. Wait a minute — I'll show you. I made a bit of a chart last summer — went out there in my motorboat and took a lot of soundings all round the island and between the Dutchman's legs, where the regular charts don't show the detail. Here!" He spread the paper on the table, and Eckles peered, and Dahl leaped down from the berth for a close look.

"See there — the breeches, the legs straddled and one a bit shorter than the other. That's where we go, in there between the Dutchman's legs, like going into a dock. There's a good five fathoms' depth for about a ship's length and then a shelf that levels off at two or less — all these are high-water soundings, understand. The bottom's mud, like most of the island, but right in the middle of the shelf is a ledge of rock set flush with the mud. Get the idea? As sweet a spot for a little job of barratry as ever you saw. We run in there at full tide or, better still, a bit on the ebb. She shoves her bow up on that soft mud shelf, and the rock slits her bottom open like a can opener as far back as the engine-room bulkhead. No farther, Dahl, in case you're wondering. Your firemen won't even get their feet wet. She'll bring up her stem hard against the face of the island itself at that point. I measured all this carefully, so I know. If we choose the time right it'll be over in five minutes and then we launch the boat and make for Port Barron."

"What if there's a sea running?" Eckles mumbled, staring at the map.

"If there's a big sea running we won't try it at all. We'll

keep right on for another load of coal and try it again next trip. But with any ordinary sea we can beach the ship and launch the boat and take our time — she'll be lying there practically in a dock with the tide on the ebb. That's the beauty of it. And the first gale and flood tide'll beat right over the Dutchman's legs, drag her off the ledge and down she goes. There's nothing to worry about. I've figured the whole thing out."

"The insurance people or the wreck chap," Eckles quavered again. "Suppose they question me about blundering into a place like that. What do I say?"

Sax's lips curled. "You'll say you were taking the inside passage to save the long run out around Topsail and Frigate. The ship's been through the Race before — they can check that with the lightkeeper on Frigate if they're curious. They won't quibble over taking the Race at high tide for the inside passage. It's a good seamanlike choice that any master but you would take without turning a hair. Oh it's all safe and sound — even your precious ticket. There's been wrecks galore on those islands in time past. This'll be just one more. Chances are the underwriters won't even question it. If they do you'll know what to say — a snow squall came up and hid the islands, the tide set you to loo'ard, and you struck before you knew it. I'll be there to keep your courage up."

Eckles thought on this for a time. "All right," he sighed in a resigned voice. "I'll have the boat overhauled and swung out ready to launch when the time comes."

"You'll do nothing of the kind. That's what the insurance blokes might call a 'suspicious circumstance' if they happen to collar any of the crew. That's not likely to happen, of course. Before they can get around to investigating the wreck the crew'll be paid off and scattered to hell-and-gone. But I'm taking no chances there either. The crew

292

won't know a damned thing. When the time comes I'll take the helm myself — for the run through the Race, see? They've seen me do that before. That takes us close in by Dutchman anyhow, and we'll be hard aground before anyone knows a thing." He added, "Satisfied?"

The captain licked his lips. "We'll be in ballast — riding high — you realize that? With any amount of wind or sea she don't handle easy when she's light. You tell him, Dahl."

Dahl laughed excitedly. "She'll handle well enough. Sax knows. Have you forgotten, Eckles, he brought her light as a tin cup across the whole of the North Atlantic? The winds we had? The seas we had? Was there anything in the Devil's knapsack that we did not have? So now this, what is this? Nothing. You will see. By Gott, Sax, I love you. You are a man. You care for nothing. You are mad enough to be a Pomeranian like me, or a Finn, who will do anything."

Sax chuckled. He jerked his head at Eckles. "All right, you can take that bottle now and go." Eckles made a swift clutch at the rum and departed almost at a run. Dahl got down from the berth and sprawled on the settee. He took another pull at the schnapps.

"Now tell me, Sax, now he is gone, that poor old fool, what means all this?"

Sax tucked away carefully the penciled chart of Dutchman. Calmly he said, "You know what trade's been like ever since we brought the ship across. Trade! There's no trade any more. When I took over that firm in Port Barron I thought I could run it as a straight old-fashioned business proposition. I thought I could make a good square go of it. For a time, by God, I thought I was old John C. himself. But I hadn't reckoned with the shape the world was in. I could buck men and the sea but I couldn't buck 1929 and the hang-over that's brought things to this pass. Why, right now, at this minute, every bank in the States is busted flat — did you know that? There's a panic from New York to Frisco. The richest nation in the world, and not a bank door open anywhere. So help me, sometimes I wonder if I'm awake and not just dreaming things. Well, in one way or another I fell to loo'ard of the bank in Port Barron and a lot of other people, and now things have come to a head. I've got to get a bunch of money fast. I've got to have at least twenty-six thousand dollars just to pay off the bank and some others before they slap a court plaster on the ships and properties. That's about what I paid for the *John* in Stettin but I couldn't get half that for her now. Right now I doubt if I could give her away, the shape she's in. But there's thirty-five thousand dollars' insurance on her. So you see? God bless the underwriters."

Dahl smiled and held up the bottle. "To the underwriters," he said, and drank.

"And now," Sax went on, "I suppose you're wondering where you're going to fit when this little job's over. I'll tell you. You know that auxiliary schooner I built for package freights about the coast? She's been laid up since fall. She hadn't even earned her wages — it was as bad as that. Well, I've spun you some yarns about that rum game I was in. I remember you said I was a fool to leave anything that paid such good money for such good fun. So I was. So I'm going back into it. There's St. Pierre with good booze cheap for cash, and there's Boston, dry Boston, right across the mouth of Fundy. The U.S. banks may be closed but there's still a lot of thirsty money around and it talks louder than ever. Right now it's saying, Nolan here's your chance. So I'm taking it, in the *Roger,* and you're coming with me to run those good big diesels. With this insurance money from the *John* I can save my properties — including the schooner — and still have plenty to finance me for the rum trade. I hear the Yanks are taking the dry law off their books, but it can't go into effect for seven or eight months. In that time I can make a haul — with luck I could make a fortune. So I can promise you five times the pay you're getting now, and all the schnapps and excitement you want. That makes you sit up, doesn't it? Okay — but don't light that cigarette now. I don't mind it out on the deck but I hate the stuff inside, you know that. If you must poison yourself, Dahl, stick to schnapps."

Dahl grinned and tucked the cigarette behind his ear. He drank again.

"A Finn!" he exclaimed a little thickly. "You are even more crazy than a Finn, Sax. Even Finns love tobacco and schnapps."

～ ～ *Chapter 36*

T HE ship came down Fundy against a deep and regular swell. There was no wind. The sharp cold had changed the grimy slush on her decks to a hard black crust in which every footprint had been preserved as if in cement. The bulwarks, the bridge and wheelhouse, the boat on its chocks, the derrick gantries, the winches, all sparkled with frost. The parted waves sweeping back from her stem painted a new boot-topping along her sides, this one of ice. From the funnel a black rope trailed over her wake as far as the eye could reach. She sat high on the sea, with her propeller thrashing the surface whenever she dipped in the trough. The sky was covered with a high layer of gray cloud through which the sun gleamed faintly now and then like a worn silver dollar tossed up for a bet and defying the law of gravity. The hands off duty were thankful to stay below. Even in the wheelhouse, the only enclosed part of her bridge, the air was frigid, for the Germans who built her had been concerned with war, not comfort, and Sax had refused the expense of a steam radiator there. The helmsman stood muffled in all the clothing he could cram on, gripping the spokes in hands covered with two pairs of woolen mittens, fisherman-fashion, and stamping his sea boots on the grating to keep the blood stirring in his toes.

Eckles and the mate, a phlegmatic young man from Newfoundland, where the sea is always comfortless, wore parkas, with the fur-trimmed hoods drawn about their faces. At intervals they stamped up and down the wheelhouse past the man at the helm. Sax leaned against a frame, staring forward through the plate glass as if he could see beyond the thin undulating line where gray sky met gray sea. In his fur-lined overcoat and fur cap he looked incongruous there, like a squat and swarthy Russian from the winter steppes, unaccountably sent to sea. Occasionally Eckles or the mate stepped over to peer at the compass and check the course. Not a word passed except the perfunctory phrases of one helmsman relieving another and stating the course, or a brief exchange when the mate went below at the end of his watch and Eckles remained in charge. For hours on end the only sounds were the hiss of the sea at the stem, the steady thumping of Dahl's engines, the thrash of the screw, an occasional rumble of the steering engine and at long intervals the clatter of the ash hoist. The *John C. Caraday* moved on her course as if her entire life were mechanical and the silent group in the wheelhouse merely spectators.

296

Sax looked down at the foredeck, at the battered bulwarks and hatch coamings, the winch with its frozen black grease, the worn paint of the booms and posts and beam of the gantry. She had taken a beating for many months in his service and she was about to perish in an obscure corner of the world, a whole ocean away from the scene of her birth, but he had no sorrow for her and no pity. She had served his purpose, none too well, and now he was done with her. She was nothing now but a floating check for thirty-five thousand dollars, payable on Dutchman. But he was not unmoved. Indeed, he was exultant. Here on the bridge, about to pull off another good neat trick, he felt himself again. He smiled when he thought of the end of *Albertine*. That had been too easy, too soft, too small a bit of barratry after all to give the proper kick. Up here on this rugged coast, in this kind of weather, taking this kind of chance — this was the stuff. He was glad that he had Dahl. Dahl could appreciate a thing like this. And he saw himself and Dahl adventuring gloriously in the *Roger,* quenching the thirst of Boston and the busy towns about it for spot cash, the kind of thing he and Dahl were meant for, not the dull and unrewarding business of common trade that other people bothered with.

When darkness came he reduced the speed to Slow, for the ship must linger through the night so as to approach Dutchman at first light, when his careful calculations showed that the tide would be at high-water slack or the beginning of the ebb. He turned in with an easy mind on these affairs, but when he had switched off the cabin light and drawn the blankets about his chin he thought of Rena and her lover. At once the brooding hate and bewilderment were back. His familiar devil arose within and jeered at him for the fool of the world, letting that clever old woman put him off again. One fraud abetting another. What truth was there in anything that artful woman had said? Except that Rena was hurt and ill — he had checked with Bannister on that before leaving for St. John. Never mind those final words of hers that still buzzed in his skull and stung like wasps. Think of the rest — the rest was plain enough. The old fraud had gone out to warn them and they'd been running to the boat, that guilty pair, when Rena fell and upset everything. It was hard to picture Rena hurt and ill, she was always such a healthy specimen, and his mind refused the attempt. He lay there longing for the sound white flesh he remembered; and when he thought of it warm and secret in the old cottage in the wood for all those months and pictured it rapturous in the arms of that sneaking loafer at the Head, it was more than he could bear. He turned restlessly in the bunk, sweating with rage. And after all what had he promised Rena's mother? Nothing. Not one damned word. A phrase came into his head, he had read it in an old court case somewhere — "judgment deferred." He repeated it aloud in this darkness throbbing with Dahl's engines and it had a satisfying sound. Because they couldn't run away now. At any rate Rena couldn't, and surely that fellow would be fool enough to stay with her. You might say they were prisoners together at the very scene of the crime, like a pair of mice trapped under a tub. You could defer a lot of things in a case like that. You could even take your time.

Before dawn he was on the bridge. Eckles was there and the helmsman. He called a calm good morning to both, and when Eckles replied Sax saw at once that the man was drunk. The old fool! He had saved the rum for this time when his principles — his principles! — must go by the board. Well, what did it matter? Within half an hour the lighthouse on Frigate appeared like a morning star against a mat of black cloud sailing up the sky with the dawn itself, and soon the island was standing up boldly, and Topsail to the north of it, and nearer at hand the low dark patch, now hidden, now reappearing with the undulations of the swell, which was to be the *John C. Caraday's* last berth.

Sax spoke to the helmsman. "Shift your course to nor'east by north. We're taking the inside passage." The man flicked a glance at Captain Eckles but he obeyed without question. It was well understood in the ship that when Nolan was aboard he was captain, whatever Eckles might feel and however the articles read. "I'll take the helm myself before we get to the Race," Sax added casually. The man nodded stolidly. That too had happened before. The ship plodded on. The new course brought the deep swell on her starboard side and with the dish bottom of her Baltic designers she rolled like an empty cask. In another hour Dutchman was plain on the port bow, the low points of the muddy legs, the fringe of ice that marked the tide. The sky to the south and east was heavy with rapidly moving clouds but there was no wind yet upon the sea. Dahl came to the bridge. He had been down to the engine room to see that all was running well for the supreme moment. His sallow cameo face glistened with sweat that quickly cooled in the frosty air of the wheelhouse; but he was dressed for the cold, and his blue eyes, bloodshot from last night's schnapps, had the eager look that always came when Sax was at the wheel on an adventure.

As Dahl appeared Sax moved to the grating behind the wheel. "All right, Bannon, give me the helm. You may go below for a smoke." The helmsman stepped aside gladly enough. His boots rang down the iron ladder and along the foredeck. With his hands firm on the spokes Sax inspected Dutchman carefully. The legs of the trousers opened towards the southeast. It was necessary to approach the westerly leg, the short one, and at the proper moment to swing hard up northwest, allowing for some leeway when the ship came across the tide. He heard a mutter from Eckles and, turning, saw him gazing towards Frigate, where the sky was now open-and-shut, with moments of pallid sunshine and then the gloom of black cloud masses still working up swiftly from the east. From one of these black squalls a white curtain hung down to the sea. Sax laughed. "There you are. That makes it perfect. Anyone ashore can testify there were snow squalls the morning she struck. And anyone that knows the ship can testify she wasn't fitted with radio, so there was no chance of a bearing from Gannet Head. You won't even have to lie — you and your bloody principles."

Dahl was looking through the glass ahead. "The tide seems well on the ebb," he said, without concern, but as if it gave the affair an added interest. He pointed past Dutchman towards the inner passage, where the characteristic waves of the Race were showing their frothy white peaks. Sax frowned. The Race was a thing that lived on a fixed schedule with the tides. At high tide, when all was slack, the passage between Dutchman and Topsail and the Whales was a passage like any other, in which the water had no movement except the surface waves created by the winds. As the tide began to fall the great surge out of Fundy began to break and toss in a tentative manner over the main shoals, still quite deep, that lay about mid-passage. And as the water dropped and the other shoals began to drag at the belly of the outgoing flood, the area of the overfall, with its confused masses of water swirling and leaping, grew until it occupied the whole length of the

300

passage from Dutchman to a point well on towards Gannet Head.

For the space of a minute Sax was disturbed. An error? After all that careful planning of time and distance and the ship's speed and the tides? Impossible! A solution came to him. "It's this swell running in from the south across the tide. Makes the passage boil a bit. You see some funny effects sometimes, even towards the Head, where there's no overfall at all. See there — the shore of Dutchman. The tide's just on the ebb, no more. You can see for yourself." Dahl looked. The high-water mark seemed clearly shown by the ice rim on the muddy banks. He shrugged and cast another curious glance towards the Race. These tremendous tides were a mystery. In the Baltic there was no such thing as a tide, not enough to notice anyhow, and a shoal was a shoal. When you saw water break you knew the bottom was not far below. A tide so huge, so powerful, that it tumbled over itself in a depth of many fathoms — *wunderbar!*

Sax held on his course with confidence. A glance to starboard showed him Topsail with its dark wood, and he could see the ice wall reaching high with a crest built up by the flung spray of nor'westers in the bitter weeks since Christmas. Far beyond Dutchman he could see the low line of the cape and the white blink of its barrens covered with snow. At times, as the ship lifted on a sea, he thought he could make out the far faint smudge of Port Barron's morning fires rising straight up in the frosty air.

As the ship moved on he watched with wary glances the advance of the snow squall dragging its thick white veil across the sea. Frigate was blotted out already and Topsail soon would go. He took his marks with care. As the first gust of wind ruffled the sea about the ship he was ready to swing up into Dutchman. He put the helm over swiftly, dragging on the spokes as if he could move the rudder by his powerful hands alone. The steering engine clattered obediently. As the snow closed in he had a good look at Dutchman ahead at half a mile, and he noted the rate of leeway, for the ship was now across the tide. It was stronger than he expected and he shifted the course to northwest by west.

Now was the anxious time. His remark to Eckles about the snow had been flippant, and indeed he was not alarmed. But it was a little awkward that it should have closed down just at this moment. He calculated swiftly. Three minutes at full speed should do it — five at the outside. He counted off the seconds in his head, with his gaze traveling swiftly between the compass and the forward glass of the wheelhouse. The snow was very thick. In a minute the deck was white. The forecastle could be barely seen. Three minutes — and nothing. Four minutes and nothing. Five and nothing. Six! Eight! Eight — and Eckles crying suddenly in a high cracked voice, "You've missed it! Too much leeway! You're running past the island to the east — must be!"

An access of fear had sobered Eckles thoroughly, and now in this moment of crisis all the instinct born of his years on the sea, of his manhood in the better days, came out in him. He stood with the parka hood thrown back, stabbing a finger towards the port side, where in his own mind he could sense the low shape of Dutchman sliding past behind the snow. At another time, and with more time, Sax would have snapped his usual, "When I want your advice I'll ask for it." But he now knew what had happened himself, and Eckles's cry was like an echo of the warning signal in his head.

His mind revolved quickly. What now? Keep on this

course for a safe distance and then swing west around Dutchman for another try? Too chancy. Too many muddy flats that way. You go barging about there in this snow and you'll stick her nose on a bank, and there you'll sit like a fool, where the first flood tide and a couple of fishing boats can take her off. What, then? Swing her off to the east, where all's clear and good deep water. Make your circle there and come in from the southward for another try — this snow squall will pass in a few minutes. He dragged the wheel over to starboard. Again the steering engine clamored. The wind and snow came ahead as the ship swung into the east. The white flakes spattered on the wheelhouse windows and clung there in masses, slowly falling away. Steadily the bow came around to the south, and there Sax held his course. Make sure this time. A good offing to the south'ard and then swing her up. He heard voices on the foredeck. The forecastle door was open and two or three men, made curious by these maneuvers, peered forth into the snow. But there was nothing to see and it was cold standing there in their shirts. They dived back into the forecastle and the door closed with a clang.

Ten minutes. Make it fifteen and be sure. Odd, the difference in the motion of the ship. The steady southerly swell on which she had ridden towards Dutchman should now be smacking on her bow. But it was not. The ship rocked uncertainly once or twice. Suddenly she began to dance and lurch. In the whirl of snow alongside, in the dim compass of visibility from the bridge, black pyramids of water seemed to rise up, white-tipped, hissing, thumping against the starboard side like fists. At times the dance brought her screw out of water and the thing raced as if determined to fling itself off the shaft. When Sax heaved on the wheel for the swing up west and northwest the ship was slow to answer. He felt — and they all felt — the ship in the grip of a force to which her engines were nothing.

"You're in the Race," Dahl said calmly. The voice of Eckles came accusingly. "Fool! Did you think you could play ring-around-the-rosy about the head of the Race — in a light ship — at tidefall — and not get into it? Swing — swing, man — you'll have to run the Race now and trust to that devil's luck of yours." The old man, in a frenzy, seized the nearest spoke of the wheel and attempted to wrench it out of Nolan's hands. Sax moved quickly, all bull ape in a moment. He struck the captain a blow of such force that it threw him on his back, silent, with his mouth gaping and the upper plate of his false teeth hanging absurdly from the corner. His eyes were turned up and showing the bloodshot whites. Sax could hear Dahl laughing, a thin cackle, as he seized the wheel once more and swung the rudder over to port. He snapped, "Haul that old rum-pot away out of my sight — the chartroom."

Run the Race? Nothing else for it now. He was still amazed that the ship should have made so much leeway at a time when according to his reckoning the tide was just on the ebb and the Race only beginning to stir. One thing was sure, the current was running strong here, by some freak of the sea. Impossible to buck the thrust of that. For a time the screw and rudder seemed to have no effect at all. Dahl, watching Sax's face with amused eyes, seeking the fear that ought to be there and finding none, had a whimsey that the ship was drifting beam-on down a huge chute of some kind, with an angry giant dashing buckets of water against her starboard side. But at last the stem came around. With her bow pointed down the stream the snow once more sprang from ahead. The driven flakes seemed to converge on the wheelhouse windows as if the whole purpose of this white storm was to blind the ship now running in the great salt torrent.

Sax was not afraid. He was angry. Silently he raged at the turn of luck that had so thoroughly upset his plan; at Eckles for the truth of that accusation made in the heat of the old seaman's heart; even at Dahl, standing there beside him, staring at him with the curious and delighted smile of one lunatic watching the antics of another. Aloud he cursed the snow. Squall? This is no squall. We've walked smack into a March blizzard. The flakes were coming larger now, and moist, matting on the windows and clinging there. He snapped at Dahl, "Stop grinning and slide open the glass before me there so I can see."

As Dahl drew the panel aside the full rush of wind and snow sprang into Sax's face, but it was possible to blink the flakes from his eyelashes from time to time and catch a quick blurred glimpse of the forecastle thrusting its white wedge into the storm. He called the chart to his mind. The course of the passage was not long, it was five miles at most, running east and then southeast as it trended around Topsail Island towards the cape. Questions sprang in his mind without hope of answer. How far have we gone down the Race? What's the actual stage of the ebb? Should I try to swing her head southeast now? In another minute? In three? Five? Are we in midstream or on the edge, and if on the edge, which side?

On the last point he felt a glimmer of assurance in the wild motion of the ship. She must be going right down the middle of it. Like an empty can tossed into a millrace the ship rose and fell, careening, staggering on the lumpy waves of the overfall and veering this way and that as she encountered wide and powerful eddies in the brute rush of the tide. Sax heard a clatter of boots behind him and then the voice of the Newfoundland mate uttering shaken words.

"Is — is everything all right, sir?"

Sax snarled over his shoulder, "Of course it is. Get out. Get up for'ard, you and one or two others — up on the fo'c'slehead and yell if you see anything."

The man departed on the run. He cried something to the men, who had crept out one by one, muffled in parkas and Mackinaw coats, and were huddled now in a group in the lee of the forecastle itself. Two of them went up on the forecastlehead with him and clung there in the dash of spray, in the stinging snow, peering under their up-raised hands.

Sax looked at the polished brass of the engine-room tel-egraph, thought a moment and rejected it. Daren't re-duce speed now. Need her full ten knots to manage her in the eddies. And the Race itself must be running close to five. No doubt about it now — misjudged the tide's turn here among the islands and kept the ship dawdling too long in the night. He gritted his teeth when he thought how cocksure he had been last night, turning in when he should have been checking and rechecking his tide tables and his reckoning — and lying there thinking of Rena! All his difficulties seemed to come back to women some-how. They had begun that day in Nassau when he saw Ellen Carisfort and wanted her. From that moment he had determined to be something he was not, a bloody gentle-man, and where had it got him? And what? Port Barron and Rena Caraday! And now within two years — two years almost to the day — he had lost his money and his woman, and, what mattered more than women or money, he seemed to have lost his luck. Fool! Fool! After all that time in the south, all that sweat and scheming, all those wild risks boldly taken and won, to chuck away his luck for a creature like that! A woman of Class! He seemed to see Ellen and Rena together, laughing behind their hands and whispering "Monkey Eyes," like those girls in Port Barron all that time ago.

But now his inner devil asserted itself with a touch of his old unconquerable spirit. He shook off those morbid and fruitless self-reproaches as he shook the plastered snowflakes from his face. To hell with all that! You're not done yet, Sax. Not you — not Sax Nolan. You've been through worse than this and come out grinning, Sax. You'll beat 'em all yet — the Race, the underwriters, Halkett, the bank, those penny-grabbing outport merchants with their duns and judgments — yes, and that scheming mother-in-law of yours, and Rena and her lover. Beat 'em all! All!

From the forecastle came a cry, a thin chorus of wild voices borne on the wind and flung into the open wheelhouse with the snow. Sax could not make out what they said. Instinctively he took a fresh grip on the wheel. And then, blinking rapidly, he saw through the whirl of flakes a white shape dead ahead. It was long and low, rising to a hump towards the left, like a great fish breaking water. Like a whale. The Whales! Dahl cried out to him and together they tore at the wheel. There was no time to think, no time to guess which of the three Whales it was, no time for the ship to answer the rudder, no time for anything.

The *John C. Caraday* struck the tail of the rock where the current swerved, so that it was not a head-on collision but a glancing blow. The shock came first under the bluff of the bow at the port side and threw everyone off his feet. Sax and Dahl scrambled up, with the ship under them shuddering and still driving on with the full thrust of her faithful screw and the torrent of the Race. The hull rode partly up on the rock as it passed, so that the deck listed

307

sharply to starboard, and there was a tremendous rumble and snarl of torn plates below that pierced the storm and reverberated in the empty holds. The sound and the rending passed along the whole port side. Then it ceased. The icy shape of the great stone fish slid away and disappeared in the snow astern. The ship was wholly water-borne again and she came to an even keel, driving on for a few moments as if nothing had happened, as if rocks struck at ten or fifteen knots were nothing, as if the ersatz plates and rivets of a hasty wartime job in Stettin all those years ago were proof against anything, even that.

But the passage of the rock had torn open the whole port bilge. She was like a codfish slit for gutting and she filled almost at once. To Sax, clinging to the dead wheel, the ship did not seem to sink so much as the sea appeared to rise. As he stared forth into the snow he could see the frothing black humps of the Race leaping high about the hull. There was a rush of men shouting and stumbling along the deck and up the ladders towards the funnel and the boat. Through the after windows of the wheelhouse he could see the cook with a wild face, apron fluttering, tugging away at the gripes that lashed the boat firm on its chocks. And he marveled, amazed that the cook or any of these fools should think they could launch the boat in the time they had, or that the boat could live a minute in the Race if they did, or that they could get ashore anywhere on the islands, where the ice walls would be looming through the snow. He heard Dahl's insane laugh then, and saw him pointing to the frantic men about the boat and then downward towards the stokehold. The sea must be rushing in there as it was everywhere. He had an instant vision of that flood of icy water rising about the fires and the old boiler vibrating under a full head of steam.

The explosion came at that moment. A geyser of scald-

308

ing steam shot up through the fiddley gratings. The whole deck about the funnel seemed to bulge, to lift and fly apart. The funnel, the fiddley, the boat and the struggling figures about it all vanished in a blast of steam and smoke and debris. The wheelhouse windows were shattered and its whole after bulkhead torn away. Dahl was a bloody heap that did not move. Sax remained, stunned, crouching against the wheel standard, and seeing an apparition in the doorway of the wrecked chartroom, the figure of Eckles, his white hair blowing in the gale, his chin daubed with dribbles of blood. He gazed sternly at his owner, like an old prophet confronting Evil, and lifted a long accusing finger, saying something inaudible in the uproar of wind and sea, of air and steam whistling out of the last invaded crevices of the ship, of dim clangs and thumps and one far voice screaming like a girl.

This vision, this spectacle of the old seaman curiously dignified at the moment of death, as if he were the spirit of all men who live honestly by the sea, who accept its dangers, its rigors and its loneliness and yet make no compromise with cunning or chicane — this was the last Sax saw of his crew, of his ship, or of the world in which he had been born, in which he had struggled for so much. The Race, triumphant, poured through the gaping windows and bulkheads in a solid wet rush. As the cold flood closed about him Sax still had no room for fear. He was filled with a wild and bitter protest against the injustice, not of this alone, but of life and women and the world. He had meant well always, he was sure of that. And he had been cheated, he had been cheated after all.